BOOK 2 OF THE LEGENDARY ARTIFACTS SERIES

OF HUNTERS AND MAGI

CHRISTOPHER J. HARRIS

PROLOGUE

Two thousand years ago

CASSANDRA, MOTHER SUPERIOR of the church of Kyrie, ascended the staircase of the main cathedral, headed toward the goddess Kyrie's throne. Her white linen robe swished against the marble stairs as she rose. The rhythmic sound of cloth against stone was a reassurance to Cassandra and served as a link throughout her life. She had always grown up within the walls of the church, had always worn the same garments, and had always heard the slight rustle of not only her religious robes but those of the other sisters.

She gave three solid knocks on the oak door leading to Kyrie's seat of power.

"Enter," a powerful, yet matronly voice answered.

As Cassandra pushed the two double doors inward, the hallway was bathed in the reds, blues, and greens of the stained-glass windows that decorated the ceiling. Instead of seeing Kyrie at her throne, she was instead on the balcony, facing toward her capital, the city of Corinthe. Kyrie turned as Cassandra knelt in front of the goddess' throne, casting her eyes down to the stone floor. Even the Mother Superior should not offend the Goddess by looking her in the face.

The soft swish of Kyrie's robes was slow and methodical as it proceeded to Cassandra's position. A gentle breeze cooled her cheek as the goddess passed and then took her seat.

"You have not brought your blade with you," Kyrie said. "Even I can see that. Do you know why I'm blind?"

"Because you are justice and justice cares not for appearance or demeanor," Cassandra replied. She had rarely been gifted an audience with the goddess and Cassandra wondered what would cause Kyrie to call upon the Mother Superior.

Kyrie issued a wry laugh. "Yes, that is what we tell our followers. It makes a fitting story, but no, it's not the truth. Do you wish to know the truth?"

"I ... I ..." Cassandra stammered, unsure how to answer. Would it be sacrilegious to question the teachings of the church, or worse to not accept information given by the goddess herself? "I wish to know anything you think would make me a humbler servant."

"What do you know of the pantheon's origins, or how the first four came to be?"

Cassandra considered her answer. She truly did not know, only that she was taught the gods and goddesses have always been. "Before the universe, there were only the first four gods. Laevin, yourself, the trickster Chivas, and Marianna of the oceans. Laevin and you birthed the two full god siblings before creating humanity. And your grandchildren, Lau'O'Penake and Defurge, were born after humanity came into being."

"Before the first four, there was the void. The source of all the universe. The first four were caught in that void, surrounded by the beginnings of the stars and planets. It was a miserable existence, so when one day an explosion spewed all the matter of universe across the vast reaches of space, we deities fled as fast as we could, stealing magic as we did so."

Cassandra's face flushed as she listened to the explanation. These were not the teachings of the church, but this was the goddess. Was Kyrie testing her, waiting for her to refute the tale? But above questioning, there was only one more heretical act: to disagree with a deity.

"The void, as we called it because despite containing all the beginnings of the universe, was completely dark. Even as far as we fled, we could feel the void's hunger, its desire to reclaim the stolen magic and subsume the first four and never make the mistake of giving us a chance to escape again."

"Does the void threaten you still? Cannot the deities destroy this force?" Cassandra cursed herself for asking but found herself drawn up in this forbidden knowledge. Why was the goddess telling her this?

"No. The void is a fixed point in space, but we cannot approach, because it would draw us into its embrace, forever trapping us again."

Kyrie continued, "When my daughter Fria was born, we learned of her ability to see all of time and the myriad possibilities of fate. In every branch of fate, Fria explained that it would be important to have the ability to create souls with the void. If a goddess were to sacrifice something of significance, toss it across the vast reaches of space toward the void, we could create souls that fostered its powers."

"And you gave your eyes to create such a soul?" Cassandra asked, looking up a little so she could see the hem of Kyrie's robes.

"Yes, to create what Fria called a void walker. You may look upon me, my child."

"Why would you need to create a soul with properties of the void?" Cassandra asked. She raised her head slowly until she cast her eyes upon the face of her goddess. The corner of Kyrie's mouth turned up into a grin, almost as if she knew Cassandra was disobeying doctrine by looking upon her.

"The Ywaigwai, despite being our servants, threaten to disobey and possibly supplant us as deities from time to time. They rely upon our magics to sustain them, but one Ywaigwai has learned how to exist absent the magic of the gods. She has learned that a pact with a mortal with magical aptitude can sustain her for some time. That rogue Ywaigwai now roams the mortal realm, disobeying us and making pact after pact with mortals."

"Why not destroy the Ywaigwai?" Cassandra asked, carefully memorizing the features of Kyrie's face. She seemed placid most of the time, but her grins—when they momentarily surfaced—seemed so foreign to how Cassandra thought a deity should behave.

"Yes, we could. But then that would be a signal to the Ywaigwai that they were something to be feared, and that the deities themselves would be required to put them down. Eventually, the Ywaigwai might band together, and we would face a war of divinity. The casualties would be numerous and shake not only the mortal, but *all* the realms, soul and divine included."

"And instead, you have created a void walker to bring the Ywaigwai to heel?"

"Yes, very smart. All the sisters in the church of Kyrie can command my magics. Why do you think I let you, one with no magical aptitude, be appointed to the position of Mother Superior?"

"My devotion?" Cassandra asked. She had always wondered why but had never questioned. That would be sacrilegious. "And you gifted me with the Rune Blade and Armor to make up for my inability to use magic."

"The Rune Armor and Blade would be pretty gold baubles in the hands of a mortal. In the hands of a void walker, however, they are tools to help hone the gifts of the void. Do you remember the time you caught lightning on the tip of your blade and thrust it back at your opponent?"

Cassandra forgot herself and rose quickly. "Wait, are you saying …?"

Kyrie slowly nodded. "You are Mother Superior no longer."

Cassandra quickly fell back to her knees and cast her gaze downward. "I'm sorry; have I offended you, my goddess?"

"No. You shall leave the church and hunt down the rogue Ywaigwai, Val. She appears as the marble statue of an angel. No one within the church must know the truth of your departure. But I shall not cast you out in this world with no allies. Form a group to keep your secret—only they shall know what a void walker is—and prepare to bring any rogue Ywaigwai to justice. You are the Mother Mercy, now."

Chapter 1

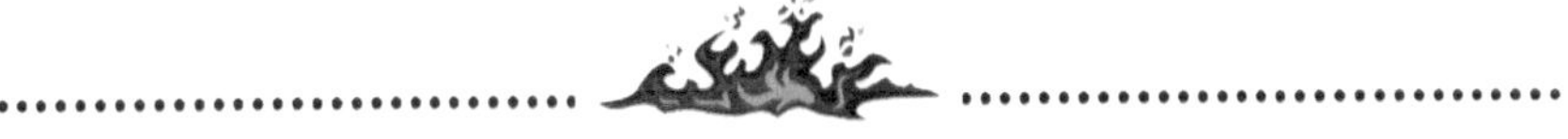

Three weeks after the release of the mad god Defurge

Bronwyn Amyna, hopefully still the captain of the Emestrian royal guard, knelt next to the skeletal remains trying to ascertain the cause of death. It was not the first dead body she had seen. In Emestria, she had investigated murders, but it was the first she had seen in months. The skeleton had already been picked clean by scavengers and many of the bones were scattered about among the clothes of the deceased.

She fingered a rib bone; there were signs of predation—uneven breaks in the bones—but there was a precise cut in the middle. Too even to be made by the crunching of bone by a larger animal, and too deep for rats or vultures to cause. The wrist and anklebones also had indications of man-made weapons; they were splintered, but there were bladed cuts as well.

In the pocket of the pants, a piece of paper peeked out. Bronwyn dropped the rib bone and removed the note, unfolding it with difficulty as blood had dried in several places and stuck those sections together, ripping the paper. Between the age of the writing, the tearing, and the dried blood, very little information was legible.

She did her best to ascertain what it once said. It started as almost a taunt, beginning with "Dear" and then the first letter of a word lost to the paper's rips, followed by the word "scum." The next sentence was even more broken up by stains and rips, with only the words "son", "alone", and the phrase "more pieces." The next two or three sentences were only bits of letters here or there and were impossible to decipher. Finally, the note seemed to be signed, but Bronwyn could only make out the second word of the signature: "hunters."

"There's another over here," Defurge called from twenty feet away.

Bronwyn put the note back in the deceased man's pocket, rose slowly, and then headed to where Defurge waited. The former god's medium-length, silvery hair blew in the breeze. No nation had citizens with silver tresses; maybe it came from Defurge's time as the incarnation of the god of fire and madness.

She looked at the other set of skeletal remains, taking a cursory glance. Nothing about this skeleton stood out to her, but given the state of the carcasses, she guessed they died around the same time.

"Could the creature Miro described have caused this?" Defurge asked.

"No, the creature he warned us about, the cassolisk, petrifies its prey before consumption. Think of a big dumb bird that likes to eat rocks. These two were probably killed by bandits. The other body had signs of man-made weapons. This body seems younger." Bronwyn turned to see the forest, their intended destination, then looked to the sky. "We should get moving, get deeper into these ruins before nightfall. The bodies are weeks old; hopefully whoever did this is long gone."

"Well, I doubt we have to worry about bandits. Having the god of fire by your side pretty much guarantees safety." Defurge chuckled and started to walk northeast with little fanfare. She cast another glance at the other skeleton, then followed him.

God of fire and madness, Bronwyn thought before chastising herself. Defurge had once been just a man but had come upon a gem that made him an incarnation of that god of madness. He had no memories of his time as the god of fire, and the actions he committed during that time were a product of the insanity that gem caused, not his fault. But now, he wasn't really even a god. He was … well *something*, but definitely not a god. Still, there was a feeling she couldn't shake about the corpses. If she weren't so relieved at being away from the library she had just come from, that feeling would have bothered her.

Here, away from the Library of Laevin—a place once inhabited by the now departed gods—she felt like herself. Breathing in the clean air, she didn't feel the same weight on her chest, and even if the bodies had been fresh, they wouldn't have filled her heart with the same dread she experienced when thinking about her return to the library.

Wordlessly, the duo walked to the northeast for another two hours before Bronwyn suggested making camp. The ruins of the town petered back down to the occasional stone foundation coated in vegetation. The forest was still a quarter-day's travel away, but she didn't want to enter it at night. The last time she had fought at night in a forest didn't turn out too well, and she didn't have Miro with her this time to make sure she stayed alive.

Back in Emestria, Bronwyn, Miro, and Clara had been ambushed at night by a pack of Emestrian wolves, beasts as large as horses and ferociously ravenous. Bronwyn had been pinned by four of the animals, and it was only because Miro entered his curse and tapped into the full energies of the Ywaigwai that made him into a magus, that she survived. Although he saved her, he had completely lost control and almost killed Clara and her. It was only through the sacrifice of a spirit guardian, an animal blessed with divinity, that he was stopped.

Bronwyn still didn't quite understand the magi's curse. Miro never explained it well and admitted to knowing little about it. But when a magus underwent great times of strife—physical or emotional—the being that lent its power, the Ywaigwai, would flood the magus with magical energy, killing all life around it, including the magus. Then the Ywaigwai could come and claim that magus' soul. There was no way to exit the curse once it was fully entered, and thankfully the two times Miro had almost entered the curse, something had intervened.

Miro. She wanted him here. Despite her being the one who commanded that he wasn't allowed to leave the library, she still wanted him here. They had traveled together for two months, and she found herself missing their fireside chats before arriving at the deserted Library of Laevin, where they had made their base of operations. That choice, the one that he shouldn't fight alongside her anymore, seemed like a distant memory and she still had trouble rectifying her thoughts in the moment with her current feelings.

They had fought Defurge, been sucked into the very gem that once gave Defurge his abilities, then made a deal with the entity contained within the gem to destroy it, but Miro lost control of his powers. Bronwyn tried to tell herself the decision was sensical—that Miro was too dangerous, that his magic could overwhelm him—but after they exited the gem, when she had decided to kill him to protect the rest of her group, he hadn't resisted her. She shuddered thinking about the look in his eyes, the way he welcomed death—but she also remembered the way his eyes had clouded, him about to enter his curse. But he didn't. He struggled against the force that would have endangered her, but she had still been filled with some foreign compulsion to strike him down.

Bronwyn shook her head, dismissing the nagging feeling as she put her pack down and started to set up camp. Defurge needed directions on how to erect the tents, but with a simple wave of his hand, he caused the wood they gathered to light in a bright blaze. Former gods of fire were somewhat useful. It made up for the fact that his knowledge of the world was limited. When Miro and she had agreed to destroy the gem and free all the former incarnations' souls from being prisoners from within, the phoenix, one of the incarnations still sane in the gem, used her power to liberate Defurge of his madness. Part of that boon was that he lost all memories of his time as a human and a god.

After ensuring that Defurge had satisfactorily followed her orders in erecting the tent, Bronwyn retrieved ingredients for the night's meal from her bag: rabbit, potatoes, onions, carrots, and some spices. She poured her waterskin in with the meat and vegetables and set a pot above the fire to heat and simmer. A nearby rock made a good sitting stone, and she removed her steel greatsword to inspect it for any nicks or burs to polish out.

As she sharpened, she said, "Since this creature Miro described is dangerous, I need to know what you're capable of before heading into battle."

"Although my powers as the god are locked off to me, I still have the abilities of the phoenix at my disposal. I can create fire, usher it forth, and even imbue my weapon with it." Defurge indicated toward the whip at his hip.

"We should probably look into finding you a more suitable armament," she replied, not taking her eyes from the six-inch-wide sword she sharpened.

"Are you offering yours up?" he asked.

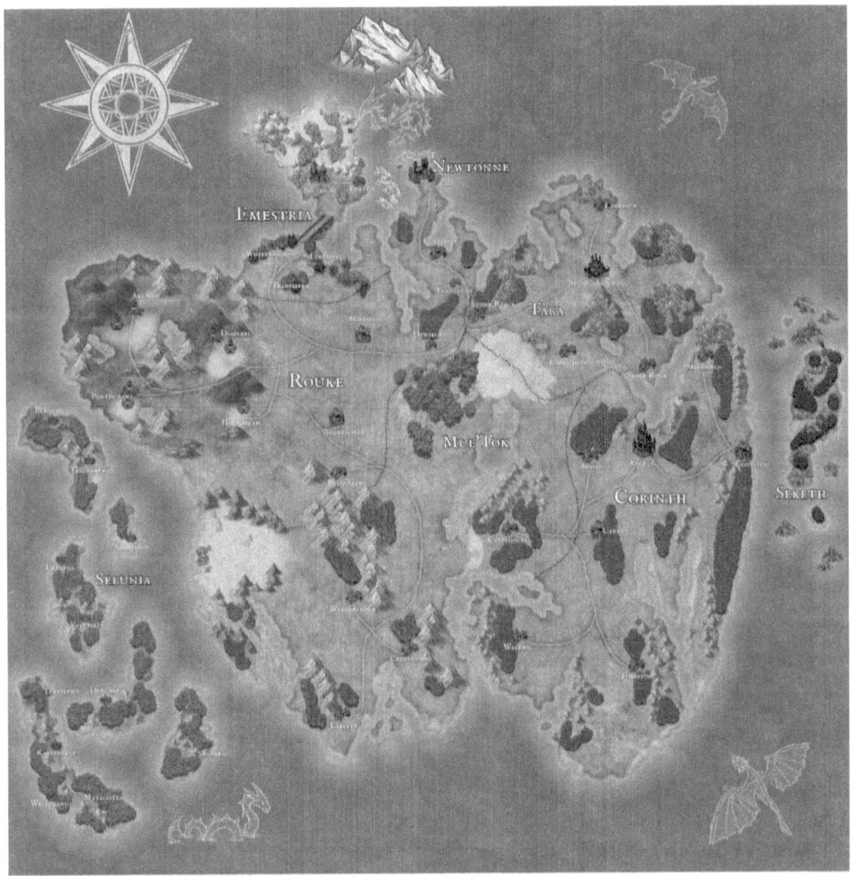

"No, but if you could utilize something like this, that would be helpful. Perhaps we could start you off with a spear."

Defurge extended his hand and Bronwyn hesitated before tipping her blade in his direction. With one hand, he gripped the hilt, then raised it. Honestly, she was a little surprised that he effortlessly hefted its weight. Most people required two hands to lift the weapon and needed both to wield it proficiently. The only reason she was able to switch to a one-handed stance was because she had exercised so diligently, and the fact that she was Emestrian. Long ago, the goddess of ice, death, and fate, Fria, sired many demigods and requested they settle in the same region, bolstering the bloodlines and making Emestrians the strongest of the people in the world, Primerra. Still, she had never seen an Emestrian swing a sword like hers one-handed; no one trained as hard or as regularly as she.

Defurge swished the sword in the air a couple of times before offering it back to Bronwyn. She readily took it; although not the greatsword her father had wielded in the Battle of Lynnfield fifteen years ago, it was similar, and she liked to think she would have one day inherited his blade if he had outlived the war. Only three people survived the monster—or weapon, or possibly something else—that destroyed Lynnfield and the armies occupying it. Miro, the Invincible Hero King Bryant, and one other, a friend of Miro's.

Although the battle of Lynnfield had been fifteen years ago, Emestria found itself in conflict with the neighboring nation of Rouke once again. Relations had always been strained between the two nations, and it was just a matter of time before they found themselves locked in conflict. This time, Rouke had brought the fight to the heart of Emestria, severing supply lines and trying to starve the country into surrender.

"Thanks, but I prefer my whip," Defurge said.

"Your whip won't be as effective in combat."

Defurge leaned back casually before replying, "It's not my bladed lash that's dangerous, it's the fire that I can create on it. I can ensnare a target from a dozen feet away and burn it to ash. With a sword, I'd be limited to a couple of feet. I can produce flames that travel that far. Seems like a waste."

Bronwyn nodded at the assessment. She had yet to see him fight without his godly powers, so she wasn't sure of his skill, but there was a feeling she had around him, a comfortableness, a desire to be agreeable; he was quite charming. Not in a romantic way, she had no time for such idle thoughts. She was trying to save her homeland. This quest to recover the legendary artifacts was supposed to be Emestria's salvation. No, it *would* be Emestria's salvation. "Hopefully fire will be enough of a deterrent for this creature. I don't know about the magical, but normal animals avoid fire, so maybe just emitting it for some time will allow us to explore the area and retrieve the artifact unmolested."

"What is so important about this artifact?" Defurge asked. "You said Miro had identified a dozen artifacts that you've been tasked to recover, but you're following a vague lead to seek this one out."

"King Bryant tasked us with recovering as many artifacts as possible, to make Emestria a nation no other would dare attack with their power. Emestria, my country, is besieged. The nation of Rouke is trying to starve our people by cutting off our trade supplies and occupying our farmland. The Horn of Garanhir is supposed to make food. With it in Emestria's possession, we can weather the siege until the winter is over and try to negotiate with other nations for help come spring. Then we'll have time to recover more artifacts."

"Or you could return with a god at your side, and I could lay waste to the army."

Bronwyn cringed before replying, "I think Miro might have a problem with that tactic. His wish is to limit callous loss of life."

"Is it callous if I'm saving your people by destroying your enemies?"

"If we find this artifact, it won't be necessary to kill thousands. And besides …" She allowed the thought to die on her lips, but Defurge's narrowed eyes convinced her he wasn't going to leave it incomplete.

"Besides what?" Defurge asked.

With a sigh, she replied, "Well, do you really think you can destroy an entire army? Clara, Miro, Issaroh, and I were able to best you in combat. And you were working with the powers of the god, although diminished. Now you're telling me that you don't have access to that very power, only that of the phoenix."

"I had been trapped underground for four hundred years. I must have been weakened, which is the only reason you succeeded."

"Why don't we see how well you fight before committing to a one-man war? From what I understand, if you were to fall in battle, the next one to pick up your gem would become the new incarnation of the god of madness, except that the phoenix would not be able to temper their insanity. She indicated she could only do it once because when you died, she would turn mad as well. I'd hate to see that gem passing from person to person, each one wreaking more devastation."

Defurge waved his hand dismissively. "No one's getting my gem. I'm the last Defurge there will ever be. You'll see how well I fight."

"Yes, because we'll look for the artifact to destroy the gem after we find the one that makes food here," Bronwyn said.

Defurge tensed and seemed cautious about replying to Bronwyn. When he finally did speak, he asked, "That old scholar, Issaroh, told me that nations used to have patron gods and goddesses. Was I Emestria's patron god?"

Bronwyn snorted. Defurge narrowed his eyes. "No, Emestria's patron goddess was Fria, goddess of ice, death, and fate."

"I know what my family's realms of influence are," Defurge chided.

"Well, you didn't know how to erect a tent. How am I supposed to know everything you do and don't know?"

With a quick shake of his head and a dismissive hand flick, Defurge said, "Did Rouke worship me? Is that why they are fighting Emestria? To prove that their god is stronger?"

"No one fights for the gods and goddesses anymore. They abandoned us, and I'm pretty sure that was a good thing. Just Laevin and Defurge's battles destroyed entire cities and killed thousands of people."

"You mean my battles? We created you and you forsake us just because we're not actively bestowing our gifts at the moment?"

"You created nothing. If anything, that gem around your neck is the real god Defurge. You have the personality and powers of him because you picked it up. As we say in Emestria,

'Giving a child a sword makes them a warrior naught.'"

"Tomorrow, you'll see a warrior god in action."

"Defurge, I—" Bronwyn tightly gripped her temples as an intense headache roiled through her skull. The pain was so directed, she found herself unable to remember what she was going to say. "I need to lie down. We have a long day ahead of us. You can debate godhood with Issaroh; that's his strength. I'm just the one that pokes bad things with sharp sticks."

"Oh, sorry to hear you're not feeling well. I didn't realize our conversation was bothering you so."

The headache brought on strange sensations of the feeling of fresh snow crushing beneath her boot and the smell of the first stew of winter. She felt guilty for belittling Defurge's power and lessening his being. After all, he didn't ask for any of this. It was another stray, incongruous thought she found herself having more and more of these days. "No, it's nothing. I'll finish making dinner and then we'll retire."

Bronwyn returned to making her soup, and the conversation turned from less tense subjects. She would have given anything for Clara or Issaroh to be here. They would be a small consolation to the man she really wanted to be here, Miro. How ironic that she was the one who said he couldn't accompany her on trips like this, but all she felt was a desire to have him beside her. She trusted him, but yet she didn't, but in her deepest self, she did. Every thought in her head told her she had done the honorable thing in restricting him to the library, but her gut and her heart told her he should be here. But Defurge was here; that was something, right?

The idea of confronting a dangerous enemy with an untested variable was not pleasing. Issaroh refused to fight, being a magus like Miro. Issaroh worried that he could lose control and endanger others around him. Clara had been … Well, she had been difficult ever since their battle with Defurge. It was like she was trying to get into an argument with Bronwyn every time they chanced conversation. It was unlike her.

But then again, Clara was always a many-sided coin, and Bronwyn was starting to realize that Clara may have deeper feelings for Miro. Feelings Bronwyn couldn't understand. She didn't think they were romantic, but still, Clara seemed to have this protectiveness toward him, and at the same time was seeking his approval in her actions. It was a stark contrast to how Clara acted with him before coming to the library, or even in the first week of their residence. At least Bronwyn's next obstacle was physical—something she had plenty of experience dealing with.

CHAPTER 2

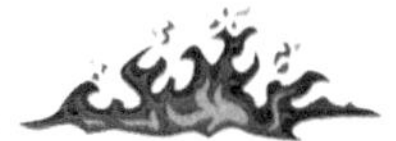

THE SCATTERED REMNANTS of the ruined village gave way to what could have been farmland at one point, but all that remained were patches of long grass interspersed with wildflowers and fragrant bushes. Bronwyn and Defurge continued their trek toward the dark forest that Miro had indicated was the last known location of the demigoddess Gwyndlyn Garanhir. It had been over five hundred years since the demi-goddess went missing while trying to rid a town of a particularly dangerous pest, the cassolisk, that resided northeast of the ruins they found themselves in.

The artifacts were gifts from the gods and goddesses to their demi-godly children. It was unlikely that Gwyndlyn Garanhir wouldn't have the item on her at all times. If this was the place where she was finally defeated, then it was where the Horn of Garanhir was most likely to be found.

"How are we going to know what this creature looks like?" Defurge asked.

"Miro showed me a couple of sketches. You'll know it when you see it. The skin is supposed to be pebbled with protrusions, and what appears to be feathers are sheets of stone along its back and wings."

"Do we have to worry about it flying around?"

"No, apparently the bird is flightless, too heavy, but it's important that if we do encounter it, make sure it doesn't bite or claw you. The venom causes flesh to petrify."

"Basically, keep it away from us?"

Bronwyn nodded and unsheathed her massive greatsword, keeping it at her side as the scattered bushes started to give way to tall, dark, walnut trees. Despite being almost noon, the thick canopy prevented much of the sun from reaching the forest floor. The ferns were thin in some areas, leaving her to believe that game still traveled through here. If that were true, perhaps this creature wasn't that fast … then she thought about the large constricting snakes she hunted in the swamp surrounding the Library of Laevin. They were ambush predators, making up for their lethargy by dropping down on prey from above.

Trying to ascertain where anything was in the canopy was difficult. A tangle of tree limbs and thick swaths of leaves left ample room for a predator to hide. Although Bronwyn was carefully watching her steps, rolling her heels as she walked and avoiding branches, Defurge marched through the underbrush, creating plenty of noise. A harsh look and her finger to her lips were enough to cause him to moderate his stride and attempt to follow her example.

"Where is this artifact supposed to be?" Defurge asked in a whisper.

Bronwyn stifled a sigh and replied, "I don't know. We'll just have to investigate."

"It could take days traipsing around the woods. Do you even know what it looks like?"

"Like a curved horn made of brass with raised dimples along its surface."

Bronwyn stopped suddenly, almost having tripped over what appeared to be a statue. Rather than a buck standing confidently in the air—its antlers reaching to the sky—what remained was an animal's body, lying on the forest floor, in obvious pain. The mouth was open, and the limbs were contorted in such a way that she could feel the screams the creature had probably protested its untimely demise with.

She knelt and ran her hand over the shaped rock. It felt like stone, but in portions there were polished sections dug into the animal. There was some crumbling along the gashes, but most of the imperfections were smooth. How strong would something have to be to carve stone so smoothly, like a wire through cheese?

Bronwyn rose, then motioned Defurge forward. He carefully walked around the simulacrum of the dying stag.

It was only the first of the petrified animals they found; sometimes it was only a limb or other recognizable body part, other times there was nothing left besides a scattering of stones the size of her fist. Since its prey was turned to stone, the creature was probably able to eat them at its leisure. The level of detail retained in the stag convinced her that the cassolisk still roamed these lands. Weathering would have smoothed the details away long ago.

Is it possible that this is the same monster Gwyndlyn Garanhir had hunted? It would be ancient, but the other option would be a breeding population, which is even scarier. The last thing Bronwyn wanted was to be surrounded by a pack of beasts with petrification-inducing talons. Miro had indicated that it was solitary though. *Maybe a migratory species, or roaming males?*

As they made their way further into the forest, patches of broken stone became more common, and Bronwyn began to scan their surroundings with increased frequency. Some of the stones were noticeably human in appearance; she found a couple of hands and smashed faces. After a particularly thick congregation, she spotted something peculiar past a fern. She approached cautiously, her grip on her sword tightening. Unlike the other hardened figures they had seen so far—grey, like granite—this one was a polished, gleaming white.

Bronwyn pushed the fern aside, expecting to startle the cassolisk, but was instead greeted by an outstretched arm reaching up from the ground, fingers splayed. If it weren't for the color, she would have probably never seen it. She caught Defurge's eye then indicated toward the arm with an inclination of her head. He raised an eyebrow and they both grew closer.

With another glance about the forest, she reached down and tried to pull the hand from the earth. It was solid and did not budge. "Here help me with this."

Bronwyn started to brush the lichen and dirt from around the edifice and after several more inches of the limb continuing, she became convinced that there was more underneath the forest floor. Unlike the other statuesque figures, this one was of polished white marble with thin black lines where the arteries and veins would be visible on a human. She rose, then retrieved a larger flat stone off one of the granite corpses and started to dig in haste where she thought the head would be. Defurge followed her example and scraped dirt away with a stone from where the torso might lay.

When Bronwyn's digging implement hit something hard; she worried that she might have chipped the nose on the marble façade. Dropping the stone, she brushed debris away, pulling up roots that had settled around the marble to loosen the soil. She revealed the face, not a single chip or abrasion on it, then looped her pack off her back and rifled through looking for the portrait Miro had removed from a book. Without seeing the hair, it wasn't guaranteed to be the body of Gwyndlyn Garanhir, but the resemblance was uncanny. Any discrepancies could be attributed to choices made in the artist's particular style or difficulty in the medium used.

With her heart thundering, Bronwyn compared the cheekbones in the picture and the statue, then the nose, and finally the eyes, which were open in the drawing but closed in the marble effigy. Her elation was interrupted by a racket akin to terracotta roofing tile clattering upon cobblestone streets. She twisted up from her sitting position, looked behind herself, and then quickly turned, checking for the source of the noise. Defurge likewise backed up against her and started to undo the clasp on his coiled whip.

The sound occurred again, and Bronwyn estimated its distance to be close and to the north. She motioned for Defurge to follow her, and they proceeded to the south, finding a couple of trees to hide behind but still within sight of the marble statue. The last thing she wanted was to be chased through the forest and risk losing what she had happened upon by pure luck. Peering carefully around the tree, she looked for the source of the noise, which seemed to be steadily approaching their location.

The six-foot-tall cassolisk slowly came into view. It appeared to be a large flightless bird, its body held above the underbrush by two thick, mottled grey legs. The neck was long, and the bobbing head had a beaked snout with wicked serrations along the edge. As the creature shook, the stone-like feathers on its back and wings grated against each other and reproduced the sound Bronwyn heard earlier.

Round eyes on either side of the creature's head were as big as Bronwyn's fist. Its head dipped down to the forest floor, and it appeared to be sniffing around the dirt. However, it didn't seem to be their scent it was interested in, but instead when it found the chunk of granite Defurge had been using, the bird-like creature clasped the rock in its beak, raised its head, then crushed the stone, causing it to crumble in its mouth. Despite the grating, crashing sound, it didn't have any difficulty in destroying the hard material.

Bronwyn tensed as the cassolisk cocked its head to one side, then the other, staring at the arm of the marble statue. Bobbing and stepping tall with its taloned feet, the animal made its way toward the edifice, seemingly curious. When it reached the marble, it knocked its beak along the length of it before opening its mouth around the limb. Although it had no complications with the previous stone, the creature violently clacked its beak against the black-veined, alabaster limb. Having made no headway, it increased the distance between its legs and then jerked its head aggressively back and forth across the arm. After a minute or so, it turned its attention to the fingers of the hand but had just as little luck trying to liberate them. Then it let out a sharp shriek before smashing its snout upon the arm quickly in succession.

"Why isn't it able—" Bronwyn silenced Defurge's question with a wide-eyed stare, but it was too late. The cassolisk twisted in their direction, the pupil of the eye that faced them dilated, then it issued another shriek and charged toward them.

"Chivas!" Bronwyn cursed as she timed the creature's fast dash so she could round the tree before the cassolisk arrived. She underestimated the speed at which the creature turned and no sooner had she rounded the tree than it snapped its beak at her. She brought her sword up and deflected the incoming bite.

She had lost track of Defurge trying to get away, but the crack of Defurge's whip was soon followed by the flaming lash sailing through the air. She continued rounding the tree, attempting to keep the creature on the other side of it, seeing Defurge standing exposed facing the cassolisk head-on. The advantage of being behind it was eliminated for him as the bird-like animal turned quickly, then jumped back as his whip sailed toward it.

Undeterred, Defurge raised a hand and a billowing column of fire burst forth but fell short of where the cassolisk had hopped back to. With a screech, the cassolisk flipped one of its wings in his direction. A handful of stone feathers hit the ground in front of him, but he didn't move and when the creature took a step forward to send a second volley, Bronwyn knew that not only would the cassolisk's attack reach him, but that his vision was obscured by the flames he was still conjuring with his hand.

"Watch out!" Bronwyn yelled, dropping her sword and running toward Defurge. He didn't even seem to hear her, and she was forced to tackle him, both interrupting his blazing stream and knocking them to the ground. Thankfully, the stone feathers flew high and only caught the trailing end of Bronwyn's cloak. Her luck ran out there, as the cassolisk was quicker to react than the two of them.

Bronwyn rolled away from the creature's stomps and snapping beak, tossing Defurge further back in the process. But the cassolisk effortlessly hopped over her, requiring her to roll in the opposite direction and cutting her off from Defurge. Wishing that she still had her sword, she tried to unclasp her cloak. Maybe if she could trick the creature into stepping on her cloak, she could pull the cloth out from under the cassolisk and knock it off balance.

Before she could try and accomplish the maneuver, a taloned foot was just about to come down on her. Bronwyn brought both arms up to intercept the attack, aiming the block for the middle of the creature's foot. The talons wrapped around Bronwyn's higher forearm, and she jerked the lower one away, avoiding the venomous tips.

The mass of the creature was phenomenal, and as it pressed its hindlimb down, she was forced to brace her pinned arm with the second, all the while trying to avoid getting scratched. Struggling against the weight, she had no defense as its beak rocketed toward her unprotected face.

The sudden stop to its movement surprised Bronwyn till she saw the flaming lash wrapped around its neck. The coils tightened and she felt the bulk of the creature lift off her. Accomplishing what she had failed to do, Defurge yanked the whip again, causing the cassolisk to lose its balance and stumble away from her—forcing the creature to release her from its grip. She stifled a scream as one of the talons tore through her leather sleeve and grazed her skin.

Once it was off balance, Defurge was able to get close enough. A spout of flames engulfed the creature, but despite the heat it seemed to recover and turn its attention back to him. Bronwyn fumbled for her knife, trying to forget the pain in her forearm.

Bronwyn couldn't see Defurge drop his whip, she just noticed that he raised a second hand and the gout of flame doubled in intensity. Panicked, the cassolisk wheeled around, either attempting to run or confused by the fire. Defurge advanced again, and this time she was forced to roll away from the increased potency of his blaze. She thought she wasn't far enough away and felt some of the heat on her clothes.

When she had rolled a couple of times and turned to face the cassolisk, it was noticeably stumbling. Defurge was almost on top of it and Bronwyn was about to yell out for him to be careful when the cassolisk slumped to the ground. He didn't stop with his conflagration and continued to burn the creature, causing the surrounding plants to shrivel and lace with bright red embers.

Looking in between the ripped leather and at the cut in her arm, Bronwyn saw a small trickle of blood and the skin around the gash looked whiter. She rose and put the arm down to her side, keeping the injury flush against her body. "I think it's dead," she said.

"I'm just making sure," Defurge was now standing on top of the creature. The flames would have licked at Defurge's person as well, but he was seemingly unaffected by the heat or fire. It curled about him and didn't make contact with his billowing white shorts or vest.

The flesh of the cassolisk crackled and popped and a thick milky fluid leaked from its eyes. Bronwyn said, "It's dead. Help me with finding the artifact."

"Bronwyn, we could dig here all day and probably not find it. Why don't we return with Miro, Issaroh, and Clara? Now that the cassolisk is gone, there isn't as much worry about them entering combat."

"No, we have to find it now," Bronwyn ordered. She didn't bother brushing the dirt off her clothes; she didn't have time. Judging by what Miro had said, she'd need to get to him or Issaroh quickly. She didn't want to alarm Defurge, though. There wasn't much he could do. Miro and Issaroh controlled healing magics, the only thing that could slow the venom's advance.

Checking to make sure she hadn't been burned by Defurge's fire, she was surprised to find some of her tunic singed, but none of the flames seemed to have been strong enough or affected her long enough to burn her skin. Despite several spots of burnt clothing, the flesh underneath was still fair without any blisters.

Bronwyn made her way back to the statue, and with increased intensity started to dig around the marble corpse. Defurge joined her shortly after. Bronwyn still listened for the now tell-tale sign of the cassolisk's rustling feathers, but she trusted Miro to be right in the fact that they were solitary creatures. She uncovered the top half of the head and moved down to the feet as Defurge finished clearing the torso. Once they had enough of the body out of the ground, The two of them worked together to lift the figure. Now, with it completely liberated, the resemblance to the portrait was unmistakable. Bronwyn checked the statue for any trace of the cornucopia that Miro had described.

Apparently, the legendary artifacts that they were seeking were indestructible. Nothing short of the gods or another artifact could destroy one. Clothes and gear had long ago been destroyed, so Bronwyn began digging in the dirt where the corpse had been. She shoveled muck out desperately, feeling the numbness in her arm start to spread to her elbow and hand.

She continued excavating, now aided by the fact that her hand was stiff and had no sensation in it. It dug into the ground with the same effectiveness as her earlier stone. She ignored that aspect; she had to recover this artifact. Miro might not go back to get this artifact if something happened to her. Her hand felt more like a claw at this point.

"What's wrong with your hand?" Defurge gasped, now that he had turned his attention to Bronwyn.

"It's nothing," Bronwyn replied, clawing faster.

Defurge grabbed her forearm, and all Bronwyn could feel was the restriction in her movement. "It's not nothing. Your arm is rock hard."

Bronwyn tried to yank her arm away, but now even her elbow's range of motion seemed stiff. "I'm fine. We need to find this."

"You're not fine. You're turning into stone."

"I'm fine!"

Defurge yanked Bronwyn to her feet and despite her strength, she felt the muscles of a former god forcing her to do his bidding. "We have to get back to Issaroh or Miro. They might be able to do something."

"No, we need it now!" Bronwyn argued, trying to free herself.

"We're leaving." Defurge pulled her away and forced her to follow him. Looking down at her arm, it had started to take on the pearly, polished color of the marble figure they had just liberated.

CHAPTER 3

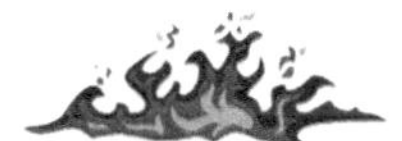

THE STONE STOPPED moving up Bronwyn's arm within hours of fighting the cassolisk. At first, she worried that was some indication that the venom had seeped further into her system and was affecting major organs. But her breathing never became labored, her heartbeat never slowed, and she didn't feel any other negative side effects. In fact, after that couple of hours, she started to regain some feeling in her hand, and the stiffening in her elbow dissipated. An hour away from their proposed meeting point with Issaroh, the color had even reverted. That was good; she didn't need Miro or his former mentor fussing over her with magic.

By the time the sun set, all the ill annoyances of the venom seemed to have worked their way through Bronwyn's body and she wished they had stayed to look for the artifact. Especially now that a return to the library was imminent. Even when Bronwyn spent a couple of hours hunting in the surrounding swamps, she found herself dreading returning to the structure. It was probably the tension between her, Miro, and Clara.

But she had felt that way before the fight with Defurge. It was the homunculi and golems that were the caretakers of the library, but aside from the homunculi that were always lingering around Miro, they didn't bother her that much anymore. Maybe it was the noises and shadows she sometimes experienced while walking the breadth of the stacks, or possibly the fact that being surrounded by all the gods' effects polluted her dreams. Every night she had dreams putting herself into the gods' stories. That's right—it was the noises and weird dreams. That's why she didn't want to go back.

Still, each step felt a little heavier than the previous one. The next breath always seemed a little shakier. Bronwyn struggled against the feeling and with difficulty was able to ignore it. Issaroh still hadn't arrived, and confident that her body had processed the venom, she was willing to entertain the questions Defurge had been asking her on their day trek back to the ley line Issaroh was supposed to pick them up from.

"Are you okay?" Defurge asked, probably for the fiftieth time.

"I'm all right, look." She raised her now flesh-colored hand and rotated it back and forth, showing Defurge how it had regained its natural pallor.

"How? I thought Miro said it was fatal if you were envenomed."

"As they say, it's just a flesh wound," Bronwyn replied. But there were other thoughts on her mind. Miro had said in the past that she could resist magic, an ability he didn't understand, and something that Issaroh had dismissed. She might talk to him about this situation, but she didn't want Miro to know. He tended to become overly excited about anything he didn't comprehend. From legendary artifacts to her supposed magical resistance, he could display this frantic, slightly scary energy when he was intrigued by something. Lately, he had been more reserved, almost non-communicative at times, his eyes a little dull, but that was preferable to the way he could be when agitated.

"Was that the demigoddess that you two were talking about?" Defurge asked, pulling Bronwyn away from her current line of thought.

"Most likely. It matched the portrait as far as I could tell."

"Why was it marble? Why not the same color as the other ones?"

"I don't know. Ask Miro. Maybe demigods were of stronger stuff than regular mortals." A nagging part of Bronwyn wanted her to pay more attention to that, but her mind was quickly overwhelmed by thoughts of returning to the library. The feeling she got whenever she thought of the gods since coming to the library.

"If I had managed to get scratched, do you think I would have turned to marble? Or something more fantastic, being a god and all?"

Bronwyn sighed, then groaned. Even Defurge's mention of the gods made her head throb a little. She had yet to have any dreams about Defurge though. Thankfully, their conversation was interrupted by a bright blue glow that forced her eyes closed. As the light dissipated, Issaroh's form came into view.

Issaroh was of dark skin, a little lighter than Defurge's, the white hair of his head and beard neatly braided. Although he was over four hundred years old—a claim Bronwyn first thought was some weird trick but now had come to accept—he only looked to be in his late seventies.

Miro, likewise, didn't show his age. Even though he was approaching forty, he appeared as young if not younger than her, not a day over twenty-five. Something about being a magus, about immortality. However, if they were truly immortal, how come Issaroh indicated his physical age had advanced rapidly in recent years? Would Miro appear to be twenty-five, then over the course of a couple of years look to be seventy? If that were the case, it still would be long past her life when that happened.

Issaroh turned to Defurge and Bronwyn, seemingly surprised by their presence. "Did you find it?" he asked.

"No. We had to leave early because Bronwyn got scratched by the cassolisk," Defurge said.

"What? Where?" Issaroh rushed toward Bronwyn.

"I'm fine. The venom wore off before it had a chance to take hold." Bronwyn raised her hand, rotating it back and forth as she did with Defurge, even though Issaroh didn't know where she had been wounded.

Issaroh's brows pinched together, and he slightly shook his head. "I should try some healing just in case."

"It's fine," Bronwyn reassured, pulling her sleeve up to reveal the small scratch that had caused her momentary difficulty in moving her limb. Issaroh's look didn't change, and she tried to say something else to take his attention from her arm. "We weren't able to find the artifact, but maybe if you, Miro, and Clara returned with us, we could do a more thorough search."

Issaroh sighed. "It was a bit of a longshot to begin with. Perhaps Miro has made more progress in researching Gwyndlyn Garanhir. Just because this was her final resting place doesn't mean the Horn of Garanhir was taken with her. It wouldn't have had much effectiveness in hunting a cassolisk and there is no guarantee that even if she took it, someone didn't retrieve it afterward."

Bronwyn wanted to argue, wanted to tell him that this was the closest lead they had, but perhaps Miro had found something else out.

"Gather close and let's return to the library," Issaroh said, gesturing for them to come closer. Bronwyn didn't want to; she needed to stay here and look longer. Yes, that was the reason she didn't want to go back; it had nothing to do with the library or the tension in her relationship with Miro and Clara. She debated arguing, but ultimately Issaroh was right, and a reprieve to continue researching might yield more results than her and Defurge remaining here, digging for days.

Issaroh chanted, "Ramun, god of time and space, worldly traveler, bless this journey, Summa." Bright white-blue runes formed on the ground surrounding them, bordered by a similarly colored circle. The magic increased in intensity until Bronwyn shut her eyes. Even with them closed, she could still see the light through her eyelids. Then she felt untethered, the world around her and its external stimuli disappearing. Birdsong, the smell of flowers and grass, and the crisp wind were all replaced with the sounds, sights, and smells of the swamp that surrounded the library of Laevin.

Bronwyn's stomach churned as the light died down. The nausea no longer caused her to vomit, but she still was off-balance when the magic faded. The ability to teleport was useful but could only be cast at ley lines—convergences of magical energy. Even then, the sorcerer needed to intimately know the lines and have visited them previously.

Opening her eyes, she concentrated on the distant horizon, taking measured breaths as she waited for the queasiness to dissipate. The ley line was right outside the library's entrance. It was on the southernmost section of the swamp, where the land wasn't as muddy and the canopy of trees wasn't as thick. Still, the grass was caked in mud wherever they stepped. In the side of a hill, obscured by rocks, a tunnel led down to where the library now lay.

Issaroh and Defurge walked toward the library ahead of her, not as affected by motion sickness as she. They disappeared from view before she felt sufficiently stable and proceeded inside. The grotto leading inside was about ten feet high, large enough for the golemic tenders to traverse. Packed soil blanketed the floor. As she proceeded, the temperature cooled, and the humidity started to dissipate. Her breathing came easier as she came upon the broken doors of the entrance.

Bright yellow, unnatural light bathed the library's interior as Bronwyn proceeded through the doorway. Crystal chandeliers hung from the ceiling, providing most of that artificial light, but sconces on the walls protected little glass bulbs that provided the same illumination. Stacks of books extended as far as the eye could see, and in the middle of the hundreds of feet-long building, two spiraling staircases led to the second floor, where the bath, chambers of the gods and goddesses that sometimes resided here, garden, kitchen, and dining room were situated. The gods had used this structure as a halfway point between the divine and mortal realm, acclimating to human forms before they visited their creation, humanity.

When the gods quit the world after Defurge, the god of fire and madness, destroyed the city of Dalmarask four hundred years ago, the deities concluded that their presence brought more destruction than benefit to mankind. When they did that, the magic that held the library aloft in the sky faded and the building sank to earth. It landed in the region of Mul'tok, but the weight of the library caused it to sink beneath the ground, pushing water to the surface and creating a swamp.

As Bronwyn tracked mud onto the stone and carpeted floor, a large ten-foot golem came by with a broom to sweep the dirt away. The headless golems looked humanoid, but only had three fingers on each hand. Their bodies were firm and hard, like fired bricks. Miro and Issaroh indicated that the constructs were powered by magic and required no sustenance or sleep.

Having lost sight of Issaroh and Defurge, Bronwyn headed to the back of the library to find Miro. She always found him in the same spot, where the information about the legendary artifacts they were hunting must reside. When she had first arrived, she had trouble navigating the maze of books and tomes, but after residing here for a month, she now easily made her way through the assorted stacks, choosing the most direct route. Miro was exactly where she expected to see him, surrounded by a half-dozen homunculi, the other caretakers of the library.

For the most part, the golems did their jobs, but the homunculi seemed to be broken. There once was an artifact kept in the library, The Eye of Sleepless Dreams. Since it was removed over a hundred years ago, the homunculi had been erratic. Some still tended to their given tasks, but others performed functions that served no purpose. In the room that they used to write the history of the world, a dozen of them sat at a table motionless with dried inkwells and quills suspended above pages.

The ones cloistering near Miro swayed slightly back and forth, staring at him intently. Short in stature, their thin bodies were wrapped in dark leather. Beady little eyes and needle-like, sharp white teeth added to their unsettling nature. Their vestigial wings aided in balance as they hopped about with overly long arms and truncated legs, like gorillas. The ones now standing near Miro were probably waiting to replace the book he now held in his hand, a red cover with gold filigrees along its border.

Miro flipped between two pages, too engrossed in the tome to notice Bronwyn's presence. She cleared her throat, but he did not look up or acknowledge her.

Bronwyn said, "I didn't find the artifact, but I believe I found the body of the demigoddess. I'd like to convene a meeting with the five of us to decide what to do next. Have you uncovered anything new in your research?"

Miro didn't answer, only turned back several pages, his eyes still fixed on the book. His movements were slow and measured. It seems like he was in one of his dour moods. He vacillated between three different emotional states: scary manic energy, concerning fatalism, and then his normal self, the person Bronwyn thought was the real Miro. It was difficult to tell why he went through these varying personalities, and Bronwyn worried that he would need another intervention.

She had previously sat him down to insist that he return to regular sleep and meal breaks. When he first arrived, he seemed to either forget or not care about them, researching until he passed out from exhaustion. She took a step closer to take Miro's book and attention. The stench of his body was overwhelming. He likely hadn't bathed in days, despite the most luxurious bath in the world being upstairs.

The stacks always smelled of leather, vellum, and some weird herb that Bronwyn could never place. The third smell she assumed was the homunculi, but sometimes she caught the scent off Miro, and it might be some type of cologne. When she reached for the tome, he stepped back, not doing anything else to acknowledge her presence. The surrounding homunculi flinched as she reached again, probably waiting to replace the books as a normal librarian would. They often did things properly, but then other times they would repeatedly remove books, return them, and then remove them again.

"Miro, can we talk?" Bronwyn asked, having given up on trying to take his book. When he didn't answer this time, she emitted a frustrated sigh. Judging by the three days of stubble on Miro's chin, he had likely not been taking care of himself the entire time she was gone. She hoped that Clara's newfound closeness to him, something Bronwyn still hadn't made sense of, would cause Clara to try and support him as Bronwyn used to, but Clara either lacked the ability or concern to look after his health.

"Miro," Bronwyn repeated, opting to wave her hand above the book, rather than trying to take or close it. "Look, I'm not going away until you talk to me."

That at least got some reaction and Miro finally turned up to see Bronwyn. He blinked slowly, dark bags underneath his different colored eyes, one blue, the other green. His shoulder-length brown hair was greasy, and she hoped he would return to taking care of himself, otherwise she'd probably have to force him to bathe. His skin was pale, and she worried he wasn't eating either. She gritted her teeth as he continued to blink, the dullness in his eyes fading a bit.

"Bronwyn?" Miro asked, like he hadn't noticed her till just now, another frustrating habit he had in this place.

"Did you hear anything I said?" Bronwyn asked.

"Bronwyn? When did you get here?" he replied.

With a groan, Bronwyn decided that whatever game he was playing today, she had no desire to participate in it. "I'm going to get Clara, Issaroh, and Defurge together and decide what to do next. Do you want to join us, or do you plan on just sitting here, reading, and ignoring your need for sleep, food, and hygiene?"

Miro turned back down to his book, beginning to read again.

"Fine. I tried." Bronwyn turned, stifling her anger, not wishing to give him the satisfaction that his immaturity was bothering her. He had served in the Emestrian army during war and lacked any discipline whatsoever. Perhaps when she returned to Emestria, she'd find out if the officer who trained him was still alive and ask that officer how horrible of a recruit

Miro had been. At least he was attending to his duties and researching artifacts. She could put up with a small lack of discipline as long as he served his purpose.

Bronwyn made her way to the carpeted staircase that led to the second floor, probably where she could find Clara. The natural oak of the decorative banisters at either end of the stairs was protected but not diminished by clear varnish. The carpet running up the staircase was likewise ornately fashioned with gold bordering the sides of the red material.

As Bronwyn turned the corner into the bedroom Clara had been occupying—the former bedroom of the goddess Lau'O'Penake and her godly husband Ramun—Bronwyn noted the sense of calm the room evoked. Lau'O'Penake was a deity of nature, and the room was decorated to evoke images of wilderness and animals, from the bed posts carved like vines to the many tapestries of picturesque landscapes.

Clara lay on her stomach on the bed, her light-rose-colored hair hanging down, obscuring her cheeks. This was the first time that Bronwyn had seen her in a dress, one of the ones the goddess Lau'O'Penake had left in her wardrobe situated against the wall. The garment looked large on Clara, even though it was a short summer shift. She was only four and a half feet tall at most. She claimed that she was just born slight in stature, and it wasn't a physical characteristic of the people of her destroyed homeland, Lynnfield. Floral patterns and lace decorated the fabric, making it totally out of place for Clara's character; she was a smuggler and former pirate, not the type to wear dresses. Skirts were fashionable in Newtonne, the town she called home, but Bronwyn had never seen Clara wear one.

Bronwyn cleared her throat, "Clara."

Clara spared a glance before returning to the book she held between her hands. She rarely mentioned what she was reading, but the few times she had, she indicated that the books she read were the stories of the gods and goddesses. The library contained all the stories and histories ever written by mortals, recorded by the immortal scribes who had penned no new books since the Eye of Sleepless Dreams was absconded.

"Don't you knock?" Clara asked, sparing Bronwyn another glance.

"Without any doors in this place, knocking seems like an awkward notion."

"Oh, so you're allowed to ignore common courtesy? I get it."

Bronwyn realized Clara's behavior now was still a product of Bronwyn's actions when she threatened Miro after their fight against Defurge. But Bronwyn had been pulled into the gem he wore around his neck. When they first returned, she thought Clara and her relationship hadn't deteriorated to the point of hostility. She thought Clara had understood how Bronwyn was confused and afraid at the time.

Being inside the gem around Defurge's neck was jarring. There was no natural light or sound in the place. Everything was dark and the phoenix that resided within threatened not to release her from the prison. When Miro had been attacked by the monks and almost entered his curse, Bronwyn had been thrust back into the world so suddenly, she could only react out of training. Miro was a threat, and threats needed to be eliminated.

Miro didn't end up succumbing to his curse, but if he had, it would have been a death sentence for him and anyone near him. She thought he could have killed them, and even when she noticed that he wasn't going to enter the curse, he begged her to kill him.

Stifling a sigh, Bronwyn said, "I was unable to recover the Horn of Garanhir. Issaroh, Defurge, and I are going to convene a meeting to discuss next steps."

"Why? You're just going to do whatever you want anyway. It doesn't matter what I say."

"Clara, that's not true. I always take your opinion into account."

"Right, you're always right. I forgot about that."

"Do you want to join or not?"

"I don't see the point; you never listen to me."

"Okay, if you're not going to come with us, could you just encourage Miro to eat something or take a bath, it looks like he hasn't done either since I left."

"You're always so critical of him."

It didn't deserve a reply, and Bronwyn wasn't going to even try and deign it with a half-hearted refutation of Clara's points. It was obvious that Clara was set on being confrontational and Bronwyn wished to play that game as little as she wanted to entertain Miro's of ignoring her. She walked to the table next to the bed and noticed that Ferdinand's cage was covered. The messenger falcon was a prized possession of Clara's, given to her by

Bronwyn's king, the Invincible Hero King Bryant. "Why is Ferdinand's cage covered?"

Ferdinand responded to his name with a subdued shriek.

"He's annoying; he won't shut up."

"Perhaps you could take him out hunting? He might enjoy that."

"So now you're telling me how to take care of my pet?"

Bronwyn turned to leave. "Check on Miro. I'm going to meet with Defurge and Issaroh."

Both Clara and Miro's behavior had become increasingly exasperating and hostile over the last couple of weeks. Bronwyn had hoped that things would return to normalcy given time, but tempers only seemed to get worse every day, despite her apologies and explanations.

Before tracking Issaroh and Defurge down, Bronwyn decided to take a small respite to let her own emotions level out. She retreated to the room of the goddess Fria, a utilitarian domicile with only a bed, wardrobe, nightstand, and odd crystal. The crystal dominating the majority of the room, situated exactly in the middle, appeared to be a sculpture of ice, which only made sense, given Fria's areas of influence. It was a light-blue, semi-reflective surface that warped and obscured the dimensions of the room behind it. Bronwyn walked to the wardrobe, to take out the jewelry box she had previously found.

A small smattering of jewelry was contained within, but a singular piece always drew her eye. The thin, silver chain with a sapphire pendant reminded her of the sea ice that surrounded her home country during the winter. She set down the box—a web of mirrored surfaces on the exterior and interior. Picking up the necklace, she held it in front of her body, entranced by the way it moved. She stared at her reflection with the pendulating necklace. She didn't dare undo the clasp and don the delicate ornament; Bronwyn didn't wear jewelry. Still, she had a strange fascination with it and often stood in the mirror admiring how it would hang on her neck, long enough to be concealed by her tunic, but she never wore it. It quieted her mind in this place in an unexplainable way; only the baths seemed to do the same.

Shaking her head, Bronwyn dismissed the hold the bauble had over her and replaced it, tucking the jewelry box back where she had found it. Her legs were sore from standing motionless, gazing at her reflection on the semi-mirrored surface of the ice sculpture. As she walked out of the room, the heaviness she always experienced here returned, probably a product of the swamp's humidity. She made her way down the stairs to the study Issaroh had transformed into his bedroom. Having been alive when the gods and goddesses still resided in the mortal realm, Issaroh felt too reverent to stay in their former domiciles.

Bronwyn found Issaroh and Defurge sharing the space, Defurge pestering with questions he had most likely asked a thousand times. He seemed to enjoy annoying the older man, especially when he claimed to still be a god. Issaroh sat at his desk, penning in one of the books he kept stacked atop it. His bed, not as big or extravagant as the ones in the gods' and goddesses' chambers, was situated against one wall. There was also a chest at the foot of the bed and a table in the middle of the room, which Bronwyn could find him at most days.

Issaroh wrote furiously in the book he had opened, abandoning the normal elegant script that she had seen him pen in previously. The fact that he was ignoring Defurge's questions, which didn't seem to deter Defurge from asking them, led Bronwyn to believe whatever he was writing was fresh in his mind, and he worried about losing his train of thought. Still, what she wished to discuss was important.

Defurge stopped his questioning, looking at Bronwyn as she entered. She gave him a cursory smile before saying, "You have a point Issaroh, even if the artifact is in the forest where we found Gwyndlyn Garanhir's body, there is no telling how long we would have to dig to scour the location for its resting place. You mentioned that the artifact, the Eye of Sleepless Dreams, once resided here and could be used by mortals?"

Issaroh looked up from his writing, "Yes, the Shi'en, the people that have it now, use it to show them visions."

"So, I might be able to use it to discover where the Horn of Garanhir currently resides?"

"Possibly, but the Shi'en warned that a mortal using it could cause them to become insane."

"It might be a worthy risk if I can uncover the actual location of Garanhir's horn. With Rouke's siege on Emestria, the biggest concern is starvation. Since the horn is supposed to create food, that artifact is the most important to retrieve. Have you finished the map of possible locations these nomads might frequent?"

"No, I've been a little busy lately. This time of year, they could be at a lake to the southeast, about a three-day trek."

"I'd appreciate it if you could prioritize this map, but maybe I should travel out to this lake to see if they are there. Even if they refuse to part with the artifact, they might be willing to let me use it. I'll depart tomorrow since the sun is probably down by now." Bronwyn wasn't certain if it was, but she felt like she was staring at that necklace for hours.

"I don't know if heading out tomorrow is the best idea," Issaroh said, turning back to his writing.

"Why not?" Bronwyn asked.

"Just wait a couple of days, I'll have a map by then," Issaroh replied, not taking his eyes off the book he was penning.

"You've said you'd have that map finished in a few days for weeks now."

Issaroh signed his name on the back of the notebook he was currently writing. "There, done. Now I can turn my attention to this map."

"Will you? Still, there wouldn't be any harm in Defurge and I heading to the lake to see if the Shi'en are still in the area."

"Just wait a couple of days. It will save you time if you have alternate locations to scout rather than losing the three days in travel."

"I'm supposed to stay here, just waiting for the map?"

"Just a couple of days," Issaroh promised.

"And what do I do in the meantime?" Bronwyn asked.

"Perhaps you could visit with Miro; ensure he's taking care of himself."

"That's probably a duty left best to Clara at this point. I'm not his keeper. If Clara wants to be the one close to him, she can step up and be his warden."

Issaroh grimaced then turned his head down, massaging the bridge of his nose. "Can you just stay for a few days and make sure Miro is doing all right?"

As Miro's former mentor, Issaroh had a vested interest in Miro and Bronwyn understood the older man's concern. "Two days."

"That should be long enough," Issaroh said with a sigh.

CHAPTER 4

MORTALS ARE A funny thing, Defurge thought. *Their minds can be complicated, but at the same time, they can be absent of any thought altogether.* "Well, well, grandfather, this book says every time we fought, you won," Defurge said as he tossed the book he had been reading at the marble statue of the god Laevin. "How did that work out for you? Now you're gone and I'm still here."

Defurge had chosen this room as his residence in the library. It only made sense. This is where the "arbiter of the gods" once slept. Now that Defurge was the only god left on this accursed rock, that made him the de facto king of the gods. Sure, the mortals hadn't come to accept it yet; they still thought him some lost vestige of divinity, but he still wore the gem and could, if he figured out how, tap into the full powers of a god at a moment's notice.

"At least they think you're gone. I haven't decided if you are. I mean why else would you lock me up and leave? Now here I am, in your precious library, surrounded by your precious humans." Defurge shook his head, staring at the doorway. "They're interesting. I'll give you that. But they're broken. One's mind is completely dead, the other is a woman trapped in the mind of a child, and the third's mind is plagued and assaulted with dire warnings. Only the old man seems to have any idea of who he really is."

Defurge kicked the book on the ground before one of the homunculi could retrieve it. "Bring me more books about Ywaigwai and magi. Prioritize anything that Chivas has written on the subject."

The homunculi stopped retrieving the book and looked at Defurge, cocking its head back and forth.

Defurge said, "You heard me. Now go."

The creatures didn't always do what they were supposed to do, but when Defurge gave orders, they followed them. They knew he was a god and obeyed him while ignoring the others.

Chivas' writings were few but particularly interesting, especially on the subjects of Ywaigwai and magi. He had taken copious research notes and proposed many interesting theories that he hadn't explored. The god of souls was the one that came up with the idea of Ywaigwai, divine messengers and servants who subsisted on a fraction of the power of a god.

The old man thought himself the oldest magus alive, but Chivas wrote about the theory thousands of years before Issaroh was born. In one case, a Ywaigwai wished to be free of the gods and began making magi until the goddess Kyrie sent a champion to silence the wayward servant. But Chivas proposed that the combination of a human soul and the divine power of a Ywaigwai fused by a god's power could result in a hybrid divine creature.

Defurge headed back into the main hall of the library. Miro, the magus without a single thought in his head, continued reading his books, trying to find knowledge that would never come to him.

Shaking his head, Defurge started toward the study Issaroh had made his home. It seemed since the gods departed, all their creatures became broken. Only this man who had been alive when they still roamed the world had any semblance of sense.

Issaroh was sorting some old notebooks on his desk as Defurge turned and hopped up onto one edge of the desk. Issaroh moved slowly. Over four hundred years and he was still alive. A blessing from the pact he made with a Ywaigwai long ago. Defurge wondered what color his hair had been before being robbed of it by age. Could it have been silver like his? The man's complexion was the closest to Defurge's.

"Good morning, old man," Defurge said.

"Good morning, Defurge," Issraoh said, as he rolled his eyes.

"Is that how the gods were greeted in your day?"

"No, we usually said your lord or ladyship. And that is how I would greet a god if I ever had the chance to meet one."

"I am a god. The only god left in this tattered world. What is it with all of you denying my divinity?" Defurge chuckled.

"I don't have time for your nonsense today," Issaroh said as he finished stacking the notebooks and headed out the door. "I've got training to do."

Despite the limitations of his abilities, suppressed by the meddlesome phoenix and monks, if he were to unleash his full power, no mortal could deny his divinity.

Defurge strolled behind Issaroh as he met Clara. The duo headed out of the library to a clearing with the god in tow. Watching them do magic was entertaining.

Magic. Such an inconsequential thing. A borrowed moment of a god's power. Yet, mortals lauded it and acted as if it was the pinnacle of human endeavors. But, Defurge reveled in being under the sun, and having some slightly amusing spectacles to entertain him seemed like a good way for a god to sunbathe and be entertained.

The old man and short woman walked to an area outside the library where they used to train. It was fascinating watching mortals laud this power that they could never really grasp. These two were practicing the magics that his twin sister, Lau'O'Penake. once employed. Where she could move the very earth with a mere thought and gesture, these humans were required to chant and make signs with their hands, weaving runes into complicated patterns. It seemed like a supreme annoyance.

This area, a small clearing of muddy grass and misshapen earth, was bordered by a thick canopy of trees to the north that obscured the swamp. The ground was interrupted in places where the two hopeful sorcerers had wielded the magic his twin sister once employed. It wasn't the first time Defurge had observed their practice.

The library was horribly boring. The most exciting thing he had done was fight that stone bird, which was a waste of his powers. But the phoenix—the entity that granted his current control over fire, since the gem's abilities were deemed too dangerous to wield—insisted that he stay with this splintered group of mortals so they could uncover the artifact that would destroy the gem around his neck.

Defurge didn't see what the big deal was. The previous owners of the gem had gone mad, and Defurge at some point was also insane, but now that the phoenix had lent her power to hold the gem's maddening influence at bay, there was no real point in destroying the source of a god's abilities.

"I thought we could practice shaping walls today," Issaroh said to Clara before stepping and facing away from her. "Lau'O'Penake, goddess of nature and rebirth, guard my allies, Fragma Petra."

The incantation required several runes to be traced in the air, in a rough circular pattern. The places Issaroh traced the runes glowed with a brown light before finally dissipating. Earth rumbled as a wall forced itself from the ground. Its height was irregular, with half-sized walls every five feet of its twenty-five-foot length. In the other portions, eight-foot-tall sections obscured Issaroh as he walked along the wall.

"I find this formation is very effective when trying to attack from the gaps. You can prepare spells while hiding behind the larger portions, step into the gap, then finish your magic and send it off toward an enemy. Of course, its uses aren't limited to magic; you could also protect your allies as they use bows, crossbows, or even rifles."

Clara didn't respond to his lecture and instead was transfixed by a dragonfly zigzagging through the clearing. Issaroh cleared his throat and tried to repeat the instruction, but speaking louder didn't seem to snap Clara out of her daydreaming.

"Clara," Issaroh said, addressing her directly. This finally caught her attention and after a few eyeblinks and a shake of her head, her attention returned to the task at hand. Issaroh seemed to be oblivious to the library's effect on the other mortals, how it robbed them of thought at times and made them act unlike themselves. Clara had lived forty years but acted more like a child when the library's hold was strongest. Mortals weren't meant to live among divinity. Defurge still hadn't figured out why Issaroh seemed immune, and Bronwyn seemed the least affected, only experiencing an intense unease that didn't alter her personality significantly.

"Yes, sorry, I was … distracted," Clara said, shaking her head and bringing a hand to her temple to massage away some imaginary pain.

"It will be important to learn the different modifier runes to shape your spells. There is more variety in modifier runes in the Fragma Petra incantation, but mastery of the basics can have surprisingly effective results."

Clara nodded along, but her eye was still drawn to the dragonfly, now zipping around her periphery.

Issaroh didn't seem to notice his pupil return to a lapse in attention and continued, "Most sorcerers fail to grasp the importance of the modifier runes and don't bother to learn more than the most straightforward of them. Form a wall; protect your flank. It's an important spell, but the uses are numerous. You could use the modifier rune to form a flat plateau, which could be used to cross dangerous obstacles or to bridge a gap between two sides. You can change the parapet wall into a stairway that would allow you to ascend to a lofty perch."

"Uh-huh," Clara responded blankly, now turning her attention to a cluttering of wildflowers taking root at the base of one tree.

A bead of sweat formed on Issaroh's forehead, and his skin flushed. He took Clara's hand, concentrating her attention. "It's not just the Penakian discipline you should learn. You have Defurge and Miro with you now. Miro lacks a strategic mind; maybe he'll learn to think like that one day, but you, you could learn how to combine the three of your abilities to a devastating degree. Working in concert …."

Issaroh took a rag from his pocket and blotted his forehead, his breath shortening as he continued to talk.

"Okay," Clara said, her tone as flat as the previous reply.

Issaroh sat on one of the half-height portions of the wall, pulling Clara to sit beside him. "He needs help," Issaroh said. "He needs guidance that I was never able to give him …."

Issaroh's breath shallowed, and he wiped another deluge of sweat from his forehead, then around his neck. "But, with you and Bronwyn, you both could help him. Even though he …."

Issaroh breathed deeply before continuing. He put his hand to his head, seemingly to steady it. "He learns magic easily and is the most impressive healer I've ever met, but he fails to see how to work as a team, how to combine his talents in the disciplines with others."

Issaroh dropped his cloth, then gripped his left arm. "Clara, would you mind fetching Miro for me? I just remembered something I need to tell him."

Clara nodded and absent-mindedly rose, walking back toward the library.

Defurge approached Issaroh, sitting beside him, taking Clara's place. Issaroh's eyes fluctuated between dilation and contraction. "What seems to be the problem, old man?" Defurge asked.

Issaroh only responded with deeper, measured breaths, so Defurge probed his mind. "You're not well, are you?" Defurge asked. "Oh, you're really not well."

Issaroh gripped his left arm tighter.

"How did I miss that? Could you have been clouding it from your mind, or did you not know this was coming? But then you asked Bronwyn to stay for two additional days, and here we are, exactly two days later..."

"How did you?" Issaroh asked, barely managing the words between breaths.

"I guess that will just be one of the questions you take with you to the next life." Out of the corner of his eye, Defurge noticed a stark white horse with a horn jutting from its head, the Ywaigwai that had come to collect Issaroh's soul. "But then I guess there is no next life for you, having sold your soul for immortality and power."

"I never wanted ...." Issaroh's head slumped a little as his eyes closed before snapping back to attention.

"And now your master has come to collect his reward for your service." Defurge gestured toward the Ywaigwai, now stamping its hooves, obviously impatiently waiting for its promised sustenance.

"Now, I could help you. I could preserve your soul."

Issaroh's eyes widened with hope.

"But you'd have to do one thing for me. Admit that I'm the only god left and dedicate yourself to my worship."

"I'd never ... you're not a god."

"I am, and I could make you one too. Chivas wrote extensively about the relationship between divinity, magi, and Ywaigwai."

"You can't read," Issaroh said.

"I told you I can't. Probably a mistake to hold up in a library with all the world's knowledge in it. With a little bit of my essence, I could bind you, your soul, and that Ywaigwai together as one. You'd be an immortal with a portion of a god's powers. You'll rebuild the pantheon with me. You could be my new ... not Laevin, I already have someone picked out for that. Perhaps Chivas? You could be my new Chivas. Imagine the power."

"I never … I already made the mistake of one infernal bargain, and I'd rather consign myself to oblivion than make a deal with you."

"Hmm, too bad." Defurge sought out the memories of Issaroh's recent conversation and clipped the moorings, separating the thoughts from his mind. He'd prefer to rebuild his pantheon with those he knew first, but the last thing he wanted was little godlings challenging his right to rule.

With the conversation forgotten, Issaroh turned to see the Ywaigwai in his periphery. "Please, get Miro."

"Why? Do you wish him to try and heal you, to keep your death at bay a little longer? No, that's not it." Defurge probed a little deeper, peeling back Issaroh's panic and searching for the deeper meanings. "You're just going to accept this? All this power, this bid for immortality, and you're not even going to try and fight?"

"Please, get Miro …." Issaroh managed between ragged breaths.

"Don't worry old man, I'll take care of your favorite pupil."

"No," Issaroh snapped, his exhaustion seeming to take a backseat to his worry. The worry for his pupil who he had at one time thought of as a replacement son. "You leave him alone."

"You know, I was the god of madness and fire, but without my madness, I'm just the god of fire now. Why wouldn't you want someone like me looking after your precious Miro?" Defurge was honestly curious, not just taunting the old man this time.

"I don't trust you," Issaroh said, his voice steadying, but his heart still failing.

"Well, it's a pity you won't be able to tell anyone." Defurge delved deeper into the old man's mind, then severed his ability to convey his worry to others. "You know, I've never watched someone die before. I guess I have, but I don't remember any of the people I've killed since the phoenix locked those memories away when curtailing my madness. It will be a new experience to watch someone die, probably the most interesting one I've had."

"I swear if you—" Issaroh attempted to stand but found himself falling to his knees instead.

"You'll do nothing," Defurge replied, walking away and sitting on a nearby boulder, sensing Clara and Miro's imminent return with Bronwyn following behind. Miro, at seeing his mentor on his knees, hurried his pace.

Then Defurge felt it, Miro's fog dissipated, and a beautifully brilliant range of emotions emerged. Love, hate, sadness, anger, worry. It all assaulted Defurge in such a deluge it was overpowering, enough to render him speechless. That was strength that could be harnessed, utilized, and weaponized. A brilliant candidate for the new Laevin. Defurge watched with glee as Miro grabbed Issaroh's arm and helped him to his back, laying him on the muddy earth.

Miro began to weave his hands, forming runes in the air above Issaroh. "Seraph, goddess of life, love—"

Issaroh grabbed Miro's hands, preventing him from tracing any further runes. "No, it won't help me, only endanger you."

Despite the old man's frailty, he held Miro's hands tightly. "Miro, I'm so sorry. I've tried to be good to you, but I've failed you so much. I always thought of you as the son I failed, and I'm a coward for not telling you about that sooner."

"No, Issaroh, let me help you," Miro pled, trying to rest his hands free.

"Please, Miro, let me have some courage in this moment. I love you. I love you as a father loves a son, and I'm sorry I didn't say it sooner."

Miro tried to pull away from Issaroh harder, wishing to free his hands again. "No, no—"

"We all have our time. Mine is now. Let me …." Issaroh fought for another breath. "Please Miro, look to Bronwyn and Clara; let them help you like I never could."

Issaroh glanced momentarily at the Ywaigwai waiting in the distance.

Miro's eyeline followed Issaroh's and Miro let go of his mentor's hand, rose, and yelled, "No! I won't let you take him!"

The Ywaigwai stomped its hooves in defiance as lightning started to snake around Miro's body, starting at his hands then running up the back of his arms. His eyes turned white as he snarled at the former pet of a god. "If you try and take him, I'll destroy you!"

Defurge had never seen the often-mentioned curse of the magi. Miro started to tap into the full strength of the Ywaigwai that had given him its strength. The hair on the back of Defurge's neck prickled at the idea of seeing a Ywaigwai fight a magus. What greater measure of strength, a Ywaigwai versus another Ywaigwai's thrall? Miro's mind was alive with a hatred so complex, so strong, that Defurge's chest thundered with excitement. But then, Bronwyn stepped up and grabbed Miro's hand.

"Miro, you can't," Bronwyn pled, squeezing his hand tightly. And disappointingly, Miro's rage seemed to dissipate. "Maybe there is another way."

The fog over Miro's mind returned and it died depressingly once again. Bronwyn walked toward the Ywaigwai, her steps measured, deliberate, but non-threatening. She approached until she was within ten feet of the creature before stopping. "Issaroh said your name was Brontidus. Please, don't take him, not now," Bronwyn bargained.

Brontidus whinnied and shook his head, his mane flapping right, then left.

"Give him a little more time. We need him."

A snort from Brontidus indicated his displeasure at the request.

Bronwyn continued her parley with the divine being, but Defurge's attention was now brought back to Issaroh, him still trying to depart his final words. Miro knelt dumbly beside Issaroh's body, his mind blank again. Clara's mind was a little more exciting but still subdued. It was her hand that Issaroh grabbed next.

"Please, look after him. Convince Bronwyn to help you. He's a good man. I'm so sorry that I didn't tell you how much time I have left."

Clara didn't respond, only sniffled and grabbed Issaroh's hand tighter.

"In my study, I've been compiling my knowledge on magic, writing down all the spells I know along with more complex ones I've never been able to master. You'll …" Issaroh blinked slowly. "You'll take care of him, right?"

Clara looked to Miro, then back at Issaroh, "I need to go back to the library."

Clara tried to stand, but Issaroh held on to her. "Clara, please, promise me you'll look after him."

"I just need to get back to the library," Clara said, her eyes glossing over.

"Please …." Issaroh asked, but then realization started to creep into his mind. "Wait, Clara, what's wrong?"

"The library," Clara said, tugging with determination, trying to free her hand.

Issaroh grabbed Clara's arm with both hands, forcing her to look at him, and then his eyes went wide in shock. "Who are you?"

Clara wrested her arm free, then started toward the library, ignoring Issaroh's questions. Miro also seemed to be pulled back toward the library and left his mentor's side almost as suddenly. The hold the library had on each of these souls was so powerful that even the death of someone they cared for was overwhelmed. Another couple of weeks, and the two souls would be unable to leave altogether, regardless of what outside influence was trying to rest them away. Mortals really couldn't handle divinity.

Issaroh's shock turned to terror and frantically he looked for Bronwyn, reaching out to beckon her toward him. However, Bronwyn was still arguing and pleading with the Ywaigwai and could not hear the old man's feeble attempts at getting her attention. His voice was now little more than a raspy whisper. Defurge approached again and knelt, bringing his ear close enough to hear the desperate attempts at last words.

"Does it always take people this long to die?" Defurge asked quietly.

"She … right … tell her … wrong … this place … them …" Issaroh managed, each word harder to make out than the last.

"Now, where's the fun in that? Maybe when I've grown tired of this particular situation. When I've learned all I need to in this treasure trove of knowledge you've gifted me with."

Issaroh tried to say something more, but the words caught in his throat along with his breath. His eyes fluttered as his chest tried to pull in more air, his diaphragm unable to function without the oxygenated blood required. He was fearful as his body started to spasm, and then it turned only to little twitches as his arms and legs went limp. Defurge watched with rapt attention until a whinny from the Ywaigwai caused his concentration to wander. The Ywaigwai shook its mane, reared up on its hind limbs, then turned and started in the opposite direction of Bronwyn.

Bronwyn's shoulders slumped and she yelled, "No, come back!" For a moment, her arm shot up to her sword on her back, but it retreated in defeat, mimicking the rest of her body posture. Even her steps to follow the creature were slow and short; she knew there was no way she could catch a galloping fraction of immortality. Even if she could, after a quarter of a mile, the creature bled into mist and dissipated into the air.

Bronwyn stared at its last location, then hung her head and shook it. She brought her right hand to her eyes and wiped away tears. Defurge was about to leave, head back into the library or somewhere he could sunbathe in peace when Bronwyn turned after five sullen minutes alone. Her eyes were slightly red as she walked toward Defurge and he decided to stay, just to see what she meant to do.

Bronwyn stood above Issaroh's body for a minute, as Defurge stared at her, waiting to see what she would say. "He's gone ..." she finally said, half question, half statement.

Defurge nodded in reply.

Bronwyn only now seemed to notice Miro and Clara were no longer here, "Where are they?"

"They went back into the library."

"Even Clara?" Such an odd question. Did this mean she expected Miro to leave, but not Clara? Defurge tried to probe her mind, but it was a jumble of conflicting emotions, not as beautifully complex as Miro's, more akin to muddy water as opposed to Miro's which were like oil on the surface of water, a mesmerizing rainbow of whirls and eddies.

When Defurge didn't answer, Bronwyn shook her head, tears beginning to well in the corner of her eyes once again. She slowly closed her eyes, holding them that way for a half minute until a single tear rolled down her right cheek. She wiped it away and said, "Do you think you could stay here, with Issaroh for a couple of minutes? I'll be back soon."

Defurge wanted to argue with her, to tell her that guarding a corpse was below the concern of a god, but he knew that such a remark now would be seen as callous and make further games he wished to play more difficult, but not in the fun way. He nodded and she walked past him, back to the library.

Mortals must not have a good concept of time, because it was a half-hour before she returned, with a lamp, a couple of shovels, white cloth, and a more somber attitude. Wordlessly, she first positioned Issaroh's body, crossing his hands over his chest, and closing his eyes. Then she laid the cloth down next to the body and repositioned the body over the cloth before starting to tightly wrap it. She motioned to Defurge and they used the cloth to cradle the corpse as they headed back toward the library's entrance. They laid it down to the side of the entrance, about a hundred feet to the right of the cavern that led to the library. She walked ten feet away from that spot, closer to the swamp, then started to dig.

She didn't ask Defurge, but some physical labor would feel good, a chance to use his godly muscles and marvel at his own strength. Despite their combined efforts, the grave took a while to dig. They went three feet down into the thick, clay-like ground, Bronwyn's boots becoming so caked in the stuff that there were several inches stuck to each sole. By the time they had finished, both their shirts were soaked in sweat, the fabric sticking to their bodies in the humidity.

After lowering the body, they started to layer the dirt and mud back on top of it, only taking a break long enough to light the lantern as dusk set in. Bronwyn didn't even ask Defurge to light it, a simple task for him, but instead used a match to spark its wick. Night had fully set in when Bronwyn used a shovel to pry a portion off a nearby boulder and stick it into the head of the grave, jutting into the air. They both stood, looking down at the piled dirt, now several inches higher than the surrounding terra. Bronwyn crossed her hands behind her back.

"It's weird they're not here, isn't it?" Defurge asked, the first utterance outside their mouths since this began aside from grunts and other exertions of labor.

"People grieve in their own way. I can understand Miro, his desire to shut down, to ignore the pain, but Clara …. No, I've never been around her when someone she knew died. Maybe that is her way as well. She said she *needed* to stay in the library, so perhaps she didn't want to show emotion around us. She'll visit in time, and grieve in her own way. I know she will."

It sounded like Bronwyn was trying to convince herself more than she was trying to convince Defurge. "This is what it all comes down to? Four hundred years and he ends up in the ground, food for worms?"

Bronwyn shot Defurge a disapproving glare, then cleared her throat. "He was a good man and tried to live a good life. He made mistakes; we all do, but what's important is that he tried to do the right thing. Perhaps now, he can join the family he said goodbye to."

"Without a soul?" Defurge asked. That's what the Ywaigwai came to claim.

Defurge expected Bronwyn to anger, or argue, but instead, she sat, buried her head in her hands, and shuddered. Defurge probed her mind, and it wasn't as muddy as last time, but several thoughts dominated her still. Sorrow at Issaroh's passing. Concern for how Miro would react. Worry that her great mission, to recover the Legendary Artifacts, was now in even more jeopardy. Defurge did something he had done on several occasions, and he tied Bronwyn's thoughts of Defurge to some of her favorite memories: roast boar, the crisp air on the first snowfall, and hot pine tea after a long day in the cold. He then put his arm around her, and she put hers around him, burying her face in his shoulder. Defurge stared into the dark night, a smirk on his lips. He couldn't leave the mortals; the phoenix threatened to rescind any power she gave him if he did, but having a troupe of players entertaining him as he contemplated how to start a new religion sounded fun.

CHAPTER 5

Bʀᴏɴᴡʏɴ ᴡᴏᴋᴇ ᴀɴᴅ made her way to the wardrobe in Fria's bedchambers. It had become a morning and nightly habit. She bent down and retrieved the mirrored jewelry box and removed the sapphire necklace. As she held it in front of her while looking into the reflective surface of the ice sculpture in the middle of the room, she watched the necklace gently sway back and forth, the image imitated in such a way that it looked like she was wearing it.

She would never wear it; it was too expensive and it made little sense to fight with a priceless gemstone suspended by a delicate silver chain around your neck. Still, there was something about it, something about it that none of the other pieces in the box seemed to elicit in her. Maybe it was the way it reminded her of home. Or how it complemented her blue eyes. Perhaps it was just a desire to do something mundane with some time of her day, to let her mind wander, and let the responsibilities on her shoulders give way to something that was absent time.

If Miro and Clara visited Issaroh's grave, then they never did when she was around. She understood it. On top of their difficulties, losing Issaroh so soon after meeting back up with him, there was no doubt in her mind that all those feelings had just resurfaced. It had made life in the library more difficult than it had previously been, and the stress was beginning to fray her nerves. Clara left the baths the second Bronwyn entered. Miro refused to talk to her. When Bronwyn cooked, no one besides Defurge showed up for her meals. When Clara chanced to cook, if Bronwyn came to get a bowl, to share in a meal, any comment she made was turned around on her.

The added stress had only caused more nightmares to fester, always absurd situations with gods and goddesses. Non-existent whispers plagued her ears when she traversed the library alone, and she was always alone in the library now, both Clara and Miro eschewing her company. Defurge sometimes came to talk with her, and it was pleasant, but he didn't seem to grasp mortality or didn't really know Issaroh, so talking about the loss was awkward around him. She needed to leave, just for a bit.

She had meant to leave, but the day before she had decided to venture out, Issaroh passed and now it seemed wrong to continue her quest when Clara and Miro had lost so much so suddenly. She worried it made her seem callous, that she cared more for her people than she did for her friends. She was the captain of the Royal Emestrian Guard; her people were her responsibility. Miro and Clara had their reasons for being on this quest, but saving Emestria—that was what was important. She could not return without Emestria's salvation.

But Issaroh was gone, and she couldn't help that But she could still help her people from starving to death. She would not stop mourning Issaroh if she continued her journey, and having something to clear her mind would help with the healing process. Being in this environment though, feeling guilty about Clara's and Miro's inner thoughts about her, that wasn't helping.

After watching the entrancing dance of the necklace, Bronwyn replaced it gingerly and started to go through her pack and determine what she'd need to bring with her on this trip. She decided on two weeks' worth of supplies. There was a lake a couple of days' walk southeast of the library that Issaroh indicated the Shi'en might make their home during this time of the year. Two weeks would give her enough time to arrive at the lake, and if they weren't there, branch out to another possible location, or find tracks, then arrive back. It would also give Miro and Clara time to grieve without her, so they could concentrate on their feelings for Issaroh, rather than those of Bronwyn.

Once she had gone over her list three times, Bronwyn headed outside her room. She spared a glance toward the corner that dominated Miro's time and groaned. She didn't want to talk to him. But she had promised

Issaroh that she would look after Miro, which seemed absurd. *He's a grown-ass adult.* He didn't need to be coddled. But a promise was a promise.

Bronwyn's ears heard every little noise as she made her way toward Miro. Secretly, she hoped that some innocuous fumble would give her a plausible excuse to avoid talking to him right now. But with each step, she closed the distance between herself and the barbed conversation she knew she'd have. She rounded the final corner. Each step was one closer to saying something she'd dissect over and over again.

Miro turned the page of a red leather-bound tome with gold filigree in his hand. He replaced it, but took it off the shelf a moment later, probably wanting to re-read some bit of knowledge he missed. Or perhaps like her, it was difficult to hold onto thoughts right now. He might be re-reading the same passages to do something normal, or at least familiar.

She waited until she was within fifteen feet to address, him and even this far away, the smell of his unwashed body was overpowering. Homonculi lingered around him, gently swaying. His skin looked almost gray, and his eyes seemed lifeless and dull. "Miro, do you mind if we talk for a bit?"

Miro turned a page, turned it back, then forward again, reading on.

"I went out to visit Issaroh yesterday and put some flowers on his grave. I don't know if you've been out there yet, I understand if you're not ready, but I made a headstone. I haven't engraved anything. If you want to, we could do that together, or you could do it with Clara. I think Issaroh would want it."

"Issaroh?" Miro's attention diverted from the book momentarily, he cocked his head, then returned to his reading.

"I think I'm going to spend some time away, maybe a week or two. A nomadic tribe, the Shi'en, has an artifact that can give prophetic dreams. I can use it to find out where the Horn of Garanhir is."

"Issaroh?"

"I know. I miss him too. Maybe you and Clara could do something to remember him, together, while I'm gone. I understand that there are a lot of feelings, especially after my actions when we fought Defurge."

Miro didn't reply. Even now, he childishly took his feelings out on her, poking and prodding her patience, waiting for it to fracture. Bronwyn clenched her teeth hard, worrying that biting her tongue any longer would crack a tooth. Measured breaths reminded her that as much as she was feeling Issaroh's passing, Miro had known and been much closer to him for longer. Slow, methodical breaths allowed her to continue without indulging her anger.

"Miro, I'm devastated by Issaroh's passing. He was a good man, and I had come to rely on his wisdom. I can't imagine the complexity of emotions you're wrestling with right now, and I know he loved you despite your somewhat rocky history. But right now, I'm more concerned about you. I don't know if my leaving will be better or worse for your grieving process, and I'll stay if you ask me to, but maybe time by yourself is what you need."

Miro turned another page. Bronwyn's fists clenched and her knuckles whitened. She wanted to return to her habit of barking orders and ignoring emotional needs. Miro needed to do what she wanted him to.

"It's just, we both know that you have your moods. You go from excited to subdued sometimes and that can last for weeks. I can't imagine what Issaroh's death is doing to you, and I already felt like you were in one of your more dour states. Please, eat, wash, and sleep while I'm gone. Talk with Clara, and spend time with her; you two are closer than before. I can't lose you too. Issaroh is already so much."

"Issaroh?"

Bronwyn gritted her teeth and willed the tears to stay in their ducts rather than show her hurt that given her feelings Miro still wanted to play ridiculous games to punish her. "Miro, I'm being honest and open with you. I'm trying to be understanding, but you know I'm also mourning and you pushing my buttons like this is too much."

"Issaroh?"

"Fine! That's how you want this? I don't care if I have to throw you in the bath, force you to eat, and pin you down in the bed till you sleep. I'm not going to let you self-destruct, that's the last thing Issaroh would have wanted." Bronwyn tried to curtail her anger, but it was just becoming too much. She was about to turn and walk away when Miro decided to push her one more time.

"Issaroh?"

Bronwyn roughly grabbed Miro by the collar and hauled him close, causing his book to fall from his hands. Miro reached out to it as he said, "My books."

"You'll have plenty of time to read after your bath." Bronwyn started upstairs, pulling Miro after her as she rose the spiraling staircase that led to the upper chambers of the library. Miro struggled at first, weakly, but soon his only protestation was a continued muttering about his books. When Bronwyn made it into the smooth marble bathing room, she spun Miro in front of her, putting his back to the square bath.

"Is this what you want? Do you want to make me your warden?"

"My books," Miro weakly replied.

Bronwyn pushed Miro back into the bath fully clothed, his robe fluttering as he fell flat on his back and was momentarily submerged. He righted himself, his feet trying to find the steps, as he flailed his arms.

"What the hell, Bronwyn?" Miro shouted.

"Oh no, you don't!" Bronwyn shouted back, wading into the water, grabbing his collar once again, and pulling him onto a step so he could find purchase on the bath's floor. "You're not doing this again. You are not going to come apart; you're going to take care of yourself. You told me once that you don't break your promises. You promised me to help Emestria, and if you truly are a man of your word, you won't let Issaroh's death take that trait from you."

"Issaroh? Oh gods, Issaroh, he's dead." Surprising Bronwyn, Miro wrapped his arms around her and then buried his head in the crook of her neck.

"Issaroh." Miro's voice cracked as if he were digesting the information for the first time. Maybe he had been somehow blocking these emotions, and now he was forced to address them.

Bronwyn felt the need to soften, to comfort him, but she couldn't encourage this behavior. He needed discipline. "I know. You miss him. You loved him. But I need you. I need you to help me. All of Emestria needs you."

Miro shuddered as he attempted to suppress his sobs. The moment was almost affectionate until Bronwyn heard Clara yell from the door of the bath. "What are you doing? You're always trying to hurt him!"

Bronwyn let go of Miro momentarily and turned to see Clara turn and march out of the bath. "Wait, Clara, it's not…"

But she was already gone.

Bronwyn turned back to Miro. "I'm sorry, I need to explain to her," she took his head in her hands, "But I'm coming back, and we can talk about what the next steps are."

She waited for Miro to nod in recognition and when he did, she let him go, then turned to leave the bath. Her clothes floated around her body in the water, then clung tightly as she left. Puddles were left in her wake and her boots slapped noisily against the rugs on the stone ground. Inside Clara's room, well, really the former room of Lau'O'Penake and Ramun, Bronwyn found Clara face down on the bed, her face buried in pillows.

"Clara, it's not what you think." Bronwyn tried to explain. "He's hurting and he was trying to bury that hurt, which was causing him worse pain. He needs to talk to someone, he needs someone to look out for him right now, and maybe that's not me, maybe it's you, but he needs someone."

"Why do you hate him?" Clara accused, taking her face momentarily from the pillows before reburying it.

"I don't—" Bronwyn was interrupted by the pathetic chirp from the corner of the room where Ferdinand's cage lay, covered by a cloth. The noise came again, a noise Bronwyn had never heard from the overly proud falcon, and she ignored Clara as she approached the cage and uncovered it.

Ferdinand lay huddled at the bottom, his feathers fluffed and ragged. He looked up to Bronwyn, mucus accumulating in the corner of his eyes, then gave another chirp, begging her.

"Clara, what's wrong with Ferdinand?" Bronwyn asked.

"I don't know!" Clara yelled back.

"When's the last time you took him hunting?" Bronwyn asked.

"Why do I have to do everything? I can't stand him with the constant noise he makes," Clara complained.

"Clara, that's not true. I didn't realize that Issaroh's death was hitting you so hard as well. Why don't I take him out to hunt, then I can bring him back."

"Take him forever, I hate him," Clara shouted as she moved to the bedside table, took the enchanted messenger stone, and threw it at Bronwyn. She caught the feebly tossed stone easily and stood dumbfounded. It made no sense, despite claiming the bird was not very bright, Clara still talked to it like a child. It was more than an animal to her, it was her friend and confidant.

Bronwyn had vastly underestimated the degree that which Clara and Miro had been grieving or avoiding grief, and the only explanation she could come up with was because of her presence. She promised she'd come back and talk to Miro, but at this point, would that just enrage Clara further?

Bronwyn didn't know how to help Miro or Clara. They didn't want to talk about their grief, but she did know how to fix Ferdinand. Given some food, the bird would be back to normal in no time, she hoped. Without discussing any further with Clara, Bronwyn took the falconer's glove, stone, and cage and left the room. Clara only wanted to yell at Bronwyn, and as much as she wanted to help her friends, she refused to be the punching bag of their pain.

She hoped to find Defurge, the only person not overwhelmed by Issaroh's passing. Perhaps his inability to understand mortality would allow him to be a good moderating factor as Clara and Miro grieved. At the very least he could make sure they were taking care of themselves.

As she left the library, Bronwyn snatched a couple of wildflowers and made an impromptu floral arrangement. Defurge sunned himself nearby and Bronwyn ignored the curious traces of his glance as she bundled flowers together. She laid the flowers at the head of Issaroh's grave and looked again at Defurge to see if he was listening.

"I know. I know I promised that I'd stay and take care of him. But I can't anymore, Issaroh. I know what you'd probably say; I need more patience. Clara and Miro, they don't want me around anymore. Maybe if you were still here, you could help. I can't though. I just really can't. Emestria needs me and my opportunity to help them is slowly closing. I can't afford to be wallowing in grief and frustration. I hope you'd understand."

Taking a moment for herself, Bronwyn closed her eyes and tried to concentrate on the external stimuli of this place. The sound of leaves brushing in the wind, the peaty smell of swamp water, a swirl of water from a fish or crocodile moving beneath the surface, and the pathetic chirp of a falcon that needed to eat something as soon as possible.

"Have they been out to visit him?" She asked Defurge, who was splayed on a boulder near the other side of the entrance. Defurge hadn't completely disrobed this time; he still wore his short clothes as he turned his attention to Bronwyn. He shook his head in answer to her question.

"Defurge, I can't stay here right now. They're still too distraught. Dealing with me and Issaroh's passing is too much for them."

Defurge stood. "You're leaving?"

"Yes, I'm sorry. Can you watch over them, try and get them to come out and visit his grave? I know it's a lot to ask, but me being here only makes things worse."

Defurge nodded and Bronwyn leaned forward to kiss him on the cheek. A thank you, but still, a gesture that seemed completely alien to her. She didn't know why she felt compelled to give it.

Defurge leaned back a little surprised before answering her, "I will. How long are you going to be gone?"

"I'm not going far, but I think it's best if I stay away for a week or two. I'll come back and check on them to see how they're doing. If they're still not better, it's best I keep my distance. Is there any way you could take a look at the books? Try and find an item that could help my country with their current food shortage?"

"I'm sorry. Although I've inherited some of the phoenix and monk's memories, complex tasks like reading aren't in my repertoire."

"Oh. Well, maybe I'll take some of the books when I return."

There was more she wanted to say. But they exchanged nods and Bronwyn headed into the swamp.

She dispatched the first creature she could find, an adder. Normally she wouldn't eat them—too little meat—but finding Ferdinand food as quickly as possible seemed like the best bet. She slapped a mosquito after it had already sucked some of her blood. It made her worry that perhaps there was some other reason Ferdinand was ill. Perhaps he had contracted some tropical disease. They needed Ferdinand to communicate with her king once they had procured artifacts. Communication was key in the affairs of the state.

Retreating to the outskirts of the library, she cleaned the snake. Once Ferdinand was placed haphazardly on a downed tree, she laid the meal beside him. The bird looked at the dead reptile with trepidation.

"Eat," she said, hoping the bird could understand her. *Clara and Miro can talk to animals with their magic. They use normal words. Can Ferdinand understand me even if I can't understand him?*

Ferdinand nudged the lifeless body before starting to pick pieces of the white meat stained with blood. Her mother always said time and food heal all wounds. She was rather rotund, so it might have been a coping strategy after her husband's death, but Bronwyn always found it to be true.

Once the raptor slowed its consumption, she tried to return him to his cage using the falconer's glove. He resisted and it was only when she roughly gripped his talons that he finally relented. Bronwyn draped the remainder of the adder on the perch and headed back into the swamp to find a more suitable meal for herself.

The crocodilians were skittish around her. They dove into the water before she could even get close. She had probably killed too many of their brethren for them to want to defend their territory. Goading them into a strike at the water's edge posed too much danger.

It wasn't long before she spotted a constrictor coiled in a tree. They often tried to ambush targets from above, using their weight to pin passing prey. Bronwyn waited under the tree for the creature to register her presence. When it tried to strike at her, she feigned back before slicing its head. It fell and its coils writhed on the ground, absent a head to direct their wrath.

Reptile meat spoiled quickly, so she only cut off what she could consume. She tossed the remaining four feet into the swamp. A meal for the crocs; perhaps this would make them linger the next time she came looking for a meal.

With little knowledge of the surrounding geography, Bronwyn made for the southeast to the lake Issaroh had indicated was nearby. She had taken some fruit and three days' worth of water with her. If she didn't find a new source of clean drinking water, she'd return to the swamp to boil and strain more. Returning to the library was an unpleasant prospect.

As the sun started to disappear, Bronwyn made camp. After cleaning the constrictor, she draped it over the fire. She let Ferdinand out of his cage. He had finished the last of the adder. A little uneasy on his footing, he perched in the tree above her tent. There was no need to keep him caged.

The homing stone's magic would ensure he stayed nearby unless sent to deliver a message.

The meat sizzled and dripped as Bronwyn turned it every couple of minutes to ensure no part got too singed. Satisfied it cooked thoroughly, she picked small handfuls off once they had cooled. The meat contained little fat to season itself. With any luck, she could start trapping tomorrow night and catch something more appetizing. A break from snakes and crocs would be welcomed.

Ferdinand flew the next day as she continued her trek. At the end of the second day, she found a large body of water. She half-expected the water to be salty, that she had traveled the length of Primerra and now found herself at the Southern Ocean. In truth, she had no idea how long it would take to do that. But the fact that she couldn't see the southern shore of the lake had her curious. This journey to recover artifacts was the first time she had ever left her birth country of Emestria. Part of her longed to be back there, to be ordering her guards, seeing that Solstice, the capital, her city, was running smoothly. Despite the difficulties in navigating the politics of her position, the only female captain of the guards in Emestria's history, that life seemed simple compared to what she had to navigate now.

Miro and Clara, although pleasant, were nothing like the people she fraternized with in the guard corps. Her position there earned her deference, and she wasn't subjected to swaths of seething anger when she made a call that Clara didn't agree with. At first, she thought it nice to be around others that weren't under her employ, and thus wouldn't moderate their words or actions. But now, she was having to endure the reverse side of that coin.

Perhaps it was a mistake to consider Clara and Miro to be her friends. Things now would be easier if they just accepted her as their commander, but she doubted that was possible. Miro didn't even want to use her honorific when they first met, and since leaving Emestria, Bronwyn had come to realize that Clara was very much a free spirit. She would be less willing to accept Bronwyn as her commander than Miro.

But being away from the library was a relief, at least. It was only when she was this far away that she remembered the unease she felt when they first entered. How she had investigated errant sounds that led to dead ends.

The others seemed so at home when they first entered, but it was only after they had resided there for some time that she stopped being cautious.

Ferdinand's condition improved drastically once he was properly fed. The bird didn't screech as much around her. Possibly, he understood that she couldn't talk with him like Miro and Clara did. But Bronwyn and the bird had some sort of communication.

They started hunting together. She would launch a rock from her sling to scare the nearby ducks into the air and Ferdinand would dive, striking the ducks at startling speeds. It was entrancing to watch him hunt. He'd fly high in the air until one of the mallards positioned itself in his strike range. Then he would turn and hurtle towards the earth. An explosion of feathers erupted when he hit, and both birds would plummet to the ground. Ferdinand flared his wings, slowing prey and predator's descent, then released his talons and floated to the ground gracefully. Bronwyn would then cook the duck, rewarding Ferdinand with a wing and neck for his prowess.

CHAPTER 6

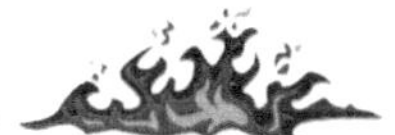

BRONWYN HAD ONLY been at the lake for three days. Three days and three dead crows. She picked up the corpse and tossed it into the lake. Ferdinand didn't even eat much of the birds. It was bad luck to kill a crow, let alone eat one. Not one for superstitions, Bronwyn was sure it didn't count if it was another bird that killed the crow.

Despite having downed the bird, Ferdinand readily took to the sky when Bronwyn decided duck sounded like a good breakfast. In truth, duck sounded like a good breakfast, lunch, and dinner. Bronwyn was spoiling herself at the lake. She never had duck in Emestria. Grouse was the closest thing she had ever eaten. Duck was rich and velvety. She had started to use the fat in cooking root vegetables.

Ducks were rather stupid. Despite Ferdinand killing one a day, they still gathered at the lake's edge in the morning, only to be scared into flight by a thrown rock and picked off by the falcon. After Ferdinand downed one for the morning meal, Bronwyn tossed a wing to him. He liked the meat just as much as her. *Must be why he didn't eat the crows. The duck proves too tempting of a meal.*

Falcons had to be like cats, prone to hunt anything that moved in the wrong way. Ferdinand perched on a nearby tree stump, patiently awaiting the cooked reward for his efforts. While Bronwyn rotated the duck, she surveyed the surrounding landscape.

This lake was a godsend. They should have quit the library long ago. They could have just stayed here and returned to the library to retrieve more books now and then. Sure, it lacked the heated bath, but the absence of the golems and homunculi more than made up for that. However, she did miss the beds in the library—the luxuriously soft mattress and smooth sheets.

Shaking her head, Bronwyn reminded herself of how she felt surrounded by the gods' effects. Comforting bed, bath, and lavatories weren't worth the unease.

She still had yet to see any signs of the Shi'en, the tribe that Issaroh indicated stole the Eye of Sleepless Dreams. During the days, she traveled along the lake's shore, half a day's walk, then back again to rest at her chosen campsite. There were some horse tracks, which might indicate the Shi'en came to the lake for water, so tomorrow she planned to head out early to that spot and wait all day, hoping to come into contact with them.

A small red shape bobbing in the distance drew Bronwyn's attention. It flew through the air, heading straight for her. Ferdinand fluffed his feathers, ready to take to the air and down the bird.

"Wait," Bronwyn said. She and Ferdinand had grown close enough that the bird followed her directions.

As the distance closed, Bronwyn recognized the small red shape. Nobles in Emestria kept these canaries for their songs and coloration. A certain diet was required to keep their feathers a fiery red. The poor pet must have escaped from some noble carriage and now approached her because of its familiarity with people.

As Bronwyn waited to get a better view of the canary or see if it truly was headed toward her, a sudden fireball engulfed the creature, startling her into stepping back. As the flames dissipated, she was surprised to see Defurge.

"Bronwyn, thank the gods I've found you," Defurge said, panting.

"How did you—"

"We don't have time. Something is wrong."

"What do you mean?"

"It's Miro. He hasn't eaten or slept since you've been gone. Clara used to be able to get him to eat, even though she is a horrible cook, but he even refuses her at this point."

"Just throw him in the bath," Bronwyn said, turning her attention back to the roasting duck.

"I watched them like you asked me to. I need you to come back now," Defurge pled.

Even Bronwyn couldn't deny there was something more to her refusal. It wasn't just the looks and hostility she would experience. The library wasn't a place for her. She hated that place now that she had spent time away from it. It was more than Miro's obsession, the homunculi, golems, or Clara's hostility. Her core didn't want to return.

She turned the spit that suspended her breakfast.

"Something is wrong. Seriously wrong," Defurge said.

With a sigh and grumble, Bronwyn emptied her waterskin over the fire. *Such a waste of a meal.*

"Okay. Let me pack."

With methodical slowness, Bronwyn packed her supplies. The knot in her stomach grew with each item she put away. Everything she stuffed into her sack only lessened the time she could spend away from that horrid place, the Library of Laevin.

Defurge offered to carry her pack as they started back toward the library.

There was a quickness to Bronwyn's steps. She forced each step further, each step faster. It was the only way she could keep herself moving forward. Every fiber of her being wanted to return to the lake, despite her closeness to Miro and Clara. Even Ferdinand shared in her hesitation. His screeches, which had been absent for most of their time at the lake, increased in frequency the closer they got. He had as little interest in returning as she did. Still, he followed her, using the currents to dip and dive through the air after them.

Bronwyn's speed had morphed from a hurried walk to a jog, then a run, as they came closer. She forced her body to lessen the distance even though it fought her every inch of the way. Defurge kept the pace easily, not even panting with the added weight of her pack.

Bronwyn's run continued as she entered the library and headed toward the corner Miro had cloistered himself in. Somehow, she knew that was where she would find him, flipping through his books. She had found him there so often; she didn't even need to give it a second thought as she turned down the stacks.

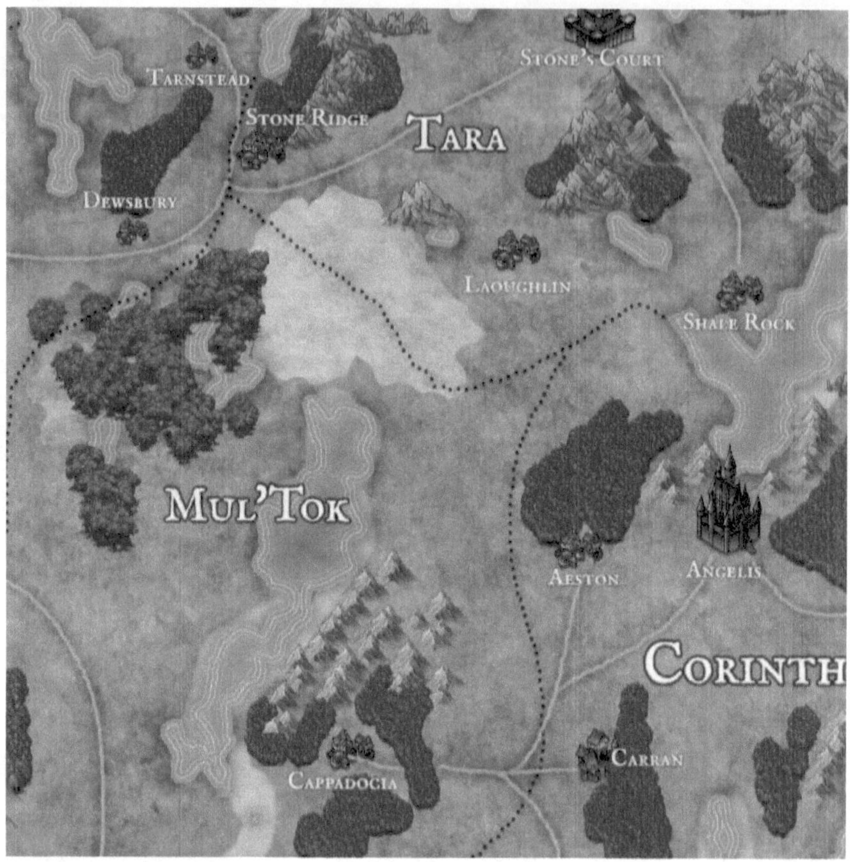

Miro's frame came into view. Removing, flipping through, and replacing tome after tome. His skin seemed to hang from his skeleton. The fair complexion, now a gaunt grey, deprived of sunlight and nutrition. Bronwyn slowed as she watched him pull out the book again. *The same book. How did I not realize it before? It is always the same book—the red leather cover with gold lacework decorating its edges. I have yet to see another book like it.*

"Miro?" Bronwyn asked.

Unresponsive as always. He is always unresponsive. Always obsessed with the books, but this same book. How did I miss it until just now?

He flipped through the book and put it back, only to retrieve it again. A silverfish ran down one of the pages. Miro quickly grabbed the insect and gnashed it in his teeth before letting the body fall from his lips.

Bronwyn had seen this before. One of the homunculi in the greenhouse garden did the same thing when she first toured the facility. Positive any words from her would go unheeded, she attempted to grab the book as Miro went to replace it.

Miro hissed and cradled the tome against his body. His eyes were dull and lifeless. The pupils were unnaturally large—inhumanly large. As she attempted to wrest it from his grasp, he yanked himself free and started to climb up the bookcase. Exactly the same behavior she had seen so many times before from the impish residents. With concern, she looked for Defurge. *Where has he gone?*

Clara would be in Lau'O'Penake's room. She was always in that room. Even that realization at this point traced a cold finger down Bronwyn's back. She raced up the stairs, glancing back at Miro until the stacks obscured her line of sight.

Taking the corner quickly, Bronwyn skidded to a halt seeing Clara on the bed. Her legs kicked in the air.

"Clara, we have to get out of here. The library, it's doing something to Miro."

"Get out of my room!" Clara yelled, her face glowing bright red. "I hate you! I wish I was never born!"

Bronwyn had yelled the very same words at her mom when she was thirteen. Bronwyn turned around and ran from the room to find Defurge. It wasn't just Miro; the library was doing something to Clara as well. She was a forty-year-old woman, not someone prone to a teenager's outbursts. She needed to find Defurge. There was definitely something wrong with this place.

Defurge was below, in the stacks. "Defurge, it's not just Miro. This place, it's doing something to both of them."

How did I miss it? The signs are so glaringly obvious. The only way I could have missed it …. Only my absence from the library allows me to see things how they truly are. Defurge doesn't know. He has only known Clara and Miro since they have been in the library. These actions would seem like their normal behavior.

"Get to the greenhouse and collect a couple of weeks' food," Bronwyn ordered. "Then go for the notebooks Issaroh wrote. I'll get Miro."

"Wait, what?"

"We have to get out of here, if this place will even let them leave at this point. Grab as much food as you can, the notebooks from Issaroh's study, and Clara. Physically force her to leave if that is what it takes." Hopefully, that's all it would take. Bronwyn couldn't stomach the idea that this place had somehow permanently tainted her comrades. At that point, what could she really do? Perhaps there was healing magic that could deal with something like this.

While hopping down the stairs, her heart pumped, and her breath forced in and out. Every hurried movement meant one less second in this cursed place.

Miro still clung to the side of the bookcase, hissing at her return. Climbing after him could threaten both of them with toppling. *If I hit my head and am knocked unconscious, will I be under this place's spell once again?*

If he loves the books so much, what will happen if I threaten one? Bronwyn removed a random tome and ripped a page. Miro ferociously raked the air, his lips tightening into a growl. It was only when Bronwyn lit the page and placed it under the book that he descended and tried to protect it.

She felt bad about it, but struggling to get him out of this place would slow their retreat. As he advanced, she grabbed his forehead in her palm and thrust the back of his skull against the bookcase. She knew her strength, and although he wasn't a full-blooded Emestrian, a half-blood could still endure more than average pain. He would be fine, she hoped as he crumpled to the ground. A bright red stain of blood streaked against the wooden shelf where his head had hit.

Hang in there, Miro.

Hoisting the surprisingly light body over her shoulder and looking back toward the stairs, she saw a bobbing waft of flame. Defurge's hair, normally silver, now undulated through the air, suspended by the fire that clung to it. Several stuffed packs hung by his forearms and a bound Clara was clutched tightly to his chest. She wriggled and squirmed, trying to free herself of his iron grip.

Bronwyn dodged down one of the stacks as she saw a golem advance. She wasn't sure if it would try to stop her, but her blade would be no match for its hardened skin. *Is Miro part of the library now? Will they try and stop me from removing him?*

The question was partly answered as three of the homunculi crested the bookcases to her sides. They dropped down, two in front of her and one behind. Clutched in their hands, they held the same blackened leather that bound their bodies. Their eyes fixed on Miro.

Bronwyn dropped him as she drew her sword and sliced at the two in front of her. The honed steel cut through their bodies easily. Bones, a thick black ichor, and powdery skin jutted from the bisected body.

Bronwyn turned to find the third assailant gripping Miro's robe, trying to pull him deeper into the bowels of the library. Bronwyn thrust her sword forward, skewering it. Whatever they were, their bodies reacted the same as any other to a mortal sword wound. It slumped and slid off her blade. She re-sheathed her weapon and picked Miro up.

Daylight beckoned her forward. Promised her escape. Defurge followed closely. They were almost free.

CHAPTER 7

As Clara exited the tent, Bronwyn tensed. Clara had been uncommunicative all of last night and today. Her gaze was fixed firmly on the ground. As she raised her head, she gave Bronwyn an uncomfortable smirk.

"Feeling better?" Bronwyn asked, sure the facial expression was Clara's and not some product of the library.

Clara sat down next to the fire and ladled some of the soup into a bowl. "I can't believe I was acting like that."

"Like what? A teenage girl?" Bronwyn asked.

"Ugh. Can we just forget this part of the trip?" Clara groaned.

"Maybe …." Bronwyn trailed off. It would be so easy for everyone to pretend everything in the library was just some product of divine infection. She wouldn't let herself off that easy. She had been trying to determine how much of her behavior in the cave, before fighting Defurge, was some errant deity's emotional baggage and how much was her own. The library had probably been affecting them all while they were in the cave. That is why Clara was suddenly affectionate around Miro. And it was the reason, Bronwyn shuddered—it was the reason Miro wanted Bronwyn to kill him.

"How did you figure it out?" Clara asked.

"Bronwyn has a theory," Defurge interjected. "She says magic doesn't affect her the same way it does other mortals. She thinks she wasn't completely under the spell, so she was able to leave the library."

"Other mortals?" Clara asked, her eyebrow raised. "Does this mean Issaroh was also under some sort of control from the library?"

"I don't know. We'll have to ask Miro when he comes to," Bronwyn said. *If he comes to.*

Clara's head shot up suddenly, locking eyes with Bronwyn. "Is he okay?"

"I hope. Whatever was happening to us, he seems to have borne the brunt of it," Bronwyn said.

So, Clara's protectiveness and possible affection weren't just a product of the library. Although Clara hadn't shown any attraction outright toward Miro, she could have been hiding those feelings. Perhaps the library made Clara accept them, or Miro almost dying brought them out. Bronwyn nodded and turned to Defurge quickly. Bronwyn would make sure Clara understood that she posed no threat to those feelings.

"I want to try and get some food in Miro. Hopefully, providing him something to eat will help him break through the hold the library still has on him."

Defurge nodded as Bronwyn grabbed a bowl and spoon. They walked to the tent where they had tied Miro down. He still writhed against the ropes. The only thing that stopped the snarling was the gag Bronwyn had put in his mouth. The stench of death permeated the tent. Bronwyn hoped it was just the lack of hygiene, but worried those imps might have been doing something else to him. Perhaps feeding him herbs or other nonsense to change him from the inside.

When they first came to the library, Bronwyn was sure that both the golems and homunculi were inanimate. That the homunculi were just leather wrapped around some shape. After seeing what was on the inside, she knew that wasn't all they were. There were bones and a black ichor that could have been some remnant of blood or organs. They were alive once.

"Sit behind him and prop him up. Won't do us much good to get him out of there for him to choke on a carrot."

Defurge sat cross-legged on the floor and hefted Miro's body into his lap. His arms wrapped tightly around Miro's torso, preventing him from struggling. Bronwyn straddled his squirming legs as she pulled the gag off his mouth. Using the spoon, she mashed the vegetables she had boiled. She avoided taking any of the meat when she poured the bowl; Miro abstained from eating mammals or birds.

After blowing on the spoon, ensuring the meal was sufficiently cooled, she brought the food toward his mouth. Miro stopped his hissing and clamped his mouth shut. A sigh escaped Bronwyn's lips. Hopefully, the smell would do something, convince him to eat. Before the spoon could even touch his lips, Miro rocketed his head backward, slamming it into Defurge's nose.

"Damn him," Defurge yelped.

"Are you all right?" Bronwyn asked, pausing trying to feed Miro.

"Yes." The normal suave tones of Defurge's voice were replaced by a nasal whine. "I don't think it's broken, just bleeding."

Defurge repositioned, keeping one arm around Miro's torso and bringing his hand to Miro's head. Pinning Miro's head against his chest, Defurge nodded, signaling it was safe for Bronwyn to try again.

Bronwyn put down the bowl and gripped Miro's jaw, squeezing until he opened his mouth. She tried to feed him and Miro's teeth grated against the wooden utensil. Miro seemed more intent on eviscerating the spoon than eating. Mashed carrots and boiled potato bits slid out of the corner of his lips. Frustrated, Bronwyn pulled the spoon away.

"Maybe I can just get him to drink the broth," Bronwyn offered.

Defurge nodded again and helped tilt Miro's head. Bronwyn took the bowl in one hand and forced Miro's mouth open with the other. Little by little she dribbled the soup between his lips, taking breaks to make sure he was swallowing and not letting it run into his lungs. When most of the broth had been emptied, Bronwyn put it down and got off Miro's legs.

"You can let him go," Bronwyn said. "I'm going to stay with him a bit."

Defurge replied, "I'm going to go get cleaned up."

Defurge extricated himself from Miro. The blood had dripped down Defurge's chin and now stained his shirt. He brought his finger up to his nose to help dam any remaining blood flow.

With pity and sorrow, Bronwyn replaced the gag, halting Miro's grunts and groans. He squirmed until he was on his side, but now his movements were arrested to the point that he was unable to return to lying on his back.

Looking at the back of his head, Bronwyn removed the bandage she had placed earlier. Dark blood still stained his hair from where she slammed him against the bookcase. She wetted a rag and blotted it away. It seemed to have stopped actively bleeding. Then she began to wipe away Defurge's blood, which now stained the back of his shirt.

They had removed Miro's robe. For the best. He would have been upset if it had been stained with blood. It was the one they bought in Newtonne. The compromise Clara had him make since she told him he couldn't wear the red privateer jackets the captains of Newtonne did.

Grabbing a second rag, Bronwyn poured some more water on it and blotted the sweat on his brow and neck. Miro stopped wriggling and forced quick breaths from his nostrils. She ran her fingers up the back of his neck and his breathing slowed.

"You're a piece of work, you know that, right? You only seem to be satisfied if you have me mad or worried."

Bronwyn turned over and ripped another strip of cloth from the bottom of her tunic. She re-wrapped his head wound and waited for him to resume trying to escape. He just lay there, having exhausted himself with his futility. Bronwyn traced her fingers up his neck again and felt a small ridge at the collar of his shirt. She let her finger linger on the raised, smooth skin.

How'd he get this scar?

When Bronwyn exited the tent, Defurge and Clara were taking turns singing. Defurge a low humming tune and Clara some bawdy tale about some pirate captain having a peg leg for a penis and making wooden fish babies with a mermaid. Bronwyn shook her head.

"Am I missing the sing-along?" Bronwyn asked, dropping the bowl and rags she used to wash Miro.

"I was just telling Defurge about a tune we sing about Newtonne," Clara said. "And he was showing me the song the monks in the gem sing for him."

Defurge faced Bronwyn. His nose seemed absent the blood.

"Your nose," Bronwyn remarked.

"Cauterized the wound," Defurge said, his voice having regained its natural charisma.

"He inhaled fire up his nostril and blew out smoke," Clara said.

Bronwyn sat back down at the fire. "Defurge, would you mind keeping a watch on Miro for a bit? I don't want him to be alone tonight. Just in case he frees himself and tries to go back to the library."

"No problem," Defurge said before looking at Clara, then Bronwyn, and nodding resolutely.

Bronwyn waited a couple of minutes after Defurge left before asking, "How much of the library do you remember?"

"Not a whole lot. The stuff I do remember, it was like I was behind my own eyes, screaming to be let out."

"Do you remember Issaroh passing?"

Clara's eyes were half-lidded as she gravely nodded her head.

"Do you think Miro remembers?"

"I don't know. I can ask him when he comes to if you'd like."

"Yes, maybe it would be better coming from you. And the cave?" Where they had fought Defurge, where Bronwyn had almost decided to kill Miro.

Clara nodded her head with a frown.

"I wanted to …."

"Bronwyn, we were all out of our mind in that place. I know that wasn't you."

Bronwyn hid her smile, knowing she shouldn't be let off that easy. "I need to tell you something. Before I left Emestria with you, the first time, General Tiernan ordered me to kill you or Miro if I ever thought you were a danger to Emestria."

The pained look on Clara's face hurt more than anything that could have been said.

"And obviously, I never felt that way about you. But after the wolves, I was worried about Miro. And I think in the cave, I got scared, or the library's magic clouded my judgment. I made my decision about Miro, that I don't think he was a danger to Emestria—or us. I wouldn't let him hurt us if he was."

Clara sighed but seemed to try and lighten the mood. "He does go around being helpless all the time, doesn't he?"

Bronwyn let her own smile bleed through. "Yes, he does." Taking a big breath, Bronwyn continued, "And I wanted to let you know that there is nothing between me and him. And if you feel—"

Clara raised her eyebrows comically, tilted her head, and broke into a fit of laughter, tears pooling at the corner of her eyes. "Oh gods no. I thought he was some father figure while we were in the library. No offense Bronwyn, but he isn't my type. He's a bit of a dolt. If you had met Atien in Newtonne, you'd see how far off he is from the men I normally associate with."

"Yes, I hear Atien was rather dashing. Wait, what do you mean 'no offense?'" Bronwyn asked.

Clara shrugged and gave a wry smile. "Well, maybe you'll get to meet Atien after we've found all these artifacts and return to Emestria." Clara sighed. "I'm going to miss the baths."

"Me too."

"And the bed, it was so comfortable."

Worried, Bronwyn asked, "You don't want to go back, do you?"

"No, no, no, no. Being stuck in my own mind once is already bad enough. It's just that … Issaroh said he left me something."

Bronwyn turned to Defurge's pack and flipped through the stack of notebooks until she found the notebook Issaroh left for Clara. She handed it to her, and Clara clutched the book, sitting back down. She opened it and was reading something on the inside cover.

"I figured they were safe since they weren't really part of the library."

Clara turned up to Bronwyn and a tear rolled down her cheek. "He wrote me an inscription." Clara shuddered a little. "I don't remember him dying. I mean I do, but it's like I didn't know who he was when it happened. I knew I was sad, but not why. It's just so horrible that he died and none of us knew what was going on. Wait—how are we supposed to find the artifacts if we can't use the library?"

"I've got a plan. But we'll talk about it in the morning. Let's just all try and get a good night's sleep."

 Chapter 8

Bronwyn had taken first shift for watch, and as such, she was last to wake. As she pulled the tent flap aside, she saw Clara, Defurge, and Miro all sitting around the fire, sticks with charred vipers wrapped around them in their hands. Miro didn't look great. Emaciated, dehydrated, and sleep deprived. Still, he was sitting up on his own, eating, and at least nodding along in the conversation.

"Morning, Bronwyn," Clara said, a bright smile across her face.

"Morning." Bronwyn walked to the fire and took one of the sticks next to it. The blackened meat would have little taste outside of the crunchy char that clung to it. Bronwyn brushed off some, the burnt meat caking away on her fingertips.

"Sorry, I think I was a little overzealous in catching them," Defurge said.

Bronwyn started to ask, "Did you make sure to remove—"

"Yes, yes. Miro was very explicit in how they should be prepared in cooking them. Well, in finishing cooking them," Defurge straightened his posture with animated eyebrows.

Biting into the snake, Bronwyn was not surprised there was little taste to it. The meat had very little flavor of its own, now that was overpowered by the former incarnation of fire's exuberance in catching them. *I have to tell him to lay low on the pyrotechnics now that we're out of the library.*

"Clara, I think I saw a small stream a thirty-minute walk from here. Let's go fill the waterskins," Defurge said, grabbing them.

As Clara left, she turned, showing Bronwyn the same wry smile from the previous night. Bronwyn rolled her eyes and shook her head slightly. She turned back to the fire and approached Miro. His legs started to jostle. He didn't want to have this conversation any more than she did.

"How are you feeling?" Bronwyn asked.

"Like I was trampled by a herd of reindeer," Miro replied.

Bronwyn chuckled at the comment so reminiscent of home. "That's understandable. Just make sure you're eating and drinking properly for the next couple of days. You'll be back to your old brooding self in no time."

Miro let out the tiniest start of a chuckle.

"How much do you remember?"

"Honestly, very little. I remember looking for the gem, and the tablet, but after that, everything becomes hazy."

"Did Clara talk to you …"

Miro let the pause linger and Bronwyn was almost tempted to finish her sentence when Miro answered what she was afraid to ask, "Clara asked me if I remembered why Issaroh wasn't here with us. There was so much that seemed surreal about the library. Part of me wished that his passing was a dream. But I couldn't even lie to myself about that. It felt too real. I remember the Ywaigwai, of rising to fight it off, then you stopping me."

Bronwyn averted her eyes and swallowed. "What about the cave? Did you remember that?" A small part of Bronwyn hoped that he wouldn't remember, that it would be easier to explain herself if Miro didn't recall, or if it felt like a dream to him.

Miro nodded his head and Bronwyn's excitement died. She stared at the ground as she picked another piece of the snake off and chewed on the meat, giving herself time to think of what to say. "I'm sorry. I don't want to give excuses. I know why I did what I did, and I wish I could say it was because of the library, but in truth, I was worried that you were going to lose control. If not then, then some other time."

"It's okay," Miro said, his voice flat.

Bronwyn sighed heavily. "General Tiernan gave me orders to kill you if I ever thought you were a danger to Emestria."

"I figured they would have told you something like that, especially after the banquet. You weren't exactly subtle with your implication of marching up there and telling them everything."

"Subtlety is not my strong suit. Why did you come if you thought I might have been given those orders? Did you think me not capable of acting on them, or that I would be unable to do it?" Bronwyn asked.

"No, because I knew you could." Miro sighed this time. "Why do you think I lived in isolation before you came to find me for this expedition? I could have left Emestria, gone somewhere they didn't know me, and lived a normal life, but I didn't. I wanted to be where I couldn't hurt anyone. The only reason I left is because I trusted you, trusted you to be able to stop me if you needed to. I felt safe because you wouldn't let me hurt anyone. You'd kill me if I ever became a threat."

"What?" Bronwyn turned suddenly to Miro. Unlike Clara, his face wasn't haunted by the same pain.

"My life is in your hands. It has always been. I trust you to kill me when the time comes."

"Miro …." Bronwyn turned as she squinched her eyes, trying not to let her shock at the statement show. "It's the library. It's still making you feel that way. You were being turned into one of those homunculi. An eternal life void of emotion, food, and sleep would be enough to make any human lose their value for life."

"No, it's not that. I once asked Issaroh if his Ywaigwai talked to him. He had no idea what I was saying, so I figured it didn't. Mine does. At night, the dreams are of the things I've done. And it's not just the things I've done. It haunts me with things I'm *going* to do. People I'm *going* to hurt. They're not like prophecies or anything, but it shows me hurting the people close to me, like you and Clara. Not even with my magic sometimes. Just with my bare hands."

"Well, I don't believe that."

Miro's head quickly swiveled to look at Bronwyn.

"I mean, I believe that your Ywaigwai torments you. I don't believe you'd hurt me, or Clara." Bronwyn gulped and tried to crack a joke. "Besides, you're not a match for me with your magic. How could you expect to take me with your bare hands?"

Miro laughed and rubbed his eyes. "Thanks."

Bronwyn tossed the last of her serpent into the fire, the tail too crunchy to eat. "You know, you don't have to be getting so upset all the time and turning into a lightning ball with an absurdly deep voice. I'll protect you."

"You'll protect me? I think I saved you from the wolves and Naani. And probably from the hydra too."

"I had the hydra under control. Naani doesn't count because it was your fault she was traipsing about the tundra unsupervised. I can't argue with the wolves, but you didn't give me a chance. I took out the god of fire, chaos, and madness. I also saved you from becoming a homunculus cursed to replace the same book over and over for all of eternity."

"Fine, I'll give you that, but I still contend I saved you from Naani as well."

Bronwyn crossed her arms and let out a satisfied sigh. "I missed this."

Miro raised an eyebrow before asking, "Why was I turning into one of those things while Clara seemed to be taking on aspects of the child goddess Lau'O'Penake?"

"I don't know. Maybe because Clara was sleeping in Lau'O'Penake's room while you were falling asleep among the stacks all the time. Maybe it was based upon our personalities." Bronwyn stammered, "N-not that your personality is like the homunculi, just maybe it's not like the other gods."

"*Right*," Miro turned his lips down in a faux frown. "Without the books, how are we supposed to find more artifacts?"

"I have a plan. First, we're going to a lake. It was only when I was there that I truly felt free of the library. After a couple of days of fattening you back up, we're going to go looking for one of the nomadic tribes. Issaroh said they stole something called the Eye of Sleepless Dreams because they could use it to have prophetic dreams. We could ask them to use it so we can find the artifacts. I saw some tracks at the lake, so I think they must be near there. If they haven't moved on. But it's a start."

"Sounds solid." Miro turned around and stared in the direction Clara and Defurge headed. "So, Defurge ...."

"What about him?" Bronwyn asked.

"I don't know. You and Clara seem to be at ease around him."

"Well, he is quite charming," Bronwyn said as she turned around to look in the same direction as Miro. "Maybe you could learn a thing or two from him."

"I don't know. I haven't had much time around him. What is he at this point? A god, a human, something else?"

"Not a god anymore, but I think he's still immortal, or at least not going to die of old age. But the powers of the gem, those of the god, are locked off to him. But he still has control over fire, a gift from the phoenix so he's not completely undefended. He's strong, maybe as strong as me." Bronwyn angled her head downward so Miro couldn't see her mischievous smile.

"Ah yes, you full-blooded Emestrians love to boast about your strength."

"Our muscles are as thick as the frozen tundra and our bones as hard as rocks."

"You know it's a bullshit title. The demi-humans were half-blooded gods and after hundreds and thousands of years, even the most pure of noble bloodlines are not full-blooded."

"Sounds like something a half-blood would say." Bronwyn couldn't resist the gentle ribbing. It reminded her of a time before gods of madness, homunculi, and golems.

"I don't think I trust Defurge."

"He's the only reason you aren't a homunculus right now. He came and got me when he saw you were in trouble. Don't be jealous just because you can't dominate all of Clara's and my time."

Bronwyn stood, seeing Clara in the distance, and waved to her. Miro turned back to the fire, hunching over as he continued to pick the meat out from his breakfast.

Duck sounds really good right now, Bronwyn thought.

Chapter 9

Defurge had just finished hoisting his pack. He blinked and reopened his eyes to find himself inside the Soul Gem once again. With a grumble, he made his way up the stairs leading to the pedestal the phoenix and monks called home.

The Soul Gem was composed of two areas. The prison was a giant approximation of the gem's real-world appearance. Each facet of the gem held one of the previous incarnations of the god—their souls trapped within for all of eternity. The only three former incarnations that retained their sanity resided on the platform Defurge now approached.

A translucent red pane of no thickness stretched twenty feet in either direction. The two monks were lost in meditation, as always, but the phoenix was seated in her human form at the stone table in the middle. Instead of the apples she had there when Miro and Bronwyn visited, the phoenix now had an assortment of all the foods Defurge had been eating.

"Why am I back here?" Defurge asked.

The phoenix, a remarkable woman with a long thin neck, arms, and legs, stood. Her billowy red hair came down to the middle of her back. She was beautiful if you found women attractive. She was also difficult to work with and overly concerned with trivial matters.

"I need to talk to Bronwyn," the phoenix said. "Now that the man is out of the library, the monks were able to properly probe his past. I need to warn her of what he's capable of."

"No," Defurge answered plainly. "This is my body. I will continue to feed you the memories of the food and sun, but I am the one that lives out there."

"I warn you, current incarnation. It is my power that keeps the gem's grip at bay. It is my powers that you now rely on." The phoenix's red eyes narrowed.

"And I am holding to my part of that bargain. I'm following those witless humans on their adventure to find the artifact to destroy the gem. But I don't want you out there conspiring with that woman. What do you see that is so special in her? Why do you think her able to stave off the gem's madness if needs be?"

The phoenix remained resolutely silent, crossing her arms and flashing a subdued smile. Defurge used the power of the monks to try and pry the information from her mind.

"You'll find their abilities don't work on me," the phoenix said with grinning eyes.

"Fine, keep your secrets. As long as you keep secrets from me, you'll stay in here." Defurge turned to leave. It was only the voice of the monk that stayed him. They didn't normally talk.

"You must be careful of the one they call Miro," the monk with the long braid of black hair said. The tattoos all over his body vibrated color with his voice, ink fading from red to orange and back again at the words. "He will try and claim the gem for himself."

"I'm not worried about him," Defurge said, continuing to descend the stairs.

"And the little one, Clara. You mustn't trust her either. The gem has a strong hold over mortals. You must keep their minds occupied if they should show interest in it," the second, completely bald, monk added.

"Stop trying to convince them you're a god," the first monk warned. "It will only bring trouble."

Defurge spun to face them. "I am a god."

"Former incarnation," the second monk said.

The first monk added, "Yes, former incarnation. Remind them."

"Defurge." Defurge opened his eyes at Bronwyn's voice. It had only been a second in the real world. Time worked differently inside the gem.

"Yes," Defurge answered, biting back his frustration.

"Are you okay to carry that much? I know it's a lot, but Miro is still pretty weak."

"Well, I am a god after all." Then a wicked idea came into Defurge's mind. A wicked idea made sweeter because of the words of the monks. Just like when the mortals thought of him, they would think of things they liked, Defurge decided to give them another prompt.

"Former incarnation of a god," Bronwyn corrected.

Defurge smiled at his cleverness. Traveling with humans was bound to get boring quickly. It was best for him to come up with as many games as he could. Defurge smirked and Bronwyn nodded. Despite her immunity to magic, Bronwyn was not immune to his ability to sway the mind. He had proved as much to himself by compelling her to kiss his cheek when she left the library.

Bronwyn and he were carrying the heaviest loads by far. Clara was only carrying about a half-load because of her size, and Miro, being severely malnourished, was given nothing to carry. That left Defurge with twice as much to lug around as Bronwyn. From god to pack horse. Given his strength, though, it was a tiny burden.

"Ferdinand," Clara called out to the falcon circling above.

Clara held out the bird's cage, calling its name several more times. Regardless of how many times she yelled, the bird didn't descend.

"Don't worry Clara, he's just a little mad about the library," Bronwyn reassured. "Given some time and food, he'll come down."

Bronwyn walked up to Miro, looking him over. Inspecting him to see how far they could travel today, no doubt. Miro seemed to shrink under her gaze. Seemingly satisfied, Bronwyn hoisted her pack and walked to the front of the group.

"It's about a two-day walk to the lake. We'll take it slow. Stop every couple of hours. We'll break at midday and get some lunch."

Bronwyn stepped forward and the party seemed to be drawn up in her wake. Defurge walked in back, keeping eyes on Miro and probing his mind as he did. Miro looked back frequently at him, a visible annoyance across his brow.

While they walked, Bronwyn used her sling to fling rocks at gophers that popped their heads from their holes. They were the size of two fists and didn't look very appetizing. The rocks didn't help with the prospect of their palatability. When she did manage to hit one, only one out of every five throws by Defurge's count, she crushed their skull. Little drops of blood dripped from their caved-in heads as they hung upside down from Bronwyn's belt.

When the sun was in the middle of the sky, Bronwyn pointed to a tree that would provide suitable shade.

"We'll stop there, and I'll make lunch," Bronwyn said, grabbing the rope the varmints were tied to and raising it.

"Ferdinand, come down," Clara yelled to the sky, thrusting her gloved hand up to make a perch.

The bird seemed to finally have decided to forgive her, but as he dove, he sailed above Clara's hand and instead headed toward Miro. He backpedaled and put his arm up in defense. The raptor flared his wings and dug talons into Miro's forearm. He winced but didn't try and shake Ferdinand free. The bird screeched loudly at Miro.

"Don't be like that," Miro said.

Ferdinand repositioned himself on his outstretched arm, cocked his head back in Clara's direction, then let out another ear-piercing, but quieter caw.

"She didn't have any control over it," Miro explained. "It was magic. Like with your homing stone. She couldn't control it."

Bronwyn was now walking toward Miro and the bird with some haste. Her free hand was extended towards Ferdinand's talons when he pitched off Miro's arm and flew back in Clara's direction. Clara held her glove out, and the bird alighted. It now gave Clara an earful of noisy protestations.

"I know, I know, I'm sorry," Clara apologized, pulling her hand closer to her body. She fished something out of a pocket and proffered it to the bird. Ferdinand took the scrap of meat and pinned it underneath his foot, ripping a small piece free.

Miro was rubbing his arm where the falcon had landed. "Let me see," Bronwyn said. Bronwyn took the sleeve of his robe and shirt and pulled it up. Blood was dripping off his arm from where the bird's talons had dug through his robe.

"It's okay," Miro said. "Seraph—"

Bronwyn interrupted his cast, grabbing his arm and preventing him from making the runes. "No magic, just for a while."

Miro paused but nodded. Bronwyn ripped a strip of fabric from the bottom of her tunic. It was getting considerably shorter, and now Defurge could see the slightest hint of her bare stomach when she raised her arms. If Miro insisted on continuing to get hurt, pretty soon Bronwyn would only have the cloak to hide her upper torso. She wrapped the fabric around Miro's arm, fastening it tight enough to elicit a whine from Miro.

"Don't be a child," Bronwyn said, dismissing the complaint of pain. "You're Emestrian for goddesses' sake. Act like one."

"Defurge, we'll gather some wood and get a fire going. Can you help Clara with that?" Bronwyn asked.

Defurge replied, "If it's all right with you, I'd like to get some sun. We're in no hurry. I'm sure Clara will be able to handle it."

Without waiting for a reply, Defurge slid his pack from his shoulders and laid it down on the ground. He only took off his vest this time as he splayed out in the grass beneath the noon heat.

"I think I'll stay back here with Defurge if you don't need me," Miro said.

Bronwyn raised an eyebrow. "No magic," she reiterated.

Miro waved her off and sat down next to Defurge. He propped his elbows up on his knees. He almost looked like those homunculi of the library they left.

"How are you doing it?" Miro asked.

"Doing what?" Defurge feigned ignorance.

"Making them comfortable with you. So at ease around you."

"It's just my charming personality." Defurge's face lit up as he smiled.

"We both know it isn't. It's not magic. Bronwyn should be immune to that."

Defurge thought for a second. "Hmm, so it's not working on you?"

Miro sighed and picked up a blade of grass. He held it between two fingers, ripping it in half down the middle.

"I hear them," Miro said. "Rummaging around, trying to whisper things to me. The monks are not as intrusive as they were in the gem, but I know it's them."

When Miro and Bronwyn had come to the cave searching for the gem Defurge wore around his neck, thinking it a trap to catch Miro's Ywaigwai rather than the font of a god's power, they entered the gem after incapacitating Defurge during their initial fight. Of course, they couldn't claim the power as long as Defurge still lived. But the monks found Miro threatening and worried he would try and claim the gem, so they probed his mind and attacked him psychically.

"Interesting," Defurge mused. "It's an ability the monks possessed. Not magic, not of the gods. When Bronwyn and Clara think of me, they think of things they like: roast boar, the first snow, the feel of the waves, and the smell of the salt in the air."

"You're influencing them …." Miro's voice was low and grave.

Defurge laughed. "The monks and phoenix agree that it is best to keep this expedition moving forward. That all of us trusting each other is in the best interest of everyone."

"I won't let you," Miro said, going to stand.

Defurge gripped Miro's arm. "You know, in the library and the cave, we couldn't read your mind. It was too deadened by the library's influence. But since we've been out, you've been an open book to me. I'm not the only one with secrets. I know what you did."

Miro's eyes widened and his jaw slacked and elicited an almost imperceptible tremble as he looked back at Defurge.

"You and I are kindred spirits in a way," Defurge said, knowing how much it would pain Miro to hear it. Defurge had destroyed an entire city when he was at the full strength of his powers and under the gem's maddening influence. Miro likewise blamed himself for Lynnfield.

"What are you—?"

"You have your secrets, and I have mine. They can just be secrets between us, or they can be secrets everyone knows about."

Miro hesitated before sitting back down. "If I think for a second that you might cause them to come to any harm, I don't care if I never see them again. I will expose you. The only reason I don't now is because Bronwyn will have to assume control of that accursed gem. I don't want her to risk getting stuck in that prison. A fate you should also be trying to avoid."

"She wouldn't have to if someone else took the gem from me." Defurge angled the gem in Miro's direction, so the sun glinted off its rough but mirrored surface.

Miro shook his head and looked away. "I have no desire for power."

"That's not what the phoenix and monks think."

"They're wrong." Miro massaged his wounded forearm.

Defurge looked at the bandage, blood beginning to seep through. "Why don't you just heal it?" Defurge asked. "Why are you letting a mere mortal tell you what to do?"

"Because she asked me not to." Miro gave Bronwyn a friendly wave as she looked back at the two of them from afar. "And don't let her hear you call her that. That *mere mortal* defeated you in the cave without the use of her sword."

Miro grinned at Defurge this time. With a flourish of his hand, Defurge signaled his acceptance of the point. "You four had me at a disadvantage. I was unable to summon my hellfire from underground. If the fight were to happen now, above ground—"

"She would have your head on the end of her sword before the first ball of fire hit the earth."

"You have a lot of confidence in her abilities. And some admiration for her. Quite a bit. Are you fond of her?"

"No, Bronwyn is a good person. I'm not."

Calling Miro a kindred spirit must have got underneath his skin. Defurge had only talked to Miro for five minutes and it had been the most amusing conversation in the time he had been free. Maybe there was a benefit to Miro not being susceptible to the monk's gifts. Wishing to ponder the implications before engaging further, Defurge stood.

Miro was stimulating in a way the others weren't. Miro was protective but also believed Bronwyn and Clara were his equals, if not more. Defurge sensed Miro's fear about Bronwyn in particular. *Why is he afraid of her? Does he believe she stands a chance against me, Defurge, the god of destruction?*

Defurge said, "I think they're ready for me to light a fire."

"I'm keeping my eye on you," Miro said, staring Defurge down.

"Is that a threat?" Defurge asked with giddy excitement.

"No, we're all working together, right? Pursuing the same goal, the destruction of the gem?"

"Right." Defurge began walking toward the tree and heard Miro following behind.

Bronwyn had cleared away the grass, creating a small firepit. She had heaped some broken branches in a loose pile. Now she was rubbing a stick against a piece of bark, blowing on some fibrous material to get a spark.

Defurge stepped forward and held his hand out to the sticks. The woosh of fire startled Bronwyn, but she nodded in appreciation. Putting the bark and material back into a pouch she looked up to see Miro.

"Thank you," Bronwyn said.

"Why have a god of fire around if he can't light your campfires?" Defurge asked.

"Former incarnation of the god of fire," Bronwyn and Clara answered in unison.

Bronwyn stood and approached Miro, holding out her hand. "I didn't use magic," Miro said. Bronwyn's hand lingered.

"Humor me," Bronwyn replied. Miro sighed and proffered the wounded arm, and she pulled up his robe, inspecting the wounds for any unnatural healing. Defurge chuckled and shook his head.

Clara looked up at Miro. "She was just afraid you'd let Defurge talk you into cauterizing the wound. Wouldn't want to *mar that pretty skin.*"

Clara laughed nervously after she said it. Miro chuckled as well. Defurge stared at the display. Nothing they said was particularly funny. He probed Clara's mind to understand what she was saying. Repeating the words of a drunkard in Newtonne that had teased Miro about not getting a tattoo; It still didn't make the comment funny.

Bronwyn seemed to share Defurge's bewilderment. She wasn't laughing either. In fact, she seemed rather perturbed by the joke. She released Miro's arm, and he quickly covered it back up.

As their meal cooked, Miro continued staring at Defurge, his sour expression comical.

Once the rodents were well done, Bronwyn handed them out. One to Clara, Defurge, and Miro. She only took some of the boiled vegetables for herself. Sitting down next to Miro, she looked at the gopher he still hadn't touched.

"Do you not want it?" Bronwyn asked.

"I just thought I'd offer you some first," Miro replied.

"No, that's alright. You need it. Until we find a suitable source of meat that you will eat, I won't hear any complaints about consuming mammals or birds. You're too weak to make this trek without any meat in your belly. That's an order."

Miro grumbled, "Please, take some Bronwyn."

Bronwyn breathed heavily as she used a knife to sever the last quarter of the rodent.

"Do you only eat rats and snakes?" Defurge asked. He gave Miro a pointed stare as he continued, "I thought you would like to eat something more substantial than vermin."

"I'll set some traps tonight and we might catch something else," Bronwyn said. "When we make it to the lake, there will be plenty of fowl. Miro could probably get some fish as well. He usually abstains from eating birds and mammals. But it doesn't make much sense to carry a large kill while we're traveling."

"Speaking of which," Miro said. "How did you survive for four hundred years in that cave? What were you eating?"

Defurge's grin widened. Miro took the bait. "Well, I don't need to eat."

"You don't need to eat?" Miro asked. "But you take our food and complain about it?"

"Miro," Bronwyn chastised.

"No, he's right. I didn't realize you were so starved. I don't need to eat. I still feel hunger and miss sustenance. Still, maybe it's best if I don't eat anymore."

"There's plenty of food," Bronwyn said, casting a disapproving glare in Miro's direction.

Miro looked at Defurge. Miro's jaw clenched and Defurge only offered a pleasant inclination of his head. Even if Miro did try and tell them Defurge was influencing their minds, it would be hard for Miro if Bronwyn believed he was doing it out of spite.

After lunch, they resumed their lazy journey to the lake. Bronwyn had no luck trying to catch more vermin, but Ferdinand managed to down a couple of doves. Defurge thought about goading Miro into another outburst but decided on a more subtle approach. After they had all gone to sleep, except for Bronwyn, Defurge waited for her to return to camp after setting her snares.

Defurge parted the tent he shared with Miro. Bronwyn was sitting next to the fire. She turned to see Defurge and a look of shock registered on her face. Not who she was expecting. Defurge made his way to the fire. Her thoughts quickened as he sat next to her.

"Trouble sleeping?" Bronwyn asked.

"Just a little cold." Defurge put his hands forth and caused the fire to blaze in intensity. "The phoenix misses the fire, as do most of the denizens of the gem."

"Can you talk to them? The phoenix and the monks?" Bronwyn had asked this before and Defurge indicated he had no contact with them, but his comment seemed to signify that had changed.

"At first, no. But now a little bit. It's difficult to explain." Defurge started to shape the fire into the form of a woman, twirling and spinning, her dress fanning out into wisps of smoke.

Bronwyn watched the display. She leaned forward, looking into the fire, the light reflecting off her eyes. Physically, she was pleasant. If one went for that sort of thing. She shook her head, and the spell of the display seemed lost on her.

"I'm sorry about having to share a tent with him. He has night terrors."

"I'll be fine. I don't need much sleep. Being a god and all."

"Former incarnation of a god," Bronwyn said.

"Right, former incarnation."

"Earlier … well he just takes some getting used to. But he's not always like that. It must be the library."

"Think nothing of it. He's entitled to his opinion of me. I mean, he barely knows me. It's just …." Defurge said. At first, he worried she wouldn't try to get him to continue.

"What?" Bronwyn asked.

"I don't know. I probably shouldn't say anything. It's just … I remember our fight in the cave. Even when I was fighting against you, I couldn't believe the way you moved. The grace in your strikes. How you dodged my attacks. Then with the cassolisk, you proved yourself more than capable as well. I don't see how he doesn't realize that."

"What did he say?" Bronwyn asked, her posture straightening.

"Nothing. I don't want to start trouble. I'll just say, I'm glad you're here. I think you and I can work well together."

The low guttural sound from Bronwyn's throat reassured Defurge that the anger was more than mental. Her knuckles cracked as she flexed her right fist, then the left.

"Is there something between you two?" Defurge asked.

"N-no," Bronwyn stammered.

"Oh, so him and Clara then?"

Bronwyn laughed. "Definitely not."

"But you two are ravishing women. Surely traveling for so long together, he must have expressed a desire to one of you."

"We're compatriots. Miro understands that. We're here to help people, and that's what we're concentrating on."

"But what's a stolen half-hour during the day if it makes life better?" Defurge turned to Bronwyn. His red eyes locked with her blue. "That's what I plan on doing. I don't know what will happen to me once we destroy the gem. I may return to being mortal, or I may perish. I plan on enjoying the little bits of life I can 'til then."

Defurge kept his stare locked onto Bronwyn's for another thirty seconds. Just long enough for her to not want to break it first. Long enough for her cheeks to redden by the tiniest shade.

"Goodnight," he said, standing to return to the tent.

"G-goodnight," Bronwyn repeated after a short pause.

Defurge walked back to the tent with a wicked grin. If he was going to be stuck with these mortals, he'd need to be entertained. Despite her so-called immunity to magic, Bronwyn didn't seem to have any defense against his ability to sway minds. This would make her an interesting plaything.

Chapter 10

As Bronwyn pulled the tent flap open, she was dismayed to find only Miro sitting around the fire. He looked worse than yesterday, probably because she had him carry a half-load. With his hostility toward Defurge, it didn't make much sense for Defurge to have to shoulder Miro's burden more than he needed to.

"Good morning," Miro said, an easy-going smile across his face.

"Morning." Bronwyn surprised herself with the animosity in her voice. She hadn't meant for it to sound so confrontational. Avoiding eye contact, she walked to the fire to see how much of this morning's breakfast was saved for her. It was just vegetables. They could wait.

"How did you sleep?" Miro asked.

"Eh, fine. I'm going to go check my traps. I don't want to hear any complaints about what I bring back."

Miro seemed perturbed at Bronwyn's short answers, but she didn't want to talk to him this morning. She couldn't believe he had belittled her combat prowess in front of Defurge. The conversation after the library led her to believe he did admire her strength, but obviously, Miro felt the need to boast around another man. How boringly typical of him. She had yet to see his behavior around other men outside of a guard in the dungeons of Emestria and Issaroh and was disappointed it amounted to dismissing his female companion's skill.

The three snares only yielded a single hare. Ferdinand would have to catch a duck tonight. When she returned to camp an hour later, Miro was gone and Defurge warmed his hands over the fire. Bronwyn grabbed a bowl and what remained of breakfast and sat down. Defurge joined her shortly after.

"Where's Miro?" Bronwyn asked.

"I don't know," Defurge replied. "I came back to camp, and he just got up and left. I asked him where he was going, and he ignored the question." Defurge would need time to acclimate to Miro's moods; he still seemed perplexed by Miro's behavior.

Bronwyn rolled her eyes and slightly shook her head as she speared a potato and brought it to her mouth. "You'll get used to him. One day he is a joy to be around, the next it's like pulling teeth," Bronwyn said before biting into the potato.

"I'm sorry. That must be hard for you to deal with."

She brought her hand to hide her full mouth as she talked. "Thank you, at least someone understands."

Defurge smiled broadly and asked, "Would you like to spar today? I thought we could both do with a little bit of exercise. Get our minds off the previous days."

Bronwyn swallowed. "How can we spar? You only have the whip. I doubt it would be much use against my greatsword."

"Indulge me."

After Bronwyn finished her meal, they decided to find a suitable location. Defurge insisted on an area with plenty of open ground. He would need it to have any chance of using his whip effectively. Standing twenty-five feet apart, Bronwyn gripped her sword with both hands and held it in front of her in an aggressive stance.

"I'll be at a bit of a disadvantage. The whip is best for grappling, but with the barbs, I can't risk cutting you. I'll also be without my fire."

"Those sound like excuses for why you're going to lose." Bronwyn grinned.

Defurge shrugged before uncoiling his whip and giving it a few practice cracks. The razor-sharp metallic barbs glinted in the sunlight; they were braided into the leather. Bronwyn hadn't noticed them when they first fought since his whip was engulfed in flame. It made her glad he hadn't managed to land a blow. At the very least they would cause considerable tissue damage, and depending on how tight the grasp was, he might be able to cause damage to muscle and tendons as well.

"Ready?" Bronwyn asked, shifting her weight to her dominant foot.

"Ready."

The second Bronwyn pushed forward, the whip shot toward her face and forced her to duck. She retreated out of range to regain her footing.

Defurge stepped forward, cracking the whip at her sides. With all his attention focused on her, she had difficulty progressing toward him. She would have to force him into range. As he snaked the whip towards her, she ducked and thrust her sword into its path. His weapon wrapped around hers, and she wrenched her blade aggressively, catching him off-guard.

Once there was slack on the whip, she stepped on it, pinning it to the ground. She spun her sword around, casting off the coils, only to parry with the blade, wrapping more of the whip around her steel. She pulled again and Defurge came tumbling forward. He grabbed her waist as he closed the distance.

Heat radiated from his body. Bronwyn felt as if it were flowing into hers.

"This is the part where I would use my fire," he said, releasing her waist and stepping back. "I'm not like the sorcerers you're used to fighting, I don't require runes or invocations."

"I could still do this," Bronwyn dropped her sword and spun to Defurge's back, placing a dagger right where his kidney was. "This would be a fatal strike. All I have to do is retreat and you will bleed out."

"Impressive," Defurge complimented. "Again?"

As they continued training, Bronwyn was able to best him three out of five times, but he adapted to her tricks well. If he managed to wrest her sword from her grip, it became almost impossible to close the gap. If she ever had to fight him, she would be glad Clara and Miro would help. Bronwyn worked up a healthy sweat during the hour they trained and excused herself to enjoy the lake water.

In the water, she found Clara, already bathing. With a quick glance in either direction, Bronwyn tossed off her garments and stepped into the cool lake.

Chapter 11

THEY HAD BEEN at the lake for the better part of a week. As Clara finished studying and training for the day, she re-read the inscription Issaroh had left for her.

For Clara,

So, you may continue your training. I'm glad the last student I had the privilege of teaching was you. You brightened the few days I had remaining. I'm sorry I didn't tell you how soon my time would be up, but I wanted you to enjoy your studies without having to worry about how much time we had left. You'll make a wonderful sorceress one day.

—Issaroh

Clara closed the notebook and wiped a tear from her cheek. It was still so hard to accept that not only had he passed, but he did so with his two pupils afflicted by the library in some way. He must have felt so alone in his final moments. Clara clutched the book to her chest, then put it in her pack. Her frustration with her training occupied her mind on the way back to camp.

But it wasn't just Issaroh's passing that weighed on her mind. From what Clara could remember last in the library, she had been concocting a plan to help Scarlette, her daughter afflicted with a blood disease. She squeezed her hand tightly, letting her fingernails dig into her palm. The decades-old habit of distracting her body from emotional pain with physical sensation was ever more soothing after being out of her mind for so long. Had she done this at all while her mind was distracted by the library?

At first, becoming a magus and using the magic to keep Scarlette healed herself seemed like a good idea, but after Miro's warnings and Issaroh's description of what he had given up to obtain that sort of power, Clara concluded that any deal with godly beings would result in the loss of what she cared about most, a daughter that didn't even know Clara was her real mother.

Issaroh had talked about powerful magic, and Clara wished that some of that magic had been included in the books he left Miro, but after "borrowing" and scouring the contents without Miro knowing, she found no spell that could permanently cure Scarlette's illness, only one that could treat it. This was already the healing her bastard of an ex-lover was paying for.

Maybe there was hidden knowledge the Church of Kyrie was keeping to themselves, but even if she put a team together to infiltrate their libraries, she wouldn't even know what to look for. If she had been more in control of her thoughts towards Issaroh's end, she could have pressed him for more information. Now that lead had evaporated alongside her ideas of becoming a magus.

There were only two avenues left for Scarlette at this point: either find an artifact able to cure her illness, or somehow convince Miro to treat Scarlette himself. Convincing him would be hard considering the fact she didn't want to tell Miro who Scarlette was. The shame that she was unable to provide for her child, that she left home convinced she would have the means to make enough coin to provide, and still came up short would be too much for Scarlette to bear. This left identifying an artifact that could cure Scarlette's illness, somehow finding a way to convince Miro and Bronwyn that they should pursue that artifact, and then stealing it away in the night, never to return.

Miro and Bronwyn had protected her in the wilderness of Emestria, but she was a prisoner in that endeavor. But if it weren't for Bronwyn, she would still be stuck in that library, stuck behind her mind, unable to remember the things that mattered. Could she repay that kindness with betrayal?

Clara resolutely shook her head. *It's not betrayal. Bronwyn's priority is Emestria, Miro's is in stopping war, and I do not doubt that both of them would put more mundane concerns like a mother caring for her daughter on hold if their priorities were in danger. Why should I sacrifice my desires given that neither of them would likewise give me the same consideration? To have the protection of your child be the most important thing in the world to you. They can't know. They'd never understand the feeling as you look into your child's eyes for the first time. The way that you would gladly undergo any hurt the world could provide to spare the life you cradle in your arms a fraction of that pain.*

Still, Miro was immortal, and if there was some way she could convince him to help Scarlette without him knowing who Scarlette was, wasn't that the most honorable way forward?

No, honor was for knights and kings. Clara was a pirate and a smuggler. She made her choice long before Bronwyn was first looking at other girls and boys with a gleam of attraction in her eye. There were few real "happily ever afters" in life; Clara had sacrificed or missed her own long ago, but she would be damned if her actions would diminish the chance that Scarlette could have the same opportunity she once did. *A way forward is what Clara needed right now, and the most reliable way forward was on the path Bronwyn and Miro were currently on. Find more artifacts, make herself useful so Bronwyn and Miro need her, and when the time comes ….*

"When the time comes …" Clara muttered to herself, followed by a sigh. "When the time comes, you do what you need to do, because they'd do the same to you, and you can't forget that. Don't let their naivety infect you."

Clara returned to her magical study, pushing thoughts of what she would have to do to the back of her mind. She was trying to practice the modifying runes of the stone wall spell. Issaroh had extensive notes detailing the effects of the modifiers and how they could shape the wall into more complicated configurations. Even with his notes, it seemed to require a lot of practice. She had created a curved wall so far, as well as a short flat one that served as more of a plateau than anything else. Right now, she was trying to cast a parapet-type wall, which was increasingly difficult. It required keeping the wall at two different heights in regular sections. It seemed like the most useful of the configurations. Clara could cast spells from behind the wall, peeking out to direct them when needed.

Unluckily, learning any new spells proved to be even more difficult. It wasn't just runes. She had gotten the runes right on Tremma, a spell Issaroh used while fighting Defurge in the cave. It had caused the cave to shake and stalactites to break free from the ceiling. But even with perfect form, nothing happened after the runes faded. She wished she could have seen Issaroh cast it like a regular sorcerer. The only time he had used the spell, he cast it as a magus, requiring no incantation or runes. She was sure if she could see it just once that would help her figure out where she was going wrong.

As she approached the lakeside camp, Clara saw Bronwyn sitting alone at the fire. A gentle breeze caused the smoke to waft haphazardly. The loons' tremolo still filled the afternoon air, so Bronwyn likely hadn't hunted another one of their kin for dinner—yet. Underneath the shade of a large willow tree, Clara spotted Miro in the distance. He had a pole in his hand, fishing for his dinner.

"Don't you usually take a bath after training with Defurge?" Clara asked as she sat down at Bronwyn's side.

"Miro's still fishing," Bronwyn said. "I'm going to wait until he's done."

The neckline of Bronwyn's tunic was wet with sweat. Defurge and she pushed each other harder every day. They must have been finished a while ago though; Bronwyn's face lacked the normal red pallor of exertion.

"Well, he's got to catch his dinner," Clara offered as a way of apology to Miro.

"Or he could just eat what the rest of us do."

Clara breathed out heavily as she put her hands on her hips. "Don't you think you're being a little cruel to him?" The words surprised Clara herself. Why did she care? Bronwyn leaned back, trying to force a look of shock. She stammered, trying to object to the characterization. "Does he even know why you're upset with him this time?"

"He should."

"How is he supposed to know if you don't tell him? So what? He's been a little rude to Defurge, but I don't see why that gives you reason to be mad at him. They got off on the wrong foot."

Bronwyn crossed her arms and groaned. "He's been a little rude to everyone, including me."

"Maybe, but I have to wonder how he's handling everything. He's only known us for several months and it seems the only two friends he had in this world—Naani and Issaroh—are now dead. I can't even imagine how hard it must be for him to accept Issaroh's passing without being able to remember it." Clara stood and brushed some dirt from her lower pant's leg. "It's been a week. Either tell him why you're upset or forgive him. We don't have time for this."

Bronwyn hung her head at the admonishment. Clara wasn't sure if the act was genuine or not, but Bronwyn would probably lend a little weight to the words. With not much else to do, she decided to join Miro and fish. As she walked over, she kept asking herself why she even cared. What does it matter if Miro and Bronwyn act like two children? Was it born from her feelings that she should be the one guiding the twelve-year-old Scarlette through relationships at this point in her life, or was it about something else? Perhaps it annoyed her because these two couldn't understand the burdens she shouldered. Or perhaps, lying and obfuscating the truth had become such a habit at this point, that she didn't even know why she felt or did certain things. One thing was for sure, regardless of whether she wanted to steal an artifact or convince Miro to help her, it was important to see how Miro was doing.

Miro didn't even register her presence until she sat next to him. He turned and almost seemed surprised to see her.

"Have an extra rod?" Clara asked.

Miro said, "This is the only one I have, and it's not even that effective. Actually, most of the fish I catch are from the basket." Miro pointed toward the lake shore. Nestled among some reeds growing at the border of water and dirt was a woven basket secured with twine to a stick. The top of the basket was protruding from the water's surface. Small currents in the water indicated there must be a couple of fish in there already.

"Oh, then why are you bothering with the rod?"

Miro shrugged. "Something to do, I guess."

"You could always join me for training and studying. Have you taken a look at the books Issaroh left for you?"

"A little. Looked up some spells. Studied the runes, but haven't tried anything. Bronwyn doesn't want me to use magic right now." Miro gazed out across the lake. "Probably for the best. It's hard reading them. Not physically but …."

"I know. I still shed a tear or two whenever I do." Clara understood the point of asking him to refrain from magic after the library, but now the request seemed punitive. Bronwyn and Defurge trained with their weapons. Clara trained with her magic, but Miro was just forced into this pattern of uselessness.

Bronwyn's concern was understandable, if Miro overly taxed himself, he could enter his curse. Clara had only seen it once before. He became something else, created a sphere of electricity around his body, and attacked everything around him. Issaroh said the only reason Miro survived was because the spirit guardian, Naani, gave her life to incapacitate him before he could fully enter it. But what did Bronwyn expect him to do here by the lake while they just all waited for him to regain some strength?

Did Miro even know the spell to treat Scarlette's condition? How would he learn it if Bronwyn restricted him from learning more magic? Clara reached over and gripped Miro's hand. She squeezed it and rested her head on his arm. Miro's muscles tensed but relaxed after a couple of seconds.

"Clara, what are you doing?" Miro asked hesitantly.

"Don't get your hopes up you dolt; it's not like that. You just look like you need a friend today," Clara replied.

They sat there for the next half-hour, watching Miro's line float along the water's surface. Miro was right, it served no purpose. Clara wondered if there was even bait on the hook.

"What do you think of Defurge?" Clara asked.

"Why do you want to know?"

"Just curious as to your opinion."

"I don't know what to make of him," Miro said. "If I knew the person before he acquired the gem, and his reasons for doing so, it might be easier to decide one way or another. I've tried to talk to him, but he seems more interested in witty banter than actually discussing anything of substance. You and Bronwyn seem quite taken with the god of fire and madness."

"Former incarnation of the god of fire and madness. Yeah, she'll see through that soon enough. Just taking her a little while."

Miro turned and tilted his head. "What do you mean?"

"You know, Defurge and I have never disagreed about anything. It's almost like he knows exactly what to say on every occasion." Miro nodded along slowly. "I've learned that if someone never disagrees with you, they're either manipulating you or intend to ask for a favor. Usually, a favor you would normally have no intention of granting. It's just taking Bronwyn a little longer to figure that out."

"If she does."

Clara smiled and squeezed Miro's hand again. "We're going to be leaving in the morning. It will be good for all of us to get back on the road and have a goal in mind."

CHAPTER 12

DEFURGE DIDN'T EVEN bother making a show of going to bed with Miro and Clara. Bronwyn had grown quite fond of their nightly talks. They discussed their training, with him always offering her effusive praise of her prowess. Last night they started brainstorming ways to work more in concert with each other when they saw combat.

Bronwyn nervously rubbed her thumb over her outer thigh. As Defurge sat next to her, she couldn't help but notice how warm his body was. The heat he radiated would make an Emestrian summer seem tame. Bronwyn got up to stoke the fire and sat back down, a little closer to him.

"We leave tomorrow, then?" Defurge asked.

"Yes, it is a pity to quit this lake. Once we're on the move again, we might have little time for training, at least not like we have been."

Bronwyn bit the inside of her lip. She hoped they could continue to train, if only for a half-hour every day. *A stolen half-hour.* Bronwyn remembered Defurge's words.

Defurge said, "I'm going to miss it. You're so beautiful in battle."

Defurge turned to Bronwyn, his eyes intense and bright. The fire reflected in them, made all the more vibrant by the red of his irises. Bronwyn swallowed as her heart fluttered.

"Thank you," she said, her voice a little raspy.

This was the most direct compliment he had ever given her. Eager to feel the heat from Defurge's lips, Bronwyn leaned toward him. His gaze turned down to her lips. She wanted to wet them; they were probably so dry. Bronwyn tilted her head and closed her eyes. But when his lips didn't meet hers, she reopened them to see Defurge leaning away from her.

"Oh, my goddesses," Bronwyn said before clapping her hand over her mouth. "I'm sorry, you're always complimenting me and talking about how good we are together. And then the thing about taking time out of the day to enjoy life …." Bronwyn turned away, placing her hands over her reddening cheeks.

"No, it's my fault. I didn't realize I was giving you mixed signals. I compliment you because you are a great fighter and do move gracefully. I thought you knew."

"Knew what?" Bronwyn expected him to go into some long diatribe about his complicated past like she had grown used to with Miro.

"You're not the type of person I'm attracted to," Defurge said. "You and Clara are both ravishing women, but I can appreciate beauty without needing to be romantically involved."

"What type of person are you attracted to?" Bronwyn asked.

"Male and preferably immortal like me. Someone more like Miro."

Bronwyn blinked in shock. "Miro? I thought you two hated each other."

"Well, we bridged that gap. Our conversations are much more positive of late. And when he was in the gem, something happened with the monks. I can hear his thoughts and feelings. We have this connection that I haven't experienced, and it is very spiritual in a way." The corners of Defurge's mouth turned up as his eyes brightened.

"I honestly didn't know." Bronwyn chuckled at her obliviousness. Strangely, the rejection didn't bother her much. In a way, she understood why Defurge would be attracted to Miro since they were alike in how long they might live. It wouldn't make much sense for either of them to be involved with a "mortal," as Defurge put it.

"I've never really considered it, but do you think he likes men?" Bronwyn asked.

"I don't know. You've said he hasn't expressed feelings to you or Clara, and he's been with both of you for a long time. Maybe there is a reason for that?"

Bronwyn thought back to what the phoenix said about him losing someone he loved. *Did the phoenix ever say it was a woman? What about*

Issaroh? He talked about Miro meeting back up with someone from the war and going to start a life together in the north. I'm pretty sure he said it was a woman, but that was in the library. Can my memories be trusted while I was there? But then there was the way that Miro and King Bryant acted together.

"Hmm. That might explain a lot. Has he expressed any interest in you?" Bronwyn asked.

"He plays everything so close to the chest, Even with the link, I'm unable to gauge a reaction from him. It's his move to make. I made myself available."

"What is it like, your connection?" Bronwyn asked.

"Most of the time I can't hear anything substantial. Now and then, I can make out some words or thoughts. When he's upset or excited, he is less guarded. In the library he was a void; it was like his mind was dead. I didn't even realize we had the connection until he recovered."

"And he knows?" Bronwyn asked.

"Yes. He says he can tell when I'm probing him. It's not like I can do it without him realizing I'm snooping."

"In that case, it doesn't seem that harmful. Why are you telling me? Because I tried to kiss you? You could have just told me you weren't interested." Bronwyn blushed.

"I didn't want you to fret over why I rejected you. I also thought you might be able to provide some insight since you two had spent a considerable amount of time together before I arrived."

"If you can't tell what he's thinking with your connection, then I have no idea what is going on in that mind of his. You're right, he's secretive. It becomes downright frustrating at times. I wish he would be more straightforward about things. I've always been."

"Anyway, I'm off to bed. I guess I'll see you in the morning." Defurge rose to leave.

"Wait, before you go, can you answer one question for me?"

Defurge halted and raised an eyebrow.

"His past. Do you know what happened? Why he continues to focus on it and punish himself?"

"I know. I can't tell you. But if you ask me, he lets himself off too lightly." Defurge went to the tent he and Miro shared. Before ducking in he looked back at Bronwyn one last time. That same strange smile on his face when he told her he liked Miro. He must have wanted to tell someone and was now feeling a sense of relief.

As Bronwyn finished up her watch, she picked apart every interaction she had with Miro. *Am I missing something? I missed it with Defurge, taking his praise as a sign of desire. I thought his insistence on enjoying the few moments together was directed at me, but perhaps he meant Miro all along. Defurge spends equal time with all three of us. Miro favors me, but maybe that is the same reason that Defurge confided in me.*

Miro called him King Bryant the Betrayer. Is there some other meaning to that than Miro's insistence King Bryant broke a deal? The way they talked to each other at the castle was strange. Did they have a relationship that ended badly? I'm sure Issaroh said Miro met up with a woman after the war. Perhaps he enjoys the company of men and women?

It would have been nice for Miro to let me know he was bisexual. We could talk about it—something we have in common outside of artifacts, combat, and regret. I haven't mentioned anything to Miro about my previous relationships either. Perhaps if I do, he might share with me as well.

Clara was right. It was time for Bronwyn to either tell Miro why she was angry or forgive him. Bronwyn woke early the next morning during the beginning of Miro's shift. She sat on her bedroll yawning and rubbing the sleep from her eyes for a couple of minutes. It had been a while since she rose early. She dressed quickly and quietly slipped out, careful not to wake Clara, who also shared the tent. As she exited, she saw Miro tending the fire. Holding her hands out to the fire to warm them, she approached.

"Morning," he said, seemingly surprised by her presence.

Bronwyn sat down, not next to him, but on an adjacent log. She chose a spot where the smoke didn't obstruct her view of him.

"Morning," Bronwyn said, fighting back a yawn. They sat for a bit as Bronwyn warmed her body and blinked her eyes, trying to fight off the drowsiness of rising early. "You've been spending a lot of time away from camp with Defurge."

Miro chuckled. "I've been lecturing him on the moral implications of power and use of it. I used to have the same conversations with Art …

King Bryant in the academy." Miro's abandonment of his nickname for King Bryant was a surprise. Especially since it seemed to be a conscious effort. He corrected himself, without so much as a glance from Bronwyn. "And I've been practicing."

"Magic?" Bronwyn asked. She had asked him not to cast. It was dismaying to hear that he was doing it without even talking to her.

"Not casting, just the runes, so I can use it if I need to. Start pulling my own weight around here."

"I never felt you weren't pulling your weight. Sure, your magical repertoire is a little limited, but it gets the job done. I'm the only one that can't use magic in the group. If you and Clara keep improving, my sword is going to become useless."

"Are you kidding? That's the only reason I'm trying to learn more, so I can support you better in battle. If I started to work with you, like you and Defurge have been, our fights wouldn't always be so close. You wouldn't need to be the one always bailing us out.

"There is one spell I've been studying. It slows time for ten to fifteen seconds. That's enough time for me to get off a second spell, but not much else. With your ability to resist magic, you would probably still be able to move normally. That amount of time for you would be enough to devastate an opponent. It's pretty complicated, so I doubt I'd be able to invoke it in short repetition, otherwise it would be possible to chain it one after the other. Imagine what you could do with a whole minute, uninterrupted."

"A stolen moment in time ...." Bronwyn said, contemplating the revelation. One spell for him, and a dozen quick strikes for her. If he had commanded that ability with the wolves when they were attacked in Emestria, they would never have downed her.

"Have I done something to upset you?" Miro asked. Bronwyn was taken aback by Miro's question. It seemed to come suddenly from the quiet moment and was wholly unrelated to the conversation. "I know I've been in a bit of a fog. It took a lot longer for me to shake the library than Clara, but I thought when we were free of that place, it would be like before. Lately, you've found reasons to not be around me."

Bronwyn held in her sigh. *Have I been so obvious that even he picked up on it?* She was unsure how to answer, so the question hung in the air. She waited so long, Miro seemed to grow impatient with the silence.

"Is it because of what the phoenix told you, about my past?" Bronwyn tried to make eye contact with him, but he looked away.

"No. I told you I'd stop asking you about it," Bronwyn said. The statement was terser than she meant it. She was certain after they fought Defurge that Miro had some role to play in Lynnfield's destruction, an ancillary role that he blames himself for still, but how could he? Looking at his body now, still frail and recovering, how could anyone like him have that much impact on the world? He would have been a man just in his twenties with the ability to heal others magically. But … then why did he torture himself so?

"Do you think I'm not appreciative of what you did for me in the library? I am. I thought I was demonstrating that, but maybe I wasn't direct enough. I owe you my life. It sends shivers down my spine to think about what that place would have done to me. I know I have you—partly Defurge, but mostly you—to thank for that. Only you would pick up on the way that place was changing me."

"It's that." Bronwyn sighed. "Not that you aren't appreciative, but that you're not more direct with me. I'm always honest with you. I put myself out there, but you are always so secretive. Not just about your past, but other things. I never know where I stand with you. Are you going to be in a good mood today and treat me with respect, or are you going to be sour and a pain? Even before the library, that's how you interacted with me. In the beginning, I excused it, but then the closer—I mean the longer we were traveling together, the more it started to bother me. Then Defurge came along, and I saw how I deserved to be treated."

"You're right," Miro said with a slight frown. "I've been a poor friend. I let my own feelings cloud not only how I behaved toward you, but also Clara. But you and I spent more time together, so you had to bear the brunt of it. I'm sorry I made you feel that way. You've been kind to me, and I took advantage of that kindness. Looking back, I'm ashamed of the way I acted. I promise to pay you more respect going forward. You deserve that."

"Thank you." Bronwyn nodded. "It's nice to hear you say you're sorry, but you know that doesn't mean all is forgiven. I'm glad you're working on your attitude, but words are easy, action is harder." It was a start. Miro rarely apologized for his behavior, let alone promised to do better. When he was erratic in the library, searching for the seal that would allow him to find the Soul Gem, she had sat him down and gave him strict rules to follow before she allowed him to go after the gem. He had obeyed, but never apologized for his behavior. But she was doubtful this round of contrition would last longer than any of the others.

"And Defurge?" Bronwyn asked.

"Maybe I owe him an apology as well. He did save me from the library by getting you. Although his attitude rubs me the wrong way at times, I've been trying to be more cordial with him. We have to work together to destroy that gem."

"That's good. I think you'll find that Defurge has a lot of respect for you."

"And you. You two seem to enjoy each other's company as well."

"Maybe too much." Bronwyn chuckled, thinking about her failed advance the night before. Miro raised an inquisitive eyebrow. "It's nothing, only a misunderstanding we had." Bronwyn stood. "I'm going to check my snares and start packing up. You might want to catch some fish for the road as well. We're going to try and find these nomads. If their tracks haven't faded too much."

"Ready to quit my company already?" Miro joked but then paused with a concerned look. "I'm sorry, old habits."

"No, it's all right. The ribbing isn't what I was talking about." Bronwyn shook her head. *Just when I think he's starting to understand. So close, yet so far. Maybe he will never really understand me.*

Chapter 13

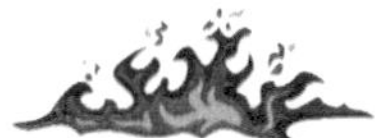

After the second day of trying to follow the nomads' tracks, Bronwyn worried that she had either lost their trail or they had moved their camp. At first, the tracks headed north but then veered northeast. To the best of her knowledge, they appeared to be hoof prints, but they weren't shodden. The further they got from the lake, the fainter the impressions became. Tracking wasn't something she needed to be intently familiar with in the royal guard.

She could tell the direction the horses' hooves were headed in and little more. For all she knew, the tracks could be days or weeks old. She had no idea how long tracks would remain in this unfamiliar terrain.

The ground surrounding the swamp was soft, with a clay-like quality. It stuck to Bronwyn's boots and needed to be scraped off at the end of the day. The further they got from the lake, the more the ground seemed to dry up. The impressions were getting fainter, and she was having increasing difficulty finding them.

"They're over there," Defurge said, pointing to the north. Bronwyn stared in the direction he indicated, and it was only after several minutes that she noticed small wisps of smoke.

"How can you be sure that's them?" Bronwyn asked.

"I sense several fires. It's some type of community of people."

He can sense fire? If they truly were where Defurge indicated, then they would be hard-pressed to reach them during the day. Bronwyn didn't wish to approach at night. They might think their small party meant to raid them. If they were hostile, Bronwyn would want the daylight to prevent themselves from being surrounded. There were few trees in the plains they now found themselves in, but at night the lack of visibility could allow a foe to surround them, especially since these people had horses and greater mobility.

"We'll camp here for the night, and approach them tomorrow," Bronwyn said, turning around to see Miro and Clara nodding along with her assessment. *Now the question is, who will approach? Of course, I will go. Having Clara along with me might help our group seem unimposing. Her small stature can be mistaken for a child at a distance. Without knowing the tone of their skin and whether it is uniform, it might help to have Defurge with us as well. If they also have darker skin, they might be more receptive to someone that resembles them. I don't want to take Miro, his brash nature has the greatest risk of setting us up on the wrong foot, but at that point, leaving only him behind doesn't make much sense.*

"In the morning we'll approach," Bronwyn explained. "I won't don my armor, so we shouldn't appear too threatening with our weapons. Defurge and Miro don't carry any of note, and Clara's axe and my sword will probably just be viewed as a way to protect ourselves." No one argued with her assessment, so Bronwyn gave a nod and they started to make camp.

Bronwyn debated finding some game in the morning to offer the nomads but worried that they might view this land as theirs. Perhaps they wouldn't take kindly to others hunting on it. Instead, the four members of her ragtag group pooled the remaining dried fruits they had. If they had any chance of these nomads letting them borrow the artifact—if they even had it—a gift might help. They advanced toward the camp from the south. Bronwyn scanned the horizon for movement as they did. If they happened to send riders out, Bronwyn wanted to greet them, rather than having them circle and flank her.

When she was within eyesight, Bronwyn waved at what she guessed were two guards. She hoped the gesture would be seen as friendly. It was not returned, but as they were still a couple hundred feet off, it was possible the guards did not see. She repeated the wave when they were a hundred feet away, and it went unanswered again.

From this distance, Bronwyn could accurately assess the size of their encampment. There were four pavilions, which seemed to be made of stitched hides strung between poles. They must only be semi-nomadic, moving seasonally or when there was sparse game in an area.

There was a herd of horses, kept in by some sort of corral It was difficult to tell exactly how many people lived here. They moved busily about their day, going in and out of the structures frequently. Based upon the structures and the number of horses, Bronwyn estimated at least thirty people. Assuming half were men, that meant fifteen fighters. Unless of course the women were also trained combatants. That number would be reduced by how many children or individuals too old to effectively fight there were.

At each of the cardinal directions, two guards were stationed. They held spears with shiny metal tips. *That bodes well. If they are truly nomadic, they likely don't have a forge and craft their own iron. They must take part in trade outside their group.* The guards continued to stare as Bronwyn approached, but they did not sound an alarm, and no one mounted to meet them. Bronwyn tried waving again and shouting, "Hello." But they still did not react.

When they were within thirty feet, Bronwyn stopped. She did not want to advance any further. She would be able to talk to them without yelling at this distance, but still be far enough away to take up a defensive position if need be.

"Hello," Bronwyn said again. No response, they only continued to stare at her. The nomads wore an interesting type of armor Bronwyn had never seen before. It was two-toned leather, stitched on top of each other so the border of each piece was black, with a smaller section of brown on top. The armor seemed to be in four pieces and was interlaced on the front, back, shoulders, and waist. The upper torso was completely covered, but the bottom was only covered by a long leather skirt with four breaks in the front, back, and sides. It would allow for freedom of movement, but also protected the front and back of the legs. Underneath the armor, they seemed to be wearing long cloth.

"We were hoping to talk to you and brought some fruit in kindness," Bronwyn said, indicating to the sack they had put the remaining dried fruit into. Their presence seemed to be drawing a crowd. The other guards in the four cardinal directions didn't move, but the villagers were starting to congregate and move slowly south. The majority of the population wore a single piece of cloth, fastened around the neck and wrapped around the body. A belt, of either braided leather or cordage, was secured around the waist. The wrap stopped at the knees, exposing the lower legs. The garments probably provided relief from the hotter climate of Mul'tok.

More people approached their position and started to talk in an unfamiliar language. Bronwyn listened as best she could to the murmurs, trying to determine if any of the words sounded hostile. It unnerved her, not knowing how this interaction was playing out.

The village had varying skin tones, from rich tan to almost as dark as Defurge. There were two dominant hairstyles in the camp. The first was hair grown long and braided down the back. The second was shorter with tight braids on one side of the head going from front to back. The hair on the other side of the head was either extremely short or removed completely. Children seemed to have long, unbraided hair. Perhaps the hairstyles were only adopted after coming of age.

At first, Bronwyn assumed the longer hairstyle was worn exclusively by women, but one of the guards in front of her had the short hairstyle and features that were distinctly feminine. Most of the women wore the longer style, but some men did as well. An equal proportion of men wore the shorter style, but two women seemed to have adopted it. There seemed to be some significance to it that Bronwyn couldn't place.

"Can I try something?" Miro asked, stepping in front of Bronwyn. Bronwyn shrugged. He couldn't do much worse than she had already.

"We," Miro placed his hands on his chest, then indicated to the rest of the party, "brought you some fruit." Miro took a couple of dried apricots, put them in his palm, and extended them toward the guards. They only raised an eyebrow, continuing to stare at him.

"We are looking." Miro put his hands over his eyes and pantomimed looking around. The gathered crowd started to smile, and a couple of children broke out into giggles. Bronwyn tried to keep a straight face.

"For the Eye," Miro put both hands in front of his eyes, forming a large circle, "of Sleepless Dreams." Miro rested his head against clasped hands and acted out sleeping. Even the adults were laughing at this point and all the children were giggling and speaking among themselves, some mocking Miro's gestures. Bronwyn had to clasp her hand over her mouth tightly to avoid joining them.

Finally, someone stepped forward, putting an end to Miro's attempts at diplomacy, much to Bronwyn's relief. She was biting her lip to prevent herself from openly laughing at Miro. Miro's eyebrows knitted and by the tension in his jaw, Bronwyn could tell he was clenching it.

"Okay, I have to stop you there," the man said chuckling to himself. His hair was sandy-blonde and adhered to the shorter hairstyle. "I was pretty sure you were going to resort to talking louder and slower, but I have to give you credit for the hand gestures. That's a new one."

"Oh, you speak the common tongue," Miro said, ignoring the laughter.

"From where I'm standing, my people speak the common tongue. I just happen to know your foreign language." The man frowned upon saying this.

"Oh, I'm sorry. I didn't mean for it … I guess what I meant was, you know our language," Miro said.

"I won't hold it against you. I take it this is your first time meeting my people, the Shi'en?"

"Yes, is it that obvious?" Miro shrugged. He shifted on his feet and didn't seem to meet the man's gaze.

"Most of the nomadic tribes have their own language, but many of us are bilingual, to facilitate trade. Usually, people with experience present themselves then wait to be addressed by one that understands their language." The man smiled and didn't seem to take any offense to Miro's attitude. Bronwyn knew this would result in a foul mood from Miro. She hoped he'd stay true to his word and not allow a small setback change how he treated others.

"I'll take you to our village elders. They can talk to you more about the Eye. We will not part with it, but the least we can do is provide you with an explanation of why." The interpreter turned and started to walk further into the encampment.

Bronwyn and Miro looked at each other, and then followed. Bronwyn turned to see some of the children approach Clara. They looked disappointed when they got close and discovered she was an adult. Clara smiled, squeezed both her hands shut, then extended them which the children took, and led her away to a field with some type of brown leather ball.

Defurge didn't follow. Bronwyn thought it was probably for the best. She hadn't felt the draw of the gem since she first touched it, but she didn't know if that was because the phoenix was somehow masking its allure, or if it was only because she had experienced it already.

"What's your name?" Miro asked the interpreter, quickening his gait to catch up.

"I am Malik. We're going to see one of our elders, Liman." Malik brought them to the center of their village. Around a small fire, three individuals with grey hair sat across from two younger men. The younger men still had the long hair of children and hadn't adopted one of the two hairstyles Bronwyn saw the other adults wearing. When Malik approached, he said something to the man in the middle who then seemed to dismiss the younger men. The three elder individuals wore none of the hairstyles Bronwyn had seen in camp so far. Their hair was shorn very short; even one person who appeared to be a woman wore it this way. Bronwyn wasn't sure if it was a status symbol or for comfort.

"Excuse me Liman; we came here to talk to you about the Eye of Sleepless Dreams," Miro said.

Malik seemed to interpret Miro's words, speaking to the three elders. He then pantomimed Miro's gestures at the village entrance all while explaining in his native tongue. More laughter erupted from Malik and the elders. Wiping a tear from his eye, Malik said, "I'm sorry. I couldn't resist."

Bronwyn turned her head away from Miro. She was having increasing difficulty not taking joy in Miro's embarrassment.

Miro tightly crossed his arms; a low grumble emanated from his throat. "Yes, very funny," Miro said.

Bronwyn stepped forward, unwilling to risk Miro becoming hostile. "We came to ask if it would be possible to borrow the Eye of Sleepless Dreams."

Bronwyn went on to explain their quest and their belief that the Eye could lead them to find an artifact to help Emestria. Malik exchanged words with the elder. Liman spoke at length to him. Bronwyn tried to listen for repeated phrases and the rhythm of the language to ascertain if the response was favorable or not.

"The Eye is important to my people. Long ago, we used a berry in our coming-of-age rituals that caused visions. It only grew in the northeastern section of the swamps of Mul'tok, around an island. A white dragon took up residence in that area over a hundred years ago and still guards it. Now we use the Eye as a substitute, but it is both a curse and a blessing. The Eye answers our questions but shows the user the worst things imaginable for its gift. Using the Eye twice will cause someone to go mad, and sometimes even exposure to it once is enough to break the mind. As such, we cannot share it."

Bronwyn waited to see if Malik had more to say. "What if we slew this dragon? Then you could have access to the berries again. Would you be willing to lend it then?"

Malik's eyes widened and his brow furrowed. He slowly turned to Liman and translated her words. Liman and the other elders looked at her, their lips tightly turned down. Malik imitated the tone of the response. "You can't possibly be serious. There is no way you would succeed in such an endeavor."

Bronwyn didn't know much about dragons, but she did know white dragons used to live in the north and had an affinity for ice. They would probably be susceptible to flames, and she had the former incarnation of the god of fire on her side. Bronwyn straightened her posture and raised her chin, trying to display confidence. "I am serious. If we return with proof of its death and some berries, will you let us use the Eye?"

Malik translated her boast. Liman responded and Malik said, "We can't stop you, but know this: we will not retrieve your bodies."

"You won't need to, we don't plan on dying," Bronwyn said. Malik shared her words one last time before approaching Bronwyn.

"This is a bad idea. That creature is immense. You don't stand a chance against something like that. You're not even wearing armor," Malik pleaded.

"I bested a spirit guardian, a hydra, and an incarnation of a god. I never needed armor then, and I doubt I'll need it now." Malik shook his head, looking to Miro, likely thinking that Bronwyn was exaggerating the things she had fought. Miro shrugged and nodded in agreement with her assessment.

"I'm sorry you feel that way," Malik said. "You seem like good people. You will find the creature in the northeasternmost reaches of the swamp. It makes a large pool of water its home, only revealing itself to ambush prey. Are you sure I can't convince you?"

Bronwyn shook her head, and Malik extended his hand to show them the way from the village.

As they walked, Clara joined them. "Bronwyn, do you notice anything about those three horses?" Clara pointed to three large brown horses among the skinnier black mustangs. Clara raised her eyebrow in inclination. "They only have three single saddles on the post to their enclosure."

"Those horses look familiar," Bronwyn said, trying to broach the subject as artfully as possible. "We had released three horses matching their description at the far edge of the swamp several months back."

"We found those animals wandering the plains," Malik responded with a calm, measured tone. "We knew they were domesticated. Whether they are the same or not, I can't tell you. But if you left them there, you gave up any right to them when you didn't return."

"Of course," Bronwyn agreed. "With the use of those mounts, we could travel to the swamp and return sooner. I'm sure your people would prefer our hasty return."

"I may not be able to deter your reckless course of action, but I'm not about to loan you three horses to feed the beast any more than you already will. It will have enough to eat, gorging itself on the four of you." Malik spoke gravely.

"Of course. We'll return in a few days. If this creature is as formidable as you say, we can merely turn around and return. Maybe then we can find some other bargain that would allow us to use the Eye, just once." Malik only shook his head again, lowering it as he turned and left them at the village edge.

Bronwyn waved goodbye in a friendly manner. By her estimate, it would take them a day and a half to reach the swamp again. A couple of hours to scout and plot how to take down the dragon, and they could be back in three to four days. She explained her plan to Clara and Defurge. Defurge seemed hesitant until Bronwyn reminded him that he was the former incarnation of the god of fire and a white dragon would be susceptible to his abilities. Clara was eerily excited. She was already talking about the message she would send back to King Bryant after she slew a dragon.

CHAPTER 14

BRONWYN DREADED GOING back into the mosquito-infested swamp. Thankfully, they didn't have to progress through much of it to find the large body of water at the northeastern point. The four members of her team crouched through the underbrush, attempting to avoid detection from above. There was an island in the middle and a channel of water cutting around it, creating a lake-like feature. As she approached, Bronwyn saw the giant, white-scaled creature. She estimated its size: thirty feet in length, the last ten of which was a huge muscular tail. Oddly, its legs were short and stubby and its wings non-existent.

"That's not a dragon," Clara said in frustration, standing upright in the brush. She squeezed her left hand into a tight fist.

"Shh," Bronwyn cautioned her, taking note of how angrily Clara seemed to be making fists.

"It doesn't even have wings. It's just a crocodile." Bronwyn stood at this point as well. The reptile warmed itself in the sun, holding its angular snout open. Small birds dashed in between its teeth, picking the remnants of its last meal from them. It cared little about the noise they were making, and its eyes remained shut.

"Why did they call it a dragon?" Bronwyn asked as she looked to the sky, half expecting a large, white serpent to descend, snatch up the crocodilian, and carry it off.

"Maybe the word is the same in their language?" Clara offered. "Or it ambushed them, lunging from the water when they saw it. They would have been running so fast they wouldn't have spent time properly identifying it. Not to mention, an albino crocodile would be unexpected and rare. As a baby, it would have faced incredible pressure to avoid detection, the white scales ruining any chance of camouflage. Probably why it's so big; had to grow up fast to defend itself so it didn't become a snack for something else." Clara sighed loudly.

"This is great. It's not a dragon," Bronwyn said, then looked at Clara who kicked up a clod of dirt. "You're disappointed?"

"I wanted to see one," Clara replied with a half-hearted smile.

"What do we do?" Defurge asked standing up.

"Crocodiles are ambush predators and territorial," Clara said. "We could hang around the shore but would run the risk of being caught unawares. It might be best to bait it close to the water's edge and annoy it enough to elicit an attack. It would be at a considerable disadvantage fighting on land."

"All right, I'll hunt a snake or something." Bronwyn headed into the surrounding swamp on the lookout for prey.

After decapitating a large constrictor, she fished a rope down through the first foot of the esophagus. Bronwyn used her knife to make an incision and tied the rope off, making a loop. The plan was simple. Toss the carcass into the water to make a splash, draw it out, and dangle the last couple of feet. When the crocodile got close, pull the snake to land. Once the crocodile was on land, Defurge and Clara would begin to attack it from range, drawing it further ashore.

"Or I could just electrocute it," Miro said.

Bronwyn turned to Miro, concerned. "I thought maybe you would sit this one out. You're still not up to full strength and I don't want you to become ..." Bronwyn struggled with her words, "overly upset if things go sideways." Her phrasing did little to prevent the shame and embarrassment his face conveyed.

"I can't just let you all fight and stand idly by," Miro spoke calmly, his voice straining to hide his masked frustration. "Let me pelt it with spells from a distance, keep it focused on me."

"No magic," Bronwyn said abruptly. "I'm afraid it might be too much of a strain." Bronwyn thought for a bit, not wanting to wound his pride too deeply, but also not willing to concede her concerns. "Can you use a bow?"

"Yes." Miro rolled his eyes.

"Take my bow." Bronwyn pulled the bow from her pack, strung it, and gave him the quiver. "Try to keep it coming towards you, but maintain distance. If it starts to get too close, run away."

Miro sighed. "Bronwyn?" Bronwyn knew an arrow would do little against a creature that size. In truth, Defurge and her would be doing most of the heavy lifting, with support from Clara.

"Please," Bronwyn said, lightly touching his arm. "For me?"

He reluctantly nodded in agreement and took the bow and arrows from her. As the others approached the shore, he stood back, weapon in one hand with an arrow ready to be nocked.

Bronwyn approached the water's edge. The crocodile was still sunning itself, but she didn't know what else lived in this swamp's waters. If something else tried to attack, she would be the fastest and best at escaping an ambush. Clara and Defurge held the other end of the rope. Bronwyn cast the seven feet of reptile into the water, performing a perverse hammer throw, swinging the awkward dead weight of the snake. The first two throws were met with no response. On the third, the crocodile pushed itself forward, sliding down the embankment into the brackish water. Bronwyn left the shore and joined Clara and Defurge. Slowly, they pulled the rope attached to the snake's carcass. Bronwyn wanted to leave about a foot in the water until she saw the white head beneath the surface, then she would give the order to withdraw the bait quickly.

Patiently, she waited until the white head came into focus beneath the murky water. Bronwyn began teasing the snake away as Clara readied her spells and Defurge drew his whip, his flames running speedily down the length of it.

To Bronwyn's chagrin, the crocodile forced itself aggressively from the water, catching the end of the snake before she had time to withdraw. It snapped its jaw shut, severing the last three feet of the meal. Luckily, it lunged a second time, trying to catch more of the prey in its mouth.

Clara cast rapidly, her invocations running together, lobbing stone spells. These weren't like the clusters of rocks she previously hurled. They were large, solid, and appeared sharp. Defurge began to crack his whip at the creature's eyes, attempting to blind it. The monster seemed to have little interest in fighting them and retreated to the water. Bronwyn left the bait on the shore, just out of reach, and drew her greatsword. She positioned herself above the snake, ready to leap out of the way if necessary. Defurge continued to crack his whip on the water's surface.

Bronwyn was barely prepared for the crocodile when it lunged. The creature used its massive tail to propel itself quickly ashore, bringing most of its body onto land. Bronwyn was forced to use her sword to ward off its attack as she leapt backward. She found herself pushed off balance and landed on her knees and one hand. She swiftly rolled to the side, avoiding teeth as the creature twisted its head, attempting to crush her between trap-like jaws.

Defurge stepped forward and brought his whip to bear in earnest against its head. Bronwyn recovered and advanced. She struck, sidestepped, and dodged to the left to allow Defurge's whip to strike where she used to be.

"Lau'O'Penake, shield me, Fragma Petra." Clara erected an odd-looking stone wall. Instead of being a single length of stone, a barrier composed of ten-foot sections of rocky clay with three-foot gaps in between each section forced itself from the ground.

Clara ducked behind the hard protrusions of earth, muttered a spell, and then stepped into the gap to lob another stone projectile at the reptile. She looked to be aiming for the head and eyes, but the beast was surprisingly quick.

As Bronwyn sliced at the creature's side, an arrow struck its tail, deflecting off its armored hide without doing any real damage. Another arrow rebounded off its scales as Bronwyn jumped back from the creature when it attempted to catch her in its jaws again.

Eventually, one of Clara's stones struck the creature's eye. It turned its attention to her. Clara ducked back behind one of the stone walls.

The creature rammed the earthen barrier. The massive, bony-plated head caused the structure to collapse, showering its face with rocks and clay that easily weighed twenty pounds.

Clara drew her axe and in a big overhead swing, brought its entire weight to bear against the tip of the creature's snout. A resounding crack rewarded her efforts as her axe split the bone and armored skin.

Bronwyn used Clara's diversion to go for the soft scales of the crocodile's underbelly. She charged and swung her greatsword in a large arc, slicing into a good three feet of its underside. She looked with satisfaction as the muscle protruded and red blood began to seep. Defurge whipped the rear left leg, lassoing it.

"Defurge, stand back," Bronwyn yelled.

"I've got this," he replied confidently, ignoring her request. Defurge pulled but didn't manage to trip the crocodile. It responded by whipping its large tail toward Bronwyn. The force of the move heaved Defurge forward, upsetting his balance. Bronwyn ducked the tail as it sailed over her head. She saw Defurge wheeling into range of the muscular appendage and rushed to his aid, pushing him to safety. However, the maneuver left her ill-prepared as the crocodile's tail swung back.

Bronwyn braced her sword against the hit. She was able to absorb most of the initial impact, but the sheer size and force of the appendage sent her tumbling back. With a terrifying splash, she felt the warm water of the swamp engulf her body.

Bronwyn righted herself in the water. With her feet touching the bottom, her head was barely above water level. Drawn by the sound, the crocodile ignored Defurge's and Clara's attempts to divert its attention and turned, then dove gracefully underneath the water, its powerful tail propelling it toward her.

Bronwyn felt her sword, heavy in the water. She eyed the closest shore and started swimming. If she dropped her weapon, she might be able to quit the swamp, but that would leave her defenseless and in range of its lunge. At the very least she could turn in the water and bring her blade to bear against its jaws. She felt her heart pump and sink to her stomach. *I can't believe this is how I'm going to meet my end, against a stupid crocodile people thought was a dragon.*

Bronwyn looked to the shore. Miro had dropped his bow and was starting to run toward her. She swam in earnest. *He says he can electrocute it. If I can just get to him ….*

"Defurge, a hand," Miro called out, still running toward Bronwyn.

The flame died from Defurge's whip and sailed toward Miro. Miro brought his arm up into the whip's path. The weapon wrapped around his arm. He twisted his hand around it, holding it in his palm.

"Fria, goddess of ice, death, and fate, the vigilant eye, aid my passage, Fragma Frios." The wall materialized, just above the water's edge and

Bronwyn swam to the icy bridge in earnest. Perhaps she could get up in time, be able to take more of a defensive position, or attempt to swim around it, giving her a protective barrier and hopefully enough time to retreat.

"Ramun, Tempus Dallates!" Miro shouted as he ran forward. The crocodile, Defurge, and Clara all froze in place as Bronwyn took the opportunity to clamor up the wall, gripping the other side to hoist herself up.

The world, only stopped momentarily, now appeared to be speeding up again. As she turned around to bring her sword up into a fighting stance, Miro ran atop the wall. He braced himself, using the whip, as his feet glided over the water and ice. He slowed as he approached Bronwyn, the length of the whip at its maximum.

"Great, now we'll die together," Bronwyn said, ready for the crocodile's lunge.

Miro grabbed her waist and pulled her close. Miro whispered hotly into her ear, "My pleasure."

Shocked, Bronwyn looked into his eyes as he embraced her. She stifled a gasp as she felt this energy about him. The same energy that encased him when he saved her from the wolves. Sparks were traveling from his body to hers wherever their skin touched. Her skin prickled and the hair on her arms and neck stood on end.

"What are you doing, you idiot!" Bronwyn yelled as the world began moving at its regular pace. *There are worse ways to die,* Bronwyn found herself thinking, tightening her grip around his waist. She could feel the pulse of his heartbeat next to hers. A second was all the time needed for the crocodile to continue bearing toward them at full speed.

"Get me out of here!" Miro shouted to Defurge as he pulled his whip back sharply, knocking Miro and Bronwyn prone against the ice but beginning to propel them forward along the slick surface. Bronwyn managed to swing her sword against the beast's muzzle, doing little else but annoy it. It crashed against the end of the wall, splintering the ice.

Bronwyn noticed the blood in the water and worried the crocodile had taken her leg. *No, they are both still there.*

She looked up to find the source of the blood cascading over her body. She remembered then that Defurge's whip was covered in razor-sharp metal braided into the leather. The sleeve of Miro's cloak only protected the upper portion of his arm. The lower portion was bleeding badly. The skin and muscle were cut into, and the bones of his wrist were visible.

Miro winced noticeably when they finally came to a stop a foot from shore. When Defurge released the whip, it snaked clumsily from Miro's arm. Bronwyn helped Miro to his feet and turned to face the crocodile as it changed direction—toward them.

The monster had no real sense of the wall and swam against it, causing the ice to crumble, but slowing it enough for Bronwyn to prepare. With a push, she forced Miro back from the water's edge.

"By the goddesses, heal yourself!" Bronwyn shouted, turning to see the blood pouring from his arm. His face was white, and she readied herself to catch him if he fainted.

"May I?" Miro asked sarcastically before beginning an incantation. "Seraph, goddess of life and love, lend me your aid, heal my wounds, Lagos Medus." Green runes encased his arm and bound the lacerations closed.

His face is still pale, but at least he isn't losing any more blood. "You think you can still manage some lightning, Sparky?" Bronwyn asked, preparing her sword to defend them.

"I've got something better. Buy me some time and keep your blade low!" He yelled loud enough for everyone to hear. "Defurge, I need a lightning rod."

Defurge nodded, picked up his whip, and called out to Clara. "Give me your axe."

Clara hesitated but lobbed her weapon in the air toward him. Defurge whipped the axe from the air and brought it in a large arc above the beast's head. He cracked the whip, sending the axe down, lodging itself in between the crocodile's eyes with a satisfying *thunk*. The crocodile hissed and whipped its tail once more at Bronwyn before turning its attention back to Defurge. Bronwyn was ready this time, ducked the first strike, and flipped backward over the second attack.

"Lau'O'Penake, goddess of nature and rebirth, shield my ally, Fragma Petra!" Clara called out as she erected a barrier concealing Miro from the creature's line of sight. The remainder of her previous, odd-shaped wall collapsed, but she was far enough away to not be in any immediate danger.

Bronwyn heard Miro from behind the wall but couldn't see the runes. "Laevin, lord of the skies, god of lightning, arbiter of the gods, let your voice rage from the heavens and blanket my foes in your fury, Levos Thyella!"

He had never used an incantation this long. The rapidly coalescing storm clouds surprised her.

The next thirty seconds were met with the sound of Bronwyn's sword hitting and defending against the creature's strikes, then the very sky seemed to growl in anger. The first two bolts of lightning missed and struck tall trees instead. The next three connected with the metal pry bar of Clara's axe. The third only waylaid the creature, but by the time the fourth and fifth hit, the smell of burnt flesh was beginning to permeate the air.

Almost as quickly as they had formed, the clouds started to part. The crocodile slumped against the ground and Clara and Defurge still stood in attack stances. Bronwyn had only seen lightning like this from Miro twice before, when he almost killed them all by entering his curse, and she ran around the stone wall, her sword ready.

Instead of the pale blue eyes and the levitating madman she had seen during the fight with the wolves in Emestria, Miro leaned against the stone, exhausted but otherwise okay. She went to him and put his good arm over her shoulder, supporting his weight as she brought him out from behind the earthen rampart. Helping him down so he could sit, she cautiously approached the crocodile. Bronwyn walked toward its left front leg and pressed her sword deep into its body until only the hilt was visible. She calculated that's where its heart would be. Satisfied as the rich purple blood poured from the wound, she pulled her blade free.

They all breathed a sigh of relief. Bronwyn went to the beast's jaws and used her knife to pry a few of the seven-inch teeth free. Defurge mounted the skull and heaved on Clara's axe, attempting to liberate it. The lightning had melted the pry bar side of the weapon with its intense heat. It still glowed a faint red. Clara searched along the shore for bushes. She found one, with bright purple berries and put a handful into her pouch. Defurge then handed her the axe, and she looked at the warped metal with a scowl.

CHAPTER 15

"I'm glad you came to your senses," Malik said as he greeted Bronwyn at the village entrance. He smiled, looking happy to see her.

"Not quite," Bronwyn said, stepping forward and holding out her hand. Opening it, she revealed a half dozen seven-inch teeth she had pried from the crocodile.

"And there are these," Clara said, joining Bronwyn and pouring out some berries from her pouch.

Malik cocked his head, raising an eyebrow, "No. It could have lost those, and you managed to pick some berries while it was away." He shook his head and set his jaw. His eyes narrowed as he looked at Bronwyn.

"There is the giant, dead body of a flightless white dragon that argues otherwise. It will take the scavengers weeks to pick the body clean. Send some scouts; confirm what I tell you." Bronwyn smiled. *Of course, he can't believe me. He can't believe because I can do things normal people can't. We all can. Together we can do the impossible.* Bronwyn glanced at Miro, hiding a smile.

Clara had suggested that they continue to call it a dragon. She said it was to avoid insulting the Shi'en. She looked just as confident, despite the agitated Ferdinand pacing on her glove.

Malik turned from them and then said something to one of the guards. The guard left and headed for the horse pen, taking another villager along with him.

Malik said, "We're about to eat. You can join us. When the scouts return, we'll see how truthful you really are." He eyed Bronwyn but extended his hand forward and stepped to the side, inviting them into the village.

Defurge came with them this time. Some of the children came up to Clara, but Malik intercepted them, telling them something before they turned away with tight little frowns. Bronwyn looked about the village; it was less inviting than the last time they were here.

Once dinner was served—a type of spiced stew spooned over rice—Bronwyn noticed how the Shi'en ate. They sat around in circles, talking. The groups were usually separated by hair type, with children eating in the longer, braided hair circles. The elders were joined by a mixed group. No one came close to Bronwyn's group, who ate by themselves off to the side.

"Not exactly the welcoming party I was expecting," Clara said, trying to get Ferdinand to eat. He screeched and refused to take the bit of meat she offered.

"Is the food not to his liking?" Bronwyn asked.

"He's been agitated since the fight with the crocodile. I think he also ate a crow this morning," Clara replied.

"He did that a lot when I left the library," Bronwyn said. "Is it a stress response? He only ate very little of them with me though."

"I don't know, he's just been yelling "danger" and "crow" all the time." Clara shrugged, putting the meat into her mouth instead. Even though Clara and Miro could talk to the bird through their magic, Ferdinand's speech was difficult to parse a lot of the time. Clara once explained that the bird usually only gave a couple of words to indicate what it wanted.

"Funny bird," Bronwyn said, shaking her head. She took her hair and tied it up with a strip of leather, then started to eat her meal. She looked toward Miro, who averted his gaze. He was sitting close to Defurge, and whenever she caught them in conversation, it was quiet and conspiratorial.

"Defurge, why did you decide to join us this time? Aren't you worried about ...." Bronwyn pointed to her chest, trying to indicate his gem.

"I was close to the guards last time, and I didn't see them looking at it. Nor did they ask me about it or try to get closer. Maybe the phoenix or monks are muting its draw."

Bronwyn nodded. "That's good. We'd be at quite a disadvantage if we couldn't go into populated areas with you." Bronwyn looked back at Miro. His head was down and eating his food without saying anything. Bronwyn glanced back at Defurge, gesturing toward Miro with a nod and putting her hands up slightly.

"Tired," Defurge mouthed. *That makes sense. His arm was in ribbons. It probably took a lot for him to come save me like that,* Bronwyn thought.

The Shi'en slept together in the pavilion-like tents. Bronwyn didn't feel like they were welcome to join, so they unfurled their bedrolls and slept around one of the fires. They even kept watch. Bronwyn didn't think there was anything malicious about the way the Shi'en were treating them right now. The Shi'en probably thought their group was trying to trick them into using the Eye. She would be suspicious too.

In the morning, they found yet another dead crow, untouched, with Ferdinand standing over the body. Clara picked Ferdinand up onto her falconer's glove with a sigh and slight shake of her head. When Bronwyn tried to ask Malik if they could help with the day's chores at all, he refused and asked them to stay near the fire they slept around. Bronwyn couldn't wait for the scouts to return.

The scouts finally returned shortly before dusk. They rode their horses directly into camp, right up to where the elders sat. Bronwyn smiled as their voices carried over the rest of the village's sounds. She may not understand their language, but she knew excitement when she heard it. She leaned back onto her hands and crossed her legs slightly as Malik approached, his steps a little too quick.

"How?" Malik asked.

"I don't carry this big sword because it matches my eyes," Bronwyn said.

"But ...." Malik's look of shock was almost as funny as Miro's frustration when they first arrived in the village.

"It's a good story," Clara said.

"You'll have to tell it at the feast tonight," Malik replied, beaming.

"A feast? What's the occasion?" Bronwyn asked.

Malik only laughed and extended his hand, gripping Bronwyn's forearm and pulling her to her feet.

As the meal was prepared—it was much of the same as the previous day, but they also served a type of fermented honey—Clara regaled Malik of the battle. In Clara's version of the story, the "dragon" was mortally wounded after Clara split its skull in two with her axe. Other than that, it was close to the truth. She left Miro's part out. Bronwyn looked to Miro, to see if his exclusion was causing him any undue frustration, but he merely continued to look at his feet. It worried Bronwyn.

After eating, more fermented honey was brought out. Everyone seemed to be in good spirits—well, almost everyone. Miro sat at the edge of the village, staring out at the stars. Malik was talking with the elders and came by a short time later with something wrapped in soft, thin leather. He handed it to Bronwyn. She opened it slowly. A delicate, golden, oblong ring had thin spindles crisscrossing it, suspending an opal in the middle of the design.

"We may use the Eye?" Bronwyn asked.

"You may have it. Now that you've slain the dragon, we will be moving back to our ancestral home, to guard it. We have no more use of that *thing*," Malik said with derision.

"Is it truly that horrible?" Bronwyn asked. Malik slowly nodded, concentrating intently on Bronwyn. "How does it work?"

"Before resting, you place the Eye on your chest, clasped between your hands. Concentrate on the question you want answered. The Eye will show you visions, the last of which is usually the knowledge you seek. Never use it twice. Avoid using it at all if you can." Malik spoke gravely. Bronwyn nodded.

She first went to Clara to share the news. She was among a group of younger-looking adults, that still hadn't adopted one of the two dominant hairstyles. Clara was happy to hear they recovered the Eye and said she'd send Ferdinand off tomorrow with the news. However, she was preoccupied with the young adults. They were going to consume one of the berries to experience their coming-of-age rituals, a rite that was being extended to Clara because she slayed the dragon.

For some reason, Bronwyn didn't want to tell Defurge. She couldn't understand the nagging feeling. She attributed it to wanting to tell Miro to cheer him up. Bronwyn grabbed a couple of horns of the fermented honey and headed out to where Miro sat. He turned when she approached. She raised the hollowed horns, and he turned back to the night sky. Bronwyn frowned, but sat next to him anyway, handing him one of the horns. He sipped on it, not saying anything.

"You've been avoiding me," Bronwyn said, sipping the thick mixture as well.

"No, I haven't," Miro said, failing to meet her gaze.

"You've been talking to Defurge the whole way back. Now you're out here looking at stars instead of enjoying the revelry with me."

Miro sighed. "I'm sorry."

"It's okay. What's bothering you?" Bronwyn asked, setting down the Eye.

"No, I'm sorry. I told you I was going to try and be better, but the minute you ask me to do something, I go behind your back." Bronwyn blinked at him and widened her eyes. "I shouldn't have used magic."

Bronwyn paused before saying, "No, I owe you an apology." Miro raised his eyebrow comically. "Stop that, I'm trying to be serious."

Bronwyn suppressed a chuckle and looked up at the stars, thinking it would be easier to say if she wasn't looking at him. "I was wrong. I shouldn't have made you stand off to the side. You had a good plan, and I ignored it. You were an asset, and I failed to utilize your abilities. It wasn't fair, or smart, of me. I was overly confident in my and Defurge's skills. The battle would have been less dangerous if I listened to you." Bronwyn sighed as she got the words out. She had been trying to think about what to say their entire trip back. The whole ordeal started when Defurge didn't listen to her, but Miro did. *If I only trusted him in the beginning ...*

"Thank you." Miro paused for a while before continuing. "I understand why you don't want me to use magic. You're afraid I'm going to lose control."

Bronwyn turned to Miro. "No, I'm not. I thought I was, but I realize now that it is out of a desire to be overprotective. When we were in the cave ..." Miro gulped and shifted away. "I saw the curse try and take over your body twice, but you forced it back. Then today, I felt the same energy around you, but you didn't even let it start to take over. If you can maintain control in that emotionally charged of a situation, I think you have more mastery over it than you think."

Bronwyn turned to Miro and nodded. He bobbed his head slightly in appreciation. Bronwyn leaned her body against his and sighed. She felt a slight tingle in her skin as she grew closer. "That was amazing, the way you and Defurge fought together. You and he have this connection. It makes me jealous that you can think and move together as one."

Miro tensed. "You and Defurge work very well as a team. You were striking with your sword, and his whip was filling the space you left. There is nothing to be envious about."

Bronwyn's heartbeat increased in tempo. "I'm not jealous of you having a link with Defurge. I'm jealous that he has this connection with *you*. That he gets to hear what you're thinking all the time."

"He got the raw end of that deal. Trust me, no one wants to be digging around up here for information." Miro lightly rapped his skull with his fist.

"I wouldn't mind knowing what you're thinking sometimes." Bronwyn turned to Miro, waiting for him to look back.

"It's a mess better left alone." Miro's smile disappeared.

"What about when you're thinking about something or someone fondly? I'm sure it's not all doom and gloom when you're thinking about someone's company you enjoy." Bronwyn waited for a reply, but when none came, she stopped leaning against him. "You know, you can be really dense sometimes. Why would you think I'd get mad at you for using magic to save my life?"

"Because I gave you my word that I was going to be less difficult, and then the next thing you ask me to do, I ignore. You could have rescued yourself just fine, but I had to do things my way." Bronwyn had hoped to stir some type of emotion in him, but he refused to react. His response was logical and emotionless.

Bronwyn used her hand to tilt his head toward hers, feeling a spark as her skin touched his. She stared intently into his eyes, hoping to get the message past his thick skull. "No, I couldn't have. I figured I had two options: drop my sword and swim for land or try and fight in the water. If I dropped my sword, I would be left defenseless even if I made it to land. If I fought in the water, I may have been able to deflect a blow or two, but

I would be *dead*. But then, you came and got me. You saved me, practically cutting your arm off in the process."

Miro spoke quietly, "I'm glad I did. I wouldn't have been able to live with myself if something happened to you."

He gazed into her eyes and Bronwyn waited for him to lean forward, unsure if she would lean away. Miro turned, cleared his throat, then stood and brushed off his robe and pants. He walked away, going to join Defurge. Bronwyn bit her lip and rolled her eyes. She stared up at the stars, only returning to the village when her horn ran empty.

Later that night, Bronwyn lay in one of the Shi'en tents, uncomfortably close to Miro. They had been invited to stay in the elders' tent tonight. An honor, she was told.

"I'm sorry; do you want me to leave?" Miro whispered.

"Why would I want you to leave?" Bronwyn asked, confused.

"You told me to never go in your room, even if it meant I had to sleep in the streets. I figure this counts as your room as much as the inn in Newtonne did."

After their first night in Newtonne, Bronwyn had imbibed too much rum and passed out with Miro still in her room. She thought the worst when she woke the next morning undressed, but later realized nothing nefarious had occurred. She still gave Miro an earful and warned him about ever sharing a room with her in the future. Bronwyn nudged him playfully. "Stop being a pain and go to sleep."

Bronwyn lay looking up at the top of the tent, trying to sleep. She wasn't sure if Miro was awake as well. She closed her eyes, listening to the sound of crickets and the breathing of all the people around her, and drifted off.

Bronwyn woke to Miro's cries a short while later. They weren't as loud as they were in the library, or maybe hearing them didn't pain her as much anymore. His breath was ragged and interrupted by moans and grimaces. Tears pooled in his eyes and trailed down his cheeks. Bronwyn extended her hand, brushing the hair on the side of his head. He turned away from her, clutching his chest before letting out another wail. It woke some of the Shi'en, but they just shook their heads and returned to their slumber.

Bronwyn ran her fingers through the back of his hair, like she had in the library. It calmed him there, but he continued moaning and sobbing here. *Come on Miro. You saved me. Please, just let me help you sleep.*

A sudden jolt stung Bronwyn's fingers and caused her to wince in pain. Then she was falling, or it felt like she was falling. When she re-opened her eyes, the tent was no longer dark. She soon realized this wasn't the tent she had fallen asleep in. To her right was a bed on a simple frame. Furs were heaped upon it, and not just wolf hides, but those of snow leopards and other animals she couldn't identify. To her left was a large chest, with expensive dresses peeking out from the sides. Behind it, a dressing partition and a full-length mirror.

But it wasn't her reflection staring back at her; it was Miro's. He looked less worn down by life, and somewhat happy, but his eyes still harbored sadness. He wore a uniform, the crisp attire of a lieutenant, but with a blue cloak over his shoulders, a hood bunched up around the neck—a support mage's uniform. King Bryant had said Miro was a support mage in the war. A sound caused her attention to turn. Suddenly, in front of her, a man stood.

He was tall, at least a head taller than Miro. His large arms were supported by his broad chest. He walked so close that she was forced to look up to see his face, but then her head was pulled down to the ground. *No, Miro is forcing my head down. I am sharing Miro's body. I can see what he sees but have no control over his movements.*

The man's large hands caressed Bronwyn's cheek and pulled her vision back up to his eyes. He had a short beard and tussled brunette hair. He looked similar to the portraits that King Bryant had commissioned of himself in the war but more handsome and rugged. He seemed to have a glow about him.

He doesn't seem *to glow; he* is *glowing. His silhouette is outlined with a soft red haze.* Then Bronwyn felt something at her chest. Delicate fingers snaked around to her front and began pulling at the buttons of the uniform.

Something soft and warm pressed against her neck. The scent of lavender and vanilla wafted from a woman's blonde hair. Another soft kiss on her neck from the woman and Bronwyn looked back into the man's eyes. There was passion there, but also coldness. As the man's head lowered to Bronwyn, her eyes shut.

When they reopened, the man, a younger King Bryant was on the ground, fifty feet away. He was pinned beneath a soldier's boot. It was difficult to make out anything aside from his face, staring at Bronwyn, as men kicked and beat him. A scream drew Bronwyn's attention to the left. There, the blonde-haired woman lay, her face round and beautiful with plump lips. A man was on top of her. Her screams were cut off as the fabric from her robe pulled at her throat before ripping. Her shirt followed soon after. She clawed at the men as they pinned her arms above her head.

Bronwyn's eyes were heavy as she looked down. Thick, dark-red blood coated her hands as she tried to hold the entrails spilling from a large gash in her stomach. She slumped forward, her face scraping against the hard cobblestone of the road. And Miro forced her eyes shut. *Not yet Miro. I need to see what happened.* Bronwyn struggled to re-open her eyes.

But when they did, the sky was red, with black clouds streaking across it. Bronwyn was on her knees, surrounded by grey ash. She dug her hands into it and as she raised them, the ash slipped between her fingers. It was deep, and as it fell to the ground, it puffed into the air, fine and powdery. Bronwyn doubled over, sobbing in the thick burnt remains, ash clouding her lungs.

The ground seemed to slip away until Bronwyn was standing at the edge of a cliff, her hands outstretched, looking at a falling body. It was the blonde-haired woman, a white dress billowing around her as she fell. She could feel Miro's pain and his love. He blamed himself for this. He was the reason she was falling. *No, you didn't, Miro. Did you?* Soon, only a soft red haze where the woman had disappeared beneath icy waters remained.

The blue sky was eclipsed by a dark shadow, undulating in the air, floating. The shape had no real form, or she couldn't see its form. *Maybe I'm not meant to see it*, Bronwyn thought.

"Why won't you let me die!" Miro screamed. A low, deep chuckle vibrated the ground as Bronwyn pitched herself over the cliff. The fall was broken in thick snow, pooling around Bronwyn's knees—her knees, not Miro's. Bronwyn looked to her chest, to see her dented breastplate. Next to her, in the snow, was her greatsword.

She looked up to see Miro yelling at a giant snow leopard. It looked like Naani, but Naani had been missing one eye. This cat had both of them. Then Miro's attention snapped toward her. Miro's beard was shaggy, and ice clung to it. *This is the day we met. The day when he healed me.*

Instead of the measured stride Miro had used to close the distance in the real memory, he charged. His eyes were white, and his lips curled back in a snarl. He moved too quickly, almost like a feral beast as he tackled Bronwyn. Bronwyn tried to push him off, tried to free herself, but he was too strong. *Miro isn't this strong.*

One hand grabbed her neck, cutting off her breath. As she brought at first one, then two of her own hands to pry his free, he doubled his efforts. Both his hands clasped her neck tightly as he squeezed.

"Miro …" Bronwyn managed to squeak out. "It's … me—"

A roar cut her off as she felt her body yanked to the side. Miro was off her, pinned beneath the leopard's giant paw. His body began to crackle with lightning as the leopard quickly bit into his head. His body turned into the black smoke of a bonfire and floated away. The leopard bounded back toward Bronwyn. Bronwyn reached for her sword, but before she could get it, the leopard was lying in front of her, its side rather than its face or claws obscuring her view.

"Get on. You're not supposed to be here," the leopard said in a deep, yet somehow feminine voice.

"Naani?" Bronwyn asked.

"Quick, before he returns."

Is this what Naani's voice sounded like? Bronwyn had expected it to be harsh and grating.

Bronwyn grabbed onto Naani's fur and hoisted herself onto the leopard's back. As she did, she saw shapes start to materialize around her. At first, it was just a dozen, but soon there was a sea of Miros all staring at her with hatred. Bronwyn looked down to her sword. She let go of Naani's thick fur with one hand to lean over and pick it up, but before she could, Naani leapt into the air.

Bronwyn's hair whipped around her as Naani bounded toward the clouds.

"You aren't supposed to be here. Only bad things live here," Naani said as the clouds parted. Something floated in the distance, too far off to determine what it was.

"Where am I, Naani? Is this my dream?"

"This is his nightmare. Good things can't be here."

"But you're here Naani. You're his friend."

"And he thinks he killed me." Bronwyn's heart sank.

After Naani died, Miro asked, *"Did I kill Naani?"*

And Bronwyn coldly replied, *"More or less."* She wasn't sure if you could get motion sick in a dream, but nausea made her stomach lurch. *No, this isn't motion sickness. It is guilt for what I said to him then.*

Naani died trying to save Clara when Miro had entered his curse. It was only Naani's attack on Miro that was able to subdue him and bring him out of the curse. Without Naani, they'd all be dead. Bronwyn didn't ask any more questions. She only held tightly to Naani's fur until they slowed.

They were on the floating thing. It was like an island, suspended in air. It sloped upwards, to a thicket of trees. A cheery song floated in the sky. The flute that made it must be in front of her. This place felt familiar somehow.

"Come, she wants to talk to you." Naani ran toward the trees.

"Wait, who wants to talk to me?" Bronwyn asked as she ran after Naani. Despite her size, Naani deftly weaved between the trees, and Bronwyn soon lost sight of the great cat. Instead, she followed the music of the flute. That was the direction Naani was going.

The trees parted and she found herself at the end of the island, a large flat rock in front of her. Surrounding the rock were two figures, next to their own smaller stones. Past them, Naani lounged regally. Behind her, the grass of the island dropped off. Bronwyn slowed as she looked at the figures. They were at least nine feet tall.

The man took the flute from his lips. He wore a dark suit, and his even darker hair seemed to be plastered to his head, thick spikes clasped around his head like the black-footed talons of a bird. The woman wore a fur robe, and her skin looked frostbitten. The bright blue of her lips drew Bronwyn's attention for only a moment before it was drawn to her right eye. The entire eye socket was encrusted in ice.

The woman turned to Bronwyn and said, "This is very dangerous."

"Who are you?" Bronwyn asked.

"Not very bright, is she?" the man in black asked, taking a seat on the nearby stone.

"Chivas," the woman chastised.

"She may not be very bright, but she's interesting," the dark figure commented. "She talked to Brontidus."

The name sounded familiar, but Bronwyn couldn't put a face to it until she remembered that was the name of the Ywaigwai that had come to claim Issaroh's soul. The memory seemed so distant, even though it was only a week ago.

"Approaching Ywaigwai, walking through dreams, and she's here when she isn't supposed to be. I warned you about this plan, Fria," Chivas said.

"And the time for warnings and misgivings has long since passed," the woman replied. She glanced over her shoulder, looking at the expanding black speck in the distance. "I didn't expect you to seek us out this early."

"Wait, who's us? Where am I?" Bronwyn asked.

"You don't recognize your gods?" Chivas asked.

"Gods? The gods are gone. They left us hundreds of years ago." Bronwyn looked at the woman, then the man. She had seen plenty of depictions of Fria in the library and an illustration or two of Chivas. She had also experienced more dreams than she'd like involving the gods and goddesses, but this felt more real somehow. Still, their semblance was striking. "Is this another dream left over from the library?"

"We left the mortal realm, but I made sure to leave echoes of myself and Chivas to provide some guidance," Fria said.

Both figures looked at Bronwyn like she was an idiot for asking such a question.

"Stay out of his dreams. Don't use the Eye; let Miro," Fria said.

"Let Miro? No, he'll use it to find some way to trap his monster or some other silly thing. He won't use it to save Emestria."

Chivas gave a condescending look toward Fria. Then they both looked back toward the speck in the sky, which had grown considerably since the beginning of their interaction.

"We don't have a lot of time," Fria said. "You know what we are, and you know that if we've taken the time to talk to you, what we say is important. Let Miro use the artifact. That will be the way to save the world."

"The world? I don't want to save the world. I'm here to save Emestria," Bronwyn argued.

"Let Miro use the artifact," Fria reiterated.

Chivas interjected. "Fria, we've spent enough time here. We need to leave. She's been here too long already."

First the man, then the woman looked back toward the black void in the sky. It continually grew larger and seemed to be pulling in the space around itself. Now the far reaches of this island seemed to ribbon off and swirl into its expanse. The man's silhouette grew hazy, turning to black smoke that seemed to be pulled toward the point in the sky before it dissipated completely.

"Wait, where are we?" Bronwyn asked. "Why am I here? Is this Miro's dream? Are you part of Miro?"

"We can't answer your questions," Fria said, looking apologetic. "But we can offer advice. Just don't use the Eye, let Miro. You will not find the artifact if you use the Eye. If you use it, all you'll find is pain. Trust him. That's the only way this is going to work."

The dark mist of the man coalesced for a second, then said, "We've said what we can. We are not supposed to be interacting with mortals, and we are not supposed to be making Void Walkers."

"What's a Void Walker?" Bronwyn asked. Bronwyn found her eyeline drawn to the black hole, now the size of one of the figure's heads.

"It's too late for any of that. What is done is done." Fria walked toward Bronwyn, and Naani rose to her feet, circling the two women, to Bronwyn's backside.

"You *have* to trust him," Fria said. "You can't use the Eye. What you did here is very dangerous. You must stay out of his dreams." She looked back at the void, which now seemed ready to suck the island into its blackness. Little dots of light sparkled in it. "Quick, you have to go. Take this."

She held a silver chain with a sapphire hanging from it. It was the necklace from the library. Bronwyn had spent hours staring at that necklace in the reflective surface of the sculpture in Fria's room. Bronwyn stared at the gem oscillating back and forth. Wisps of mist seemed to fall from it as it glowed faintly. "What is it?"

"It will guard your memories from those who seek to steal them."

"Miro?"

The woman's brows knitted together as she held the necklace in both hands. She undid the clasp and put it around Bronwyn's neck. "Promise me you won't take it off. Last time you left it at the library, we went to great lengths to retrieve it. *Don't take it off.*"

The woman knelt, leaned toward, and embraced Bronwyn, cradling her head, much as her mom used to do when she was young. Fria rose to her feet, stepped back, and lifted Bronwyn's face, holding it in both hands, then leaned in and kissed her forehead with a tear in Fria's good eye. The tear hardened and chipped before it turned to mist.

"I'm sorry. I wish there was another way," Fria whispered.

Before Bronwyn could reply, she felt herself yanked off the ground. Naani had her tunic in her mouth and pulled her away. The island and its inhabitants disappeared from view as Naani ran from the void in the sky.

Bronwyn opened her eyes to the sound of Liman's snoring. She looked to see that Miro had quieted. *Stupid library. Now it has me having idiotic dreams.* Then a cold sting brought her attention to the jewelry around her neck. Beneath her tunic, she saw the faint glow of the sapphire.

Chapter 16

Bronwyn's group left the Shi'en first thing in the morning. The Shi'en had already begun packing up their camp to return to the outskirts of the swamps now that the "dragon" was dead. They had ridden two hours to the east to find a small clearing to use the Eye of Sleepless Dreams. Clara had been forced to buy the horses back. Apparently, the Shi'en's goodwill at slaying the dragon did not extend to horses. Clara didn't even have enough money to repurchase the third horse from them. At least they threw in the two-person saddles they used for riding.

The horses were now tied to a single tree in the area. Defurge and Clara had just finished erecting tents in front of the horses and tree, and Bronwyn had dug a firepit. It was still early in the morning, but she wanted a clear view of her surroundings while someone used the Eye. She didn't want to use it in the presence of the Shi'en. She couldn't place exactly *why* she didn't want to, and absent-mindedly fingered the sapphire pendant of her new necklace.

"That's nice. Is it new?" Miro asked.

Bronwyn looked down at the necklace, now resting outside her tunic. It must have slipped out during their ride. Having access to horses again was a godsend. She took the jewelry with two fingers and put it back underneath her tunic. It was cold against her breast. Bronwyn replied, "Yes. One of the Shi'en gave it to me."

"It matches your eyes," Miro said, looking at her intently.

Bronwyn smiled but shook her head. She looked back down at the Eye of Sleepless Dreams in her hand and wanted to return to the topic. "Malik said we just hold it on our chest when we sleep. The user concentrates on the question they want answered, then when they fall asleep, they'll receive visions. The Eye will show you horrible visions, and only after that will it answer your question."

"No thank you," Clara said, standing up from the campfire and raising Ferdinand on her falconer's glove. She had just finished penning the missive to King Bryant explaining they had slain a dragon and obtained another artifact. Ferdinand seemed to resist flying off. Bronwyn worried there was something wrong with him; he had killed two more crows today. With another thrust, Ferdinand flew from Clara's hand, rose into the sky, and headed to the northwest, toward Emestria.

"What does it even mean, 'It will show us horrible visions?'" Defurge asked, drawing Bronwyn's attention back to the discussion at hand.

Bronwyn shrugged. "Each one of us can only use it once. Using it twice can cause madness."

"I'll do it," Miro said, stepping forward.

Bronwyn looked to Defurge. Defurge shook his head and said, "The phoenix and monks have tempered the gem's madness, and if that thing is a legendary artifact, it could very well undo their work. I doubt you want me to return to being the mad god and raining fireballs from the heavens."

"Clara?" Bronwyn asked.

"I'll do it," Miro reiterated.

"No. I refuse to use it," Clara said.

Bronwyn turned back to Miro. She didn't want to say what she was thinking. They couldn't risk him losing control. "Malik said even one use can cause madness."

"I'm already mad, so I should be safe," Miro said with a chuckle.

"Miro, this is serious. I'll be the one to use it. You said I have some immunity to magic. If this thing works with magic, I'll probably be the best candidate." *It was just a dream. Someone gave me the necklace while I was drunk. It can't be real.* Bronwyn felt the cold sting of the pendant on her chest.

"Bronwyn, every night I'm tortured by nightmares. What this thing can probably do is nothing compared to what I put myself through. Let me." Miro extended his hand forward, waiting for her to place the Eye in it. Bronwyn hesitated, bringing the Eye closer to her body reflexively. Her skin tingled as Miro placed his hand on her bare arm. "Please."

Bronwyn remembered the conversation before the fight with the crocodile. She had asked Miro to use the bow and when he disagreed, she asked him, *"Please."*

How can I trust him with this? He showed me in the library how much he wants something to trap his monster. He will be more likely to look for the hammer to destroy Defurge's gem than he is to find something to help Emestria. She closed her eyes, gritted her teeth, then handed the artifact to Miro.

While Defurge lit a fire, Miro retreated to his tent to rest with the Eye. Using it during the day, as opposed to night, would be preferable. If someone were to approach their camp, Bronwyn would see them far in advance and be able to prepare an adequate defense. Despite this time away from Emestria, she was proud she still thought like a guardswoman.

Quiet, restless hours passed, and Bronwyn stared in at Miro in his tent, and asked, "Anything?"

"No updates since the last hour, when you asked me," Miro replied, opening one eye to look at her.

"How will we know when it's working?" Bronwyn asked.

"Maybe interrupting me every hour is preventing it from working," Miro said.

"Right, I get the hint." Bronwyn turned to leave.

"Bronwyn, we've got one shot at this. Regardless of what you hear or see, don't wake me. I need this to work." Bronwyn nodded, and Miro closed his eyes, breathing out heavily.

Back at the subdued campfire, Bronwyn joined Clara. She was teasing her hair out of the tight braids the Shi'en had put into it after the coming-of-age ritual. Defurge was out sunning himself. Apparently, this was the ideal time to feel the sun's heat.

Bronwyn absent-mindedly took the pendant from her tunic and rubbed it between her two fingers. It would not warm to the temperature of her hand.

"Let me see it," Clara said, noticing her. Bronwyn held the pendant up for Clara to see. "Cute. Take it off, let me get a look at it."

Bronwyn went to undo the clasp but hesitated. "Come over here and look. The clasp is such a pain to get on and off."

"I'll just put it back on you," Clara said. "Are you afraid I'm going to steal it?"

Bronwyn raised an eyebrow. "Right, 'cause I want you awkwardly fidgeting with it. Stop being lazy and just get off your butt to have a look."

Clara stood and walked over, taking the pendant in her hands and looking at it intently. "No one gave me any jewelry. You'd think the slayer of the dragon would be given the greatest honors." She let it go and it swung back to Bronwyn's chest.

"Maybe they didn't have anything that would go with your eyes." Bronwyn blushed the second the words left her lips. She did not mean to say it. The words just forced their way out.

Clara grinned. "Oh, is that why you're afraid of me taking it? Because Miro finds it fetching around your neck?"

"No." Bronwyn tucked the pendant back into her tunic as Clara sat down next to her.

"What was it like?" Clara asked. "When he saved you."

"It was terrifying. I'm about to be eaten, and then I have to rely on some crazy plan of his to get me free. I'm still surprised it worked." Bronwyn shifted her gaze to the fire.

"You didn't look terrified with his arms wrapped around you."

Bronwyn rolled her eyes. "Not this again. Clara, I'm here to help Emestria. Miro has his reasons. They just happen to align with ours right now." Bronwyn looked back to the tent. *Hopefully, they align right now.*

"Yes, but what about just a stolen half hour of the day," Clara teased, mimicking Defurge's words. Bronwyn turned to her, eyes widening. "We sleep together in tents not fifteen feet from the fire. Do you really think all your late-night conversations are that secret? Half the time you don't even wait long enough for me to fall asleep."

Bronwyn put her head in her hands. "Tell me you didn't—"

"I did. I can't believe you tried to kiss him."

Bronwyn shook her head, wishing she had bigger hands to hide in. She looked out toward Defurge, lounging in the sun. "Haha, I'm the fool. He even said himself that he was giving me mixed signals."

"But you see the way he looks at Miro, right?"

"I guess I didn't."

"He looks at Miro the way Miro looks at you." Bronwyn frowned as she looked at Clara then shook her head. "Maybe you should have traded that necklace for another horse. The two of them are going to be riding together until we can get another one."

Bronwyn grumbled.

"I'll stop. You're right though; I probably would have tried to steal it."

Bronwyn turned to Clara. She cocked her eyebrows and grinned, then said, "I would have given it back eventually. Just like I do with the books."

"The books?" Bronwyn asked.

"Yeah, Issaroh's books about magic."

"But he gave you the one about the Penakian discipline. Why would you need any of the others?"

"I've been looking at them, trying to figure out ways to use the elements and spells together. To create different combinations. Like we did with the earth walls when we captured Defurge." Bronwyn nodded, focusing on Miro's tent and not Clara. "Of course, I put them back, so Miro doesn't even know I've taken them. Not too sly, that one."

Changing the subject, Bronwyn asked, "Have you had any strange dreams since leaving the library?"

"No," Clara replied, suspicion in her voice. "Why do you ask?"

"What about while you were there? Did you have any weird dreams while in the library?"

"Nothing I can remember …. What have you been dreaming about?"

Bronwyn forced a chuckle. She wasn't the best liar, so she concocted the first semi-decent story she could think of to explain why she would think her dreams were strange. "I keep dreaming about the homunculi, but they aren't like they are in the library; they're dancing in the woods."

"Egh … gross," Clara said, returning to teasing her hair out of the braids.

"Why did they braid your huair that way, instead of a single braid down the back?" Bronwyn asked.

"This marks me as a man and warrior." Clara grinned. "The Shi'en divide their tasks into masculine and feminine, but your birth doesn't dictate what you'll be responsible for. When you come of age, you choose by adopting one of the two hairstyles. The longer braided hair down the back is for caregivers and mothers."

"Is that common?"

"I've heard of something similar in some of the cultures of Selunia, but that has more to do with whether a woman is born into the family or not. The Shi'en believe the soul doesn't always match the physical body, and which side is dominant determines your gender. The soul is also able to change dominance during life, so your hairstyle can change to indicate your soul is shifting."

Bronwyn nodded before absently rising to go check on Miro again. She clenched her hands and sat back down, then tapped her foot as Clara started to say something else. Bronwyn stared at the tent and Miro's partly obscured body.

It wasn't until nightfall that the screams started.

CHAPTER 17

BRONWYN PACED BACK to the tent, unable to drown the sounds out. Most of what Miro said was too unintelligible or garbled to understand. Now and then something would slip out that she could decipher. "No, I'm sorry, please," or some variation was all she heard. After another hour, she couldn't bear it any longer and returned to the tent to check on Miro. His eyes were wide open, and tears streamed down his cheeks as he cried, pled, begged, and mumbled. She wanted to rip the Eye from his grasp, but she couldn't. He asked her not to. She wanted to wipe the tears away or blot the sweat from his brow, but if she woke him, this would all be for naught.

When Bronwyn returned to the fire, she threw more fresh branches on. The hiss and pop of the leaves competed with Miro for attention. Thankfully, Defurge emerged from the other tent.

"Can you see into his mind?" Bronwyn asked. "Try and help him?"

"I've tried to see what he's seeing. It's all flashes of red, gray, and black," Defurge said, walking to the fire. He put his hands out to it, increasing its intensity and drowning out some more of Miro's sounds. "The shapes make no sense and seem to be glimpses of things in the visions. I can't keep trying. The monks are losing their focus when I try, and I'm hearing faint whispers from the gem. I worry it might take control again. I'm sorry. The phoenix and monks warn if it takes hold, I'll lose my mind again.

"It's my turn at watch. Try and get some sleep. Clara stuffed cotton in her ears and laid clothes over her head, which seemed to help."

"I can't listen to him. But I can't just stand here and do nothing or try and sleep." Bronwyn went to the tent and lay down next to Miro.

"Bronwyn, what are you doing?" Defurge asked.

"If I can't sleep, at least I can watch to make sure he's okay," Bronwyn said. She waited until Defurge returned to the fire before she slowly brought her hand toward Miro's temple. *It was just a fluke last time. A stupid dream born of the library and paranoia,* Bronwyn thought as her fingers inched closer. *Let me see.* Bronwyn touched her fingers to Miro's temple and her vision flashed white.

Miro shook his head. He must have trailed off in thought. *What am I doing? Right, checking the White North for any stragglers that had the misfortune of trying to find salvation up here.* He snapped the reins, and the sleigh continued forward. Particularly harsh wind and snow bit at Miro's skin and he pulled his cloak and robe tight against his body. Visibility was poor, and he was about to give up his vigil and return home when Naani yowled loudly.

Naani had been getting worse ever since her eye was taken by hunters. Miro tried to keep her close to his cabin as much as he could, but she still felt the need to complete her duty to protect the forest. Time and time again he counseled that she mustn't kill people, and she never had, to his knowledge. His heart sank as he hoped it was the wolves trying to expand their territory again. Naani would have little trouble convincing the stragglers to stay out of her forest, but Miro would help in case she needed it.

When Miro heard the first man's cry of pain, he knew the worst was happening. Quickly, he unhitched the reindeer from the sleigh and proceeded with all haste to where the noise originated. Naani, a snow leopard as large as a small house, was in the distance, clawing and pouncing at armored men. In the snow, a child had collapsed. She seemed to be moving, and there was no blood around her body. As Miro rode past, he grabbed her cloak and swung her onto his reindeer. The child gripped his waist instinctively, but let her grip relax and then leaned back.

She faintly cried, "No, not that way. The monster is that way."

If Miro had the time, he would have stopped to calm her, but dealing with Naani was the priority. Miro gasped as the extent of her rampage came into view; the worst had happened. Half a dozen men's bodies were strewn in the snow, their blood staining it. Several dead horses lay in front of a splintered caravan. Naani was still battling the lone survivor. She was fast and deftly evaded Naani's blows. When she turned and he saw her face, his heart skipped a beat. *Serra? Serra is back? How can she be back? No, it isn't Serra. Serra can't move like that. She's too quick and agile. And her aura is different.*

"Naani, no! Naani, stop!" Miro screamed at the top of his lungs, but the wind drowned out his voice. The woman leapt back from Naani's attack, but she left too much distance between her and Naani. She had lost her advantage. Miro readied to cast the ice wall to protect her, but his hands were moving so slowly, and his voice was garbled. He couldn't cast in time.

The woman turned to try and run from Naani. The leopard's claws raked deep into the flesh of the blonde woman's back. Dismounting the reindeer and running, Miro's feet were waylaid by the thick snow.

"Naani, no!" Miro yelled again, but the wind drowned out his voice. Naani couldn't hear him. He skidded to a stop when—to his horror— Naani crouched in front of the woman and dipped her head down. Viscera snapped from the woman's body as Naani raised her head. Tears streamed down his face.

"Naani, stop. You have to stop," Miro said, his voice choking. Naani turned to him, her chin wet with the woman's blood.

"Don't worry, it's not your friend," Naani said cheerfully, organs and muscles falling from her mouth as she spoke. She put her head back down, turning it sideways to bite back into the woman.

"No, you can't!" Miro cried.

"They were hurting the flower-haired girl," Naani said before continuing her grisly display. She had never done anything like this before. It was too much to forgive. He would have to do what he'd been avoiding for so long. What he should have done before this day. Miro ran, hoping to save the woman, knowing the gesture was futile.

Naani had disemboweled the unknown woman and was hungrily eating from her midsection. Somehow, the woman was still alive.

"Please, help," she said, reaching her hand out to him. "It hurts so much." Her body spasmed in pain. "It's eating me. It hurts so much."

Miro grabbed her hand. Blood pooled around her mouth. She should not be alive. Miro's voice caught in his throat as he forced the words free. "Naani, please stop."

He held the woman's hand tightly, unwilling to let go and turn away in her last moments. Tears froze against his cheek as he tried to push the cat's head away from the stranger's body.

Naani looked back at him, tilting her head to the side. "There's plenty of meat if you want some. Cut a piece for yourself. The legs look tasty."

Miro yelled and screamed at Naani, to no avail. He tried to cast spells, but the words wouldn't come to him. The runes jumbled in his brain and refused to form.

"It stopped hurting, but I'm so cold," the woman said looking at Miro one last time, her eyes growing pale and lifeless. This was probably the child's mother, and he now found himself searching the near whiteout conditions for the one person he was able to save. He ran back to the child, to shield her eyes from the sight, but she had already picked up a walking cane and limped toward him.

"No, look away," Miro begged.

"You killed me," she replied. Now Miro realized it wasn't a child, but a woman. Her height had confused him in the panic of the moment.

"I'll get you back to the city. I can keep you safe," Miro said, removing his cloak and wrapping it around her body.

"They'll kill me in the city. She was the only one trying to protect me. And you killed me." She pushed the cloak and Miro away from her.

"I'll keep you safe," Miro said, trying to find some way to forgive himself and make this right. "I have a cottage north of here. I can take you there. I can heal your leg,"

"I'd rather die out here in the cold than go anywhere with you two monsters." The woman turned and walked away. Miro reached out for her, but the snow obscured his vision. One minute she was there, the next she disappeared into the blizzard. Her words echoed with him.

"*I'd rather die out here ....*" He knew she would in this cold. *I want to lie down in the snow and freeze to death. But Raithe won't let me. He won't let me die. Now, I have to kill Naani. I'll spend hundreds of years out here, alone, until finally, he lets me die.*

The vision cleared from Miro's memory; only the deep-seated horror remained as the next dream unfolded.

"Geometric patterns!" Issaroh yelled. Issaroh and Clara's walls went up without fail, but Miro's didn't materialize. The front of their pyramid was exposed. Clara and Issaroh had no defense when the god of destruction buffeted his fiery wings forward, engulfing them almost immediately in its hellfire.

They had come to this cave expecting to find an artifact that once captured the god of fire and madness, Defurge. But the stories were wrong, the rumors only half-truths. The Soul Gem wasn't a prison able to hold a god; it was the source of Defurge's power. Miro, in his exuberance, had led them here. Maybe if he had been less excited about finally finding an artifact to trap the Ywaigwai that stole his soul, he would have noticed the inconsistencies in the tales. But like everything, he was to blame. His friends were dying because of him, again.

"Miro, help!" Clara screamed as the flames burned her very bones. Miro tried to cast something, anything, but he couldn't think. Clara and Issaroh struggled to breathe. Each breath brought with it fire that burned their lungs and throat. They died clawing at their necks. The grotesque noise they made choking on the flames was half scream, half cry.

This was all his fault. Of course, the Soul Gem would be guarded by the very same god of destruction it meant to imprison. He was too stupid, too headstrong, and they would all pay the price.

Bronwyn attempted to use Clara and Issaroh's demise to incapacitate the foe. She elbowed the back of his head, then leapt back delivering a swift kick in the very same spot. Miro knew her elbows were lethal; he had been on the receiving end more than once. Even that was not enough to knock the god unconscious. *Of course, it isn't; what am I thinking? It is a god.*

The god flung its flaming whip back at Bronwyn. The fiery lash wrapped around her waist and the barbs and fire started to bore into her body, tightening and tightening.

"Miro! Miro!" Bronwyn screamed for his attention. He diverted it from Clara's and Issaroh's bodies, now on the ground, still writhing in agony.

"My sword! Get my sword!" She cried in pain, her voice echoing off the walls of the cavern. Miro ran and found the weapon, lodged in the side of the cave. He tugged on it, put a foot against the wall, and pulled with all his might, but it would not budge.

"Miro, please. Please don't let me die like this," Bronwyn begged as the whip dug further into her mid-section until it wrapped around her spinal cord. With a quick tug, her upper torso separated from her lower. Miro looked on in horror as her lips still mouthed *Don't let me die like this.*

Miro turned to the god. Surely the god of destruction could end his torment. The god turned and began walking out of the cave. Miro ran in front of the god, forcing it to confront him. But the god just pushed him aside.

"Why! Why them and not me?" he shouted at him.

"Because you and I are kindred spirits," the voice boomed. "Together we will bring this world to its knees. They were holding you back, preventing you from realizing your true destiny."

"No, I loved them!" Miro yelled back at the god of destruction.

"Really?" the god asked. "Then why didn't you save them? Why didn't you use your magic?"

"Something in this cave is preventing me," Miro replied.

"Nothing blocked their spells. The truth of the matter is that you wanted them to die; you wanted to witness them in agony. It is your nature, as it is mine. Why else would you refuse to pull her sword out? The wall is sandstone; it crumbles at the slightest provocation. You wanted them gone. You wanted to lie to yourself and say you tried to help them. We both know you don't save people. Now come, we have a world to destroy together."

The god beckoned him forward and Miro felt the allure and draw of it. He was powerless to stop his feet from following.

Bronwyn was in the water; the crocodile had dived in after her. There was no way she would be able to reach shore in time.

"Defurge, a hand!" Miro yelled. Defurge cast his whip forward, but it didn't reach. *Or does he not want it to reach? Is he so jealous of Bronwyn that he would let this happen? Still, I can't stop; I need to try to save her.*

"Fria, goddess of ice and death, the vigilant eye, aid my passage, Fragma Frios!" he shouted and was relieved as the barrier materialized. Miro felt as if his magic had never worked, that it always failed him, always disappointed him. He slid forward atop the bridge of ice he had created.

"Ramun, Tempus Dallates!" But nothing happened. His magic failed him again—or for the first time, he couldn't remember—but at least he reached Bronwyn in time. They would have a chance on solid ground. As he grabbed her arms, the crocodile's head submerged. He attempted to pull Bronwyn up, but the minute he tried to, something tugged at her from below. The blood began to rise in the swamp.

"Don't let go," Bronwyn said, looking into his eyes, pleading.

"No, I'm going to save you. Please let me save you, just this once." Miro cried, tears flowing freely down his cheek.

"You won't," Bronwyn said calmly as more tugs attempted to free her from his grasp. "You can't save me. Please let me look into your eyes. I want them to be the last thing I see. Don't look away."

"I won't. I won't," Miro promised.

"I love you." It was the last thing Bronwyn said before the mighty crocodilian wrested her from his grip.

Bronwyn felt her spirit being pulled from Miro's body. She was relieved to no longer have to share in his visions, to be a prisoner of his mind. Then she found herself rising into the sky.

"Wait, Naani! I need to see the rest," Bronwyn said as the ground rapidly became a blur of shapes. Down below, Clara walked forward until she disappeared under the green water. Miro lay down on the ice, defeated. Defurge said something to him, but she was too far away to hear. Bronwyn looked up; her tunic was in Naani's mouth. She knew where they were going and didn't even need to look in which direction Naani ran through the sky.

Naani set her down on the island and turned to run toward the trees. Bronwyn said, "Wait, Naani."

Naani faced her. "She wants to talk again."

"Why are you here Naani? Are you part of his dreams? Is it you, or some echo of you?"

"Does it matter?"

"It does to me." Bronwyn folded her arms, trying to indicate she wasn't leaving without some answers this time. *Hopefully, the cat is less obtuse than the goddess.*

"I'm part of his dreams, but not part of them. I go where I want and try to help him when I can."

"But why? Why can you go through his dreams? Why aren't you pulled around in them like I am? Why can you bring me here?"

"Because I'm a spirit guardian. I used to think I only had two jobs—protect the eastern forest of Emestria and the flower-haired people. I forgot my third task—help the Nice-man." The Nice-man, Miro had told Clara that was what Naani called him. With that, Naani started for the trees, quickly disappearing in the blur of bark and leaf.

"Naani, I'm not done …." *What is the point? The cat isn't going to listen to me any more than the goddess will.* Bronwyn walked toward the forest, keeping an eye out for the black spot on the horizon. When she was through the trees, the two figures were there once again, arguing in a language she didn't understand.

"Shut up!" Bronwyn yelled. They turned to her, looks of derision on their faces.

Chivas stepped closer and said, "How dare you talk—"

"I said shut up," Bronwyn repeated louder. He stopped in his tracks and even backed up a step. He glanced over his shoulder. The hole was already as big as his fist. He seemed to shrink in stature.

"I don't know why I keep getting brought here, but I know you don't want me here because that thing shows up." Bronwyn pointed toward the vortex that was already pulling more of the sky into its dark embrace.

"I want answers, or I'm going to keep coming back every day until eventually that thing swallows both of you." Bronwyn scanned both figures' faces for signs of disagreement. "You told me to trust Miro, to let him use the Eye. He wasted that chance to find out how I feel about him. Clara and Defurge refuse to use it. If you don't want me to, you'll tell me where the artifact is that will help my people."

Chivas and Fria exchanged glances. Their expressions darkened. Fria said, "That's not the question he asked the Eye. Trust him, and in the morning, you'll see your faith will be rewarded."

"No, I saw his visions. The last one was of him holding me while I told him I love him."

The woman stepped forward. "That was part of his punishment, before the Eye would show him what he wanted. We tried to get you out sooner, but he was jumping all over the place."

Bronwyn was startled by Fria's words. *Does he hate me that much?* "It was his punishment to see me tell him I love him?"

"And then to watch you die," Fria said, her voice calm.

Bronwyn looked to the ground, and when she looked up, Chivas was already gone. "What do you want me to do? Why am I back here again?"

"Serina, the phoenix, already told you what we want you to do," Fria said.

"Destroy the gem? That's what this is about? Why didn't you destroy it?"

"Laevin forbade the gods and goddesses from raising arms against each other in earnest. Gods shall not kill gods."

Tiring of games, Bronwyn asked, "So, you send mortals to do what you didn't dare to do? I kill Defurge, take the gem, and then keep it away from others? Is that what you want?"

"That is one path, but not the one we want for you," Fria replied. "It will only buy more time. We're tired of sacrificing people to keep the gem hidden. We need it to be destroyed, once and for all. Then Defurge can at least have some rest."

"The Hammer of Unmaking, then? To destroy the gem?" Bronwyn's voice was cold and demanding. Miro had bargained their freedom from the gem with the promise that he would obtain the only artifact capable of destroying another.

"That is what Miro was supposed to use the eye for," the goddess said.

"What do you mean, 'supposed to?'" Bronwyn asked. "Where's the hammer?"

"We don't know. We wanted to destroy our gifts before leaving the mortal realm, but Alcides stole and hid it. Then he used the hammer on himself, so we could never find it." The woman looked to the void, now sucking at the ground of the island. "I have to go."

"Answer me one thing. Miro's visions … if they unfolded the way he saw them, would we have said the same things to him as we died?"

Fria gave a somber smile. "No, those are just the things that would torture him the most. They aren't real, just nightmares."

Bronwyn wasn't sure if she was happy or disappointed to hear that answer. "You said I was on a path. Did you put Miro on this path as well? Did he have choices that could have prevented him from the pain he now experiences?" The woman didn't answer, only turned and faded away. "Coward!"

Bronwyn found Naani at the edge of the island. Everything around her seemed to be pulled toward the abyss, but she felt no pressure from the thing. It didn't scare her like it did Fria and Chivas.

"Let's go, Naani. I'm tired of this." Bronwyn pulled herself onto Naani's back.

Bronwyn woke, breathing heavily. She sweated from the heat in her body. As she removed her fingers from Miro's temple, sparks hopped between them. Then the fire in her body abated. She heard the blaze outside the tent and peeked out to see that Defurge was still on watch. Miro screamed and she looked at him. She had done nothing to ease the visions of the Eye; he still muttered and cried.

"No, Naani. Stop," Miro whispered.

Bronwyn leaned in and listened. Most of the words were still garbled, but as he spoke, Bronwyn recognized some of them from the visions. She listened as he went through each vision, identifying them by the things he said. Then they started all over again. *He is moving through the visions over and over, like a never-ending loop. No wonder this thing makes people go mad.*

When Bronwyn was in the visions, she forgot each dream existed as she lived the next one. The only thing that stayed with her was the increasing dread and anxiety Miro felt. Now out of them, she remembered everything. *He is living out our fights, watching Clara and I die in each one, and blaming himself for our deaths. No, it's more than that. He has to watch us blame him for our deaths.* Bronwyn shuddered as she recalled the vision of the crocodile.

Bronwyn lay down, looking at the top of the tent. Despite her exhaustion, she still couldn't sleep with Miro's cries. Then she felt the cold throb of the pendant on her chest and her eyes grew heavy. She turned to see Miro still muttering and screaming, but the words were somehow muted. She yawned and closed her eyes.

Bronwyn startled awake as Miro lurched from the tent. He stumbled as he ran, and she jumped up to follow. When he was close enough, he braced himself against a tree, gagging. As Bronwyn approached, black ichor started to run out of Miro's mouth. The viscous material sizzled as it touched the grass. Miro appeared to be choking on it. Bronwyn hurriedly came up behind him and firmly patted him on the back, to help him liberate the fluid from his body.

Miro's body tensed and spasmed as more of the ooze started to pour from his nostrils and mouth. Bronwyn rubbed his back, as he had for her on the boat to Newtonne when she was overcome with sea sickness. Malik hadn't mentioned anything about this part of using the Eye. Then Miro's back arched as he breathed in sharply. He panted, gasping for breath. When he turned to see Bronwyn, he embraced her with tears in his eyes.

"You're alive," Miro sobbed, falling to his knees, still clutching Bronwyn around her waist as he cried against her stomach. "You're alive. Thank the gods, you're alive."

Bronwyn frowned and cradled his head against her body. "I'm here," she said softly.

She held him as his tears wetted her tunic. Once his sobbing subsided, Bronwyn helped him to his feet, wrapping one arm around his waist to support him as they walked back around the tents to the fire. Defurge and Clara were standing around, looks of concern on their faces. Bronwyn forced a brave smile and helped Miro sit close to the fire. His body was colder than she would have preferred.

Bronwyn picked up her waterskin and offered it to Miro. He drank greedily from it, like he had been in a desert for weeks, then looked blankly into the fire, his eyes wide and fearful. When he finally spoke, his voice was ragged and grating.

"It's near those mountains." Miro pointed at a mountain range to the northeast. "In the basement of a building destroyed by fire."

"What is?" Bronwyn asked cautiously.

"The Horn of Garanhir. The artifact that can make food." Miro looked intently at Bronwyn as he said it.

Too shocked, Bronwyn couldn't find the words. *He chose to look for the artifact to help Emestria. All that, for Emestria?* She steadied her breathing, trying to will the tears away. The goddess indicated Miro was supposed to look for the hammer. Why had he chosen to help Emestria? Every time he spoke of their shared homeland, he did so with venom-laced words. He hated Emestria and blamed it for so much, but here he had chosen to help the land he hated rather than do what was dictated by fate and destroy Defurge's gem. Had her actions in some way changed what the goddess Fria, who could see the river of fate, expected to happen?

Was there something more to the energy between them when he held her while fighting the crocodile? But no, when Bronwyn had shrunk the distance between them at the Shi'en's camp, Miro hadn't returned her desire to be closer. But then why? If not out of affection, out of a desire to do something for her, why would he look for the artifact to save the country he hates?

Miro looked at Bronwyn, his eyes red and wet. A shiver ran up his body, shaking his limbs first before it died in his core. "Is this real? Or is it another nightmare?"

Chapter 18

Defurge eyed Miro as he helped pack camp. Defurge was relieved that Miro hadn't used the Eye to find the Hammer to destroy the gem. But something unsettled him about Miro's choice to look for an artifact to help Emestria. It was incongruous with how he should have acted.

Defurge tried to peer into Miro's mind again, to see what he had seen, but the same blurred images greeted him. Something was blocking these memories. Defurge wondered if Miro could even recall what he had seen while using the Eye, but he must have been able to. He knew where the artifact was.

After loading the horse with their supplies and securing the two-person saddle Clara had procured from the Shi'en, Defurge mounted and rode his horse over to Miro. Miro stood, shaky on his feet and Defurge extended a hand, steadying Miro as he mounted behind. Bronwyn doused the fire, then mounted her steed with Clara riding behind her. Bronwyn turned her horse to the northeast and Defurge directed his mount to follow.

Defurge closed his eyes and found himself back inside of the gem. He walked up the stairs. The phoenix's hair was on fire and her eyes burned with intensity.

"What did you do?" the phoenix seethed.

"I've done nothing," Defurge replied.

"He was supposed to look for the hammer."

"What do you care? He looked for the artifact for your precious Bronwyn."

Defurge turned to the monks. "There are holes in her memory. Are you two blocking my view of her mind?"

The monks turned to him and in unison responded, "We have done no such thing. We show you all that we can see."

"How is she able to block me?" Defurge asked the phoenix. The phoenix narrowed her eyes as she stared back at him. "How was she able to move when Miro cast the spell to stop time while fighting the crocodile? What do you know about her?"

"I know as much as you do. She will help free us of this prison. Or she will kill you and become the next incarnation. If you continue to meddle, you'll find the second option more likely to happen. You don't have any idea how it feels to be in one of those cages." The phoenix extended her arm, pointing to the many facets of the gem where the previous incarnations that were driven insane resided, trapped for all eternity.

"I am not meddling. It's Bronwyn who changed your destiny by making him go after an artifact to save her homeland."

"Because of your games," the phoenix said.

"Bah. I should just quit their company and strike out on my own. I'm a god. Do you realize how boring mortals are?"

"You are not a god, and if you leave, I will strip you of all the power I lend you. You'll be no different than one of those mortals." The phoenix stepped forward, her hair beginning to rise with deeper flames.

"And then you'll lose the gem to someone else. And your sanity."

"I'll have the monks march you up to Bronwyn and tell her to kill you. Then she will take the gem. I may go insane, but you'll be here to keep me company, for all eternity. Stop your games."

"My games have no bearing on what Miro or Bronwyn do. They merely keep me entertained."

"You tried to make Miro jealous, and then Bronwyn," the phoenix said. "Now you're pushing her closer to that man. You don't think your actions have anything to do with his decision to find an artifact for her?"

"None whatsoever. I haven't pushed her."

The unison voice of the monks began again, "What is this affection toward Miro? He is not to be trusted. He will bring ruin."

"He doesn't even want the gem. He is the only one of the three that is the least bit interesting. He is immortal, like me. He is a thing to be owned." Defurge turned to leave. "Don't summon me back here unless you have something of consequence to discuss."

Defurge opened his eyes. Miro wobbled on the saddle behind him. The Eye robbed him of getting any sleep, and now Miro dozed off intermittently only to grab the saddle as he began to lose his balance. With the sun now being higher up, Defurge thought he might be able to get more power.

He tried to probe Miro's mind again. Still the flashes from the visions. The other memories were there; only the visions from the eye were obscured. He redirected his attention toward Clara. She still hummed bawdy sailor tunes to herself and dug her nails into her palm, trying to distract her mind from the memories of Scarlette, the daughter she had failed. But Bronwyn's mind was still problematic. Most of her memories were there, but there were gaps of time unaccounted for, all starting after the fight with the crocodile—after Miro had embraced her.

When they stopped for a midday meal, Miro took the opportunity to nap. After packing up their supplies, it was time to leave, and Bronwyn shook him awake.

"Defurge's horse looks tired from having to carry Miro and him all day," Bronwyn said. "Clara, why don't you join Defurge? Miro will ride with me."

"Why don't I ride with you?" Defurge suggested. "Then Clara and Miro can take my horse."

Bronwyn turned to Defurge and stammered before finally saying, "No, I'm afraid Miro is so tired he'll need someone to support him. He might be too heavy for Clara."

Clara shrugged, going over to join Defurge before he mounted his horse. Bronwyn went to Miro with her steed and helped him climb behind her. As he did, he turned to Defurge. His thoughts were glaringly clear. *Please don't. Not this, Defurge. It's too cruel.* Miro seemed to be under the impression that Bronwyn's actions were under Defurge's direction. But Defurge was finding it increasingly difficult to even read Bronwyn's mind, let alone force her actions.

"What's that about?" Defurge whispered to Clara.

"Eh, you'll get used to it," Clara replied. "They do this all the time. They'll get mad at each other soon enough and be unable to stand the other's company. Just the way they are. Every time they grow closer, the next time they fight, they grow further apart. Eventually, they're going to either be unable to stand each other's company or …."

Defurge smiled, getting a new idea for a great game. He had been trying to make the two jealous of each other but perhaps pushing them closer was the true way to pull them apart forever.

"At least we have each other," Defurge joked, worried Clara wouldn't get the sarcasm.

"Oh, my hero, what would I do without you?" Clara put her hand to her forehead, giving her best impression of a damsel in distress. Clara laughed and Defurge returned the sentiment with a hearty guffaw. He now understood why Clara and Miro laughed at her joke about the marred skin. It had nothing to do with the comedy of the statement. Rather it was enjoyable because it was something that those two shared. Bronwyn shot the two of them a disapproving look, probably misinterpreting it as some judgment toward her. Then Defurge realized it wasn't just her memories; he couldn't read what she was thinking.

CHAPTER 19

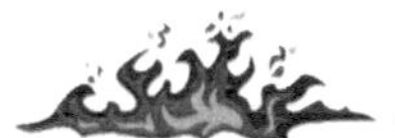

As Bronwyn rode, she purposefully let Defurge ride ahead. The idea to ride with Miro had, of course, been more than a desire to spare Defurge's horse the extra weight. She needed to find out if the visions she saw of Miro were the same. *That is the only reason I want him to ride with me.*

Once she was far enough back, Bronwyn whispered, "What did you see?" The sapphire around her neck throbbed with cold intensity.

"I don't want to talk about it," Miro said, his voice scratchy with the lack of sleep.

Bronwyn said, "You're still shaking. You need to talk."

"Bronwyn, please."

Bronwyn knew she should stop asking, but she had to know. "If we must use it again, I'm going to be the one to use the Eye. I need to prepare myself."

Fria's necklace stung her chest as its temperature decreased further.

"I saw the battles we fought together." His voice sounded numb. "Except, I was unable to save you or Clara. Each time, my magic or strength failed me. I was unable to reach you in time. I had to watch you and Clara die—repeatedly—and you blamed me for your deaths."

Miro left out the part about what Defurge said to him, as well as what he heard Bronwyn say as the crocodile ate her. The moments felt so private; Bronwyn found herself feeling guilty for her actions, even if helping was the only thing she wanted to do.

Bronwyn tried to console him. "That must have been hard." She knew it was. She lived it with him, experienced all his emotions, raw and unfiltered. *By the gods, is this how he feels all the time?* After a couple of minutes of trying to think of a way to soothe his pain, she said, "There is also something to take away from those dreams."

"What is that?"

"You said we died because your magic or strength failed you. That means you were the key to our survival. Without you, the events might have unfolded as you had seen."

"That's a rather upbeat way to look at it, but it doesn't negate the awfulness of having to watch it again and again. Bronwyn, don't ever use that thing. We can go to one of the big cities, find a real library, do some more research. Just don't ever use that thing."

Miro had refused to return the Eye to Bronwyn after its use. She didn't know how she felt about that.

"Maybe knowing what it did to you might prepare me, or I will be somewhat immune to it. I couldn't imagine having to watch you and Clara succumb to our foes, but I would be able to process it once I was awake." Bronwyn wanted to say because she had already seen it once, lived through it in his eyes, but he had suffered enough. He didn't need to know about her attempts at intervening. He would rightly be upset.

"And what if it shows you the same things I saw? You have to watch me die and blame you for it. Or you die and wonder why I didn't help you, and think it was out of some indifference I have toward you. Promise me. I still am not sure that this isn't another vision from the Eye."

"I would know when I woke it wasn't true. You wouldn't let anything happen to me. I can't promise I'll never use it; I can only promise when I do, it will be for a very good reason." It was the most she could agree to. The artifact was too valuable to not be used. There were too many variables.

"I guess that's the most honest compromise I can get out of you. Can we please stop talking about it? I'm very tired and afraid I'll say something I'll regret later."

The candidness of the statement surprised Bronwyn. "You can rest. Just lean against my back."

"I'll probably fall off the minute I fall asleep."

"Wrap your arms around my waist. I'll keep you from falling." Bronwyn reached out and grabbed Miro's hand, putting it around her waist. Like always, when she touched his skin, she felt the energy, the spark they had between them now. *It must mean something. Miro doesn't react to it. Can only I feel it, or does he hide his reaction?*

It was mind-numbingly boring as they traversed the plains. In the distance, mountains loomed, but the landscape only enunciated the fact there was little to be seen or experienced in the plains of Mul'tok. Bronwyn almost wished they would come upon a hostile tribe of nomads, just so it would break up the monotony.

When they finally decided to stop for the day and make camp, Bronwyn felt bad that Miro had been unable to sleep while riding behind her. Despite his tight clasp upon her waist and his head leaning into her back, he never nodded off. Perhaps she was partly to blame.

Anytime his grip on her waist lessoned, she brought her hand down to touch his. She could have just grabbed his wrist, protected from their touch by his shirt and robe, but she wanted to feel it. She wanted to feel the spark between their bodies. Every time her skin touched his, she was rewarded with an invigorating jolt of energy from whatever was happening between them now.

Bronwyn debated mentioning what she felt to Miro, but obviously, he felt it as well; how could he not? But he failed to react. It had only grown more powerful after the crocodile, and now she even remembered feeling the inkling of this energy after Miro had lost control when fighting the Emestrian wolves. He *had* to feel this. The fact that he hadn't reacted to her sudden withdrawals when his spark shot toward her only cemented the fact that he felt it too. They only avoided talking about it because it was a shared secret.

When they made camp, Bronwyn was unable to stop watching Miro. His movements were methodical and careful. Each action of his seemed to be moderated by whoever was nearby. He helped Clara with their tent, joking with her and smiling. He helped Defurge, likewise carefree. Every time he looked toward her, she felt compelled to mirror his grin. He rarely showed genuine happiness, so she should encourage this behavior, giving him as many heartfelt glances as he gave her. And still, as much as she tried to rationalize it, even when he didn't look her direction, while she watched him, she felt her cheeks brighten and the corners of her mouth tighten.

Bronwyn was lost in thought, remembering how Miro came to her rescue with the crocodile. It was different than it was with Naani and the wolves. Her men had died during the fight with Naani, and Miro lost control with the wolves. With the crocodile, when Miro had helped her, it was pure. That must be why the memory seemed special to her now. It was a signal that she wouldn't need to be Miro's guardian any longer. He seemed to have greater confidence in his voice and actions as well. Bronwyn almost didn't register Defurge's abrupt loss of attention as he stood quickly and looked to the east.

"What is it?" Clara asked, growing quiet as well.

Defurge replied, "Fire. A big one. In a town."

"You can tell that?" Miro asked.

"Yes, it's a couple of hours ride to the east. Just one building now, but others are starting to light as well."

"We have to go," Miro said. "We might be able to help."

"Really?" Defurge asked.

Bronwyn stood, pouring her waterskin over the coals. "Yes."

Defurge groaned as Bronwyn started to resaddle her horse. She glared at him. He rolled his eyes and threw up his hands, abandoning his protest.

CHAPTER 20

As Clara approached, Bronwyn's horse began to neigh and buck, reticent to come any closer to the burning town. They hitched them to some posts outside town before dismounting and heading further. The four of them slowed, their faces illuminated by the orange haze. Multiple buildings had already burned to the ground. At least two were still engulfed in flames. People begged and screamed, their voices barely audible over the crack and pop of burning wood. A fire line had been established, but it was inadequate to deal with the multiple sources.

"Defurge, can't you put them out?" Bronwyn asked.

"I can't extinguish flames I did not create," Defurge replied calmly.

"Miro, what about water magic?"

"I don't know anything more effective than what the fire line is already doing," Miro said.

Bronwyn failed to offer any more suggestions. Clara assessed her comrades. Bronwyn's mouth was agape, and her nose crinkled as she stared at some of the villagers who huddled on the floor. The smell of burnt flesh and hair wafted from their location. Miro's eyes darted back and forth, and his hands flexed nervously. Defurge watched with passive indifference.

At sea, fires became deadly, quickly. As a sailor, you learned to react to flames and keep your wits about you. Her friends lacked that skill.

"Bronwyn, help the fire line," Clara ordered, thinking about how she could utilize their talents.

Bronwyn nodded and rushed to join the others heaving buckets.

"Miro, what ice magic do you know?" Clara asked.

"Ice Wall and Hailstorm," Miro replied.

"Cast Hailstorm on the far building Bronwyn is concentrating on. Cast it over and over, until the fire is extinguished," Clara said before turning her attention to Defurge. "Do what you do with the campfire, shape the conflagration, keep it contained in the nearby building. I'll use stone walls to isolate it until the fire line has the far building under control."

Given their marching orders, they enacted Clara's plan. Miro weaved rune after rune casting Hailstorm in succession. Sweat beaded and ran on Defurge's forehead and his hands shook as he prevented embers from breaking away to engulf other structures. Clara erected the stone wall on two sides of the building, trapping any errant cinders Defurge missed.

It took over an hour to completely douse both fires.

The village had sustained heavy damage, and four people lost their lives. Dozens more were hurt, some of those critically.

A mother and father carried their son. He had major burns along his leg, and their home had been destroyed.

"I can help," Miro said approaching them. Their eyes traveled the length of his body from head to toe with distrust.

"He knows healing magic," Clara added. Bronwyn stood at her side, her clothes rife with smoke.

The parents nodded, but the child shrank from Miro's advance. He couldn't have been older than twelve. The burns penetrated the skin and muscle. Blood and clear fluid pooled in the cracks of the blackened, hard tissue.

When Miro placed his hands above the burns, the boy flinched and buried his head in his mother's chest. "Don't worry, I'm not going to touch your burns. This will help with the pain, but I'm afraid it won't do anything for the scarring. Seraph, goddess of life and love, I entreat you, bless this boy and heal his wounds, Ligos Medus."

The runes Miro traced in the air descended to the boy's burned leg, wrapping themselves around and seeping into the cracks of the skin. When the glowing green light disappeared, Miro placed his hand on the limb. The child tensed and looked at Miro. He rubbed his hand down the leg.

The charred skin wiped away like soot from a chimney, revealing shiny pink scars.

The mother stuttered, her eyes glued to the newly healed wounds.

"Thank you," the father blurted out, stifling a tear. The parents turned to tell others of what Miro had done, and soon a small crowd gathered. A handful of villagers carried or helped victims in one way or another.

"Please come with me," a middle-aged woman said, grabbing Miro's arm. Clara and Bronwyn followed, the gathered villagers accompanying them as the woman pulled Miro into a nearby building.

On the floor of the local inn, bodies had been laid down on white bed sheets, the victims of the fire. Two groaned in agonizing pain. Without intervention, they would not live much longer.

Miro approached the first, an older woman. Instead of her badly burned clothes, a plain white nightshirt covered her body. The trauma seeped into the bones of her legs. Her upper body was spared for the most part, but the skin of her midsection and hands peeled from her muscles.

Bronwyn stood by as the old woman whimpered in pain. Clara doubted she was still conscious and wondered what they were doing here. There was little Miro could do for someone this far gone.

Miro knelt beside the old woman and placed his hands over her, reciting his invocation and tracing the runes above. Like with the child, the green light descended and wrapped her body. Then the magic seeped into the raw, exposed wounds. Bright pink flesh replaced the red blisters and the woman's labored breathing calmed.

Clara had witnessed healing magic before, but watching him do it now, to strangers, silenced her. He was reverent, like he was performing a sacred right. In addition, he healed an entire body. She didn't think Miro could cast magic that powerful. But if he could command a strong spell like this, surely he knew the spell that could treat Scarlette's condition.

The crowd gathered at the door. Some ventured inside the inn to observe him. Miro rose and went to the second living victim. A man in his late thirties. He had burns all around his chest, hands, and face. It looked like a fireball exploded as he tried to grab it.

Then, Clara noticed the blood on the ground. At first, she thought it was from the victims, but the thick liquid still beaded on the floor, not having seeped into the grain of the wood. Her eyes followed the specks of blood up to see the liquid pooling and dripping from Miro's left arm. She gasped and Bronwyn's gaze followed Clara's eyeline. Bronwyn got in front of Miro and grabbed his hand, his blood smearing her fingers. As she lifted his arm and pulled the robe back, her jaw slacked. The wounds from the swamp had returned. They had re-opened, and Miro's face was pale.

"What ....?" Bronwyn said, seemingly confused by the re-emergence of the injury. Miro shrugged at her sheepishly and apologized with a smile. Then he gently gripped her hand and took it away from his bloodied arm. He stepped around her and continued to the man with the burns on his chest and face. He knelt and began repeating the words. Clara came up to Bronwyn, tugging on her sleeve. She turned to Clara. Bronwyn's face was as white as Miro's.

Miro only used his right hand; the left hung uselessly at his side. As he finished the spell and the man's body healed, the blood didn't drip anymore. It flowed freely from his arm.

"What's going on?" Clara asked.

"I don't know," Bronwyn said, the concern in her voice evident. "Find me some bandages."

Clara nodded and went behind the counter of the inn, throwing trinkets to the ground trying to find something to bandage the wounds. Bronwyn approached Miro again. The belt whipped off Bronwyn's body as she wrapped it around Miro's arm. She pulled the belt taught right below the shoulder. Despite her best efforts at applying the tourniquet, the bleeding didn't slow.

"What's happening?" Bronwyn asked.

"Healing magic isn't like other magics; they go out into the world and come back. Healing magic takes days to come back to you. Once you start to overuse it, the body suffers a toll."

"Stop." Miro shook his head at Bronwyn's simple request. "You have to," she argued with him.

Clara turned to see the hushed villagers, inching forward to hear their quiet voices.

"I need to help them. This isn't their fault," Miro said.

Clara couldn't understand his persistence. He didn't know these people. This wasn't his fault either.

"You're going to bleed out," Bronwyn reasoned, her voice unsteady.

Lightly shaking her head, Clara waited for Miro to say something. She wanted him to nod, agree with Bronwyn, and stop. Despite his face getting whiter by the second, he stood firm and didn't budge.

"Get Defurge. Have him cauterize the wounds," Miro said.

"What?" Bronwyn asked, taking a step back. "That's absurd."

"It'll stop the blood loss and give me more time." Miro breathed a sigh of relief when Clara came from behind the counter with some thin towels that might make good bandages when ripped. She took out a knife and began to cut them lengthwise into strips. She dropped them on the floor, close enough so Bronwyn could grab them. Bronwyn wrapped the first around Miro's arm tightly. The blood stained the cloth faster than she could apply it. Bewildered, Clara looked on.

"Get Defurge," Bronwyn said turning to Clara. Clara nodded and raced out of the room. The crowd flattened themselves along the walls, allowing Clara to go in and out with ease.

Defurge was just in front of the doorway and turned to Clara as she dashed from inside. Clara blurted, "Defurge, we need you. Something's wrong."

He nodded and Clara turned back inside, coming to sit by Bronwyn as Defurge followed. He seemed to understand the urgency when blood came into view. Defurge joined Bronwyn and Clara, kneeling beside Miro.

Miro looked at him and raised his left arm meekly. "Think you can close these up for me?"

"I'll try." Defurge held a single finger up and the flame burned bright.

Bronwyn yelled at the gathered crowd, "Everyone out!"

The villagers scurried away, and she posted herself in front of the door, so no one would see the unfolding perverse scene. Clara joined her.

"He's trying to heal people's burns, and his solution is to have Defurge burn his own arm," Bronwyn said under her breath.

Miro screamed. Clara reached over and gripped Bronwyn's shaking hand. As a tear fell from Bronwyn's eye and landed on her wrist, Clara squeezed tighter.

"He's trying," Clara whispered.

Bronwyn wiped her cheek and looked down. Her face was devoid of emotion. "What if he loses control?" Bronwyn breathed heavily as Miro screamed again. It was muffled; he must have something between his teeth, but it was still horrible all the same.

A man approached them. He had burns along his forearms. They were serious, but he would live.

"He's done for the night," Bronwyn said sternly.

"Please, they're not bad. The pain is too much," the man pushed trying to enter, but Bronwyn would not budge. Others tried to complain. Some turned away.

"He's exhausted all his energy. If he does any more tonight, he will die. He may still die even if he doesn't." This caused a couple more to turn away. As Defurge exited the inn, Clara turned expectantly. It was too short; there was no way he could have done it all.

"It's not working. The wounds seal, but reopen the minute I take my finger away. If I were to engulf his whole arm in flame ... But I'd be burning away the rest of the flesh."

Clara turned around to see Miro, still kneeling. Bronwyn's grip loosened as she did the same. The bandages had soaked through, and little drops of blood formed at his fingertips once again.

"Please, it's my little girl."

Clara hadn't seen her approach. She turned to see a woman, her arm severely burnt; she cradled a small child. Burns extended over half the child's face, scalp, and down the girl's chest. The skin resembled lava with bright red rivers running around the burned black flesh. Clara's breath caught in her throat as she looked at a mother, desperate to do anything to help her child. That feeling was all too real, all too reminiscent of how she felt when she discovered Scarlette's illness. Clara instinctively dug the nails of both hands into her palms.

"I'm sorry," Bronwyn said to the woman. Two clear lines on the woman's otherwise ashy cheeks had been carved away by tears. They still fell from her eyes. Every time she blinked a couple more would cascade down. They were quiet tears with no sobs to accompany them.

Clara knew how the woman felt. She was pretty sure she felt that way as well. To be so useless in a situation. To be powerless to help someone when you feel like you should be able to. She had felt that way the first time Scarlette got sick and now felt that way all the time, unable to help her child and having to rely on others.

"She's only seven. She's my only child," the woman's lip quivered as she pleaded with Bronwyn. "Just enough so she lives."

"Let them in," Miro said with a somewhat slurred voice. As Clara looked, his head lilted to one side, lacking the strength to keep it completely upright.

Bronwyn entered, her steps quick like when she was mad at him. But when she got close to Miro, she knelt. Clara barely heard her say, "Please." Clara stepped aside as the woman entered. "You're barely holding on as it is. What happens if you have to tap into other energy to stay alive? All the healing you've been doing will be no good. This entire town will be destroyed. Is that what you want?"

Miro smiled at her. "I'm not worried. You'll stop me."

Bronwyn shook her head and lowered it.

"I know," Miro said, placing his good hand on her shoulder. "It's not fair. It's not going to happen. I've got enough strength in me to help her. I'll be all right." Miro sounded confident, despite his inability to maintain proper eye contact. Clara wanted to believe him, but part of her was afraid.

The mother knelt, laying her child on the ground, close to Miro. "Please, you don't have to heal her completely. Just don't let her die."

The mother's eyes pleaded with Bronwyn again. Bronwyn averted her gaze. The woman turned to Miro as he slowly shifted his body toward the young girl.

At the doorway of the inn, Clara watched. Tears flowed from her eyes, and she wiped them away every couple of seconds, but Clara didn't look at Miro. She stared at the small girl. Her eyes were transfixed on the child, and she couldn't take them away. Miro began the healing ritual.

The mother only asked him to do enough to let her live, but that's not what Miro did. It was all or nothing with him. His eyes blinked slowly, and his hands shook as he formed the runes. He didn't even speak the words as the spell materialized and was absorbed into the girl's body. When the girl's eyes fluttered and opened, Miro turned to Clara, who smiled and cried. Miro nodded to her before he collapsed, Bronwyn cradling his body as he fell.

Clara found herself unable to take her eyes off the healed child. Miro healed a child, a stranger's daughter, possibly sacrificing his health in doing so. But what about his plan to save the world from war by obtaining artifacts? Did he care for a stranger more than that goal? Scarlette wasn't dying, her father was providing care, but would Miro treat Scarlette as a favor to Clara?

Guilt nagged Clara's thoughts. She had concluded that she would need to steal an artifact from Miro to get what she wanted. Why was it so hard for her to confide in him, to ask him what she needed? She'd probably have to admit she gave her child up to her father. Who really cared? Would she allow that desire—to not have anyone know what she had to do—to prevent her from asking Miro to treat Scarlette, and maybe even heal her?

Still, Clara's heart sank because she already knew the decision she would make. Any kingdom would pay an ungodly amount of money to create food from an artifact. Rouke, Emestria's current enemy, would pay a king's ransom to have such an artifact, so their armies would not need to maintain supply lines. She looked at Bronwyn and knew the hate that would fester in her from the betrayal.

But Emestria was the reason her hometown of Lynnfield was destroyed. It was the reason so many of her people were scattered across the world. So what if Rouke conquered Emestria? Other cities Rouke's army had conquered were allowed a semblance of autonomy. Those who enlisted in Rouke's army were even given citizenship and the right to choose their city's representative. Those who didn't lived as indentured servants, able to buy their freedom after years of work.

CHAPTER 21

BRONWYN MOBILIZED HER small army of villagers. First, she began the process of wrapping and unwrapping the wounds until the bleeding stopped. Around midnight, the blood clotted, or Miro had no more to lose. She checked his pulse, making sure he still lived. Once stable, they moved him to a room in the inn, one with a fireplace.

She gathered water and juice for when he woke. He would need the liquids and sugars to replenish his fluids as soon as possible. Meanwhile, she had a volunteer force of townsfolk supplying her with hot towels. She would try and keep his body temperature up.

Clara came to relieve her, but Bronwyn didn't want to leave him. But she was also tired, and her thoughts were fuzzy.

"He's not getting better," Bronwyn told Clara as she entered.

"He will. He needs time," Clara reassured her.

Bronwyn became hopeful when the bleeding stopped, but their luck started to wear thin. Despite her round-the-clock care, his pulse weakened.

"Why don't you go and get some rest?" Clara asked. "I can watch him for a bit."

"Okay. Couple of hours of sleep." Bronwyn slipped her boots off and lifted the sheets, climbing in next to Miro.

"They've offered us rooms; you can go get your own bed," Clara said.

"I need to make sure he stays warm, then he'll be all right. I just have to check his pulse," Bronwyn explained. She reached her fingers up to his neck and held them there for a bit. "Still there, slower and weaker, getting slower and weaker," Bronwyn repeated before laying her head against a pillow.

It was still night when the blanket on top of Miro and her was replaced with another hot one. Despite not stirring, Bronwyn heard the voices.

"Have you slept?" Defurge asked.

"Only a couple hours. How about you?" Clara replied.

"I laid down when the bleeding stopped," Defurge said. "Why don't you go get some more sleep? I'll stay with him until either you or Bronwyn wakes. What's that about?"

"I don't know. She was overly tired when I came in. Said she wanted to check his pulse and needed to keep him warm. She's worried about him." A book was closed and the chair's legs ground against the floor. "Make sure and change the blanket on top for the one by the fireplace every half hour or so."

"If she was concerned about him getting cold, she could have asked the god of fire to keep him warm."

"Former incarnation of the god of fire. She doesn't think he's going to make it. She wants to be there when it happens."

When Bronwyn woke again, light shone directly beneath the west-facing window. It was noon, or a little past it.

She didn't remember getting into bed with Miro. She inhaled deeply. His body didn't smell of sickness, but it didn't smell like him either. She brought her fingers back up to his cold neck. His pulse was still weak. She didn't want to tell the others, but she didn't feel the tingle when she touched Miro anymore. His spark was dying.

Movement betrayed another's presence in the room. Bronwyn hadn't moved much, and they likely didn't know she was awake. She closed her eyes and went back to sleep. She wanted to stay here a little longer. *Please, Miro, let me help you.*

Bronwyn startled when she woke the third time. She had expected to enter Miro's dreams again, to find Fria and make the goddess tell her why they made a man who seemed desperate to sacrifice himself. Someone who felt so horrible about themselves, they were eager for a chance to barter their life away for another's. But perhaps Miro didn't have the strength to dream tonight, or she hadn't come to understand and control this strange new power.

But it wasn't dreams, or the lack thereof, that startled her; it was the strange sensation at her fingertips. When she fell asleep, her hand remained close to Miro's neck after checking his pulse. Her fingers had lightly brushed his skin in slumber. She had to make sure. She brought them to his neck again. When she took her fingers away or put them back, she felt it. A slight twinge, an almost imperceptible change.

The spark was gone earlier. She put her fingers back up to his neck, this time to check his pulse. It didn't seem stronger, but it wasn't weaker. Bronwyn sat up, the blankets bunching at her waist. She turned to see Clara.

Clara smiled at her. "Feeling better?"

Bronwyn nodded and added, "I think he's starting to turn the corner. His pulse isn't weakening anymore."

"Good. Perhaps he needed you to sleep in the same bed with him all along." Clara beamed. Bronwyn could tell she put on a brave face, for her sake.

"I was really out of it this morning. I don't think I knew what I was doing." Bronwyn blushed.

"Even if you did, so what?"

Bronwyn raised an eyebrow.

"You were worried about him. You didn't want to leave his side. There's nothing to be embarrassed about."

Clara went back to reading her book, leaving Bronwyn to consider her words, re-don her boots, and head downstairs to find something to eat.

The owner of the inn knelt, using a brush and bucket of water to wash away the blood Miro left the night before. Some of the clothes used to cover bodies were heaped in the corners. The innkeeper didn't complain and smiled when she saw Bronwyn.

"Any better?" The innkeeper asked.

"I don't know. He's still not conscious, but I don't think he's worse. Thank you for letting us stay."

"Think nothing of it. Rooms, stables, and meals are on the house till he's up and about. He did a good thing for our town. And for my friend, the old woman he helped first."

Bronwyn nodded, wanting to be happy about the news. But she resented the people he saved. She hated herself for it, but she resented them. *This wasn't the worst-case scenario. If he had lost control ....* Bronwyn shuddered and tried to put the thought from her mind. "Where are we? We weren't headed in this direction, and only came when we smelled the fire."

"Bless the gods you did. Last time we had a fire that bad, it burned down half the town. This is Loughlin. Some of the villagers are holding services for those who were lost. If you want, I'm sure they'd appreciate you showing up."

"I don't know if I have the energy. Does anyone know what happened?"

"People say there was a sound in the main hall." Bronwyn sat at a table and the woman brought a plate with some eggs and sausage on it. "We had some decorations set up there for the festival in a couple days—canceled now, given the circumstances. Been having trouble with petty thievery lately, so a couple of men went to make sure everything was in order. I guess someone fell and his lamp broke. He didn't survive. The two others that were in there, they were burned. Your friend helped one of them; he got it the worst."

Bronwyn took a bite as the woman brought a cup of water and sat across from her. "The fire burned quick; we had our winter hay stored there. Most people were able to get out of their houses when the fire spread, but some were too young or old to move quickly. My friend and the young girl probably had it the worst—of those that survived."

Bronwyn continued eating, not offering much of a conversation. She was too tired to think of anything to say. The innkeeper stayed with her for another five minutes before returning to scrubbing Miro's blood from the wood's grain. Bronwyn finished her meal and left the plate on the table. She returned upstairs to sit with Clara.

"I visited the girl," Clara said as Bronwyn sat down.

"And?" Bronwyn asked.

"She's fine. Her mother's arms are still burned, but she'll survive. Just has to keep them bandaged and wrapped. The girl lost an eyebrow and the left side of her hair, but they're both lucky to be alive. A lot of the children in this town are going to have scars, so she probably won't have to deal with too much teasing."

"Bronwyn?" Miro's raspy and cracking voice asked. He held his hand in front of his face, shielding his eyes from the afternoon light.

"It's me," Bronwyn replied. "How are you feeling?"

Clara shut her book and turned to watch them.

"Did I do it?" Miro turned towards the ceiling. Bronwyn didn't need any medical training to tell he wouldn't be conscious for long.

"You did," Bronwyn said, keeping her answers short.

"Good." Miro closed his eyes. Clara and Bronwyn exchanged glances, sure he passed back out. Miro opened his eyes, forcing himself from slumber. "You know how I feel, right?"

"No, I don't," Bronwyn said. Miro didn't answer and his head lulled to the side. Bronwyn stood and placed her fingers next to his neck. To Clara, it probably looked like she was checking his pulse, which she was, but the strength of his spark would yield more information than that.

CHAPTER 22

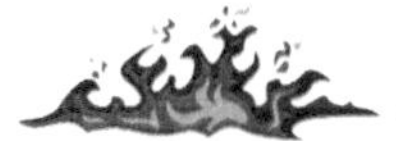

BRONWYN KNOCKED QUIETLY on the door before entering the inn room. As the door creaked open, she saw Miro still splayed in bed. A single candle on a nearby table illuminated Clara reading through some of Issaroh's notebooks. Clara peaked up over her book and nodded to Bronwyn. Pulling out a chair, Bronwyn took a seat next to her.

"Has he woken up yet?" Bronwyn asked.

"No, not since yesterday. I think he'll be fine," Clara said.

"Hopefully."

Clara closed her book, setting it on the table. "How are you doing?"

Bronwyn sighed. "Fine, I guess." Clara raised an eyebrow, prompting Bronwyn to continue. "I'm worried about him, but I don't know …. When I asked him to stop and told him I worried about him losing control, he replied that I would stop him." Bronwyn closed her eyes and shook her head before continuing. "Did he want me to? Does he really think it would be that easy for me?"

Clara half smiled. "I don't know. Why don't you try asking him for once?"

"Sure, if he wakes up."

Clearing her throat, Clara stood from the table. "Have you seen Defurge? I wanted to do something tonight."

"I think he's in his room. I guess it's my turn for watch anyway." Bronwyn picked up one of the books and started to thumb through it as Clara left. Bronwyn wasn't interested in Issaroh's writings but in the illustrations of the runes. They were the most used to her. It had been a while since she had studied runes. Even though she couldn't cast, knowing which spells her opponent was casting before the spell was finished greatly increased her combat prowess. After flipping through the first notebook, she set it down. She went to grab the next notebook, but underneath it was Miro's research on the Legendary Artifacts.

Bronwyn had reviewed his book while traveling in Emestria, but she turned to the page about the Horn of Garanhir. Few of the artifacts in Miro's book included any indication of where they might be located. The Horn of Garanhir was the same. In fact, outside of the description, there was extremely little information about it. Nothing about how to use it; the only thing it said was it increased the harvest tenfold. *But how?* Bronwyn thought. *Does it have to be in the field to do that? Or do the seeds need to be placed inside it before planting?*

Bronwyn dropped the book as Miro sat up suddenly in bed. He frantically grabbed his shoulders and then looked at Bronwyn with wide eyes. "Did you take my shirt off?"

"Um, no. Defurge put you in some less bloody clothes while we were heating blankets," Bronwyn said with her brows furrowed.

Miro sighed in relief before lying back down without an explanation. Bronwyn waited for him to say something else. "Why would you care if I changed your shirt?"

Miro turned over in the bed, eliciting a shrug and slight headshake from Bronwyn. She was about to ask again, a little more forcefully. Miro answered before she could, "I have scars from the war. I was worried you had seen them."

Bronwyn remembered that while he was in the tent after the library, she had noticed a scar below his shirt collar. "I'm sorry. Your scars don't bother me." *Physical and emotional scars,* Bronwyn thought.

Miro nodded and grunted, still turned away from her. "That's why I stiffen when you embrace me. I don't want you to feel them."

"Oh ... but we've embraced on some occasions."

"Only when I'm wearing my robe." Bronwyn always thought it odd that he kept his robe on most of the time—even while sleeping. She thought he just got extremely cold at night.

"What happened with the little girl?" Miro asked.

Bronwyn smiled, happy that she could tell him. "She survived."

"How many died?"

"Four died before we got here when the fires broke out. Thanks to you, nobody else did. You saved three people with your healing, and saved many more the heartache of losing the ones they love."

Bronwyn neglected to tell him about the other people she turned away. She didn't want him to overexert himself trying to heal them. Judging by his explanation of healing magic, for a while, any use would be too taxing.

Miro smiled and nodded.

"Are you cold?" Bronwyn asked. "I think it's time we put another warm blanket on."

Without waiting for an answer, Bronwyn left, going downstairs to remove one of the blankets they had stacked next to the hearthstone on the bottom floor of the inn. When she returned, he was lying on his back again. Bronwyn removed the blanket currently over him and replaced it with a warm one. She lightly touched his cheek—still cold.

Bronwyn sat back down at the table, intending to get back to reading the books, but then stopped and asked, "Miro, why did you do it? Why do this to yourself to help those people?"

"I needed to help them. I needed to save people for once."

Bronwyn wrung her hands. "You've helped Clara and I plenty of times."

"Yes, but we agreed to this. We knew it was going to be dangerous from the very beginning. These people didn't ask for this. They just wanted to live a peaceful life." Miro breathed heavily and closed his eyes.

"I hate them," Bronwyn admitted. Miro's eyes shot open. "I feel horrible saying it, but if you lost control, I would have been the one to stop you." Bronwyn sighed, giving herself some time to digest what she just said. "You said you wouldn't have been able to forgive yourself if you hadn't intervened with the crocodile. I won't be able to forgive myself if I have to kill you. I hope you understand that."

Miro waited an agonizingly long time before saying, "I do. It isn't fair."

Bronwyn stared at him intently. "Don't do that to me again."

Miro nodded slowly. Bronwyn stood, pushing in the chair at the table.

Miro said, "Bronwyn, wait. I hate to ask, but would you mind staying? I can't shake this feeling that this is just another vision from the Eye, and something bad is going to happen."

Bronwyn smiled and nodded, slipping off her boots before joining him underneath the blankets. Miro leaned back, a look of surprise on his face. A tear pooled at the corner of his eye and as Bronwyn reached up to wipe it away, Miro grabbed her hand, preventing her. Miro shook his head before releasing her hand. His voice wavered as he said, "This can't happen. You know I care for you, but … we're partners. That's all we can be."

Bronwyn gritted her teeth. "I … I …. You asked me to keep you company. I didn't want to, but I thought I would because you've gone through so much. I just … I can't." Bronwyn swiveled out of the bed, turning her back to Miro before getting her boots back on.

"I'm sorry," Miro said, his voice meek and soft. "I'll be fine."

"I'll go find Defurge; he can watch over you." Bronwyn left, but as soon as she got into the hallway she slumped against the wall, letting her body sink to the floor. She planned to wait there until Clara or Defurge came back.

Why am I acting like this? I'm a guardswoman. I'm here to save Emestria, not have some childhood dalliance. He's right; we can only be partners, and together we can accomplish saving Emestria. Why am I so mad when he rebuffs me?

Chapter 23

"*The phoenix requests your presence,*" one of the monks said to Defurge in his mind. He could never keep them straight. "*You said you would not push Bronwyn; she wishes to—*"

"I'm done talking to you three," Defurge said, standing. He lit his right hand, making sure his refusal would not result in the phoenix rescinding her powers. Just as he thought, he could still control the flame. The monks, however, seemed to be limiting his influence. He had been trying to push Bronwyn to Miro since Clara mentioned their tendency to grow further apart right after they grew closer. He had only been able to compel her to join him in the bed that night because of her exhaustion. The phoenix was behind it. His powers were only weakened when trying to probe or push Bronwyn, not with Miro or Clara.

A slight rapping on the door drew Defurge's attention. Clara was standing there, a smirk on her face. She said, "Come with me. I'm going to need those semi-godly muscles of yours."

Defurge cocked his head but returned the smirk.

Clara led Defurge outside the inn. The streets were quiet. Many of the villagers were probably still nursing burns and staying inside to aid in healing. He could feel the lingering heat of fire on many of the mortals here, some more than others. The mark of fire was still palpable on those that Miro had healed. Much like Miro's own back, even the remnants of fire still cried out to him.

As they walked among the burned-out hovels, Defurge picked up a stick and lit it. He had been cautioned about showing his powers in public here.

This part of town smelled glorious. The thick smell of burnt wood and flesh had yet to dissipate. Wordlessly, Clara walked on ahead, toward the source of the fire, the town hall that had stored the winter hay. The wooden floorboards cracked and crumbled under their feet.

"Miro said the horn was in the basement of a burned-out building," Clara said. "Once the fires died down and cooled, I started to investigate. None of the smaller buildings had basements, and I didn't think this one did either until I saw this." Clara used her foot to push a piece of wood up. Underneath, the foundation of the building was metal. "I probably wouldn't have noticed it, but it seems to have warped a little bit with the heat. It looks like there were several inches of dirt over the metal, then wood on top of it."

"And this is the only building with this type of foundation?" Defurge asked.

"Out of the ones that burned, yes. Seems like a good place to hide something valuable. Help me look for some break in the steel plates, or something similar."

"Should we ask some of the villagers first?"

"No. If it is here, they might not even know it exists. If they do know, they'll probably blame whoever they thought was rummaging around the night the fire started. They might think it was us if we let them know we are looking for this artifact."

"What will Bronwyn and Miro think of you absconding with a Legendary Artifact?"

"You mean the artifact I mentioned to the village leader, who then gave me permission to search for it?" Clara suggestively raised her eyebrows. Even without the ability to read Clara's mind, Defurge knew the implication. Clara would not even think about asking for permission. An admirable trait.

They worked quietly, pushing around pieces of wood, looking for places where the metal did not reflect the light completely, where dirt had settled in between the seams that separated plates. In the northwest corner, they found a plate that was significantly smaller than the others.

They removed the charred wood, then dirt, until they found an iron ring. Defurge lifted, and the wood on top cracked. It didn't seem to be attached to anything, and Defurge slid it over the rest of the foundation, the scraping making a considerable noise. They looked around to see if any lamps were lit in the nearby houses. Satisfied they were still working alone, Defurge went to peer into the hole he just uncovered. Hot air rose from the dark interior. Earthen steps led down. Clara nodded to Defurge, and he descended.

The things in this room seemed to have been spared the destruction of the fire but still had succumbed to the ravages of time. Except for where they had removed the panel, the ceiling was made of wood planks, and the metal must have been laid on top of it. What used to be a wooden bookcase at one point in time was slanted over, with the shelves laying at angles or on the floor in front of it. The stone that lined the cellar had crumbled in several places, allowing a buildup of dirt. A dozen large ceramic pots were cracked and whatever they used to hold was now so badly decomposed it resembled soil. But, in the middle of the north wall, there was a stone pedestal. Atop it, was a shiny, curved, metal horn. Defurge looked back to Clara, who had yet to descend and motioned her forward.

"It's like a kiln in there," Clara said.

Defurge shrugged and went toward the artifact. Picking it up with two hands, he admired the handiwork. It was solid brass, with small convex divots over its surface. A thin leather strap was tied to two loops of metal. Even though the room still harbored the heat of the fire, this thing was cool in his hands. Defurge turned, heading back toward the stairs. Once back atop, Clara took the horn from him and put it into a sack.

"Put the metal plate back and help me cover it back up," Clara said.

"It looks like no one has been down there in a long time." Defurge did as asked, pushing the metal plate back into place. Then they heaped the dirt back over it, pressing it down and compacting it to the best of their ability. Clara used a length of wood to smooth out their bootprints. Then they laid the broken wood back atop the dirt as naturally as they could.

"We'll wait to let Bronwyn and Miro know," Clara said. They walked back to the inn, checking to make sure no one was watching them.

As they crested the stairs of the inn, Defurge saw Bronwyn sitting outside Miro's room. Defurge tried to read her mind, to see what she was thinking, but again he couldn't—damnable phoenix and monks. Miro's mind was still open, and he quickly took a peek at whatever caused Bronwyn's absence from the room. Just as Defurge planned, Miro's rejection had driven another wedge between them.

"Clara, can we talk?" Bronwyn asked, standing up.

"Yes," Clara replied.

"Defurge, please watch over Miro for a bit," Bronwyn said, turning down the hallway with Clara. Defurge grinned, cresting the corner and entering Miro's room. He wanted to say something witty—offer to keep Miro warm underneath the blankets—but it would lead Miro to question Bronwyn's behavior more than he already was. Instead, Defurge sat at the table. Miro merely turned over in the bed and went back to sleep. Defurge used the opportunity to probe his mind without him being aware.

Surprisingly, Miro turned back over a half hour later and asked, "Defurge, are you doing this?"

"Doing what?"

"Bronwyn, are you influencing her in some way?" Miro stared intently, clenching his jaw in between sentences. "Her behavior and sudden desire to be close to me. Is this something you're doing?"

"I don't know what you mean. I stopped influencing Clara and Bronwyn long ago. Now that they trust me, there is little reason to do it anymore. It was just out of a desire to make sure they weren't tempted by the gem, but that seems to have been an unnecessary precaution."

Miro eyed Defurge suspiciously, to which Defurge just grinned in response. Miro said, "Please, don't do this. I just can't take it. This will destroy me."

"I've told you, Miro. I have nothing to do with anyone's actions."

CHAPTER 24

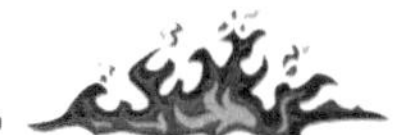

CLARA READ THROUGH Issaroh's book on healing arcana for probably the twentieth time. The spell to purify blood was complicated, but not the most advanced in the discipline. She hadn't seen Miro cast anything that complicated yet, but Issaroh had said Miro was magically gifted. If he were properly motivated, that might be enough for him to learn it. Then they could go to Corinthe and find one of those ley lines. Miro could just teleport in every week and treat Scarlette. He owed Clara that much, at least at this point.

The other option was to just leave. It may sour her plans, having to rely on Defurge's strength. Would he help Bronwyn and Miro hunt her down to retrieve the artifact? Clara would have one horse, with a light passenger. Miro and Bronwyn would have to share a horse. Clara had all the coin in this venture. She could make it to a nearby port town and find a ship to Newtonne. She doubted the three of them would be able to track her on the sea.

Clara waited until Miro turned over in the bed, signaling another bout of consciousness. After opening his eyes, Miro gave her a cordial smile. Clara said, "Miro, when does this quest end for you?"

Miro blinked and rubbed sleep from his eyes before replying, "That's a tough question. The longer we travel, the more complicated things become."

"What's the bare minimum? Save Emestria and destroy Defurge's Soul Gem?"

"And trap the thing that destroyed Lynnfield, but it's more than that, Clara. I want to stop war. I want to usher in an era of peace."

"War is not something you can stop. It's the nature of humankind."

"I think I *can* stop it. If we recover enough of the artifacts and deliver them to Emestria, then Emestria will be powerful enough to dissuade any nation from declaring war on it. From there, Emestria could make treaties with the other nations and become the middleman in any of their disputes."

Clara sighed, readjusting her chair so she could lean forward as she talked to Miro. "And what if I asked you to put off that goal?"

Miro cocked his head and raised an eyebrow.

Clara reflexively squeezed her left hand shut and concentrated on the sensation of her nails biting into her flesh. "You're going to live a long time. Longer than Bronwyn or myself. Your goal may take hundreds of years to complete, and I'm willing to help you find enough of the artifacts to save Emestria, destroy the monster you're hunting, and break the Soul Gem. But after that, I want you to do something for me."

"And that is?" Miro sat up in the bed, swinging his feet off it.

Clara relaxed her hand, took the healing arcana notebook, opened it to the page about purifying blood, and handed it to Miro. "Do you know this spell?"

Miro shook his head.

"Can you learn it, for me? And the ability to teleport like Issaroh?"

"This is a pretty complicated spell, but it's similar to the one to neutralize poisons. It might take me a while, but I could learn it. What's this about, Clara?"

Clara breathed in heavily and sighed. There would be no way to ask him for this favor without telling him just a little bit. Miro stared as Clara opened and closed her hand, pressing deeper with her nails each time. "There is someone in Corinthe that is important to me. She has blood poisoning. For my continued help, I want you to treat her."

"Clara, to treat the blood poisoning with this spell would require me to constantly have a large portion of my magic devoted to this person at all times. I don't even know if I'll be able to teleport while maintaining it without putting myself and this person in danger."

"Oh …." Clara put her head down to hide her frown. It was a good thing she hadn't told Bronwyn and Miro about the artifact yet. "I worried as much."

"I didn't say I wouldn't. Who is this person, Clara?" Miro stood, putting the book on the table before sitting back down.

Clara wanted to tell him, so someone else could help her carry the shame she felt. She tried to do best by Scarlette, and surrendering her parental rights was a horrible choice, but it was the only one Clara had that would save Scarlette. But the guilt of her child never knowing her real mother was a constant stone around her neck.

Everything she had done since then was to undo that travesty. But she couldn't tell Miro. She couldn't tell anyone, because they would all look at her differently. She would no longer be the person that they trusted and confided in, but just an opportunistic smuggler and pirate. But maybe there was another way. Maybe stealing the horn wasn't the best option. She could take the Eye instead, but this wasn't the time. She wasn't staying because it was fun to play the hero for once. Right—it was just because the right opportunity hadn't presented itself.

"I've never asked you about your past," Clara said. "Please extend me the same courtesy."

"Okay. I owe you that. If I manage to survive long enough to do the things we have planned, I'll put off my quest to obtain enough artifacts to end war and I'll return with you to Corinthe."

Clara's head jerked up and she smiled brightly, swallowing frequently to try and not cry. She couldn't believe what she had just heard. Clara whispered, "Thank you."

Miro walked over to the table and picked up his research book about the artifacts. "I'm feeling better, and I'd like to talk to some of the people about town. That mountain to the north has a unique shape and I have some similar notes about it. Who knows, we might even find this building the Eye showed me on our way. Two artifacts in as many days hopefully."

Clara nodded as she rose to leave the room and gave him privacy to change. She debated telling him about retrieving the horn, but didn't want him to mention it to the villagers in case they did know about it. Miro was too honest, too concerned about not hurting others. If anything, his asking questions could confirm whether the villagers were aware of its location.

CHAPTER 25

Bronwyn RETURNED TO Miro's room to see if he was up and about and found it empty. Clara was supposed to be watching him, so Bronwyn headed to her room next. As she approached, she heard familiar complaints from Ferdinand. He had returned early that morning. Clara's door was closed, probably as a courtesy to the rest of the inn. She knocked firmly and Clara answered.

"Quiet," Clara called back to Ferdinand as she opened the door for Bronwyn.

"What has his feathers ruffled this time?" Bronwyn asked.

Clara said, "I think it's the fire. Animals generally dislike the smell of smoke, and he keeps saying 'danger' repeatedly. I've tried to calm him, but he seems overly upset."

"Do you know where Miro is?"

"He said he was feeling better and wanted to talk to some of the villagers."

"I wish he would have said something to me before leaving. Not everyone is happy with my decisions on who to help that night."

"I'm sure he'll be fine."

"I'm going to head downstairs and get some breakfast. Once Miro returns, I think we should all get together and decide what to do next." Clara nodded in agreement. "Do you want to join me?"

"Definitely. I could use a break from Ferdinand." Clara stepped outside, closing the door behind herself, and they both headed downstairs.

As Bronwyn descended the stairs, she saw an unknown man talking to the innkeeper. His vest was clean and smart and had buttons that were a little nicer than the clothes she had seen on the other villagers. He seemed to be someone of import, and his conversation with the innkeeper was less than cordial. *A man used to getting his way,* Bronwyn thought.

Upon seeing Bronwyn and Clara, he turned his attention to Bronwyn. "Excuse me—I was hoping to have some words with you and your friends."

"I'm afraid not everyone is here at the moment," Clara replied. "Is there anything I can help you with?"

He redirected his conversation in Clara's direction. "Look, we're thankful for your assistance the other night. I was told that the man who was injured has been up and about this morning. I hate to ask this, but we think it would be best if you and your friends were on your way, if you're fit to travel."

Clara took a step forward. Despite her stature, she was never intimidated by men. A quality Bronwyn enjoyed in her. "That doesn't seem very thankful. Is there a reason you're asking us to leave?"

The man took a step back before stammering, "B-believe me, I am appreciative of your help. It's just ... not everyone, at the moment, is happy with the way things happened that night. You must understand that a lot of people aren't aware of exactly how magic works; we don't have anyone in the village who practices. I realize the danger your friend put himself in the other night. But tempers are just a little high right now, and I'm being put in a difficult position."

The man fidgeted as he spoke to Clara and his eyes darted between the two women. "A lot of people lost their homes and some sustained injuries that are going to prevent them from working for some time. The blacksmith and owner of the general store have offered to provide some of their services free of charge, as a thank you."

"We'll be taking our leave as soon as we are able," Bronwyn said. The man nodded in appreciation. Before he could leave, Bronwyn asked, "Are there any nearby settlements, or buildings outside of town? Other places that were possibly damaged in fire?"

The man, who Bronwyn had assumed at this point was probably the mayor, replied, "I can't say for sure. There was an old mill to the northeast that burned down a decade or two ago, and there is Shale Rock to the north, about a day's ride. They, like many of the towns in this area, have had their issues with fire. The weather is dry here, and lightning storms frequent the area."

Clara interjected, "Thank you. I think that's enough information to go off."

Bronwyn stared down at her. She wanted to ask a couple more questions, but the man took Clara's words as an agreement between the two of them and left quickly.

"I had more questions for him."

"Look, we should talk to Miro first. That might be enough information. Maybe he can tell us more about the place he saw the Horn."

"I guess." Bronwyn sat down in the dining area with Clara and the innkeeper brought some food by shortly after. It wasn't as extravagant as previous meals were—only some boiled grains as opposed to eggs and meat—and Bronwyn wondered if the innkeeper was starting to share in the others' feeling that they had overstayed their welcome. Did people worry that the four strangers planned to take up permanent residence in the village? What other paranoid thoughts might spring from that fear? If tempers were high, how long would it be until people started to suggest Defurge or Miro had set the fire, and the assistance provided was part of a confidence scam?

Bronwyn pushed her half-finished meal to the side. "We should go find Miro. There's no telling what kind of shenanigans he'll get himself up to unsupervised."

"Let him. He could be wandering around the village as far as we know. He'll be back here sooner or later. We should hit up the general store and Smithy and just wait for him."

Bronwyn cracked a grin. "So eager to be out of this town? What's wrong, too many good folks for your pirate heart?"

"Bah, I'm just anxious to be free of people like old stuffy pants back there. 'Sides, aren't you working on some timeline to find that artifact of yours? Or perhaps you're just hoping for one more night at the inn, eager to share a bed with him again?"

"Clara! It's not like that."

"Oh, sure it isn't. You can lie to Miro, Defurge, and yourself, but you all are an open book to me."

Bronwyn's cheeks heated in what she hoped was anger. She was the leader of this expedition and Clara was talking to her like a child. Then again, Clara was only a few years younger than Bronwyn's mother.

Clara seemed to take Bronwyn's silence as an invitation to continue, "Defurge likes to play games with you and with Miro. Miro looks to you like a little puppy dog. And you like to play soldier, forcefully ignoring the relationships around yourself."

Bronwyn responded in a louder voice than she meant to. "That's not Miro. If anything, he is hellbent on punishing himself. The other night is more proof of that than anything."

"So, punish him. Take him to bed, order him around, maybe give him a couple love taps on the rear, bugger him if he's into it. He might be into it, and maybe you'll satisfy that self-esteem complex of his. But for the gods' and goddesses' sake, just figure this shit out because I'm tired of it."

"I am not jeopardizing this mission for a roll in the hay and starting some ill-fated relationship. What if things don't work out?"

"Who said anything about a relationship? Do you think the first time I shared a bunk with Atien I was thinking of anything else than scratching an itch? No, but the sex was good, so I kept coming back. Bang it out with Miro, then if the sex is bad, no more need for longing looks."

"I'm not some wilting lily. I've been with men and women, and most of the time just to have some fun. Miro is not the 'bang it out' type."

"I've slept my way across half of Primerra. I've never met a man who wasn't up for a night with no expectations of breakfast in the morning." Clara took a bit of her porridge and pushed it to the side. "Eh, it's cold now. Shall we go find this smith, or do you want to traipse around the village after Miro?"

Rolling her eyes, Bronwyn rose from the table to ask the innkeeper for directions to the smith. She'd keep an eye out for Miro as they traveled around town.

The blacksmith's shop was relatively close to the town square. A burly man with thick muscles, he wore leather sleeves and an apron, but underneath he had no shirt on. Sweat glistened off his dark skin and shaved head. They were fairly close before he noticed them.

"Good morning," he said, putting down his hammer and the blade he seemed to be pounding out.

"Morning," Bronwyn returned the greeting and was about to ask what services he had promised to provide, but he launched into the conversation himself.

"I took the liberty of re-shodding your horses. Their shoes were in good condition, but I figured it was the least I could do. I wanted to offer if you'd like, for me to sharpen any weapons you're carrying before you leave."

How fortuitous. "Actually, my sword could do with a once-over, but we might be leaving soon."

"Look, you bring what you need sharpened by, and I'll get them done as quick as I can. Maybe a couple of hours at most. It's the least I can do."

"Thank you, I have a couple of knives I can leave with you now, but I'll return shortly with our weapons," Bronwyn said.

Clara said, "I've got an axe that's lopsided; the pry bar took some damage. I wouldn't mind you looking at it and seeing if you can do anything."

"Bring them by as soon as you can, and I'll get started."

Bronwyn and Clara returned to the inn and gathered their weapons, camp hatchet, and Bronwyn's remaining hunting knives. Bronwyn was a little dismayed that Miro still hadn't returned, but didn't want to start another conversation with Clara about his whereabouts. Upon their return, Bronwyn was surprised to find out that her weapon's steel alloy was something very rarely seen outside Emestria. Most smiths had difficulty using it for forging due to the heat needed in the fire. He could still sharpen it. Perhaps that was part of the reason Rouke was advancing on Emestria.

Clara's axe had a less-than-ideal prognosis. The smith couldn't do much for the haft besides removing the melted iron. He offered to supply Clara with another axe, but she insisted it was a gift and would prefer to just use it, even if it were a little off-balance. From there, they headed to the general store.

As Bronwyn browsed the supplies, securing rations, salted fish, and other meats, she was overjoyed to find they had soap. She had neglected to take any from the library and would appreciate the superior cleaning it provided. Bronwyn took three bars, a fourth of their stock, along with a variety of vegetables and a local tea blend. As she set the items on the counter, she thanked the keep.

"No, thank you. Last time we had a fire, it destroyed half the town. I don't care what the village head says, anytime you or your friends are in the area, feel free to stop by. I'll give you a hefty discount, just a little above cost."

"We really do appreciate all that everyone has done for us, but we were informed not everyone has a favorable opinion of our group," Bronwyn explained, starting to put the procured items into her pack.

"Eh, a small, vocal minority. They're good people, just a little upset and expecting miracles. After they've rebuilt and let their wounds heal, they'll have no problem if you and yours return. You're always welcome in Loughlin as far as me and most everyone here is concerned."

"Thank you, again," Bronwyn said, slinging her pack over her shoulder and leaving.

They had yet to see Miro around town, but upon returning to the inn, found him pouring over one of Issaroh's notebooks. He claimed he was fit to travel, and after collecting Defurge and waiting for the smith to complete sharpening their weapons, they decided to head to the northeast. Miro wanted to take a closer look at a mountain, and the man in the inn had said there was a burned-down mill in that direction.

Bronwyn dismounted her horse and said, "There's supposed to be an abandoned mill around here. We'll spread out and search; everyone pick a direction, head two hours that way, then come back." She extended a hand to help Clara and took the reins to tie to a nearby tree. "If you find the mill, report back here, then we'll all regroup and explore it together. I don't want someone falling down broken steps and getting stuck. If we don't find the artifact there—"

"It's not at the mill," Clara said, taking a pack from the horse's back.

"How do you know?" Bronwyn asked, cocking an eyebrow.

"It was in Loughlin," Clara said, pulling a curved bronze horn from one of the packs.

"But how? Where?" Miro asked.

"While you were getting your beauty sleep, Defurge and I explored the remains of the burnt buildings. I thought that the vision showed you a building destroyed in a fire, so I figured the building didn't have to be already destroyed, just destroyed when we found it."

Clara slung the artifact over one shoulder, using a leather strap to hold it. She then started to grab several apples from her bag. She tossed two to Bronwyn in quick succession, then she repeated the process with Defurge and Miro. Only Miro fumbled one of the apples, dropping it to the ground.

"Are you sure that's the artifact?" Bronwyn asked.

"Take a look at those apples. Notice anything about them?" Clara asked.

Bronwyn held the fruit up, twisting it, looking and trying to discern anything special about them. She then said, "No, just regular apples."

Clara said, "Look closer. Don't they look very similar?"

Bronwyn put the apples side by side. They were red, with some lighter yellow portions. The stems were both the same size, and the discolorations were in the same place.

"I must have had an apple in the same bag where I placed the artifact," Clara explained. "Bronwyn, toss me one of the vegetables you bought."

Bronwyn reached into one of the saddlebags and lobbed an onion in Clara's direction. Clara caught it, knelt, placed her bag on the grass, then took a knife and cut off a sliver. She put the onion into the horn at her side, then tipped it out. Several onions fell out. All of them had identical pieces sliced from them. Defurge walked over to her, dropping his apples, then picked up a couple of onions and looked at them.

"When you put fruits, vegetables, even nuts in, ten come out. I've tried putting one of the items back in, but it only seems to work once. I tried putting meat in, to no avail. I also tried some non-edible items with no luck. I was hoping it could do the same with coins. I'm still trying to figure out everything that works." Clara gathered up the onions and apples and placed them back in her bag.

Bronwyn's smile broadened as she said, "Why didn't you say something sooner?"

"I wanted to wait until we were out of Loughlin. Given that some people were wary of our motives, I didn't want the town to know we were taking an artifact from them."

Bronwyn frowned. "Did you steal this?"

Clara shook her head. "I got permission to look for it. The basement we found it in had been sealed with metal plates and looked to have been untouched for decades, maybe longer. The village likely had no idea it was even there. Still, it might have upset a lot of people, and you saw how quickly the village leader caved to pressure."

"Do you know what this means?" Bronwyn asked, turning to Miro.

He shrugged in response.

"I thought that even if we found this artifact, we'd have to wait for the next harvest season. But now, we can take the food Emestria already has. Rouke won't be able to starve us out if we can increase our food supplies tenfold." Miro finally returned her smile. "Clara and Defurge, would you mind collecting some firewood for when we make camp tonight? We're going back to Emestria."

"Sure," Clara replied, looking suspiciously toward Miro and Bronwyn. Defurge's eyes narrowed, but he didn't complain or disagree.

Bronwyn walked up to Miro as Clara and Defurge left. She pulled him into a tight embrace. He had his robe on. She whispered in his ear, "Thank you."

Miro's arms stayed at his side, not returning the gesture and Bronwyn let him go shortly after.

"You're welcome?" Miro said, his voice picking up at the end.

Bronwyn took a bite of one of the apples she still held in her hand. The skin snapped and pulled away as she bit. It wasn't as sweet as she would prefer, but it wasn't mealy, overripe, or otherwise had anything that would indicate it wasn't fit for consumption.

After chewing briefly and swallowing, she asked Miro, "Why did you choose this artifact to go after? I thought you would have looked for something to defeat your monster, or the hammer to destroy Defurge's gem."

Miro raised his right hand and scratched the back of his neck, looking nervous. "Emestria was working on a much shorter time span than Defurge or I. It made sense to look for it first."

"Is that the only reason?"

Miro folded his arms and looked back toward the forest, in the direction Clara and Defurge had headed. Bronwyn pulled him back into a quick embrace, whispering another thank you and suppressing a yelp as the spark between them returned. Miro didn't seem to react.

"Bronwyn, that mountain to the north, does it look like a bull's head to you?" Miro pulled away from her embrace, returned to his mount, took out his book about the artifacts, and flipped to a page.

"I can't really see it through the trees, and I didn't get a good look at it while in Loughlin. Why?"

Miro came up to her, showing her a drawing he had made. It looked like he traced a bull's snout, then added lines to make it look rocky. "One of the artifacts was used to slay a dragon on top of a mountain that was cut in two by a falling star. The mountain was called Twin Horn Peaks back then. The people of Loughlin call this mountain Bull's Head Summit. It's too similar to be a coincidence."

"What does the artifact do?" Bronwyn tried to peer through the trees to see what Miro was talking about. When she couldn't see much, she took his book and flipped back and forth through the pages. There was a crude drawing of a spear.

"It's called Gaebolg, but colloquially The Dragon Slayer's Spear. Apparently after slaying the dragon, they left it embedded in the skull to prevent it from resurrecting. It could still be up there."

"That's not much information," Bronwyn said, closing the book and handing it back to Miro. "Without any dragons left, it would be a useless weapon."

"Dragons were just easier to kill with it. It is rumored to crystallize the blood of anything it cuts. It would be useful on anything too big to take down with a single blow. There are a lot of wolves in Emestria. Thinning their numbers could return the White North to a more hospitable environment. It would increase the amount of game in a couple of years."

Bronwyn scowled. "Revenge for Naani?"

"No," Miro replied. "But without Naani, there is nothing to prevent the wolves from taking over the eastern forest."

"I think the Horn will be enough. We can come back and search for this spear later. We have no idea what we might encounter if we take a spear meant to prevent a dragon from resurrecting." Bronwyn looked at Miro, still not convinced it wasn't about revenge for Naani, not that she was opposed to the idea. In the back of her mind, she remembered Miro said the monster he was hunting was half-dragon, half-demon.

"It's about more than Emestria," Miro explained. "It's about recovering an overwhelming number of the artifacts. If declaring war on Emestria became infeasible due to the number of artifacts they held, then Emestria would become a powerful ally. All nations would be interested in making alliances. From there, Emestria could unify them. It would take us a couple more days to explore the mountain. Isn't this worth a small detour?"

"We'll see what Defurge and Clara think when they return." Bronwyn didn't want to outright refuse Miro, since he did find the Horn for her, but at the same time, she hoped Clara or Defurge would be able to help dissuade him.

When Clara and Defurge returned with the firewood, Miro explained the spear and the story behind it. Clara looked annoyingly excited.

"I say we go," Clara said. Bronwyn furrowed her brows in her direction. "An undead dragon is still a dragon."

"What is with you and dragons?" Bronwyn asked, frustrated.

"I just want to see one," Clara replied. "You can't tell me you're not the least bit interested in doing the same. That crocodile was such a letdown."

"I would rather never see one," Bronwyn said. "Let alone be in a cave with one resurrected from the dead."

"Technically, a dracolich can only be summoned if there is still flesh on the carcass," Miro said. "If the spear is still there, the body would most likely be bones, if it is still there at all."

Bronwyn rolled her eyes and silently groaned. Clara was supposed to help dissuade him.

"If Miro wants to go, I'll go," Defurge said.

Miro looked to Bronwyn, his eyes seeming to plead with her. Bronwyn sighed before agreeing, "Fine, but at the first sign of trouble, we leave. The last thing we need is to get eaten when we've already found Emestria's salvation."

Clara clenched her fists excitedly and Miro flashed a smile.

They reached the mountain by nightfall and made camp. They planned to try and summit in the morning. The first two hundred feet was an almost vertical climb, but once past that, the mountain didn't look too difficult.

Apparently, the star that fell also exposed a hot spring at the base of the mountain. Bronwyn hated to admit it, but the hot water made sure the trip wasn't a complete waste. She and Clara basked in the moonlight, their muscles relaxing considerably in the spring's warm embrace.

"Since it's just the two of us, would you care to explain this obsession with dragons?" Bronwyn asked, wading up to Clara to sit beside her on some flat stones.

"Nope," Clara replied curtly. Bronwyn folded her arms and furrowed her brows. "I made a promise to someone that I would see one."

"That's a pretty foolhardy response," Bronwyn said.

"I'm a pretty foolhardy person." Clara smirked at her own retort. "Perhaps you'd like to explain your reticence in obtaining this artifact."

Bronwyn blew out of sharp puff of air, causing her lips to vibrate as she did. "It seems unnecessary. We've got what I came for; it's time to go home, while I still have a home to go to."

"And what would your king say if he found out you didn't recover this artifact?" Clara asked, her smirk still plastered on her face.

"He'd ask me to return to retrieve it, but we'd probably have to wait until the winter is over to do so. I don't know if I want to be smuggled back into and then out of Emestria again. Boats are bad enough, but going through the ice flows was a thousand times worse."

"Yes, I remember how poorly you handled the seas. Maybe you should just stay in Newtonne and let Miro and I return the artifact. I *do* have an official writ of passage now. Should I send Ferdinand off with a message to King Bryant? Let him know we have a new artifact?"

"Why don't we wait to make sure we don't die on this mountain first?"

"We'll be fine." Clara waved her hand dismissively.

"That's easy for you to say; you're not the one that ends up almost being eaten by everything we fight," Bronwyn said.

"Maybe don't give Miro a bow this time?"

Bronwyn narrowed her eyes, groaning. Miro looked better, but would any use of magic be too taxing for his system? *He can control it now. Trust him.*

"You could also try not charging into battle," Clara teased.

"I'm the soldier. If I'm not charging in, that leaves the rest of you exposed," Bronwyn argued, ignoring Clara's jovial tone.

Clara slightly shook her head as she said, "You and Miro both. You just have to do everything your way. You two are a lot alike, as much as you hate to admit it."

Bronwyn set her jaw and slouched in the water. Clara laughed before grabbing the bar of soap Bronwyn had set on a stone next to the water and began to wash.

CHAPTER 26

CLARA'S BIGGEST HURDLE in ascending the mountain had been the first two hundred vertical feet. She would have gladly traded her skill in climbing rigging for Bronwyn or Defurge's strength. Even Miro seemed to have an easier time of it than her.

They arrived at the summit in the afternoon. In front of them, the mouth of a cavern beckoned ominously. The entrance stretched twenty-five feet up and forty feet wide. If a dragon folded their wings, they would have no trouble entering the space.

"Do you think it's in there?" Clara asked, grinning.

"The dragon or the spear?" Defurge asked.

"The dragon," Clara said, her eyes shining giddily with excitement.

Bronwyn and Defurge took point, with Clara and Miro following closely behind as they approached the mouth of the cavern. Once the darkness enveloped them, Defurge engulfed his arm in flame, providing light.

Wind tore at the entrance of the cave, but once inside, the air grew still. The dimensions of the cavern only increased the further they went.

Clara spied something on the ground. At first, she thought it a broken piece of pottery—an odd place for something like that. She knelt and picked up the slightly concave, rock-hard, and jagged shard. When rotated in her hand, one side reflected the light with a red iridescent sheen. She almost dropped it. To confirm her suspicions, she rotated the object in the light again. It wasn't Defurge's fire; one side of the fragment was smooth and glassy, while the other was textured and rough.

"Is this what I think it is?" Clara asked the group, causing them to turn around. At first, they stared at her, puzzled. Clara rotated the broken sliver, showing them how it glinted in the fire. Miro took it from her and turned it over. He ran his hands across both sides of the broken piece.

"It was an egg," Clara said with glee. "An egg means a baby."

Bronwyn and Miro exchanged wary glances.

"Not necessarily. If there was a dragon," and the presence of an egg increased the likelihood, "then whoever killed it might have smashed any eggs as well," Bronwyn cautioned.

Clara needed to see a dragon. When she would secretly visit Scarlette every year for her birthday, she'd entertain the child with stories of adventure, piracy, and the exotic. On the last two occasions, Scarlette had asked if Clara had ever seen a dragon with such wide eyes that Clara wished she could have said yes without it being a lie. She imagined how happy Scarlette would be if Clara returned for Scarlette's birthday in a couple of months with not only a story about seeing a dragon but with shards of a dragon egg as proof. Clara put the egg shard into her pack and let her nails dig into her palms. It was a happy sensation this time.

There appeared to be only one chamber that stretched deep into the mountain. Defurge's light failed to reach all the sides of the cavern, but Clara thought she spied more glints at the light's edge.

At the far end, dirty yellow-white bone came into view. Only a spine at first, then hindlimbs, ribs, and two sets of forelimbs, one with long spindly fingers. The body's exact orientation was difficult to ascertain. Any connecting tissue gave way long ago. The bones were piled on top of each other but followed a general anatomy. The spine got thicker as it led away from the ribs and toward the head. There was no other creature that Clara knew of that had four limbs and wings. Right in the middle of the skull, a metal and wooden handle jutted out triumphantly.

The leaf-shaped head of the weapon appeared to be serrated with three edges. A single strip of brown tattered cloth hung from the base, perhaps a battle standard. Now it only served as a testament to the amount of time the spear had remained undiscovered. Toward the head, elaborate metalwork decorated the shaft. Despite the age, the wood and metal appeared to be flawless, like they were crafted yesterday. The alloy glowed in the light with a bluish-silver tint.

Nobody moved. Even Clara hesitated to approach the haphazard pile of bones. Despite her desire to see a dragon or undead dragon, she did not wish to fight one. They all crept forward in a tight formation. When they reached the skull and it was apparent that someone would need to grab the weapon, Miro reached forward and grasped the handle. He pulled, but the spear refused to dislodge. He gripped the shaft closer to the head and wiggled it. The dragon's skull splintered and cracked little by little until Miro achieved enough leverage to liberate the artifact.

Miro stumbled back but regained his footing quickly after wresting the weapon free. Bronwyn placed her hand at the hilt of her sword, Defurge's hand hovered at his waist, ready to unfurl his whip, and Clara prepared to reach for her axe. For thirty seconds their muscles tensed as they waited.

"Nothing," Clara groaned. In her ideal scenario, the dragon would come to life, and they would run away, securing both the artifact and seeing an undead dragon. She needed to see a dragon.

"Good, let's just walk the same way we came in, so we don't disturb any of the eggs. They're probably all dead now anyhow," Bronwyn said, relaxing her grip on her sword's hilt and turning towards the light at the mouth of the cavern.

"What eggs?" Miro asked.

"The ones that are all around us," Bronwyn said. "Don't you see the light reflecting off their glassy surface?" Bronwyn pointed at some of the reflections in the distance. "Over there."

The others now took notice and despite her warnings, proceeded to walk in that direction.

"Hey, I said don't go toward the eggs! We've got the weapon; why don't we go? You can come back here and be stupid after I return these artifacts to Emestria." Despite Bronwyn's admonishments, Clara, Miro, and Defurge still walked toward the cavern wall. Bronwyn hesitated but eventually followed as well, staying within Defurge's firelight.

Clara trained her eyes on the small reflections, but they always seemed to be just out of the light. It could be an optical illusion, or mineral deposits in the wall scattering the light, creating the effect. Then they walked to one side of the cave and still no eggs or anything else that would explain the twinkling reflections.

"Idiots, we need to leave," Bronwyn said. She put her hand back on her greatsword. Miro nodded in agreement.

Bronwyn and Defurge took the lead. They plotted a course straight for the cavern's entrance. Clara stayed close behind and Miro lagged a little, walking backwards to guard their rear just in case.

Clara heard the quiet shifting along the stone, little almost imperceptible clicks. Whatever it was, it avoided the light. Luckily, they had a living and breathing torch, so there was little real danger.

Then it happened; while the others shifted away from view, one didn't. The creature stood motionless until Defurge's flame revealed it.

The strange animal belied comprehension, a type of arachnid that seemed to stand like a spider but had soft amber pincers and a shining emerald tail like a scorpion. A dull, ruby, hard shell protected the soft leathery bits responsible for movement. Eight thin legs held its curved body aloft, a foot above the stone. Although the body was only a couple of feet long and a foot wide, it tucked a fat tail equal to its body length under its belly. The armored, segmented tail ended in a barbed tip. A wet sac glistened just behind the barb.

Clara expected the arachnid to retreat into the darkness, but instead, it reared up on four of its hindlegs, extending its tail forward. With its four front legs splayed in the air, it appeared larger. It seemed to be a defensive maneuver.

"Burn it," Bronwyn whispered to Defurge. He extended his hand, and a jet of flame erupted forth. The fire illuminated most of the cavern. Thousands of tiny black eyes stared at them, the horde of creatures jostling over and under each other.

The flame surrounded the lone beast. As Defurge closed his hand, the flame died, but instead of the twisted husk of carapace Clara expected, the monster only reared up higher and thrust its tail further forward. The other creatures raced toward them.

Defurge directed his fire over the closest of the arachnids. The fire did little to deter them and lingered on their backs, creating a hazard if they came closer.

Bronwyn unleashed her steel, cutting large swaths in the advancing swarm. Arachnids were either cleaved in two or crashed into their sisters, knocking several off-balance.

Miro wielded the spear, stabbing at the soft underbelly of a foe. The body of the monster contorted and twisted before crystalline structures burst forth. Clara took note of the effect. Against a larger enemy, it would be debilitating, but against the multitude of assailants surrounding them, it was little more than a cantrip.

Defurge switched tactics, opting for his whip, cracking it against their bodies and legs. For every creature he incapacitated, two more advanced on their position. He tried sweeping the whip along the cavern's floor, tripping and waylaying the foes, but doing little else.

Clara glanced about the room. Bronwyn kept their advance and part of their flank clear, but Miro and Defurge struggled to keep the rear from being overwhelmed.

Bronwyn was twenty feet from the entrance.

Clara rattled through her mind for a solution. Walls could protect their retreat, but these things looked like they could climb quickly. Resistance to fire put most of Defurge's abilities at a disadvantage. Lightning might have some effect, but even if Miro was casting it as quickly as he could, it would only hit a couple at a time.

"Miro, cast ice wall in front of Bronwyn, near the entrance!" Clara yelled above the dirge of battle.

"What?" Miro asked. "There is barely any moisture in here. It will be too weak to do any good."

"Just do it!" Clara commanded.

"Fria, goddess of ice, death, and fate, the vigilant eye, I make this pact with you, bar our entrance, Fragma Frios." Miro cast the ice wall in front of Bronwyn effectively blocking their exit from the cave.

Clara chanted, "Lau'O'Penake, goddess of nature and rebirth, raise the earth and provide us safe harbor, Fragma Petra." Clara formed a stone wall as a circular plateau two feet off the ground. "Everyone up!"

The increase in elevation did little to bestow extra protection. The creatures scaled the structure just as easily as the four of them now did.

"Defurge, concentrate all your fire on the ice wall—melt it," Clara continued issuing edicts as Miro, Bronwyn, and she slammed their respective weapons on the creatures scampering up the earthen plateau.

An intense torrent of flame erupted from both of Defurge's hands, bearing down upon the wall. The melted water traveled down the sloped cavern, doing little more than causing the creatures to slip now and then.

"Miro, cast lightning on them," Clara said.

"Clara, I don't think—"

"Light 'em up, Sparky!" Bronwyn yelled.

"Laevin, god of the skies and lightning, arbiter of the gods, lend me your wrath, Bolta Levos" The spell snaked forward, making contact with one of the creatures. The bolt sparked and jumped along the water. Members of the horde in the water slumped to the ground, either dead or stunned. It would buy them some time.

Bronwyn hopped off the platform and continued trying to keep their exit cleared.

Clara was about to follow her when she almost tripped as one of the creatures landed in front of her. She raised her axe and brought it down.

Bronwyn was fifteen feet from the entrance.

When the second arachnid fell on Clara's back, it stabbed her several times with its stinger before she wrested it free and dispatched it. Clara looked to the ceiling. More of the arachnids attempted to position themselves above her party.

"Miro, Defurge," Clara brought their attention to the walls.

Miro thrust the spear up, impaling one of the descending creatures. He pivoted the spear and as it fell to the floor, the crystallized blood shattered, strewing body parts.

Defurge brought his whip to bear, tripping the swarming bugs before they finished climbing the walls.

Bronwyn was ten feet short of the entrance.

The rear members of the swarm crawled over the dead bodies of their nestmates, threatening to overrun them yet again.

Clara hopped off the embankment. As she landed, she fell to her feet, breathing heavily. Sluggish legs refused to heed her commands as she tried to get back up. Fiery pain seared along her back, and she reached behind to see if Defurge had possibly hit her with a stray jet of flame. Small trickles of blood streaked her hand. Another monster landed in front of her, and thankfully, her legs listened as she rose and swung her axe, splitting the carapace and exposing a dark violet ichor. A repeat of that defensive maneuver would be impossible, and deep down she knew it.

Bronwyn was five feet from the entrance.

Clara forced her legs forward. The blinding daylight and Bronwyn were just ahead. She had to escape. Miro and Defurge wouldn't leave until she was safe.

Her vision blurred, tunneling in on itself. She just needed to head towards the light. Then another dark shape appeared in front of her. Futilely, she tried to hoist her axe.

"Clara," Bronwyn said as she lifted her comrade onto her shoulder. The sound of booted footsteps nearby consoled Clara. They were escaping. Then brilliant, bright daylight.

They were free.

Even with Clara's dimming vision, she made out the figures scuttling from the cave. Clara hoped a vulnerability to sunlight caused their aversion to Defurge's fire. She was wrong.

Miro and Bronwyn said something; the unintelligible, fuzzy words made little sense. Defurge blanketed the cavern's maw with streams of flame, but the creatures still threatened to overrun them.

Clara had practiced the magic so many times, but never successfully cast the spell. She held her hands in front of her face and started tracing the runes. She concentrated, methodically making each movement of her hands. She had one chance.

"Lau'O'Penake, goddess of nature and rebirth, let your voice be heard, bring the mountains down upon my enemy, Summa!"

Nothing. She couldn't cast it while at full strength, why did she think this time would be different?

An incoming storm cloud growled, the type of sound only felt in the chest, but then the gravel on the earth jumped in anticipation. The very mountain roared. They were all airborne for a second as the ground retracted from their feet and crashed upward, forcing all to their knees. The mountain likewise reacted. From afar, the bull mountain lost the tip of one of its horns, the cavern collapsing in on itself. The rocks slammed together, crushing what remained inside.

Clara breathed a sigh of relief and let herself relax. She struggled to tell Miro the name of the girl he needed to help in Corinthe, Scarlette. A fuzzy recollection of Miro mentioning a spell being able to neutralize poison, but then she remembered Miro saying it was as complicated as the spell to purify blood—a spell Miro did not know.

Her throat was scratchy, and she was having trouble breathing. When she squeezed her hands shut, she couldn't even feel the nails digging in. *It is sad to let go, but I saved them. Maybe they will tell others I died a heroine, and possibly one day Scarlette will find out about me. She will question her father as to why she had the light-rose hair that only Lynnfield refugees had. He will lie to her, but she is a smart girl, and eventually, she'll figure it out. She'll seek out the pirate lady that visited her on her birthday, visit Newtonne, talk to my shipmates, and ultimately, find that I joined a grand quest and died a heroine.*

Bronwyn said something, interrupting Clara's final thoughts and fantasies of what the world would be like without her. Bronwyn cradled Clara's head in her arms. Bronwyn looked up to Miro, her eyes pleading. A couple of the cave dwellers tried to wrest themselves free, but Defurge eliminated the threats easily with his whip.

Miro rushed to Clara's side. Her face felt fat, and her skin and muscles burned. A searing red pain shot through her body before a dull numbness replaced it. Miro glanced at Defurge, then he looked back to Bronwyn. Clara felt her breath heavy and her head light. It was more than the thin mountain air. Her vision tunneled further as the periphery blurred into blackness.

"I think she's been poisoned." Bronwyn's distorted voice pierced through the haze. Her hands pressed against the wounds on Clara's back. "Only the creature's stingers would cause such damage."

"I can heal her," Miro replied. He started to trace the runes in the air, but then Clara grabbed his hands.

No, it is my time. It's okay that I'm letting go. If only I had enough strength to tell him Scarlette's name. But Miro is a good person; perhaps he'll seek out this girl with blood poisoning and know it has to be Scarlette.

"Isn't that healing magic? Is it safe?" Bronwyn asked.

"It is healing magic, but it's Clara," Miro said, a catch in his voice, before beginning the casting anew. Clara grabbed his hands again, preventing him from completing the ritual.

Even if he knows the magic that can purify poisons, it's complicated. He'll die saving me. He can lose control, or endanger his own life if the magic proves too difficult. If Miro dies, he can't treat Scarlette. If he kills everyone around him, no one will know of my sacrifice. No, this is the better way. I quietly pass, and Miro eventually keeps his promise. Scarlette grows up knowing her mother sacrificed herself for her friends. Maybe Miro, so touched by my bravery at the end, will honor my memory by putting off his entire quest for artifacts to help Scarlette. Did Issaroh have similar thoughts at the end?

Bronwyn's voice interrupted Clara yet again, "If you start bleeding up here, I don't know if I can get you back to safety to recover."

"It's Clara!" Miro repeated firmly. "I promised her."

Bronwyn didn't argue, but Clara refused to release her grip on his hands.

"You can stop me if I lose control?" Miro asked Bronwyn, who enthusiastically nodded and wiped away the beginnings of a tear. Miro tried to free his hands, but Clara continued to try and hold tight to them, hindering his efforts.

It's okay.

"I'm going to do this, Clara," Miro said. "I can do it now, when the poison hasn't taken hold yet, or you can continue to prevent me until you're unconscious. Either way, it's happening. It will be easier on both of us if I cast now."

So dramatic and stubborn, Clara thought, her mind slowed with the lack of oxygen. *And he will too. He'll wait for me to pass out, then ruin my heroic moment.* She released his hands, letting her own fall to her side.

"Seraph, goddess of life and love, accept not this spirit in your embrace; instead purge her of her afflictions, yield to my will, do my bidding, and rid this body of its impurities, Thayed Deliteri Medus."

Previous healing rituals required shorter incantations. These runes were complex. Normally, one or two rune circles would need to be completed for a spell, but this involved four. When they descended on Clara's body, she sucked in air, panting from the release of the ill effects of both the venom and exhaustion.

Bronwyn looked down at Clara as the burning pain returned, then waned. Bronwyn exhaled and sighed. Next, she grabbed Miro's left arm, and forced the sleeve up. He still wore the bandages from the last time she changed them. The wounds had stopped seeping, but they hadn't healed. Now, fresh blood slowly stained his bandages.

"I'll survive," Miro assured her worries. Bronwyn's hand lingered on his arm.

Clara's breathing evened out and she blinked several times. The images started to come into focus, and she made out the features of the faces of Miro and Bronwyn over her. She tried to sit up and Bronwyn held her down. She pushed Bronwyn's hands away and snapped to attention, "You idiot," she yelled at Miro once she mustered the energy.

"And you." Clara turned to Bronwyn. "I knew what I was doing! But you wanted to risk it? For what?" For once, Clara struggled to control her anger. She tried to stop him. Looking at the blood quickly staining Miro's bandages, her obvious worries were grounded in reality. There was no helping Scarlette if Miro died on this mountaintop.

Bronwyn removed a strip of cloth from her ponytail and tied the thin fabric on Miro's arm. Despite Bronwyn's help, the blood continued to gather. Bronwyn and Miro laughed at their foolishness, their eyes beaming as they stared at Clara.

"You two are the biggest set of imbeciles I've ever encountered. I swear to the gods when we're off this mountain, I'm selling that bird and I'm quitting both of you for good." They continued to laugh.

"I'm serious," Clara said. "You two are the worst."

Defurge quit his task of eliminating any beast that emerged from the rubble. None had appeared for several minutes. He smiled at Clara's frustration.

"A whole bunch of idiots," Clara remarked seeing Defurge's smile.

Clara was glad Miro used his magic, even more when it worked, and it didn't look like he had endangered his own life. What little blood loss he experienced now, he had proven himself more than capable of recovering from.

Bronwyn's actions angered Clara. Clara expected Bronwyn to try and stop Miro. Instead, Bronwyn agreed with his reckless course of action; neither of them knew it would be successful, but they both seemed more than happy to risk Miro's life for hers. If it were up to Bronwyn, Miro would have never healed the girl in Loughlin. *Why do I deserve so much attention?* Bronwyn should have argued about healing her, not the little girl. She lived much more of her life and committed many more offenses than the child. Still, it was hard being so frustrated with everyone else beaming with happiness. She relented.

"Do you think you can help me down?" Miro asked Bronwyn. Bronwyn nodded and put an arm around him.

Defurge approached Clara and offered his hand. When she extended hers, he pulled her close and gathered her up in his arms, cradling her.

"I think this is a little much," Clara complained, trying to make herself comfortable in his embrace.

"You've been poisoned to death," Defurge said with a sly smirk. "Just accept the help."

Despite her protestations, Clara's legs were still numb.

Bronwyn helped Miro as they descended. She held one of his arms over her shoulder and put one of hers around his waist. He did his best to appear healthy, but his slow movements exposed his deceit. When they stopped, Bronwyn unwrapped Miro's bandages, removing the blood-stained ones and replacing them with clean cloth further up on his arm.

Defurge let Clara down to stretch her legs. When she put her foot down, pins and needles radiated up her leg. She hoped that meant the feeling would return soon.

After Bronwyn finished re-wrapping Miro's bandages, they continued.

Dusk was beginning to set in, but they increased their pace. No one said it, but Clara knew everyone was thinking it: they had no guarantee those things were all dead.

Clara debated feigning poisoning all the time; then she would never have to walk again. She could have her own personal incarnation of a god to ferry her about.

Chapter 27

They reached the base of the mountain a couple hours after nightfall and made a proper camp using the gear from the horse's packs: two tents, a campfire, and food they had obtained from Loughlin. Bronwyn ate her dinner faster than the rest and waited for Clara to finish.

When Clara put down the last spoonful of her soup Bronwyn asked, "Clara, would you like to take a bath together? It might be a while before we get hot water like that again." Bronwyn had been looking forward to this all day.

Clara sighed, her movements were somewhat jerky. "I'm still a little tired. How about tomorrow?"

"It will help soothe your body," Bronwyn countered.

"In the morning," Clara replied. Bronwyn got in the habit of bathing with others when out and about in the world. A second set of eyes were comforting in case something was amiss.

"If you are loathe to bathe alone, I'll accompany you," Defurge said.

Bronwyn contemplated the offer for a moment. *How different can it be from bathing with Clara? He isn't interested in my body. Still, if Clara doesn't want to, maybe Miro will join me.*

"Miro, you could come with me," Bronwyn suggested. "I have soap." Bronwyn held one of the bars she obtained at the general store aloft. She attempted to hide her smile. She didn't expect him to agree, but maybe he would.

"But ...." Miro trailed off.

"We'll bathe in our short clothes. Don't be a child," Bronwyn joked. She didn't wait for his response and headed off in the direction of the hot springs. The dirt cushioned Miro's boots and the padding of his feet as he followed close behind her. She quickened her pace.

Bronwyn waited at the water's edge for Miro, worried he might have turned back. Once he crested the hilltop, she ducked behind some bushes to remove her outer clothing. When she glanced back up at him, he turned his back to her. She paused to see if he would turn around, and when he didn't, she went into the warm water in her small clothes. She debated leaving them at the shore since he didn't seem determined to peek.

"You can look now," Bronwyn called from the water. Miro walked toward the tree she removed her clothing at and leaned against it. She waded into the water a bit, waiting for him. "Aren't you going to get in?"

"It's okay. We can talk from here," Miro offered. He faced her direction but avoided eye contact.

"I'm not going to yell at you anytime I want to say something; get in the water." The idea was ill-conceived. Bronwyn thought Miro and she could have a pleasant conversation. Perhaps she should have taken Defurge up on his offer.

"Okay, but can you look away?" Miro asked.

"Contrary to your belief, I've seen a naked man before; seeing one in his small clothes will not shock me." Bronwyn stifled her amusement at his modesty. *She* should be the one concerned about *his* wandering eyes.

"Please." The word had become shorthand between the two of them. Neither set out for it to be that way, but they used the phrase when they wanted something and didn't want to explain why.

Bronwyn turned her back, allowing him to undress. She peeked over her shoulder when she felt she gave him sufficient time. His toned body was unlike most Emestrian men. He had little chest hair to speak of: a small tuft between his pectoral muscles and above his pant line. Two prominent scars, one across the chest and the other across his stomach, marred his body. The defect on his stomach extended all the way across. In his dreams, she remembered him clutching a wound across his stomach. Bronwyn mused why he hadn't healed them before they disfigured, but perhaps his magical energy was spent when it happened. She spied his left arm; the blood had hardened, forming protective scabs.

Once Miro entered the water, Bronwyn turned around. She momentarily dipped her head underneath the bath's placid surface and lathered the soap on her hand. She rubbed it across her face and held it aloft. The dirt slid off her body. When the bar left her hand, she submerged once more, washing the suds away.

Miro mimicked the procedure and handed the soap back to her but didn't speak. It made her a little nervous, and everything became mechanical. She washed her arms and body, looking at him before handing the soap back. He did the same. She turned around and cradled her hair, pulling it over her right shoulder.

"Turn around," she said, and he complied. Bronwyn removed her small clothes and held her arms over her chest. "Wash my back," she said quietly.

Miro brought the bar and placed it on her back. His breath was steady but pronounced as the slick soap glided over her skin. It wasn't as intense as before, but when his fingers happened to make contact, she felt a slight tingle. She reached behind, grabbing the soap. They fumbled with each other's fingers until she had a firm grasp.

"I'll wash yours." Bronwyn turned, her left arm still in front of her chest, the right brandishing soap.

"That's okay, I'll get it myself."

"I'll be gentle," Bronwyn recalled the conversation about the sensitive wounds on his back. Miro hesitated and she waited until he relented. He cast his eyes downward as he turned in the water.

A patchwork of scars crisscrossed and bled over each other on Miro's back. Bronwyn remembered the comment Clara made about marring his perfect skin. She now stared at it; it was far from perfect. Bronwyn looked at his left arm and wondered, *What will it look like when it heals? Is there any part of his back that isn't scarred?*

Hesitantly she brought the soap up. She wanted to pretend like this was normal, but her stomach tightened into knots as she ran the soap against his washboard skin. The scars protruded far off his body. She pretended not to notice, but every bump and wave of the disfigured flesh made her nauseous. It wasn't the skin, but rather the thought of who would do this to another person.

What can cause this many wounds? There are scars on top of scars. How long did this go on? Did someone do this, wait for him to heal, then do it over again? Was this Emestria? She always thought of the guard corps and army as two separate entities, but sometimes she sent members of the guard corps to the army. *Would people I trained be willing to do this to another human being?*

She stifled the emotions. Still, she couldn't help but let one of her fingers trace the path of the raised flesh. He winced. She made a show of washing the rest of his back, ignoring the puzzle of torment.

"What do you think of these hot springs?" Bronwyn asked. She wanted the uncomfortable silence to disappear. She knew he was uneasy, but she wanted to ignore it, hoping that not asking would indicate she accepted it without question.

"I've never seen trees like this. Their petals are so soft and blow away with the wind," Miro said, his voice low and flat.

"Clara said they usually bloom in early spring. These happened to flower early. Maybe because of the climate." Bronwyn finished washing his back.

"Makes me want to come back and watch them all year long, just to see how long they grow and bloom for."

"Maybe when this is all over, we can." Bronwyn stopped. She remembered Fria's words, and the phoenix, Serina's proclamation, Miro would give his life to destroy Defurge's soul stone. Bronwyn couldn't be making plans for the future with him.

Hesitantly, Bronwyn let her right hand run down his arm, feeling the rough texture of the already scabbed skin. The spark was stronger as she traced the lines of the scab and she almost felt like she could see it, little dabs of light in the dark water. Quietly, she asked, "Does it hurt, when you draw on your energy like that, sacrificing your health to heal others?"

Miro cleared his throat, and the words came out pained, "More than some wounds, less than others."

Less than others, like the scars on his back? "Why?"

Miro turned to face her and Bronwyn let her fingers trace their way from one scar to another, resting on his chest. She was instantly aware that she had shed her short clothes when he washed her back. His eyes, though, did not wander, and she found herself half-hoping they would. Rather than bring her arms up to shield her nudity, one remained on his chest and the other at her side.

"Why ask me? I told you, it was Clara, and in the village, I couldn't watch good people—innocent people—suffer."

"And are you not a good person? Are you not innocent?"

Miro took her hand from his chest and held it in his. Hot intense heat radiated from the contact. From passion, from something else? Was this his life force as she thought?

"No, I'm not." Then his hand left hers and he seemed to swim backward by the tiniest fraction in the hot spring's water.

A lump formed in her throat, and she felt like there were words that needed to be said but could not be spoken. Not wishing for him to retreat further, she said, "Stay like this." She turned away from him, now hiding her vulnerability, and finished washing before handing the soap back to him over her shoulder. "You can wash the rest of yourself while I get dressed."

His fingertips lightly grazed hers as she handed the bar back. The slight tickle his spark elicited in her fingertips was both refreshing and depressing.

Bronwyn exited the springs without looking back. She wanted to stay longer, but she was ashamed of her reaction to his scars. How she traced those lines of pain with a desire to show him something. That he wasn't the monster that he thought he was? That she didn't care about the scars in his mind or on his body? Was that roadmap of pain the reason he found forgiveness so hard? He had told her about war wounds on his back, but she hadn't anticipated the topography of pain he presented to her.

She redonned her clothes, keeping her short clothes apart. She had another pair back in camp. She would set these up to dry. Despite trying to force her mind away from his scars, she was unable to rid her thoughts of them. *Why would someone do that to him? Why wouldn't he tell me about something like that?* When Bronwyn heard him exiting the water, she wiped the tears from her face and hid behind a tree as she waited for him to dress.

Once he was clothed again, she came out from behind the tree. "Who did that to you?" she asked, her voice wavering. She was mad—not at Miro, but at the world that permitted abuse on that level.

"A little present from the dungeons," Miro responded with a weak smile and false bravado punctuating the comment.

"Why couldn't you heal it?" Bronwyn asked, ignoring his attempt at levity. Despite the recent lessons on the extent of healing magic, she needed to know.

"The torturers like to leave their mark. When they discovered I healed the broken bones, they found other ways. Heated iron and daggers, I couldn't fix those marks. He couldn't even look me in the face as he did it," Miro said with some semblance of sorrow.

"Why didn't King Bryant stop it?" For the first time, Bronwyn felt Miro's moniker was appropriate. Bryant the Betrayer. If he left Miro in the dungeon, subjected to this, how could he not be a betrayer?

"I don't know; possibly he didn't have the power. His brother was still alive. Or, he wanted me to give my pound of flesh." Miro stared at the ground, refusing to match Bronwyn's gaze. "I thought I deserved it for a long time. I don't know if I feel that way anymore." He sighed heavily. "Don't tell the others, please?"

He used the phrase again, the tacit agreement they subconsciously developed.

"There is nothing in the world you could do to warrant that kind of torture." Bronwyn stepped forward. She looked at his face, waiting for him to have the courage to look her in the eye.

Finally, Miro's head lifted, and he peered forward, their eyes connecting. A cool night breeze encircled them, embracing them because they refused to embrace each other. Blossoms from the trees cascaded around them like snow and the moon reflected off the water, illuminating the steam rising to the sky.

Physically, they had embraced before, but emotionally this was the closest they ever came. Bronwyn knew that at this moment if she leaned in, they would kiss. She wanted to, to feel his warm lips against hers, to feel the tickle his spark would elicit on her sensitive skin, to feel his arms wrap around and hold her close, but she sensed the reticence in him.

Miro returned her gaze, and they stared deep into each other's eyes. She knew he wanted the same as her. She could feel it in the air. Their bodies wanted to be next to each other. The necklace was so cold, it burned the skin where it lay. She felt Miro's reluctance, and he leaned away. His eyes glossed over, and he sighed.

"I can't," Miro said as he lowered his head once more.

"Why not?" Bronwyn wanted to convince him otherwise, but if she couldn't, she at least deserved an explanation.

"Because I can never be honest with you," Miro said. "I can never tell you my entire truth."

"I don't need to know it. I know you." She didn't care about his past anymore. It didn't matter. She had confirmation that his choices were never his to begin with.

"I love the way you look at me now, but one day you'll find out, and the way you look at me will never be the same. I couldn't survive you looking at me with your eyes full of hate." Miro's hands had been hovering around Bronwyn's elbows, ready to pull her close, but when he said this, they dropped to his side.

"I won't."

"It's okay. Why can't this be enough?" Miro smiled painfully.

"Because it isn't." Miro frowned and started to walk away.

"Whatever you think you did, Miro, it's not your fault. You had no choice." Bronwyn ground her teeth. "It was some plan by the gods and goddesses."

"That's a comforting thought," Miro said, glancing over his shoulder. "But I made my own choices. No god or goddess compelled me to make them." He withdrew, leaving her alone in the cold mountain air.

Bronwyn thought, *It isn't fair what he is putting me through. He decided on my reaction without giving me the chance to make up my mind. Damn the gods and goddesses and their plans and insistence on what I can and can't do. Why should I listen to their desires when* this *is what their plans do to people? They mean for this man to give his life to fix their mistakes, and who else will die in this plot of theirs?*

Whatever Miro did, whatever plan they concocted that ended with him hating himself, they mean for him to march off to sacrifice himself because of that self-hate, because he's convinced that no one who knew of his actions could love him. And I could find out. I have the tools to do it, but they have forbidden me from using the Eye of Sleepless Dreams.

But why have they forbidden me? Would knowing the truth and forgiving Miro mean that their plans would be all for naught, that Miro wouldn't sacrifice himself to satisfy their grand play? There is one path open that doesn't result in me killing Miro, but many more that involve his death. Why would they bet their entire plan on that one path, or even care for that matter, and maybe the path that results in what I want is the hardest one? Damn the gods and goddesses.

Clara sat by the fire as Miro returned to camp, his head down and his shoulders slumped. By the time Bronwyn returned, Miro had retired to bed. Bronwyn sat next to Clara. Clara could tell Bronwyn had something on her mind but didn't try and spur her into conversation. It was obvious from Miro's demeanor upon returning that something happened between them again.

"You've been borrowing Miro's books?" Bronwyn asked, knowing the answer. Clara had confided this in her when she talked about the necklace. She explained the purpose of understanding the elements as a whole, versus looking at them individually. The declaration she borrowed the books, in particular with Miro none the wiser, had interested Bronwyn.

"Yes?" Clara responded, her answer half question.

"I want you to get me the Eye."

"Are you sure?" Clara asked, glancing around, ensuring Miro was still in his tent.

"He needs someone to see, someone to tell him his past doesn't dictate who he is." Worry haunted Bronwyn's voice.

"I don't want you to do this," Clara spoke slowly and deliberately.

"I need to. He's dying inside. He punishes himself and believes he is unworthy of any semblance of a normal life. He deserves to be forgiven. He may hate me for doing it, but haven't you ever done something for someone, knowing it was the best for them, even if it would change your relationship?"

Bronwyn was determined. Clara could tell by the conviction she spoke with. She could argue with her, but part of her wanted Bronwyn to be right. If someone like Bronwyn was able to overlook the mistakes of Miro's past, whatever they may be, then maybe there was hope for others, like her. And with Miro so eagerly risking his life, it may be important to take the Eye for herself one day. She wanted to know if she could steal it from him while he slept. Unlike the books, he always kept the Eye close. Clara dug her nails into her palm.

"If I do this, you can't tell me. I don't want to know what you uncover," Clara rationalized the theft. "I mean it; I don't want to know anything you find out. Concentrate all your thoughts on him; I don't want you meddling in my past either."

"Your past ...." Bronwyn stared at Clara like a stranger. Clara was glad Bronwyn didn't press her for more details.

Clara waited until Miro's night terrors started. She slipped into the tent quietly, not waking Defurge or Miro. The Eye was always in the same bag. Miro was remarkably consistent.

When Clara emerged, she made her way to Bronwyn, who still sat by the fire. Clara held the artifact out. Bronwyn took it into her hands and Clara could see what it meant to her. She felt like she ate rocks for dinner, she was so weighed down by her shame. Miro would be devastated, but maybe Bronwyn was right. One thing was for sure, Miro needed something to change. She didn't want to gamble on this, but Bronwyn's words about sacrificing your relationship for another struck too close to home.

And could Miro ever hate Bronwyn, or her for that matter? Maybe Bronwyn was right, and Miro would stop making reckless decisions that resulted in him almost dying. Miro promised her he would help Scarlette, and he couldn't do that if he was dead. If he and Bronwyn had a falling out, they would eventually be drawn back to each other, and what if it helped Miro forgive himself?

"Keep this for me tonight," Bronwyn said, handing her necklace to Clara. She cocked an eyebrow. "I can't explain it, but it might interfere with the Eye."

Clara wondered what Bronwyn meant, but her thoughts and feelings convinced her not to ask. Her voice might betray her emotions at this moment. Clara left to get a couple of hours of sleep before Bronwyn's shift ended.

It seemed too short when Bronwyn shook Clara awake. She gave Bronwyn a knowing nod. With any luck, her visions would be less auditory. If she did happen to cry out in her sleep, Clara agreed to wake her.

Bronwyn removed her boots and laid down in her bedroll. She placed the Eye on her chest, holding it with both hands and closed her eyes. Clara waited several minutes before leaving to tend the fire.

CHAPTER 28

It wasn't like how Miro's visions were. Bronwyn wasn't reliving her own experiences, instead, she seemed to be a bystander in watching his past. Miro walked alongside the man and woman she had seen in his earlier dream. King Bryant was less handsome and the woman less beautiful. They were also absent the glowing red aura Bronwyn had seen. *Because in the dream, that was how Miro saw them. Now I'm seeing them for what they really looked like, without his affection.*

Bronwyn was like a ghost, floating through the vision. She approached Miro. He seemed happier, less weighed down by life. Then she looked closer at the woman. She had only seen her briefly in Miro's dream.

The hair was a similar color to Bronwyn's but not quite. Her face wasn't as angular, and her eyebrows and lips were fuller than Bronwyn's. She stepped back and saw the figure was a couple of inches shorter than Miro, and her gait was more stunted than Bronwyn's. Bronwyn felt a pang of jealousy. She wanted to be the one walking next to a carefree Miro, stealing furtive glances as he smiled back.

Then she heard it, the same cry she heard when fighting Naani—the sound of a man dying in battle. The three warriors raced to the conflict. Bronwyn followed—her movement dictated by their proximity.

Time blurred as Bronwyn trailed behind, obscuring the distance they traveled. It seemed as if only a second passed before they were at the source of the cry. A man, unarmored and unarmed, was pinned against the ground. A longsword thrust through his body and into the dirt, standing like a grisly battle standard. At first, only a handful of Taran and Roukian knights engaged Bryant, but soon others materialized from the outskirts of her vision.

Miro fell first. A sword sliced deep across his belly, spilling his entrails on the battlefield.

The woman fell next. They pinned her to the ground. Bronwyn had seen this in Miro's dream. The men ripped the woman's shirt and started to hoist her skirt up. Bronwyn knew this was why Emestria frowned on women on the battlefield because this is what their enemies would do to them.

Then King Bryant fell. They took his sword, kicking and taunting him. She couldn't hear what they said. Every word was garbled as if they were yelling into a strong wind.

"Please," Miro said softly. He attempted to prevent his innards from spilling forth. They slipped through his fingers.

"Please," he begged again. Bronwyn saw the battle through Miro's eyes. His vision darted between the woman about to be violated and King Bryant about to die.

"Silly child, why would you dare call upon me!" Bronwyn thought she recognized the voice; it was eerily familiar, but she couldn't place it. An ethereal figure manifested and floated in front of Miro.

The black serpent's thin body coiled over itself. Four small limbs grasped at the air, moving but vestigial at the same time. Its head was adorned with horns and its long flowing whiskers wafted through the air like smoke. She recognized those eyes. Those sickly blue eyes. They were the same color as Miro's when the curse overtook him.

"Please," Miro repeated.

"And what do you want, child of man?" The creature's question echoed off the mountains but only Miro recoiled at the voice.

"Just save them." Miro's voice weakened.

"And what will you give me, if I save them?" The creature rejoiced in its power over the dying man.

"Anything." Miro's hand reached out, trying to grab his friends despite them being too far away.

"Now listen carefully." The creature undulated forward; one of its small arms used a claw to force Miro's chin in its direction. "You will give me anything to save them?"

"Anything," Miro said, collapsing as he spoke his last words.

The black serpent rose high into the air. At first, Bronwyn thought it betrayed Miro, that this was the horror she would be forced to witness, but instead, a beam of light shot from the clouds.

When it contacted the land, the blue-white light extended as far as Bronwyn could see. Everything in its path blew away under its destructive power. Buildings, trees, plants, the attacking soldiers. They were there, but when the light passed them, nothing remained except a misshapen husk of what they used to be crumbling to the ground. Miro, Bryant, and the woman were all that survived.

The next vision came quickly. She was somewhere dark and miserable—the dungeons beneath Solstice's castle. She recognized this room. White runes decorated the cold stone and rigid bars. Miro stayed in this room the last time they visited the castle together. He claimed the runes were fake, and he told the jailors how to draw them to contain his magic. The bed was gone, and the empty cell contained Miro, several men, and a hot bucket of coals with various implements sticking out. She didn't recognize any of the men.

"How do you do it?" The man put a hot iron rod on Miro's back. Miro screamed and wailed in agony.

"There is no ultimate magic," Miro managed, hissing between his teeth.

"We know what you did. Give us the secret." The soldier removed a new poker from the bucket. This time he jabbed it into Miro. Bronwyn averted her gaze. The torturer did as well.

"Kill me and I'll tell you in the underworld," Miro said under his breath and stared at the man intently. Bronwyn smelled his flesh burning and the sound of the water bursting from his skin. She couldn't watch, even in her ghostlike form, so detached from reality.

"Put him away for the night. Maybe he'll be more cooperative tomorrow," the man holding the poker said. He pulled a handkerchief to his nose and gagged. They acted oddly for torturers and Bronwyn didn't know if they were too green, if there was something Miro was doing to them, or if the joy of torture was lost when the prisoner wanted it.

"No!" Miro screamed. "Don't you want to know how I killed them all? Don't you want to know about the ultimate magic? Don't you have the courage to find out?" Bronwyn shifted her body to gaze at his eyes. The tears flowed freely.

"I'm evil—your job is to punish the wicked," Miro called out to them. Bronwyn didn't recognize the eyes she saw, but she understood where they came from.

The interrogators took turns again; one tried to burn his chest but was so overcome by nausea, he dropped the hot knife he held and left the room. Miro was in pain, but it wasn't what these men did to him. He wanted that; he craved it. Bronwyn didn't know if he employed some magic to endure the pain, or if he just welcomed it.

When the torturers could stand it no more, they left. When Miro first told Bronwyn about this room, she thought the white runes were some sort of goodwill measure, but now she realized their real purpose. He told them about it, so they thought they had some type of protection as they did what Miro wanted them to do. One of the men turned around before they locked the door.

"You're tough, but let's see how tough the girl is." The man glanced at the cell behind him. There was the woman, her eyes full of tears, being forced to witness the horrors the soldiers inflicted.

"You even think about touching her, and I'll kill you and everyone you love." This wasn't Miro's voice; this was the voice of the black serpent coming from his body. It echoed off the walls, startling the woman and Miro's torturers. The threatened man retreated a step and tried to offer some protestation but gave up and left without looking back.

Once all the soldiers quit the dungeon, a member of the guard corps came and unlocked Miro and the woman's cell. He looked familiar. Bronwyn realized this must have been Kaleb, the guard that Miro had been so friendly with when he returned to the dungeons with her. Kaleb allowed the woman to heal Miro's wounds. Miro said nothing, only stared at the ground with self-hate as the woman wiped away the ash from burned skin, revealing scars underneath. Perhaps some of that hate was saved for the torturers, but knowing Miro, Bronwyn was sure the majority of it was directed at himself.

Bronwyn wasn't sure how many days she witnessed. The weeks or years blended, becoming routine. One interrogator was always the same, but she noticed a high level of attrition in the craft. Once one left the group, they never came back.

They entered, burned Miro, tried to get him to talk, and Miro tried to get them to continue. At the end of the session, the guard let the woman come in to heal Miro. Bronwyn tried to hear what she said to him when they were together, but it was like listening to a waterfall.

She regretted her previous judgments about Kaleb. He shouldn't be allowing prisoners to visit their cellmates, but his flexibility about the rules probably allowed him to thrive in this position.

One day, Bryant came instead of the torturers. He wasn't wearing the armor he wore when she saw them attacked in Lynnfield. He wore a finely tailored purple tunic, an elegant black velvet cloak with a furred border, and freshly shined boots. *Was this after his brother died? How strange for a king to visit the dungeons as opposed to having a prisoner brought to him for questioning. Does King Bryant know what happened? Is that why he's questioning Miro in the dungeons away from curious ears?*

"Release her. She had no hand in this," Bryant said. Kaleb obeyed and other members started to usher the woman from the room. "She is from Angelis; see to it she is on the next ship headed there."

Bronwyn thought the woman protested, but her words were still unintelligible. King Bryant approached Miro's cell. He knelt and addressed Miro. "I've made sure she is safe. I don't know how much I can do for you."

"As long as she's safe, I don't care what they do to me," Miro said between clenched teeth.

"Tell me what happened. Even I don't know. One minute we were surrounded, the next, everything was gone." King Bryant glanced around to make sure no one was close. "You died, you couldn't have survived that wound, but now here you are. How did you do it?"

Miro hesitated before he said, "It wasn't me. It's some type of creature. It destroyed the entire city in the blink of an eye. We need to find it. We need to kill it."

"We will," King Bryant replied flatly. "But then, why did it spare you? Why us three?"

"Bryant, promise me. Promise me we'll find and destroy it, so something like that never happens again," Miro pleaded with King Bryant then returned to staring at the floor and muttering.

King Bryant sighed and shook his head. "I promise you."

King Bryant left the dungeon while Miro sobbed in a corner.

Bryant the betrayer, Bronwyn thought, remembering Miro's moniker for her king. *Was this the promise that Miro said Bryant failed to honor?*

Finally, they let Miro go. They put him in exile to the north of Emestria, in the inhospitable tundra, likely thinking it was the same as a death sentence. Someone of Miro's power would have little trouble ignoring the command to keep away, but like all the other punishments inflicted on him, he welcomed it.

He subsisted for the first few days eating plants, but grew thin. He started scavenging. The first couple of times he ate a lone small animal that succumbed to the wilderness, but the third time he howled and beat his chest at three Emestrian wolves. They bared their teeth, ready to defend their kill, until he unleashed the first bolt of lightning, and they ran.

Miro camped around those kills for the next week, eating the frozen flesh whenever he hungered. The wolves never risked returning to try and reclaim their meal.

Bronwyn's uneasiness abated when Issaroh came. Miro's state of affairs broke her heart. She tried to interact with him, to soothe him, but she didn't exist in this world. Issaroh at least would be able to try and make him understand. Despite appearing thirty years younger, the way the man walked and wore his beard and hair was the same. She had no doubt this was Issaroh before rapid aging had overtaken him at the end of his life.

Issaroh had failed to accurately explain the condition Miro was in when Issaroh found him. Bronwyn watched the descent from man to animal. Issaroh did his best to reverse the situation. He created a campfire and provided a tent with a bedroll. Issaroh cooked the meat and left it out for Miro to consume. After a few days, Miro allowed Issaroh to dress him in warmer clothes and cut the pine tar from his hair.

It wasn't until the woman returned that Miro started to resemble the person Bronwyn knew. Miro's behavior drastically changed over the course of a week. Issaroh seemed happy to see Miro become his former self but upset that he was unable to coax that from him. With Issaroh, Miro seemed hollow, but with this woman, Miro appeared content. However, Bronwyn could tell the woman exuded a false sense of happiness for Miro's sake. She smiled when she spoke, but always looked on the verge of tears. She and Miro announced their plans to move further north, to make a home for themselves. Issaroh left to return to the library, most likely but told Miro he would visit from time to time.

Bronwyn witnessed the daily pitfalls of their first efforts to make a home. She saw them wrestle with Naani. Every night Naani destroyed what little progress they made in building a cabin. Winter drew near, and they grew desperate.

Miro confronted Naani and worked out an arrangement. Bronwyn always thought of them as fast friends, but even after their agreement, Naani still took out her frustrations on Miro's cabin. Before winter, they managed to complete the house and Naani stopped fighting them at every other opportunity. Naani came by frequently for food or company. Bronwyn wondered how much of Naani's behavior stemmed from the lack of Lynnfield's pilgrimage. The priests of Lynnfield traveled over the Iron Bridge, to Solstice, into the White North, and to the tomb of Alcide's. When Bronwyn had visited, there was a shrine at the base of the mountain.

Now, with the destruction of Lynnfield, there were no more priestly pilgrimages. One of Naani's divine duties was to escort the priests of Lynnfield through the inhospitable White North. That may have been

Naani's only interaction with humanity aside from scaring skittish hunters from her other duty, protecting the western forest of the White North.

Strangely, the next part was the hardest. Miro returned to a form of himself that Bronwyn recognized. He lived a simple life with the woman. They cooked, read, and took walks. Luckily, the wind still made anything they said unintelligible, otherwise it would be unbearable to observe. Bronwyn thought it would make her jealous to watch them kiss and hug, but it saddened her. Because she saw how happy he was, and she knew it wouldn't last.

The woman started to cradle her stomach beneath her hands. Bronwyn tried to close her eyes, tried to wish it away, but she couldn't. Miro sat the woman down to have a conversation and Bronwyn screamed at him to stop. Her voice had no effect. The news upset the woman, but they ended up hugging and falling asleep on their shared bed. Maybe he hadn't told her what she thought he did.

Bronwyn thought about the conversation on the lakeside and Miro's comment about hateful eyes. Then she remembered the dream, the woman falling to her death, and Miro's feeling that he was to blame. Miro would never push someone to their death, which left only one option. The woman threw herself over the cliff. Why else would she, unless she learned something she couldn't live with?

The next morning her concerns were reaffirmed. The Eye would always make you pay for your visions, and so it ensured she heard this conversation.

"Serra, please come back inside." Miro extended a hand as Serra backed away from him.

"How can I go back?" she asked, retreating further.

"I thought you understood. I didn't know what I was doing. I just wanted to protect you," Miro reasoned.

"Is that supposed to make me feel better? You didn't know you were going to kill all those people to save me?" Serra started to retreat from the house in earnest. Bronwyn took this opportunity to swoop down and gaze into Serra's eyes. Despite the horror of the situation, Bronwyn wanted to see the eyes that scared Miro. When she looked into Serra's face, she understood all his reticence. The love, hate, compassion, and contempt all swirled together, and it wasn't just directed at Miro; Serra directed as much toward herself.

"No, it's not supposed to make you feel better. But if I knew, I would have made a different choice. Please, Serra," Miro begged. His voice wavered and his eyes watered.

"If you knew, would you still have done it? All those people, just for me?" Serra continued backing toward the cliff.

"I would have tried to protect everyone!" Miro yelled out to her. He seemed unwilling to rush her. Perhaps he didn't want to startle her, but he needed to get closer if he meant to save her.

"And if you couldn't, if you had to save one person, would you still kill all those people to save one life?" Serra got closer and closer to the edge.

"It's not one life anymore." Miro hurried toward her, breaking into a brisk jog.

"I was never pregnant, I was late and hopeful; now I'm glad that's all it was. I wouldn't want to birth the spawn of a monster." Serra glanced back to the cliff's edge. She stepped back and said, "All those people."

Miro rushed forward. When Serra's arms disappeared over the edge, he dove in after her. His body became encased in the lightning shield Bronwyn had seen before, but she knew how this ended. Serra hit the sea and was pulled under almost immediately. A rogue wave pushed Miro ashore. He sputtered water from his lungs and ran back toward the inky black sea and his Ywaigwai appeared before him once again.

"Foolish boy, do you think yourself able to cheat our bargain so easily?" The booming voice rustled the pine needles and birds flew from their nests.

"Let me die!" Miro grabbed a handful of sand and flung it at the figure.

"You die when I give you permission," the voice echoed off the cliffs and ice as the Ywaigwai disappeared.

Bronwyn jolted awake. Clara was in the bedroll next to her, but it mattered little at this point. She raced out of the tent. She had remained clothed while she slept for this exact situation. Bronwyn grabbed the nearest tree and opened her mouth as the black ooze forced itself from her body.

She never asked Miro about the experience; she thought it akin to vomiting, but it was so much worse. The acidic ooze crawled from her throat, and despite her desire to rid herself of the bile, it would not be rushed. Bronwyn gagged on it repeatedly. She couldn't breathe as it left her, and she worried she would die before it evacuated.

Then a gentle hand rubbed her back, up and down, lightly, and lovingly. The hand on her back sickened her more than the ichor trying to liberate itself. Miro waited for her to finish, for the substance to leave her body, and for her to catch her breath. He walked back to the campfire with her.

He helped her find a seat on a log around the campfire and stayed long enough to make sure she was able to sit up on her own. Then he sat across from her. Only his head was visible above the fire's tips. "Did you find out what you needed to know?" Miro asked, his voice calm and unnerving.

"I don't know what's real." Bronwyn tried to divorce herself from the visions. She wasn't a part of them but somehow, they were her life. She was a witness to everything but had no reason to witness it. Deep down, her reasons sickened her.

"I still have trouble telling the difference between reality and the visions. What did you want to see?" Miro's dispassionate tone put her at ease.

"Your past, so I could demonstrate you deserve forgiveness," Bronwyn said with conviction that quickly waned the moment the words left her lips. Thankfully, the fire obscured her hands from his sight; they shook uncontrollably.

"And what did you see?" Miro asked.

"Lynnfield, you think you caused it. The dungeons, you wanted them to punish you. The cliff and Serra. He wouldn't let you die. What was real?" Bronwyn had been sure once the Eye lifted its veil, she would be okay, but now everything was a blur. She couldn't think straight.

"It's all real. His name is Raithe. The Eye showed you exactly what happened because that was the thing you'd never want to see. I killed them; I wanted them to punish me, and it's my fault she died." Miro stood. Tears welled in his eyes. "And I hoped you would never find out, so I wouldn't have to see someone look at me with those same eyes again."

Miro turned away from her and went back to his tent.

"Wait," Bronwyn called back to him. He turned and she couldn't find the words. A thousand images flew through her head; she tried to compress several months of life into one evening of sleep. The only words her brain allowed her to utter were, "All those people."

They weren't her words; why was she forced to say those words? Those were the words of Serra, the last words she ever spoke to Miro. The most hurtful words he could hear in this situation. She wanted to take them back, but they were out. There was nothing she could do now.

A pained expression crossed Miro's face. "Bronwyn, we've recovered the Horn and Gaebolg. Take those back to Emestria; they should be enough to save them from their current crisis. Defurge and I will continue and find the hammer to unmake his gem. I'm sorry."

Miro knelt in the tent to nudge Defurge awake.

"It's the Eye; I can't think straight. Please, I didn't mean to say it. I didn't mean it." Bronwyn tried to make some sense of the swirling images, words, and sounds around her. The visions were so void of external stimulation; being at their whim now was overpowering.

"It doesn't matter what you say. I never wanted to see those eyes again. I'm sorry." Despite Bronwyn's protestations, Defurge and Miro packed quickly. They took only their bedrolls and tent. Miro asked Defurge to pick up the Eye. He deemed it too dangerous to be left in the hands of Emestria. It hurt Bronwyn to hear him say it, but even more, that he said it to Defurge and not her.

And they left.

Bronwyn remained awake. She cried at first, but eventually, the tears ran out. Clara got up, or maybe she had been up all along but allowed Bronwyn the privacy of her sorrow. Bronwyn announced they had terminated their arrangement with Miro and should make for Emestria post-haste. Clara sat down next to her.

"Clara, is this real?" Bronwyn wanted it to be another vision.

CHAPTER 29

To Bronwyn's relief, Clara didn't ask her what happened. It had been two days, and Clara had yet to bring it up. Bronwyn appreciated that Clara was giving her time. They traveled east to find a road that led to Newtonne. From there, they would find a crew to take them back to Emestria. On several occasions, Bronwyn suggested they walk to give the horse a break.

Her excuse, to give the animal some rest, was flimsy; carrying her and Clara would cause little exertion. Bronwyn found herself drawn between wanting to get home, to share in her people's joy when she delivered the Horn of Garanhir, and lingering and returning slowly. Part of her knew every step she took in this direction made Miro's separation more permanent.

By the afternoon of the second day, they had barely traveled more than they normally would in a single day. Clara tried to occupy her time with reading or talking to Ferdinand when they stopped, but Bronwyn knew that eventually, she'd start asking questions.

"Once we arrive in Emestria, do you think King Bryant will return my ancestor's cloak?" Clara asked, breaking their silence. The Mantle of Alcide's was an important relic to Clara's people. So important that they hid it before the destruction of Lynnfield. It now resided in Emestria's royal vault, one country that had contributed to the events that Miro felt himself responsible for.

"I don't know," Bronwyn replied despondently.

"I hope he does. It would have come in handy with the spiderions. If I was wearing Alcide's Mantle, that bug wouldn't have been able to sting me." Spiderions was the term Clara was using to describe the arachnids encountered on the mountain.

"Don't you think the cloak is a little big?" Bronwyn sat back and stoked the fire she created. They still had several hours of daylight left, but she had decided to stop here for the night.

"I could bunch it up around the shoulders or tie it off at the bottom, so it doesn't drag. I would figure out some way to make it work," Clara said, her voice a little hostile.

Bronwyn stared at the fire, watching it grow for the next five minutes before she spoke up again, "You're pretty well known in Newtonne, right?"

"I have a reputation; people know me or know someone who knows me. Why do you ask?"

"If you put the word out that you were looking for someone, and if they showed up, to pass them a message, could you do that?" Bronwyn turned to Clara. The expression on her face was halfway between hope and sorrow.

"I can put word in with the inn and barkeeps to pass a message to me if they arrive. We don't have to wait till we reach Newtonne. Ferdinand should be able to find them. I can ask where they are going." Bronwyn was glad she decided to hold off on sending Ferdinand with another missive to King Bryant. It would be so much better to deliver the news and artifacts at the same time.

"No, he doesn't want to hear from me. I can't force him to listen ...."

Clara took a deep breath before asking, "Can you tell me what happened without giving me details?"

Clara broke Bronwyn's dam and it all started to pour out. "I shouldn't have done it. I thought if he knew I didn't care about his past, he could forgive himself. I watched him from the battle of Lynnfield for months, until ..." Bronwyn's face whitened, remembering the woman falling to her death, and Miro jumping off to join her. Tears welled in Bronwyn's eyes. "She killed herself. She called him a monster for what he did. She blamed him for everything."

"Bronwyn, please stop."

Bronwyn spoke quickly, her words almost blending together, "He loved her, and she said she loved him, but what she did. He jumped after her; I don't know whether to join or save her, but he didn't hesitate. But that thing, his Ywaigwai stopped him. And he blames himself because that's what it wants. He blames himself for everything."

"Bronwyn, please," Clara said desperately.

"He had no choice. It wanted to punish him." Bronwyn rambled. "He told me about the look in her eyes; that he never wanted to see it again and that morning he said I had the same eyes. It's not his fault; he didn't mean to—"

"Stop!" Clara yelled and Bronwyn finally began to compose herself. "It was a mistake using the Eye. I tried to warn you against it, but I understood you felt like you needed to and that there would be no stopping you."

Bronwyn peered at Clara meekly, like a scolded child.

"I'm sorry," Bronwyn muttered before turning back to the fire and tossing the stick into the flame.

"It's only been a couple of days; for all you know, they are on their way back to find us. And if they aren't, well, that's for the best. We make mistakes and we learn from them. We'll go to Emestria, we'll return the artifacts, help the people, and we can decide what to do next." Bronwyn forced a smile, and Clara un-balled her fist and wiped away the pooled tear at the corner of her eye.

"I'm going to try and do some hunting, see if I can get us some game to eat tonight," Bronwyn said. That should take her mind off everything.

Bronwyn returned from her hunt empty-handed. She had neglected her duties the last couple of days, so their fresh meat was scarce. They restocked in Loughlin, free of charge due to their heroism, but didn't want to deprive the citizens of much-needed resources, so they only took what they thought they needed for the next week.

Bronwyn planned on supplementing the produce with game, but she hadn't set snares or hunted since the Eye. Ferdinand had little luck as well; the area was strangely devoid of wildlife—except for crows. Ferdinand must be equally upset at Miro's departure because he had returned to his habit of killing crows. Maybe they would stay here tomorrow to hunt in earnest or move slowly while looking for signs of game.

Bronwyn handed out some hardtack. Tomorrow, they would focus on procuring food.

She planned to stop in towns on their way to Newtonne and buy more supplies; Ferdinand had returned with money from King Bryant on his last trip. There was a nearby stream, and they had plenty of water to fill their wineskins. Hydration was more important than sustenance.

Bronwyn jolted upright at the sound of the leaves rustling and a branch snapping; her heart jumped. *Has Miro returned?* But when she heard more footsteps, she realized several people approached. She put her hand to her sword hilt and turned to face the sound. They were still far off; their silhouettes barely visible, moving through the trees.

"Hello there," a man called out. The party continued to advance on their position. Bronwyn counted five, one with a bundle of something strung over his shoulders. He was tall, close to seven feet, and heavily built, obviously Selunian. Only Selunians grew to those proportions.

"What's your business?" Bronwyn asked, her hand still on her sword.

"I'm sorry to bother you," a woman's voice answered. "We were hunting and got separated from our horses, then two of us took a tumble in the water and lost our flint. Would you mind if we borrowed your campfire for a while? We have food we can share."

Bronwyn let them continue to approach without answering. There were two more men, one about six-foot of average build, and the other a portly man a little over five-foot-two. Two women with thin figures and long hair made up the rest of the group. Despite the Selunian's girth, he moved with determination and long strides to keep up with the others.

"Come closer, into the light." Bronwyn needed more information before making her decision. Clara stood, picking her axe up off the ground.

They were lightly armed: one of the men had a sword, the shorter man and one of the women carried bows, the other woman had a pair of daggers, and the Selunian had a bola tied to his waste. The bulge on his shoulders was a young boar they must have hunted. They all carried packs, most likely gear for tents.

The fact there were two women was comforting. She would have refused a group of only men outright. Now, she considered allowing them to join.

The average man and one of the women were only wearing light leather and tunics. He was bald and she had light brown hair.

The other woman was in a flowing garment that reminded her of a dress, only it was split at the legs to allow for movement, almost like the Shi'en's guards' robes. Her hair was black and straight, and her skin was slightly tanned. Water still dripped from her hair and her dress clung to her thin frame.

The Selunian wore a pair of loose-fitting pants and a tunic, his bronze skin a stark contrast to the others. His head was mostly shaved; a long knot of his black hair was braided and extended down his back.

They had no country's insignia on them. The other four didn't have any distinguishing characteristics to identify them as belonging to any nation. No bright red hair common in Rouke, pink hair common in what used to be Lynnfield, or blonde hair common in Corinthe.

The man with the sword and the woman in the dress shivered, their clothes soaked from when they fell in the stream and lost the flint.

"We won't be any trouble," The woman with the light-brown hair addressed Bronwyn but glanced toward Clara as well. "We'll set up camp away from you after we borrow some of your fire. We're hungry and we still have to gut and clean the boar before cooking. We're running short on daylight. Please?"

"The company and food would be welcome," Bronwyn said. *When did I become so untrusting of others? Am I like all the other Emestrians, afraid of outsiders? They appear harmless, and their story matches up with their current state of affairs. If they meant any ill will, they wouldn't have introduced themselves; they would have tried to take us by surprise.*

"Yes, that's great," the soaked woman responded.

The brown-haired woman said to two of the men, "You two clean the boar." The short man and Selunian nodded in assent before walking to the nearby stream with the boar.

The brown-haired woman then turned her attention to her two-soaked compatriots, "Dry out by the fire. Wouldn't want you two to catch a chill."

The soaked woman took the arm of the man who was also soaked and led him to the fire. They whispered to each other before she gave him a quick peck on the cheek. The simple act infuriated Bronwyn, but she did her best to hide the frustration. Miro and she never shared kisses, but what they did share was now ruined. Watching two strangers' affection was just a bitter reminder of how much she had screwed up.

"Where are you from?" Bronwyn asked.

"Everywhere," said the brown-haired woman.

The other woman put her hands above the fire, warming them, and said, "My name is Tsumi and this is Jeremiah. He's from Corinthe, a small town, not the capital. I'm from Selunia."

"And I'm Amber," the brown-haired woman said. "The short guy over there is Frank; he's from a town on the outskirts of Tara and Rouke, claiming allegiance to neither nation."

Tsumi said, "The big guy is also Selunian but from a different isle than me."

Bronwyn got the impression that the two women were battling to see who would convey information. Amber opened her mouth to say something, but Tsumi's voice from the fire cut through the quiet of the night.

"Are you from Emestria?" Tsumi asked.

Surprised, Bronwyn responded, "How did you know?"

"The claw and horns," Tsumi pointed at Bronwyn's pauldrons. Bronwyn had donned them this morning, trying to foster excitement about returning to Emestria. She thought wearing her captain's regalia would spur a more agreeable mood, but the uniform did little to satiate her unease. She had forgotten that she was wearing them.

"Yes," Bronwyn replied dismissing her apprehension. "I'm Bronwyn, and this is Clara."

"I'm from Newtonne," Clara said. "Grew up in Corinthe, but born in Lynnfield. You could say I've been all over the north." Clara got up to shake Tsumi and Jeremiah's hands.

"Did you two meet in Corinthe?" Jeremiah asked.

"I've never been." In truth, Bronwyn had never been to any of the places these people mentioned.

"Oh, but surely your parents were?" Jeremiah asked.

"No, they were born and raised in Emestria as well, as were my grandparents and as far back as I know." That was true of most Emestrians.

"But your hair," Jeremiah said. Tsumi playfully slapped him.

"I told you so," Tsumi said. "Jeremiah thinks anybody with blonde hair must be from Corinthe, I told him that's an old wives' tale. Anyway, her hair isn't blonde; it's more of a gold."

Jeremiah shrugged.

Was that what their quiet conversation by the fire was about? Bronwyn pondered.

"Well, you ladies are in for a treat," Amber said, pivoting the conversation. "That's not any boar; it's a lowland razorback. The sweetest meat you'll ever taste. They're a delicacy. Our plan was to sell it, but we only managed to get a runt; their meat is not the best. No bother though, we found their den and will be able to hunt some more when we've got our horses. Isn't that right?"

"Those boars won't know what hit them," Tsumi said, extending her hand to Jeremiah's and gripping it firmly.

"Do you hunt in this area? I tried to find some game, but the land is bereft of anything worth hunting." Bronwyn hoped a tip or two would assist her with finding a meal in the morning.

"It's the boars," Amber said. "They're highly aggressive and will go to great lengths to chase other animals out of their territory. They'll soil edible plants to deter other animals from entering. That's how we found them. But we don't usually hunt in this area; we followed a tip."

"Where do you hunt?" Bronwyn asked. "Do you live in a nearby town?" Clara had coin to purchase food if hunting was fruitless.

"We left a town three days ago to the north," Amber said. "But we don't have a regular hunting ground. We travel around, trying to find rare delicacies that will either fetch a high price or taste them for ourselves—more often than not, both."

"I can't say I've ever met an Emestrian before," Jeremiah said. "I thought your kind didn't venture south too often."

"We don't go into the greater world much, but I'm on a diplomatic mission." Bronwyn didn't want to reveal their true purpose; it might draw undue attention, or she might have to go into a long explanation about what a Legendary Artifact is. She didn't have the energy, even if Amber seemed easy to talk to. "Emestria wants to re-establish diplomatic ties with its former allies."

"Small group for diplomats," Jeremiah said.

"Don't be rude," Amber chastised. "Emestria and Rouke are at each other's throats. They probably couldn't spare a large cadre or sneak them out."

Jeremiah hung his head but brought it back up, flashing Tsumi a smile. Tsumi laughed and giggled sharply. Their behavior didn't bother Bronwyn anymore, it was so innocent and casual.

They sat around the campfire and told stories as the boar cooked. The hunters relished telling Bronwyn and Clara tales they likely rehearsed over and over. The pacing and details were so well-versed, that Bronwyn had little doubt they shared these stories anytime they borrowed a campfire.

Amber dominated the conversation, but the others' personalities were on display as well. Jeremiah and Tsumi didn't talk much, but whenever Bronwyn glanced over, their arms were either entwined or they were gifting each other with little pecks on the lips. Enele seemed to be a little slow on the uptake of their jokes. Perhaps because the puns weren't in his native tongue, but when he got the joke, he let out a ridiculous guffaw, sometimes minutes after everyone else finished laughing. Frank sat next to Clara and devoted all his attention to her. Clara placated his niceties but did not introduce new topics of conversation or encourage his compliments. To his credit, Frank wasn't overly aggressive and got the hint, turning his attention to more friendly matters.

After Newtonne, Miro had expounded at length on the charm and chiseled features of Clara's captain, Atien. A tall dashing figure with long black locks and a roguish smile. Frank couldn't hold a candle to a man like that.

As the meal progressed, Tsumi's and Jeremiah's affection seemed to wane. At times, Bronwyn found Tsumi staring into the fire distantly, picking at her meal. Jeremiah didn't try and lull her out of these bouts of seriousness, and the others seemed to ignore it as well.

At first, Bronwyn hesitated to eat much of the boar, not wanting to waste food considered such a delicacy. Clara shared her apprehension, and they only relented and started to enjoy the dinner after the third time Amber insisted they eat more.

Plenty of fat was marbled into the muscle. The meat fell off the bone and melted in the mouth. Although not seasoned, the meal tasted salty. Amber had them sample cuts from all different parts of the animal, explaining in detail what type of dishes they were used for and how best to cook them for the full experience.

"Well, thank you for your fire," Amber said after most of the meat was gone and the conversation died down. "We're going to go make camp about a half mile away. Can we grab one of your sticks for a torch?" Amber knelt and picked up a healthy piece of wood, about half an inch in diameter and two feet long.

"That's alright; you can set up here," Bronwyn offered. She would enjoy having them around in the morning. If they were headed in the same direction, they all could travel together. This was the first time in days that thoughts of Miro, or the Eye, hadn't consumed all her attention. "We only have one tent, so there is plenty of room."

"Really?" Amber asked. "Thank you, knowing my luck I was going to trip and light the whole countryside on fire."

Tsumi and Jeremiah chuckled.

Once the tents were all erected, they split up the watch, and everyone except Amber and Bronwyn headed to their respective tents. They decided on two people per shift, to break up the monotony. Bronwyn had no doubt these people bored easily. She was glad she shared her shift with Amber.

"Are you sure you don't want any more?" Amber held up another chunk of boar for Bronwyn. "The meat will be cold and bland in the morning. It only tastes good right after it's cooked."

Stuffed, Bronwyn shook her head.

"Okay." Amber took the piece and placed it on her plate and sat down next to Bronwyn.

"I'm grateful for the meal. I think I'll have to try to find a city with lowland razorback on the menu sometime in the future," Bronwyn said. She was curious ever since Amber described all the dishes. She wanted to try more than roast boar.

Amber said, "Some of the major islands in Selunia serve the meal regularly. You might find some restaurants in Angelis that are more creative with their preparation."

Bronwyn sighed and felt the weight of the day on her shoulders. Angelis was the capital of Corinthe, and Miro must be heading there now. She enjoyed the company, but now that the livelihood had died down, she was left with the same thoughts that had tortured her for the last couple of days.

"Oh honey, what's wrong?" Amber asked, turning to face Bronwyn. Bronwyn was sure she wasn't crying; maybe she was frowning?

"It's nothing. It's been a rough couple of days, and it was nice having some company."

"That's not it; I know that face. It's a man, isn't it?"

Bronwyn couldn't help herself; the tears welled in her icy-blue eyes. She wasn't used to being this emotional, but something about a stranger reading the sorrow off her face was devastating.

"Here, have a drink of this and tell me what's bothering you." Amber took two cups, tossed the contents, and refilled them with a dark red wine. She handed one to Bronwyn and took a sip of the other.

"I don't know." Bronwyn took a healthy quaff of the wine. It was surprisingly bitter, with a strong aftertaste Bronwyn didn't quite agree with.

"Hey, it's okay. The right one's out there for you." Amber brought her hand up to Bronwyn's back and gently rubbed it.

Bronwyn shuddered. It was too close of a reminder of how Miro touched her whenever she was nauseous.

"Oh sweetie," Amber consoled her. "Did he cheat?"

"No, no, it's something I did." Bronwyn drank more to prevent herself from continuing to babble and reveal everything.

"I was married once, and I thought he was the salve to heal my soul, but it wasn't meant to be. If there is the right one out there for you, it's not the one that makes you feel this way. You'll meet someone that ignites your soul and brings out the best in you."

"It was never like that. I'm not some damsel waiting for someone to give my life meaning. I am the captain of the Emestrian Guardcorps. Yet, when I was with him, it just felt like I could be both people for once." Bronwyn shuddered again, shaking off a strange feeling in her limbs. "I don't know why I'm saying all this."

"Sometimes you need to tell someone. It's easier to tell a stranger." Amber grinned.

Although Amber seemed to have the same amount of grey in her hair as Clara, there was something different about the way Amber spoke to her.

Despite her age, Clara seemed to be a free spirit, untethered in life and enjoying whatever she wanted. In a way, Bronwyn felt that she had more responsibilities than Clara and acted more maturely. But this woman, despite a lifestyle of going where she wanted and doing what she pleased, was mature and caring. Bronwyn did not doubt that if she leaned her head against Amber's shoulder, the woman's only concern would be to make Bronwyn feel safe.

Bronwyn rubbed her eyes. The firelight caused them to throb, and her eyelids were heavy. "I'm sorry, I'm not feeling so well."

"It's the wine; Taran wine is strong," Amber reassured her. "Why don't you lie down? I can finish the rest of the watch myself."

"No, I'm all right …." Bronwyn tried to protest, but her vision blurred. *This doesn't make sense, even if the wine is strong, I grew up drinking spirits. I only drank a cup of wine; I can effortlessly down three or four cups of spirits before feeling the effects.*

"I should …" Bronwyn stood but her legs were heavy, and she swayed as she tried to maintain her balance. She turned to look at Amber. A wicked smile crossed Amber's face, betraying her character.

Bronwyn spun back around to grab her sword. She had propped it against the tent. Her equilibrium failed and she fell to the ground. She attempted to cushion her fall, but when she hit, a cloud of dust erupted into the air. She struggled to stay awake and began crawling to her sword as her vision darkened.

"Thank the gods. That took forever," Amber complained.

"Is she down?" Jeremiah asked before Bronwyn slipped away.

CHAPTER 30

BRONWYN WOKE TO Ferdinand's incessant screeching. Her head throbbed, and she went to right herself to find a small pebble to toss in his direction to indicate her annoyance and quiet him. She was unable to; ropes pinned her arms, ankles, and thighs. She opened her eyes; she was still on the ground in the cold dirt. It was daylight. Fifteen feet away from her, also bound but propped up, Clara knelt with a gag in her mouth.

"This one is Gaebolg, but I don't know what the other is called," Tsumi's voice uttered from somewhere in front of her, maybe Clara and Bronwyn's tent. "I would hazard that it is also an artifact, just something about the feel and energy of it."

There was something utterly wrong. Bronwyn had surely been slipped something in her drink, and there was no reason for hunters to be knowledgeable about Legendary Artifacts.

"Gaebolg?" Jeremiah asked. "What's that supposed to do?"

"A spear with the ability to kill anything it cuts," Tsumi responded. "Why don't I give you a little nick and see what it can do?"

Jeremiah cackled. "But we have such better subjects to experiment on."

Bronwyn glanced at Jeremiah with half-lidded eyes. He looked at Clara with a predator's intensity. Tsumi parted the flap of Clara and Bronwyn's shared tent, emerging with Gaebolg in one hand and the Horn of Garanhir in the other.

The previous night, Bronwyn had failed to properly notice the hood of Tsumi's dress. Hoods were so common in Emestria, a way to keep the biting wind off the face, but in the rest of Primerra, hoods meant something very specific: the wearer knew magic. With Tsumi's offhand knowledge of Legendary Artifacts, and her dark, shaded eyes underneath the hood, the serious stares she gave the fire took on a new light. These people weren't random travelers that happened upon them. They were also hunting artifacts.

But no, if they were hunting artifacts, how would they have known to track down Bronwyn and Clara? The only remaining possibility would be that Rouke had found out about the recovery of Alcide's Mantle and learned of Emestria's desire to procure more artifacts to win the war. A traitor must have known about Bronwyn's mission and conveyed where she was headed. Of course, Rouke would send spies that weren't easily recognizable as belonging to their nation.

Jeremiah turned to Bronwyn, and she shut her eyes. She wanted to feign sleep and uncover more information, but whatever they had dosed her with slowed her reactions.

"She's awake," Jeremiah told the others.

"Get her up." The honeyed sweetness of Amber's voice was absent.

A heavy hand gripped the ropes around Bronwyn's arms from behind. Enele picked her up with little effort and Bronwyn struggled to maneuver her feet underneath her body, to rocket up and slam her head into his chest or chin. He held firm and she was only able to kneel; the position didn't provide enough leverage, but she tried. His strong arms prevented her from making any headway.

"If you want the artifacts, take them and go," Bronwyn said. She tested the ropes' strength, pulling her wrists away from each other. These strangers knew she was Emestrian, but could they have expected her to be a full-blooded Emestrian? With the give in the ropes, Bronwyn knew they hadn't factored in how strong the demigods' blood might have been in her line. As she stretched the ropes, feeling them on the verge of snapping, she caught Clara's eye, who gave a subdued shake of her head. It wasn't time to try and escape with Tsumi holding a weapon that could kill with a single strike.

Amber approached and knelt, leveling her eyes to Bronwyn's. Amber spoke calmly, "We'll take the artifacts, but that's not why we're here. I told you a lot of lies last night, but the one thing I didn't lie about is that we are hunters. We hunt demons, not animals."

Bronwyn struggled to make the connection.

"Magi," Amber said with disdain.

The thought of rival artifact-hunting parties dissipated quickly in Bronwyn's mind as she absorbed the new information. They knew about Miro.

"What's a magi?" Bronwyn feigned ignorance. Perhaps she could convince them she didn't know what they were talking about.

"We're both busy women; let's not play this game," Amber said. "You've been traveling with one. We know he has you under his spell. I saw you two at the hot springs."

"He's only a magic knight," Bronwyn bluffed, using the preferred term for a magic user from Emestria.

"A magic knight that can cast time, ice, and lightning magic?" Amber asked. "Don't make the mistake of thinking we're dumb."

Bronwyn thought back on the only time Miro used time magic, when they fought the crocodile. Up until now, the memory seemed so private; Miro had stopped time and only he and she knew what happened in that moment. But now, there had been interlopers that invaded that space. *So, they've been watching us for a while. Had they been there the whole time? They couldn't. I would have seen a campfire, or Defurge would have sensed it. They must have tracked us. There was a chance they hadn't seen everything.*

"I cast the ice magic, the other man cast the time magic, and the one you're calling a magi cast the lightning. You've got the wrong people." Bronwyn knew they wouldn't believe her, but the longer she kept them talking, the more information they would reveal.

"Stop playing dumb. She told us everything." Amber motioned toward Clara.

"Bronwyn, don't—" Clara's muffled voice was clear enough despite the gag. Frank clapped his hand over her mouth. Bronwyn didn't like the way Frank touched her. It put sinister tones to his advances the night before. *How did they capture Clara? She didn't drink any of the wine.*

"Keep her quiet," Amber seethed before returning her attention to Bronwyn. "I understand you; I do. I know that even your thoughts have been polluted and twisted. You can't admit this to yourself, but it feels impossible to even think a negative thought about your magus. I know because I was you.

"I thought my former husband was different." The sweet, charming way Amber spoke last night returned. "When I first met him, I thought him a pompous buffoon, but during our second meeting, he told me how charming he was, and I suddenly saw him that way. For a normal sorcerer, a charm spell has little use; the subject knows they've been entranced because they see the sigils and hear the incantation. A magus that is attuned enough with their powers only needs to mutter the name of the spell."

Bronwyn bit back the doubt as the words stewed. *No, Miro can't cast magic on me. He demonstrated how I'm immune to magic on several occasions.* But then thoughts of wanting to join him in the bed when he was injured resurfaced. The action didn't seem like her, but Miro was incapacitated when she made that decision. He was barely alive; how could he have cast magic on her?

"I don't know where he's going and if I did, I would never tell you." Bronwyn debated spitting in Amber's face, but she didn't want her angry—yet. She had to figure out the dynamic.

Amber shook her head and sighed. "I know how this looks. If there was another more straightforward way, I would prefer that."

Bronwyn hissed, "Keep your speeches to yourself; I have no interest in hearing them."

Amber stood, paced in a tight circle, then knelt back down next to Bronwyn. "We're not your enemy." Amber pulled up her sleeve, showing a branded italicized "M". "This is the mark of our organization; once we've neutralized the threat, we'll give you the option of receiving your own. If you're like me, you'll realize that what we're doing here today is necessary. When you show that mark around, you'll be brought before the group to pledge your sword to our cause."

"You're delusional if you think I'd let you touch me. And if I ever come looking for you and your ilk, it will be to put you on a funeral pyre."

"I told you she wouldn't listen to reason," Tsumi said.

"I'm handling this," Amber replied.

"No, you're talking her to death," Tsumi said. "If she's really under a spell like you think, there is nothing you can say that will matter. If a spell is broken with the magus' death, then will be the time for explanations."

"Give me a moment," Amber snapped, turning back to Bronwyn. The tension between the two was veiled but their tone indicated it was sharp.

"You know what this magus did. Do you know what we call the magus you've been charmed by? We call him the Bane of Lynnfield."

Bronwyn looked at Clara, trying to gauge what level of reactions she was having. At this point, Bronwyn was sure Clara had heard enough to know Miro had some hand in the destruction of Lynnfield. Clara averted her gaze. "That wasn't his fault."

"May not have been what he wished of his Ywaigwai, but it was what his wish wrought. The Ywaigwai need energy to survive. At one point, we thought just the soul of the magus was what sustained them, but then why did the magus live so long? Ywaigwai feed off pain as well. Eventually, the pain of what your magus caused will fade, and then he will need to feed his master new pain to ensure his survival."

There was no doubt in Bronwyn's words as she responded, "Miro would never hurt anyone else to save himself. If you've followed us for so long, surely you saw what he did in Laughlin."

"True, your magus seems to have a savior complex, but in a hundred, two hundred, three hundred years, will he still make the same choices? Will he choose to sacrifice his existence, or maybe he'll decide that he's immortal and that mortals live such short lives, so what does it matter if it's only a couple of years shorter?"

Bronwyn thought of Issaroh. When they first met Miro's mentor, Miro indicated Issaroh had aged rapidly in the few years since they had last seen each other. Had Issaroh discovered that his Ywaigwai required pain to feed off? Did Issaroh choose to end his immortal life rather than extend his own? There was no doubt in Bronwyn's mind that Miro would make the same choice.

Bronwyn locked her eyes fiercely onto Amber's "He would never."

"Enough of this, Amber," Tsumi said, giving Gaebolg a triad of practice swings as Jeremiah looked on enviously. "Let's get on with it."

"Yes, let's," Jeremiah said. "I believe it's my turn; you've gotten to take the last three."

Amber stood and walked off to the side, looking out to the horizon.

"Yes, but you had four in a row before that," Tsumi argued.

"You said that if I let you do the last one, the next would be mine," Jeremiah replied.

Bronwyn looked to Amber, trying to determine what exactly this argument was about. Amber still stood facing away, not reacting to the conversation. Nerves prickled along Bronwyn's spine.

"I don't care who does it. Just keep it quiet," Amber said flatly.

Bronwyn darted her vision between the other hunters. Frank nodded and started to walk in her direction. Jeremiah turned toward the fire, where Bronwyn now realized a dagger had been set in the coals. Tsumi stared with intensity at Jeremiah, then Bronwyn. Behind her, Enele stared forward, not looking down at the woman's ropes he held. As Frank walked closer, he began to pull a strip of cloth similar to the one currently gagging Clara.

"What are you …." the rest of the words died in Bronwyn's throat as she watched Jeremiah reach down and pull the dagger up. The blade was red hot. Bronwyn looked toward Clara, who didn't shake her head this time.

Bronwyn pushed up on her knees at the same time as she pulled her wrists apart. At first, she thought the ropes would hold, but as Jeremiah turned toward her with a wicked gleam in his eyes, her adrenaline spiked. The ropes snapped, her wrists finally free. Enele gasped as the ropes around her arms were the next to give.

"Grab her!" Frank yelled. Amber turned with saucer eyes as Bronwyn thrust her right leg forward, breaking the ropes around her knees.

Her first step was clumsy, but her second was determined. Bronwyn pointed her momentum toward Tsumi, Gaebolg in her hands. In the periphery, Clara rolled to the side, struggling to free herself. Bronwyn focused intently on Gaebolg, judging Tsumi's reaction speed and planning where to grab the spear's haft.

Frank and Jeremiah seemed to be frozen in time as Bronwyn dashed. She grabbed the bottom of the haft with her left hand, and as she reached out with her right, she felt a firm tug on her right wrist. With her one hand still gripping Gaebolg's haft, Bronwyn glanced behind her. The remnants of her bindings trailed behind, except for one, which was taught and gripped firmly in Enele's hand. Bronwyn yanked her right arm. Enele stumbled forward, but it still wasn't enough to grab Gaebolg with her right hand.

Jeremiah dropped the dagger, and rushed toward Bronwyn, wrapping his arms around her waist from behind. A second weight followed soon after, probably Frank.

As Enele grabbed the rope with his left hand, Bronwyn pulled Gaebolg with her left, trying to leverage the spear's edge toward Tsumi's head. Tsumi ducked, causing the spear's head to sail over hers, but it put Bronwyn off balance. Between trying to grab the spear, having Enele tugging on her wrist, and the added weight of Jeremiah and Frank on her back, Bronwyn faltered, falling to the ground and losing her grip on Gaebolg.

On the ground, Bronwyn scrabbled to try and right herself, but Jeremiah and Frank held her firmly and a third weight pressed upon her head, pinning her.

"No!" Bronwyn yelled, kicking out with her feet, the only part of her body not currently constrained.

"I told you to use double ropes," Amber's voice pierced the cacophony of grunts of exertion to keep Bronwyn pinned.

"I did," Frank grumbled "Jeremiah screwed up the knots."

"Your ropes were old," Jeremiah complained.

"Enough," Amber said. "Just get her over to the stump."

A fourth set of hands joined in hauling Bronwyn. As she thrashed and writhed, she caught a glimpse of Ferdinand flying down to Clara, hopefully trying to break her bindings. Bronwyn managed to get her left hand free as both Frank and Jeremiah tried to pull it behind her back. When she looked back to Clara, her view was obscured by the skirt of Tsumi's hooded dress. Bronwyn had enough time to look up at Tsumi as the butt of Gaebolg smashed down onto her temple.

Stars and blackness exploded across Bronwyn's vision immediately accompanied by ear-splitting ringing. The blackness didn't disappear when she reopened her eyes, so she didn't see the second strike. Dizzy, the voices and movements around her became fuzzy, indistinct.

A man's voice cut through the din in a sing-song way, like he was reciting a nursery rhyme. "Five little soldiers went off to war, four came back bloody and sore."

Bronwyn lacked the strength, or she was too well-pinned at this point; sensations were difficult to concentrate on. But then. one sensation cut through the rest, something sharp on the back of her hand.

"This one fought straight and true."

With each syllable the tip of what she thought was the dagger pressed against her fingers, one by one. There was pressure with each touch, but not enough to pierce, Bronwyn hoped. Bronwyn concentrated on the only thought that came easily: how she'd kill each one of these so-called hunters. She hadn't seen her sword or Clara's axe, so she'd need to use the weapons she had seen the previous night.

"This one deserted and was beaten black and blue."

Amber's daggers stabbed under her rib cage, piercing her diaphragm and making breathing impossible.

"This one killed the general and won a king's ransom."

An arrow in Frank's eye socket.

"This one scarred and no longer handsome."

The bola around Enele's waist wrapped around his neck till his face purpled.

"But this poor sod never came home."

Gaebolg thrust slowly through both Tsumi and Jeremiah's hearts at the same time, their bodies commingling into a crystallized monument to pain.

"He died on the torturers rack."

Jeremiah said, "Screw it, I'll just take the thumb."

"No," Amber's voice pierced Bronwyn's fantasy. "Jerund was clear that one be able to still fight after this is all done with. She'll be an asset once she's out from under the magus' spell."

Breath was hot in her ear as Jeremiah whispered, "If she let me take the thumb, I would have made it quick. Now I'm going to make it hurt as much as possible."

Her pinky was grabbed roughly, and Bronwyn tried to pull it away, but her wrist was pinned against the hardwood beneath her hand. The first rake of the serrated blade brought Bronwyn's vision back into focus. With a sadistic grin, Jeremiah pressed and sawed more of her pinky's flesh.

"No," Bronwyn screamed, her stomach seizing at the sight.

"Let's see you swing that sword missing one of these," Jeremiah said as he pulled the dagger back. The pain was a thousandfold as it splintered bone.

"No," Bronwyn futilely repeated as she closed her eyes to the pain. This Jerund, someone they must all answer to, beaten to death with the skulls of the hunters he made the mistake of sending after her.

When the dagger broke the last of the bone, the remainder of the meat of her digit was severed cleanly as the force used to cut hard tissue pressed through the rest of her soft. Vomit rose in Bronwyn's throat as spurts of blood pooled against the blade's heel. Bronwyn gagged as she retched, causing Jeremiah to quickly retreat before gagging himself. The coppery tang of the blood pooling on the stump was quickly overpowered by the acrid stench of bile. A second spurt of vomit spewed the remainder of the rotten boar from the previous night as Bronwyn lost consciousness.

Bronwyn came to with Enele's meaty palms pulling her to something sturdy to lean back against. She felt heavier, and as she looked down, she saw thick chains wrapped around her body. Her teeth were fuzzy and her mouth rancid. Amber stood in front of her with a wineskin in one hand and a wet rag in the other.

Bronwyn winced as Amber dabbed at her temple then wiped down her cheek. The cloth came away stained a reddish pink.

"I'm going to kill you all," Bronwyn said.

"Here, wash your mouth out with this," Amber said, bringing the wineskin to Bronwyn's lips.

Bronwyn turned her head away. "I'm not touching a drop of your poisoned wine."

Amber chuckled. "It's water. Have it your way if you want that taste in your mouth all day and night."

"I'll manage," Bronwyn said, turning her head to scan for Clara. At first, she thought Clara had escaped, that all the hunters subduing Bronwyn would have given Ferdinand time to peck through Clara's ropes, but as Frank shifted, Bronwyn saw Clara flanked by Jeremiah and Tsumi.

"We should cut some of her fingers as well," Tsumi said. "Give the magus a whole pouch full."

"Wait until I've had my fun," Frank said, leering and turning around to face Clara.

Amber took the wineskin away from Bronwyn's lips and turned to Tsumi. "No, I made a deal with that one."

Clara gave them the information they wanted in exchange for her safety, Bronwyn thought. She didn't blame Clara; if Bronwyn weren't Emestrian, she might have made the same deal. After all, when Miro arrived, he would have something with him these hunters would never expect: the former god of fire and madness.

"Oh pooh, pooh," Tsumi said. "We can't kill the blonde one, we can't have fun with the little one. This is boring."

"If one of you three touches a hair on her head, Enele will mete out three times the punishment on you," Amber bit back.

"Leave her alone," Enele's voice boomed. The three other hunters took a step back from Clara.

"You'll never find him," Bronwyn said. "He's long gone."

"Why do you think we followed you and not the other two?" Amber smiled and seemed happy. "Magi are hard to kill, but not impossible. Usually, we wait for them to enter their curse and neutralize them, but your magus, he has ... self-control."

Amber rose confidently before continuing, "We will send your feathered friend over there with a message your lover can't ignore. Either he returns, and we end his cursed existence, or he doesn't, and you realize you meant nothing and then help us hunt the magus down."

"When he sees what we've done to you, he will lose control and it will be all over for him," Jeremiah said.

Amber took Bronwyn's severed finger, placed it in a small leather pouch, and cinched the pouch shut. She also removed a small container, the type Clara would roll her missives into and affix to Ferdinand's leg.

"Get it down here," Amber told Clara.

Ferdinand's voice was sometimes drowned out by the commotion, but he now fluffed his feathers and made more of a ruckus as the attention turned toward him.

"Ferdinand, come down," Clara pleaded half-heartedly. Ferdinand screeched back in reply and shifted his weight on the branch, scratching the bark with his talons.

"I'll do it," Jeremiah said in frustration approaching the bird. He tried to grip the falcon's feet, but Ferdinand dug his razor-sharp beak into

Jeremiah's thumb. Jeremiah screamed in shock and used his other hand trying to grab the bird around its neck.

Ferdinand released the thumb and ducked, this time sinking his beak into the fleshy meat between Jeremiah's thumb and pointer finger. Ferdinand pivoted his body up underneath Jeremiah's hand and swung his talons deep into Jeremiah's forearm. The vice-like pressure on his tendons prevented him from closing his hand. Ferdinand might have even severed some tendons.

Jeremiah frantically waved his hand up and down, trying to force the bird to release its grip. Blood spattered the ground and nearby trees. Finally, he threw the raptor down, but Ferdinand never let go and ripped a chunk of flesh and muscle off as he plummeted towards the dirt.

The bird flared his feathers, slowing the descent.

Tsumi jumped back in horror, with some of Jeremiah's blood splattered across her face.

Ferdinand stood in front of Clara. He hissed and held his wings out, making himself seem as big as possible. Jeremiah tried to staunch the bleeding, ripping some of his shirt off and wrapping it tightly around his hand while cursing and shifting his weight from foot to foot. Bronwyn hoped Ferdinand got his sword arm. No one approached the devil bird.

"Control it, or I'll cut another one of her fingers off!" Amber yelled.

"Ferdinand, Ferdinand," Clara said. "It will be okay. You need to go find Miro, and we'll all be together again. It will be okay."

Ferdinand cocked his head from side to side before screeching.

"Ferdinand, go find Miro; he'll come and save us." Ferdinand didn't relent for a while, but Clara finally calmed him down. When Amber approached with the missive and pouch Ferdinand resumed his hostile stance, protecting Clara.

"He'll only let me do it," Clara said.

"Untie her," Amber said to Frank. Frank went around Clara's back cautiously, keeping Clara between her and the falcon at all times. Ferdinand screeched and buffeted his wings, causing Frank to flinch and dive behind Clara.

Bronwyn wasn't sure, but she thought she heard Ferdinand chuckle.

Once free, Amber tossed Clara the pouch and missive, and Clara tied them to Ferdinand's leg.

"Go Ferdinand. Find Miro." Ferdinand hesitated before taking flight. He circled the camp a couple of times, likely trying to decide whether to dive at one of them, but he flew away to the east, where they came from.

"Tie her back up and put her in her tent," Amber said. Frank nodded and went to fasten the ropes around Clara.

After getting Clara secured and dragged off, Enele lifted Bronwyn and carried her to the tent as well. Amber followed.

Bronwyn breathed quickly, with anger, frustration, and possibly from blood loss. Amber seemed to take it as fear, and said, "You won't come to any more harm. We only want the magus."

Bronwyn snarled and spat at her. "You cut my finger off."

Amber wiped the spittle from her cheek. "A necessity, to make sure the magus knows we're serious. It may not even matter. Sometimes they don't come, regardless of who we've taken. This one will probably be the same—"

"He'll come for us, and you'll regret your hand in all of this. I bet you think you're better than them." Bronwyn nodded her head back in the direction of the fire, where Frank, Jeremiah, and Tsumi talked, casting suspicious glances in Amber's direction. Enele looked back and seemed to notice this. He joined the four at the fire and the voices raised, but not enough for Bronwyn to hear over the slight ringing still plaguing her.

"I commanded men like those three once. They preyed upon the weak and took liberties when they could. I should have killed them, but I didn't have to. Miro's monster did that for me.

"At one point he commanded a spirit guardian. An animal hundreds of years old and blessed by the gods bowed down to him and did his bidding. And he's not even the worst thing that's coming for you. The one he travels with is something you've never seen in this world, and when he sees what you've done to me … the two of them will salt the earth to find and kill every last person that had a hand in this."

Amber sighed and rolled her eyes. "There is no talking to you until that spell is broken. Your other friend won't be coming. We told your magus to come alone if he ever wanted to see the two of you alive. I've lost count of how many magi we've slain, and yours is no different. He thinks himself immortal, but he'll be proven wrong, and you'll be free of his magic."

"I'll enjoy watching you die."

Amber shook her head, then rose to join the increasingly animated conversation by the fireside.

"Bronwyn, are you okay?" Clara whispered from beside her.

Bronwyn lay down in the tent, on her side. Chains dug into her, and she doubted she could get any sleep before this evening. She wanted to be well-rested when they made their escape. "It's nothing compared to what will happen to them. Whatever their plan is, it hinges on Defurge not coming with Miro."

Clara averted her eyes. "Defurge isn't coming. They made me write the note. Said in it that they had ways to make sure Miro was alone and would see him long before he arrives."

"What is the best way to get the former god of fire and madness to do something you want him to? Tell him not to. Hopefully, Defurge will be smart enough to come as something else. I saw him change into a bird once."

"Helpful trick in this case."

"It won't matter anyway. We'll be long gone before they arrive, and meet them on the road." Bronwyn turned from Clara to make sure none of the hunters had decided to check on their captives. Jeremiah was seething and poked Amber in the chest with his bloodied hand. Enele stepped forward and grabbed Jeremiah's arm, twisting it behind his back before pushing him away. "I think I can break out of these chains once they're asleep."

"How?"

"I'm Emestrian, full-blooded." Bronwyn cracked a mischievous smile, her first of the day.

"They didn't check my boot. I have a set of lockpicks in there. If you can untie me. There is a lock on your back for the chains."

"Clever woman." Bronwyn's smile faded. "Clara look—what they said about Miro."

Clara turned over, away from Bronwyn. "I don't need to hear it. If you say he wasn't responsible, then he wasn't responsible."

Bronwyn gulped, thinking Clara didn't believe her.

"What about what they were saying about magic? Is it possible Miro cast some type of spell?" Clara asked.

"No. I'm immune to magic, and he cast Chivan magic on me once to prove it. Besides, I have something that can provide a little extra protection." Then Bronwyn noticed her necklace was missing. She darted her eyes around the tent, looking to see if it had fallen off. Then she looked toward the camp, hopeful she might see a gleaming bit of silver shining in the dirt. A bit of silver swayed from Frank's belt. A pinprick of blue could be the sapphire.

"Can you make out anything they're saying? My ears are still ringing from that smack Tsumi gave me."

"They're arguing about us. Frank wants to keep us separated, have me in his tent. Amber is refusing, something about a deal. Tsumi is pressing her for the details of this deal, but Amber won't tell her."

"Wouldn't she have been there, when you told them what they wanted to know so they wouldn't hurt you?"

"I never made a deal for my safety with them. I didn't tell them much of anything. They already knew so much. Whoever this deal is with, I want to know. After we're free and have hunted them down, I'll find out."

The idea of Frank wanting Clara in his tent sickened Bronwyn and she returned to fantasizing about their deaths. Her thoughts strayed to the fight with the cassolisk, and how Defurge kept burning the creature long past its death. But then, she remembered something before the cassolisk.

"Clara, what exactly did the note say?"

Clara turned back over. "I told you the gist of it. Can't remember every little detail."

"Did they sign it?"

"Yeah, they had me sign it 'The Magi Hunters'."

Bronwyn's face grew white. "When we're escaping, if we get separated, don't come back for me. Just get to safety and find Miro and Defurge."

"Why? How dangerous can these people really be? They got the drop on us, but Jeremiah just got his ass handed to him by a two-pound bird."

Bronwyn slowly blinked and steeled herself. "We can't rely on any guarantee of safety. When Defurge and I first went after the Horn of Garanhir, we found some remains. They had been predated upon, but there were weapon marks on the bones. There was a note, and it was bloody and torn, but I remember being able to make out 'Hunters' as a signature.

I think it was another magus, and that they had taken his child. I found two bodies; one was much younger than the other."

"They killed a kid?" Clara clenched her fist so tightly the skin paled around where her fingernails dug into her palms. "Miro and Defurge won't get the opportunity to kill them. I'll do it myself."

Bronwyn had come to recognize this tell of Clara's but still didn't know what it indicated. "Is there something you haven't told me? You do that from time to time," Bronwyn motioned toward Clara's fist, "when kids come up."

"Another time. Let's get out of this first." Clara turned away from Bronwyn again.

CHAPTER 31

MIRO MOVED SLOWER today. They spent the first half of the day fishing, then had a long leisurely lunch followed by Miro studying and Defurge sunning himself. Defurge didn't mind taking their time, even if the pace meant they were purposefully not going too far from where Bronwyn and Clara might be.

Sharing time like this with Miro was something he hadn't even considered in the past. He almost told Miro about his plan for their future while they sat side by side at the lake, waiting for a bite on their haphazard fishing poles. The world needed a new pantheon, led by the last remaining god. Magi and Ywaigwai were the natural replacements for the absentee deities.

The sun passed its zenith by the time they returned to the road. Defurge groaned after Miro made yet another excuse to ride the horse to the other side to walk through the mud. The last time Miro complained the rocks might dislodge a shoe; this time he feigned spotting something of interest on the horizon.

Why does Miro play these games? These games aren't fun, like the ones I prefer. Defurge thought once they were free of Clara and Bronwyn, the stupid excuses would stop. Perhaps they were just a bad habit now. But then Defurge looked to the sky. A falcon flew in a zigzag pattern screeching in distress. *Ferdinand? And he seems to be looking for something.*

The falcon circled overhead, looking for prey. *This must mean Bronwyn and Clara are close by, probably sending Ferdinand out as their scout.*

Defurge nudged Miro and pointed to Ferdinand. "I think someone's calling your name," Defurge said. Despite his own feelings, when Miro's mind lit up in happiness, Defurge smiled.

"Ferdinand!" Miro shouted. "Ferdinand!" he repeated, this time louder. The bird ceased its screeching and made a dive, headed toward them.

"Whoa, whoa," Defurge said. He worried Bronwyn was so angry that she convinced Clara to send the bird to attack Miro. *Why did Clara agree to that?*

Thankfully, Ferdinand pulled up from the dive, choosing to land on the ground rather than Miro's arm. Still, the bird was overly excited and hopped around, making a ruckus. Defurge thought Ferdinand might only be happy to find them, but then dread overcame Miro's mind. Miro thought one word over and over, *danger*.

Miro dismounted the horse. Tied to Ferdinand's leg were a missive sheath and a small leather pouch. Miro's heart sank as he spied the dark stain at the bottom of the small bag. He took the missive off first, afraid to open the pouch.

Dear magus scum,

We've been watching you. You've been very bad. We have your friends. We've sent a present to show you how serious we are. Follow the bird, come alone, leave flaming whip boy behind, or we'll kill both the women. We have eyes on the road. Two days or we send more pieces.

--The Magi Hunters

"What does the note say?" Defurge already knew and was afraid to ask, but was helpless not to. Miro didn't say anything and removed the leather pouch; he upended it and a finger tumbled free. Miro clutched the finger tightly.

"Stay here," Miro steadied his breathing, but the anger was palpable. The dark thoughts excited Defurge.

Returning to Bronwyn was the last thing Defurge wanted, but Miro's anger intrigued him. *What would Miro do to those who threatened her and Clara?*

"What does the note say?" Defurge asked again. Defurge attempted to read Miro's mind to see exactly what type of revenge he would enact. His thoughts were jumbled and incoherent.

"They have Clara and Bronwyn. They want me to come alone." Miro grabbed the reins of the horse and helped himself back in the saddle. "Dismount."

"Wait; like hell, I'm letting you go alone. They're my friends too," Defurge argued.

"The note says they've been watching us for some time. They mentioned you specifically. I'm going alone."

"You take the horse, I'll fly. They won't see me coming." Defurge started explaining his plan, "I'll scout them out; come at them from behind. They'll have nowhere to run."

Defurge didn't need to be a telepath to sense what Miro now planned to do.

"I just can't take that risk. Stay here. If Clara and Bronwyn aren't back in three days, try and come find them. Hopefully, Ferdinand will still be able to help." Defurge reluctantly dismounted.

"Clara, Bronwyn, and *you*," Defurge replied with emphasis.

"Clara and Bronwyn."

"You expect me to stay here while you go off to sacrifice yourself? You're being irrational." Miro turned the horse in the opposite direction. Defurge was starting to understand Bronwyn's frustrations.

Miro said, "Ferdinand, fly to them; don't let me lose sight of you."

The falcon took to the sky and Miro kicked the horse into a gallop.

"I'm not going to stay here," Defurge called back at Miro. Miro pulled the horse's reins and turned around.

"If you're my friend, you will. I will risk anything for those two." Miro turned without waiting for a reply and the horse sped to a full gallop.

Defurge waited till Miro was out of sight and their mental connection severed. Miro was aware of the monks when they tried to influence him, but Defurge wasn't sure about the specifics. He opted to follow cautiously. Once the danger his subterfuge would be discovered diminished, Defurge tapped into the fire that churned through his veins. Heat began to course through him, the warmth spreading from his core to every inch of his skin. As the intensity increased, skin and bone began to burn away. With a little more concentration, the inferno began to take shape. Not the canary this time, it would be too small for sustained flight at high altitude, instead, a shape more familiar to the phoenix.

Once the body was small enough, Defurge reconcentrated his efforts on the flames, shaping them into feathers, wings, talons, eyes, and a beak. As the flames started to cool, the feathers dulled from a bright-red to a burnt brown. Defurge finished turning into a hawk and rose quickly into the sky.

Suppressing the phoenix's fire was harder in this form. The phoenix wanted to erupt forth since this shape was closer to her true self. Defurge succeeded in tamping down the blaze. His tail was still alight, and he left a trail of embers in his wake, but he would fly so high the magic would be unrecognizable.

Once Defurge was a small wisp in the sky, he flew in the direction Miro and Ferdinand headed. He soared below the clouds. It didn't take long to catch up. He glid leisurely high above. Even with the eyes of a hawk, Miro was still an insignificant speck in the distance. There was no way Miro sensed him.

Despite Defurge having refused the phoenix's requests, there had not been any decrease in his power and if anything, he was starting to gain more control over his abilities. It had been easy to pluck Bronwyn's memories of the visions from the Eye of Sleepless Dreams and find the exact worst words that Bronwyn could say to ensure she and Miro would stay away from each other: *"All those people."*

CHAPTER 32

BRONWYN FOUND IT impossible to sleep with the chains digging into her side and listened long into the night as the hunters continued to argue. Jeremiah and Frank's words became more slurred as the night progressed.

After Jeremiah exhausted his arguments and retired to his tent, the rest of the camp fell quiet. Enele guarded them most of the day, only rising when the arguments approached fever pitch. Now he sat outside the captive's tent for the first shift of the evening, or maybe the whole night. Bronwyn waited until Enele's breathing slowed and the air exiting his nostrils elicited a low nasal hum.

"Okay, now," Bronwyn whispered to Clara. Bronwyn strained her wrists and thought she could hear the metal begin to groan.

"Wait, if you break them, it might be too loud. Get my ropes and I'll try the lock first. I just need to be able to reach my boot." Clara rolled over, putting her wrists into Bronwyn's hands. Sailors usually spent their first couple of voyages learning to tie and untie every variation of knot that existed. Clara guided Bronwyn in how to quickly undo her knots.

"No, that one goes under," Clara whispered. "Pull the one that's a little loose now. Roll the other rope over that one."

Once Clara's wrists were free, she shrugged off the ropes around her arms. The slack allowed her to shimmy them up and over her head. Clara didn't untie her ankles before contorting to reach her boot and pulling out a thin black metal spike. With her senses returned Bronwyn heard the clicks of metal on metal as the spike worked the tumbler and the lock shifted against the chains. Then a louder click, and the chains slacked a little.

"Wait for me to get my feet untied, then I'll help you get them off to dampen the noise," Clara said. Soon both women were freed of their bindings. Bronwyn debated taking the chains as weapons but worried they'd cause too much noise moving in the dark.

"Okay, we leave camp and run far enough away," Bronwyn said. "They'll find us gone, hopefully later rather than sooner, but we'll be ready for them. They'll be spread out. Use your stone wall to slow them down if they start to bunch up or shoot arrows."

Bronwyn dipped her head outside the tent to make sure Enele still slept.

Clara and Bronwyn headed east from the camp. Their tent was on the outskirts, another mistake Amber made.

They skulked a little over two hundred feet before Jeremiah shouted. They had been quiet; if Jeremiah checked on the tent, he wasn't investigating a noise. He was checking on them for other, nefarious reasons.

"Okay, go; I don't think they know which way we went. If they find us, put up the stone wall. I'll use the barricade to pick them off as they round the sides." Bronwyn grabbed stones the size of her fist and cradled them in her hands.

Enele came into view first. His heavy footsteps gave away his position. He jogged and sucked in air, breathing heavily. Bronwyn grinned. Incapacitating him first would free up the rest of the battle.

"Over here!" Enele shouted, catching sight of them.

"Lau'O'Penake, goddess of nature and rebirth, waylay my foes, Fragma Petra," Clara chanted as she traced the runes.

Bronwyn smiled as Enele attempted to chuck his bola. The wall of earth would be up before the wires left his hands. Bronwyn stepped back from the wall a bit. She would use the surface as a springboard to jump up to Enele's head when he crested either side.

Bronwyn looked down as she felt something pass through her. The wires spun through her body and as she turned around, she watched in puzzlement as the bola sailed toward Clara. The bola had moved through the wall. The wires whipped around Clara's body, pinning her arms and forcing her legs together.

Clara fell, but Bronwyn rushed forward to catch her, lest her head hit something hard. She dropped her rocks in the process. Bronwyn tugged at the wires, looking for the bola's heads. The bola was glued to Clara's skin; she couldn't force her fingers underneath the wires.

"Go, leave me," Clara said. "Tell Miro her name is Scarlette."

"What? No! I'm not leaving you." Bronwyn abandoned the effort of freeing Clara. Too many footsteps were getting too close. She turned to face Enele. She lost the rocks on the ground but nearby was a sturdy enough branch. Picking it up, she rushed at the hulking man.

Enele swung at her, but Bronwyn slid to her knees, the wet grass assisting her. Enele tried to turn to grab her.

Bronwyn struck.

She brought the branch hard against the back of his leg and forced him to one knee. Then she leapt to her feet and ran at Enele again; she put one foot on his thigh and used the handy stepstool to vault her other knee up into his nose.

Enele's nose made a satisfying crunch as Bronwyn broke it. Blood sprayed forth and he fell to the ground.

Behind Enele was Tsumi, without Gaebolg. She rolled her hands in front of her and chanted. Miro had cast this magic before, and Bronwyn charged Tsumi.

"I make this bargain with Laevin, god of lightning and the sky, arbiter of the gods, Bolta Levos."

A combination of speed, skill, and sheer luck allowed Bronwyn to dodge the lightning. The hair on her arm rose as the bolt snaked around her body. A millisecond too late and Bronwyn's escape attempt would have ended prematurely.

Bronwyn closed the distance. Tsumi needed to be neutralized now; a Laevinite was too powerful to ignore. Bronwyn brought her fist hard into Tsumi's solar plexus, knocking the air from her lungs. She brought her other hand around and thrust the side of her palm into Tsumi's larynx.

Hopefully, it was permanent, but Tsumi wouldn't be doing any more spellcasting for a while.

Tsumi fell backward and tried to scream for help but was only met with a raspy whisper. She sucked in air and writhed, trying to catch her breath and scramble away from Bronwyn at the same time.

"Give it up Bronwyn; you're unarmed, and we have you surrounded." Amber held her daggers out as she rounded the wall on the end opposite where Tsumi now lay.

Amber made the first move, throwing one dagger and trying to rush Bronwyn with the second.

Bronwyn dodged the first blade, then twisted Amber's hand, the dagger falling free and to the side, and punched at Amber's stomach. Amber produced a third weapon and sliced Bronwyn's arm as she finished her punch. Amber was a little winded, but back up to two daggers.

If Bronwyn determined where Amber kept them, she could arm herself.

"Tonight didn't have to go down like this, Amber. You could walk away. I let you into my camp because the whole lot of you couldn't beat me in a fight, even if I was unarmed. Your little trick with the wine bought you a couple of hours, but that, like my patience, is gone." Bronwyn tried goading Amber into making a mistake.

"Shows what you know. We poisoned the meat. We took the antidote before eating!" Amber yelled as she charged Bronwyn. Bronwyn leaned back, avoiding the double swipe of the blades, and brought her knee hard into Amber's stomach. At the same time, she grabbed the daggers and wrested them from Amber, pushing her back with the force of her strike.

"Oh, look, now I'm armed." Bronwyn went to throw one of the daggers at Amber, but as she did it disappeared from her hand. The other dagger in her hand disappeared as well. They were both gone, and Amber wielded them once more.

"Shadow daggers. They may not be artifacts, but they're magic enough for a fight with a low-class, inbred Emestrian like you." Amber threw one trying to distract Bronwyn as she rushed toward her.

Amber tried the same trick twice. Bronwyn spun on her right foot, bringing the left around and striking Amber forcefully in the chest.

The blow lifted Amber off her feet and sent her tumbling down the incline they had been fighting above. The thud of a head slamming into a rock punctuated the sound of bushes breaking.

Wheeling around, Bronwyn caught sight of Jeremiah trying to approach them from behind with Gaebolg. Bronwyn rushed toward him, judging her distance. Rather than hold the spear in a thrusting maneuver, he held it out to the side.

Bronwyn ran in front of Clara and hopped back as Jeremiah swiped with Gaebolg. With her back foot still planted, she shouldered forward, colliding with him. Before he could bring Gaebolg around for another swipe, Bronwyn gripped the haft. She yanked Gaebolg toward her.

Bronwyn loved fighting men like this in training. They always underestimated her, even after seeing her physically overpower their fellow guards. The answer was so poetically sweet. Bronwyn brought her knee up hard into his groin. She hoped to hear a popping sound, but disappointingly, she didn't.

"Too small of a target," Bronwyn mused aloud.

Jeremiah winced and loosened his grip on Gaebolg. Bronwyn yanked again to repeat her maneuver, but as she did, she was rammed from behind by someone so massive it could only be Enele. She thought she had knocked him unconscious. Bronwyn ripped Gaebolg from Jeremiah's hands but lost her grip as Enele brought her to the ground, both of them falling on top of Jeremiah.

Bronwyn twisted in Enele's arms. Her head was against Jeremiah's chest, and she raised her head and slammed it back into him. She pulled her right arm free of Enele's grip and thrust her hand toward Enele's face, thumb extended. Enele howled in pain as she jabbed his eye, blood spurting against her face as she pressed deeper.

Enele raged backward, pulling Bronwyn's hand from his face, but freeing Bronwyn's other arm. Before he could get too far away, Bronwyn kicked out with both her legs. She tried to kick him in the chest but missed because of his violent thrashing. Instead, Bronwyn's legs sailed to either side of Enele's head. Before he could escape, Bronwyn wrapped her legs around his neck, locking her ankles.

Enele bellowed as he grabbed her thighs, reared back, then slammed her back down. The back of her head crashed into Jeremiah's front. The second time Enele did it, Bronwyn's back met the wet grass. Bronwyn gasped as the air was knocked from her lungs but didn't release her grip. She pressed harder. She wasn't choking him, but his movements slowed the third time he tried to lift her. She was cutting off the blood flow.

"Bronwyn!" Clara screamed. Bronwyn frantically looked about as Enele smashed her against the ground a third time. Tsumi stood over the prone Clara, Gaebolg dangerously close. Bronwyn released Enele's neck as the large man stumbled backward and fell to his knees, sucking in air.

Jeremiah had righted himself behind Bronwyn. Jeremiah commanded, "Stay on your back if you don't want to see your friend impaled."

Frank jogged into view now that Jeremiah had neutralized Bronwyn.

"Enele, get the bola off the little one and take her back to the fire. Tsumi and I will handle the Emestrian."

Enele went over to Clara and waved his right hand over her before closing it. The bola slackened and he reached down, picking it up and rolling Clara as he did. He then reached down and grabbed Clara by the back of the neck. "No tricks, little one."

Tsumi motioned toward Enele and made a signal of tightening something around someone's neck.

"What?" Jeremiah asked.

Tsumi repeated the motion, and it took Jeremiah a couple more tries before he nodded.

"Wrap the bola around her neck. If the Emestrian tries anything, pop her head like a zit."

With Clara incapacitated, Tsumi, Jeremiah, and Frank approached Bronwyn. Frank removed a short sword and placed it at her back. Tsumi held the head of Gaebolg underneath Bronwyn's chin.

"On your feet," Jeremiah said. "March back to camp. You try anything and we'll skewer you."

Bronwyn rose and walked carefully forward. With weapons at her front and back, and Clara under Enele's control, she didn't see any future avenues of escape. These hunters would deserve what Miro and Defurge would do to them.

As they walked back to camp. Amber climbed up the incline she had fallen down. Blood wet the back of her neck. *Damnit, I hoped she had split her head open and was dead,* Bronwyn thought.

Clara arrived back at the fire first. Enele made her kneel once again and Frank brought over some rope to begin re-trussing her. When Bronwyn arrived, Jeremiah made her kneel once again, but it seemed they had learned their lesson in trying to tie Bronwyn up. Gaebolg would need to be kept at her throat to keep her in line.

Amber was the last to congregate around the fire. She brought her hand to the back of her neck, and when she pulled it away bloodied, she began rummaging around in a sack. She withdrew a cloth and placed it on the back of her head.

"Frank," Jeremiah said after picking up a wineskin and taking a healthy swig, "we have an extra pair of manacles—get them."

"You want to put her in manacles?" Amber asked.

"She's gotten out of everything else so far," Jeremiah said as Tsumi nodded her agreement.

"We'll have to find a smithy to take them off once all this is done," Amber said.

Jeremiah crossed his arms. "We won't be finding a smithy. After that last attempt, you'd have to be an idiot to think we can just let her walk away."

"Jerund was clear; after the spell has been lifted, she will be an asset—"

Jeremiah threw his hands up and turned to Amber. "Jerund? Jerund doesn't know Jack about what is happening on the ground. Don't pretend that this is some order from above. Stop living in your fantasy world and accept the facts. When this is over, she'll need to be put down."

"I am in charge here and you will listen to me, or—"

Bronwyn jolted back in surprise as Tsumi whipped to the side, Gaebolg in hand. A thin red line appeared on Amber's throat before she frantically clasped both hands around the front of her neck. Bronwyn's eyes synchronously widened with Amber's as the first spire of crystallized blood erupted from her forearm. Amber let out a gasping scream that was cut short as her entire body convulsed and erupted grotesquely. One instant, she was there, a human, and the next, a dark red crystalline structure had taken her place; clothes and skin hung from jagged edges.

Bronwyn let out a shrill cry that she never thought herself possible of making as Enele charged forward and grabbed Gaebolg, still in Tsumi's hands.

"Jerund will hear of this," Enele roared. Blood seeped below his bandaged eye with the ferocity of his outrage.

"Amber lost her life fighting a magus, nothing more, nothing—"

Enele thrust his other hand forward, gripping Jeremiah around the throat. Jeremiah's eyes bulged and his face started to brighten.

Jeremiah struggled, gasping out, "Listen ... reason ... she was ... weak."

"You've gone too far," Enele said. He violently shook Gaebolg until Tsumi lost her footing and fell backward, releasing her grip. Before Enele could swing the weapon in Jeremiah's direction, he howled in pain. Frank's sword dug into Enele's back. Bronwyn knew that the wound was not survivable. Without a healer, the toxins released by the kidney would poison the blood. Perhaps she could convince the giant of the man to support her with the promise of Miro's healing.

The thought was short-lived when Enele lost his grip on Jeremiah's neck. Jeremiah pulled his side sword and thrust it into Enele's rib cage.

Jeremiah coughed out, "Sorry big guy—you chose the wrong side."

Frank withdrew his sword and delivered a similarly deep blow on Enele's other side. Enele swung around, freeing his chest of Jeremiah's sword and trying to bat Frank's away from his back. Frank retreated, leaving his sword embedded in Enele. He swung back around to grapple with Jeremiah, but Tsumi had recovered, and in the chaos of Enele's defense, she was able to leverage the head of Gaebolg far enough that it sank into the soft flesh of Enele's stomach. Enele's yell was cut short as he met the same fate as Amber.

As soon as Tsumi had recovered Gaebolg, she pointed it back in Bronwyn's direction.

Jeremiah reclined on the ground, sucking in breath while looking up at the twisted crystal structure that used to be Enele. He first looked to Tsumi, then to Frank, who stood unarmed.

"I can't believe that Emestrian whore managed to get through her chains and kill Amber and Enele with the Legendary Artifact before we could stop her," Frank said, holding his hands up in defense.

Jeremiah breathed heavily and looked to Tsumi, who nodded. "I knew you were a smart one. Now, how about you go get those manacles?"

Frank nodded quickly and scampered off toward one of the tents. Bronwyn stared at the dark red crystals that now took up the space Amber and Enele used to inhabit. Their personal effects were strewn about the base and Jeremiah went about picking up the bola and Amber's shadow daggers. Frank returned shortly after, carrying a handful of smooth steel and chains. He quickly came behind Bronwyn and she felt the cold metal on one wrist clamping shut, then on the other.

As Frank fastened their newest bid at keeping Bronwyn contained, her vision alternated between Tsumi holding Gaebolg to her throat and Clara, who did not say anything or move. She was like a statue with her eyes glued to where Amber had been standing.

"These are special manacles," Jeremiah said as Frank secured the second arm cuff, and another biting piece of metal was placed against Bronwyn's ankle.

Jeremiah examined one of Amber's shadow daggers and seemed to judge the balance of its weight by holding the middle of the dagger and moving his hand left or right. "You'll not get out of them. If you've been using some type of magic to increase your strength, this metal, the same in the bola, prevents magic from taking effect while in contact with a magic user."

Bronwyn's vision darted toward Clara. She had the bola wrapped around her. Had she felt it deprive her of magic? Clara cast her eyes down and did not meet Bronwyn's. The knot in Bronwyn's stomach tightened.

Frank finished securing the manacles and stepped away from Bronwyn. Where the chains had been iron, these manacles were steel. Maybe even Emestrian steel.

"You're making a mistake," Bronwyn said. Despite being drugged and tied up previously, she felt the previous confidence she tried to exude now hollow. "I suggest you leave before you find yourself embroiled in something you can't handle."

Jeremiah cackled. "Would you give it up already? Stop trying to pretend you're in control or know what's going on. Your magus will die tomorrow and the only reason Tsumi isn't shoving Gaebolg in your chest is because she wants you to suffer as much as I do."

Tsumi nodded her head enthusiastically.

Jeremiah tossed a shadow dagger into the air and caught it. "Now, tomorrow will be fun. The next weeks, even more so, but you have to pay for what you did to Tsumi and me tonight."

Tsumi pointed Gaebolg at Clara.

"No," Bronwyn yelled.

"Now, that's an interesting idea," Jeremiah mused.

Frank, who Bronwyn now noticed seemed to be a little unsteady on his feet, said, "Actually, I was thinking that maybe we could leave her for me."

Tsumi narrowed her eyes at Frank, then Jeremiah. She shook her head. Some depths were even too depraved for her. She repointed Gaebolg at Clara and grinned.

Jeremiah placed his hand on Gaebolg's haft and pressed down until the head pointed at the ground. Tsumi stared at Jeremiah as he didn't remove his hand. Jeremiah said, "We can have our fun with the Emestrian. Shouldn't Frank get to have some fun of his own?"

Tsumi shook her head as she gave Jeremiah one of the steely gazes Bronwyn had seen her give the fire the previous night.

"Don't worry about it," Jeremiah said. "We'll be so busy with this one …."

Jeremiah offered Tsumi the shadow dagger. She leaned Gaebolg against a tree and took the dagger.

Jeremiah said, "Now, how about we even the score?"

"Everything you do to me, Defurge will mete back upon you a thousandfold," Bronwyn threatened.

"Will you just shut up already?" Jeremiah said as Tsumi knelt behind Bronwyn. Tsumi grabbed Bronwyn's pointer finger and twisted it sharply. Bronwyn yelped and shut her eyes tightly. Twin streams of tears streaked down her face as Tsumi yanked and pulled the finger in the opposite direction.

Excruciating pain racked Bronwyn's body. Her hand seemed to go numb from the intensity until she felt the edge of the knife press into her skin. Bronwyn tried to pitch herself forward, to free her finger from Tsumi's grasp, but Jeremiah held her shoulders. The best she could do was manage to topple to her side, which seemed to have helped Tsumi. Hot blood filled Bronwyn's palm as she closed her fist and felt something missing.

Tsumi came around to Jeremiah and handed him her now severed pointer finger. "Wrap her hand up—wouldn't want her to be too weak to watch tomorrow."

Tsumi nodded, fished around in the same sack as Amber had, and then went to Bronwyn's back with a strip of cloth. She wrapped tightly, but the bandages wetted quickly.

Bronwyn breathed heavily as she tried to concentrate on her anger. "You have no idea what you've just done."

Jeremiah reached down and gripped Bronwyn by the hair, pulling her head far enough off the ground to slam his fist into her cheek in a downward strike. Bronwyn leaned into the punch and Jeremiah quickly pulled his arm back.

"Chivas," Jeremiah cursed as he clutched his hand. The hand injured by Ferdinand and had bandaged now clutched the one he tried to strike Bronwyn with.

"Hurts? I'm full-blooded Emestrian. My muscles are as thick as the frozen tundra and my bones hard as rocks. Punch me all you like; you'll do more damage to yourself than I."

Jeremiah mimed both his hands in a choking maneuver. "Just shut up!"

"Leave her alone," Clara shouted.

Frank took the wineskin Jeremiah had set aside and tried to take a drink, but tossed it down, dissatisfied. He fished through a pack and withdrew a dark green, glass bottle. Uncorking it, he took two quick big gulps as he walked over to Clara. In the firelight, Bronwyn saw how bloodshot his eyes were, and both his cheeks and nose were ruddy with drink.

Frank brought his hand to Clara's cheek, who turned away decidedly. "Don't be like that, poppet. Keep quiet and we'll get to spend time together later. You wouldn't want to anger Jeremiah and have him mess that pretty face."

"Don't touch her," Bronwyn yelled.

"Shouldn't you be more worried about yourself?" Jeremiah asked.

Tsumi slowly walked back to Gaebolg and picked up the weapon before walking behind Bronwyn. The spear's haft whipped against her back. Bronwyn bit her cheek as she tried to stifle a scream. She watched Frank intently as he took another drink and stumbled a little.

When Bronwyn first saw Miro being tortured in the vision, she thought Miro was encouraging the torture as a way to punish himself. Now a new possibility arose. Every time they hurt Miro, they weren't hurting Serra.

"Is this the best you two can do? Love taps? How about you, Frank? Can you actually hit like a man?"

Frank took another swig but stood dumbfounded that Bronwyn had taunted him.

"Sounds to me like she wants you to give it a try," Jeremiah said. He motioned toward Tsumi and the two lifted Bronwyn by her shoulders until she was on her knees again. "I said it sounds like she wants you to give it a try."

Frank shrugged before looking around the campfire. He grabbed a thick stick piled next to the fire for wood. As he approached Bronwyn, she grinned. Frank pulled the stick back and swung it with all his force. Blood filled Bronwyn's mouth as the strike against her cheek ripped the inside flesh.

Bronwyn spat a mouthful of blood into the dirt. "I've known Emestrian men that kiss harder than that."

Frank swung the branch in the opposite direction and Bronwyn's head lolled. "Have another drink; then you'll be able to hit like a man."

Frank didn't go back to his drink, but Jeremiah and Tsumi resumed striking her. Gaebolg was smashed into the back of her right shoulder. Jeremiah kicked her stomach and Bronwyn coughed for breath. But Frank did take another drink before he struck Bronwyn across the chest with his branch, shattering it.

Bronwyn slipped in and out of consciousness. Sometimes, the strikes came in quick succession. Other times, the hunters seemed to be resting before taking turns trying to break her. Bronwyn's right eye was swollen and hot, but she kept her left open as much as possible, watching Frank as he took drink after drink between strikes. It wasn't until he sat down and closed his eyes that she stopped goading the three. With Frank too drunk to do any harm, she finally let her mind and body rest. Occasionally, she woke from a kick but didn't say anything.

CHAPTER 33

PAIN STABBED THROUGHOUT Bronwyn's body. She was unsure how long she had been unconscious this time, but she managed to quiet her groan. Everything hurt. Every little part of her body felt like it was on fire. Her joints were so swollen they felt dislocated. Despite the gentle prodding, it felt like daggers were being twisted into her flesh.

"Bronwyn, wake up," Clara whispered. "Something's happening."

"What?" Bronwyn asked through a hoarse throat.

"Tsumi was using a spyglass. They're all over there right now." Clara nodded her head up. Bronwyn followed the movement and with her one good eye, she saw three figures standing just behind several trees. Past the trees, the clearing was barren.

"I think Miro is coming," Clara said.

Bronwyn stared intently, her vision still difficult in the morning light. Past where the three figures stood, there seemed to be movement in the distance.

"Are you okay?" Clara asked.

"Are you?" Bronwyn replied. "Did they touch you? Did Frank—"

"Nothing happened. What were you thinking last night?"

"The same thing Miro thought," Bronwyn muttered. "As long as they were concentrated on me, they'd leave you alone. Did they move us last night?"

"This morning, closer to the edge of the glen. Shh, he's coming back."

Bronwyn turned back to where Clara indicated earlier. Frank was returning alone, while Tsumi and Jeremiah's silhouettes still waited. She thought she could make out a figure walking toward them. A lone figure.

"Get up. Jeremiah wants you both to see this," Frank said. He first went to Clara and pulled her to her knees. He struggled with Bronwyn, but despite the pain, she still managed to right herself.

From above, a screech drew Bronwyn's attention. She had hoped it would be a red canary, but instead, it was Ferdinand perched above. He ruffled his feathers and seemed to be intently focused on Frank. Frank removed his short sword and rested it on Bronwyn's shoulder.

"We're going to eat that damn bird for dinner tonight," Frank said. "Falcon isn't the best tasting, but it pissed Jeremiah off."

Bronwyn was about to answer, but the figure in the distance was growing closer.

"Put your hands to your side and approach slowly," Jeremiah said. "They have swords at their fronts and backs. One wrong move, and the next sound you'll hear is the blood as they choke on it."

Bronwyn hoped it would be Defurge's voice that responded, but as he continued to approach, the blue robe with gold trim was unmistakable. "I've come alone," Miro said. "Let them go and we can be done with this."

"Continue to walk slowly. About a hundred feet forward and to your right. There is a log. Next to it is a pair of cuffs. Put the ones around your ankle first, kneel, then fasten the wrist cuffs."

"I'm not doing anything until I know they're all right."

"Sing for him," Frank said, pressing his sword into the side of Bronwyn's neck.

"Don't do anything they say, Miro," Bronwyn called out. "Wait for Defurge."

Miro's posture seemed to slump at her voice. Perhaps he was hoping that the state of Jeremiah's bandaged hands meant Bronwyn had escaped.

"Shut your mouth," Frank hissed. "Another outburst like that and he'll listen to you die before he does. Surely, you want to spare him that indignancy."

Ferdinand gave a series of ear-piercing screeches. *Fly down, attack his face. I can use the distraction … I can use the distraction ….* The gravity of the situation hit Bronwyn all at once. There was nothing she could do at this point. She could, what, roll around on the ground until Frank fought off Ferdinand, or killed Clara or herself? Frank would scream and whatever Jeremiah had planned for Miro would happen quicker.

Miro walked forward. The trees ended fifty feet away. Miro was merely a hundred feet past that. If she were free, and Miro knew, he could cast that time magic. It would be enough time to tackle Tsumi, grab Gaebolg, and then they'd have a chance. If she wasn't restrained ….

Miro knelt and picked up the matching pair of manacles Bronwyn wore. His expression was flat and somber as he said. "Let them go. I'll put them on."

"You'll put them on now, or the next thing you'll hear is their screams as we saw their heads off."

Miro knelt. The movements behind his back weren't easily discernable, but Bronwyn had no doubt he was doing exactly as he was told. Miro would gladly give his life for theirs. *No, Miro. No.*

"You have me restrained. Let them go and we can end this quickly."

Tsumi, carrying Gaebolg, and Jeremiah, with a crossbow, walked past the tree line toward Miro. Jeremiah raised the crossbow toward Miro with his right arm, and with his left hand, he groped at the pouch where Bronwyn saw him pocket her finger last night.

"I don't think we'll be letting them go," Jeremiah said. "You see, you took too long getting here, and they were problematic."

Jeremiah lobbed something from his pouch at Miro. It bounced off Miro's chest and lay in the grass at his feet.

"It's not even my finger Miro! He cut them off another victim."

Frank grabbed Bronwyn by the hair and yanked her head up. He placed his sword tight against her neck. With her head craned, Bronwyn stared directly into his hateful eyes. "One more word."

"You see, leadership has changed in the last day," Jeremiah said, continuing to advance upon Miro.

"You don't need to do this," Miro reasoned.

"I don't *need* to do anything," Jeremiah said, lowering his crossbow and kneeling in front of Miro. "I don't know if you noticed, but there is no keyhole on those manacles. That's because we just cut the feet and hands off after the wearer is dead."

The edge of the sword dug into Bronwyn's neck. A faint trickle tickled her neck. She wasn't sure if she was bleeding or imagining the sensation.

Bronwyn, I'm here. The voice was familiar, but the words weren't spoken.

Could Defurge now talk to her like he did to Miro? Despite the sword against her neck, Bronwyn chuckled. "You're too late."

"Did we beat you into—" Frank's voice cut off suddenly as the whip wrapped around his throat. Flames erupted before the whip pulled back. Blood dripped onto Bronwyn's face as Frank fell over, dropping his sword.

Bronwyn did her best to turn as Frank writhed on the ground, his voice gurgling with the blood pouring from his opened neck. "Defurge, quick—get these chains off me!"

Defurge ran to Bronwyn's back and heat radiated from his two hands as they both pulled against the ring that connected the wrist and ankle cuffs. Seconds later, the chains snapped, and white-hot links flew in front of Bronwyn. She didn't have time. She had to get to Miro.

"Get Clara free," Bronwyn commanded as she now used her liberated limbs to pick up Frank's sword. She couldn't yell at Miro. All Jeremiah had to do was raise that crossbow and fire a single bolt into his chest. She, half-hobbled, half-ran as fast as she could to get to the clearing so Miro could see that she was safe.

"I know how this ends," Miro said. "Just let them go."

"I put a similar pair on your Emestrian lover. But I'm not going to kill her before I cut her hands and feet. I have a healer friend who's going to make sure she lives once they're removed."

Miro locked his eyes with Jeremiah's. "Those are the last words, you'll ever say."

Just as Bronwyn cleared the tree line, Miro's eyes rolled white and a current of lightning broke from the cloudless sky. The energy Miro summoned not only knocked Bronwyn off her feet but was so strong it knocked even Defurge to the ground. The bright white light temporarily blinded her, but as her vision cleared, she saw Miro encircled by scorched earth. Jeremiah grabbed his crossbow and got back to his feet. The ground still rumbled as Miro stood, the cuffs snapping off his limbs like butcher's twine.

Lightning rose back up off the ground, and encircled Miro, creating a barrier. The metal melted into thin puddles of steel, hissing as they burned the green grass.

"Tsumi, kill him!" Jeremiah yelled as a bolt left his crossbow. The bolt hesitated for a moment in the energy that encircled Miro. Then it whipped into his orbit along with more dirt and debris. Jeremiah placed the cocking stirrup of his crossbow on the ground and fumbled for another bolt.

Tsumi rushed forward, thrusting with Gaebolg. Where the bolt had been caught up in the energy field, Gaebolg pierced the barrier effortlessly.

"No!" Bronwyn screamed as the weapon sank into Miro's chest. His eyes closed, and a final breath was slowly exhaled. Unlike Amber or Enele, Miro seemed to expect this end. Miro's skin was torn asunder by the blood erupting forth in crystalline structures. Tears stung Bronwyn's eyes as her grip on the sword faltered, letting it thud to the ground heavily.

It wasn't enough time. She hadn't bought Miro enough time. Taking a few unsteady steps forward, everything hurt. She needed to pick the sword back up. She needed to kill Jeremiah and Tsumi. She needed to avenge Miro. She hung her head, absently scanning the ground for the sword she had dropped. Tears and pain made it impossible to see where it lay. She'd rip the life out of Jeremiah and Tsumi with her very hands.

Bronwyn looked back to Tsumi, her grip on Gaebolg tight, Miro's body a stopped explosion of red crystal with lightning still dancing around it. But Miro's blood slowly reversed itself and time rewound, removing the spear from Miro's body only for the artifact to grow red hot and melt in Tsumi's hands.

Miro said artifacts are indestructible, Bronwyn thought, stunned. Tsumi turned as the metal dripped onto her arms. Her face contorted as if about to let out a curdling scream, but only a rasping whisper emanated from her mouth. Miro raised his right hand, and a column of white energy blasted into Tsumi, digging a trench in the ground hundreds of feet behind her, obliterating trees and bushes and leaving nothing behind. Tsumi was there, and then she just wasn't.

Jeremiah pulled up on the crossbow's strap but dropped the bolt as he stared at where Tsumi used to be. He let the weapon clatter to the ground as he started to run from Miro. Tsumi was lucky; her pain seemed momentary compared to Jeremiah's. Miro did not bless Jeremiah with that luxury. Miro raised both hands to the sky, and lighting came down. The first bolt knocked Jeremiah to his knees. The second lingered and seemed to tear away at his left leg. A third and fourth bolt gyrated up Jeremiah's body, scoring each of his limbs in the way he had threatened Bronwyn. Jeremiah tried to crawl away on the partial stumps that remained before the blood loss caused him to collapse. He retained consciousness as the energy tore through his body, inch by agonizing inch.

The torture stopped long enough to allow Miro's thunderous voice to boast, "I will dine on the agony of your soul for eternity."

After last night, Bronwyn thought she would relish in Jeremiah's and Tsumi's end at Miro's or Defurge's hand, but she had to turn away. She hadn't recognized the voice before, but after he told Jeremiah how he would live off his soul, she realized who it was. Raithe's voice from the vision—the Ywaigwai that stole Miro's soul. Bronwyn stepped from the tree line.

"That's the last of them. Miro, we're safe now. You can come down," she said, uneasy.

"This world is unworthy; it must be made to fear," Raithe boomed back in reply. "All shall know my name; all shall fear me."

Bronwyn turned as someone grabbed her arm. Defurge had freed Clara, but she seemed more afraid now than she had when Frank was leering at her last night.

Miro continued to advance toward their position. The lightning crashed into the trees surrounding them. "I am destruction incarnate; I am absolution. I am raw unfettered *rage*." The ground shook at the word rage.

"Okay, that's enough," Bronwyn repeated, a catch in her throat. Clara tried tugging her away. Bronwyn looked down at Clara's tear-stained cheeks.

"We have to go; it's too late," Clara pled. "That's not him anymore." She pulled harder. Bronwyn didn't budge. Clara let go in time and fell backward before lightning struck where she had been standing. Bronwyn ducked and tucked her hands over her head, yelping in surprise.

Clara scrambled back to her feet to run away.

Defurge stood motionless, excitement on his face.

"I've got this," Defurge said. His fiery wings and crown from when they first fought in the cave returned. Defurge yelled as his body became a swirling inferno. "You call yourself destruction incarnate? I am the God of Destruction!"

He leapt into the air, his fiery whip extending forth, wrapping around Miro's electric bubble before popping him up into the air, only to crack the whip and forcefully thrust Miro back down.

The energy dug into the ground beneath, sending dirt and rocks flying.

Bronwyn turned her back as debris pelted her.

Clara faltered. She trembled as she froze.

Defurge descended from the sky, two giant fiery arms so thick with flame they had substance, and smashed them against Miro's cage, attempting to break the barrier.

Bronwyn shook with horror as the two battled. The Soul Gem glinted and dangled in front of Defurge's neck, and she knew Miro would die; she had been told as much by the phoenix and Fria. Miro unmade Gaebolg like he would now unmake the gem. This is what the phoenix had been referencing. Miro would destroy the gem with his curse, then she would be forced to kill him: for Emestria, for Clara, for herself.

The energy field resisted Defurge's blow, and he beat his wings forward; the waves of fire pushed Miro back before Defurge raised his arms to the sky and started to bring down the stars. The small meteoroids plummeted to earth, digging trenches into the ground and casting more debris into the air.

"Enough!" Raithe boomed as lightning fell and broke the stars still falling into little inconsequential fragments. Miro extended his hand forward. The lightning picked Defurge up off the ground, and the second bolt smashed him against it.

As Defurge's body sailed through the air, Bronwyn's gaze traced his trajectory with a resigned indifference. She felt like she was in the Eye, a detached observer of the carnage. Defurge's body slammed against the trees and pummeled the earth, digging Defurge a makeshift grave. The lightning surrounded and enveloped Defurge's body with light.

Bronwyn looked back at where Defurge landed. His body lay in a shallow ditch, the gem still intact, and his chest slowly rising and falling, and she advanced toward Miro, shaken but determined.

"I am a god!" Raithe's voice boasted, but it was Miro's lips that moved. "I shall be this world's reckoning and undoing!"

"No, you won't!" Bronwyn yelled back. She didn't flinch as the lightning scoured the earth to her side. "You're not a god; you're a good and honest man."

The next bolt came down right on top of Bronwyn but split, surrounding her but leaving her unscathed, confirming her theory. Miro had to still be in there, and Miro would never hurt her, even if he thought himself a monster. "You're a poor tortured man who was preyed upon by a weak, sniveling worm of a creature that used your greatest virtue to commit atrocities in your name."

Miro raised his hand, the lightning thick and powerful before the bolt fizzled short.

"I am death," Raithe argued, his voice a little quieter.

"No, you're a silly man who talks to goats and cares more for his friends than he does for himself." Bronwyn walked forward, unphased as the lightning continued to narrowly miss, trying to deter her.

When Bronwyn got close enough, she reached into Miro's energy field, her arms passing effortlessly through it, and grabbed him by the robe, pulling him back down to her.

She pressed her lips to his and her blood grew hot as the lightning coursed through her veins and around them. It snaked its way through her hair, causing her locks to stand on end, and lifted her into the air a little until the energy dissipated, little white balls of energy snuffing out all around them. Not supported anymore, Miro fell forward, and Bronwyn did her best to catch him. She tumbled backward, her legs a little weak from last night, and caught off guard by her momentary weightlessness.

Chapter 34

The curse had been unlike any Bronwyn or Clara had seen previously. Despite the negative memories associated with the campsite, Bronwyn, Clara, and Defurge decided not to travel until Miro woke. Bronwyn argued that since she had stopped his rampage, she should stay close, in case he didn't wake up as himself.

For the first day, she rested with him. His breathing was shallow, but when Bronwyn pressed her hand against his chest, his spark was stronger than ever. Instead of a slight tingle, now the energy zapped and numbed her hand, but she couldn't stop touching him. The lightning was addictive. *What does this mean? Is it some sign that he's grown stronger, that I've helped lift his worries, or we've linked ourselves in the kiss we shared? According to Issaroh, a magus dies if they ever fully enter their curse. Miro survived, and perhaps the lightning is some residual effect of that. Is his curse still present? Can he tap into the full energies of the Ywaigwai at will because of my intervention? Or when he wakes, will I have to subdue him permanently?*

At night, sure he wouldn't wake, Bronwyn investigated the field and surrounding forest, decimated by the previous day's mayhem. She didn't expect to find anything. All five hunters died in front of her eyes, and she didn't feel sorry for them. Even Jeremiah, whose final moments seemed to last forever in her recollection. He deserved it. But those thoughts were ones Miro would not share. He valued life, and Bronwyn thought she did too, but after the last two days, she wanted to see all of the hunters die in the worst ways imaginable.

She balked when Jeremiah met his end. She felt a small amount of pity for him, but he didn't deserve pity. He deserved worse than Miro had done. He deserved to be kept alive and tormented by the god of fire and madness for as long as possible. She hadn't thought herself capable of such dark thoughts before, but they were there now. She only hoped their presence hadn't changed her.

Bronwyn touched her chest to ensure that her necklace was there. She had found it on Frank's body after they put the unconscious Miro in a tent. She had once thought the necklace was some sort of godly luck charm, but now, having heard Defurge's mind in her head, she knew what the gods wanted to keep from him. They didn't want Defurge to know that she had been communing with the gods, that there was a plan in motion by them to destroy the Soul Gem once and for all.

After the battle, Bronwyn made sure to wear the necklace as quickly as possible. She wasn't sure how Defurge's ability to talk in the mind worked, but she wanted to give him as little time as possible to discover any information about her interactions with Fria. He had given her a curious glance afterward, but that could just be Bronwyn's imagination because he helped Clara remove the manacles around her ankles and wrists. Defurge had only broken the chains previously, and Bronwyn was glad they were able to remove the manacles. She did not need to go through life looking like an escaped prisoner. The hunters hadn't accounted for the strength of a former god and a pretty ingenious lockpick. Defurge had pulled the steel apart far enough for Clara's pick to disengage the locking mechanism.

Bronwyn looked up as a trail of embers streaked across the sky. "Defurge," Bronwyn yelled.

He descended. He spent most of his time high above the clouds during the day, flying as the phoenix, flames blazing. The behavior worried Bronwyn, but Defurge assured her no one was nearby.

During the nights, he flew as a hawk, but now and then a trail of embers was visible high in the sky. He said he was scouting for people, remaining vigilant. They didn't know if a larger group of hunters would investigate Amber and her ilk's disappearance or not. As soon as Miro regained consciousness, they planned to leave.

Bronwyn knew the real reason Defurge kept his distance. The fight humbled him, and he wanted to be alone. He needed time to think.

Defurge thought himself invulnerable, but last night illustrated that his powers weren't the only thing to fear.

"Have you seen anything?" Bronwyn asked, hopeful he hadn't. The idea of another hunter, Jerund, terrified Bronwyn. They needed to get out of here as quickly as possible. "Maybe a lone person?"

"No one. I've patrolled far and wide; it's a dead zone out here. Probably why they picked this spot for their ambush; less likely to be interrupted." Defurge waited for Bronwyn to reply, but when she didn't, he engulfed himself in flames, compacting them until he formed a fiery amalgamation of the hawk. The orange-red fire shrank until it was embers, then dissipated, leaving only the bird. He beat his wings, flying parallel to the ground for a moment before heading back into the sky.

At camp, Clara sat cooking by the fire. Despite the lack of wildlife, an occasional bird flew by and Ferdinand was more than happy to pluck it from the sky. Bronwyn startled Clara and they shared an understanding nod. It would be a while before either of them felt at ease by a campfire.

Something changed in the last couple of days. Cassolisks, giant crocodiles, swarms of arachnids, wolves, and a hydra had never left Bronwyn feeling this defeated. Five people, who Bronwyn was sure she could overcome, almost destroyed everything. If Defurge had decided to follow Miro's instructions to stay behind, they'd all be dead. This battle left scars, both literal and metaphorical. Bronwyn looked down once again at her bandaged hand.

Clara rifled through the many papers she had pulled from Amber's pack. She sighed often with each new leaflet she read. Bronwyn asked, "What have you figured out so far?"

"They're organized. Every missive and note is to 'Huntmaster Jerund,' but if you have one group reporting to a single individual, reason dictates that that individual is a central figure dictating edicts to multiple groups."

Bronwyn sat by the fire and took a tin of roasted potatoes. "How do they operate? Is there anything you've read that indicates there is another group on their way right now?"

Clara groaned as she folded a piece of paper and set it aside. "I don't think so. The latest communication I uncovered was in regard to us, and unless they make copies of every missive, it's unlikely they sent it."

Bronwyn speared a potato and blew on it. She gulped, dreading the next question she had to ask, "Did you find out what the deal was with Amber that required you to be unharmed?"

Clara put the stack of papers down on the log she was sitting on. "Atien and Amber knew each other from long ago."

"Atien is one of the hunters?"

"No, he isn't. He'd never. He couldn't."

"Your pirate confidante made a secret deal to kill Miro and keep you safe."

"Atien didn't even know about Miro. We didn't talk about anything while in Newtonne, just Emestria and getting free. I didn't even tell Atien about the artifacts, just that I was doing some other work for a time that might be more lucrative."

"He's a pirate, Clara. He would probably sell all of us out for the slightest bit of coin. I'm honestly surprised his deal involved making sure you were unharmed."

"He is not," Clara declared. "There are missives from before we even left for Newtonne. The hunters were told to intercept us there. That means someone from Emestria was the original fox in the chicken coop. Perhaps your beloved king sold us out."

"King Bryant would never. My country is on the brink of starvation, and the crown has done so much to ensure we survive. This gambit to obtain Legendary Artifacts is Emestria's hope in this war. There is no way he'd jeopardize that just to punish Miro."

"Really? You're willing to cast Atien in aspersion, but think your king so noble? I'll have you know that piracy is mostly taking money from different nations to harass their enemies. Your king could have hired Atien on a number of jobs for all I know."

"I know my king is concerned for the safety of his people and the longevity of his nation. The artifacts are integral to that. He wouldn't jeopardize his nation's safety because of coin. Atien probably sold us out because they paid him enough." Bronwyn paused and judged Clara's posture. They were both heated, but Bronwyn had one last barb to discover the truth.

"Who is Scarlette?" Bronwyn asked.

"What?" Clara replied.

"Who is Scarlette? When you told me to leave you, you told me to tell Miro that her name is Scarlette. Is she one of these hunters? One of Atien's crew?"

"You need to stop asking," Clara emphatically said.

"No Clara, I need to start getting answers. There are people after us, and all I really know is that you have a pirate lover who bargained for your safety, and if we hadn't tried to escape, then your safety would have been guaranteed while Miro would have been killed."

"She's my daughter," Clara yelled, swiping her hand across some of the gathered papers. A few made it into the fire.

"Clara—"

"No, you don't get to talk right now." Clara stood and pointed her finger at Bronwyn. "She's my daughter that I've been able to hold only twelve times in her life because she was born with a blood disease, and I couldn't afford the treatments. Her bastard of a father only agreed to treat her if I let him raise her as the child of him and his fiancée. It broke my heart into a thousand pieces, but I did it because that's what mothers do."

"Clara," Bronwyn tried again.

"And I've spent every day of the last twelve years trying to find a way to make enough money so that I could afford her treatments and tell her who I was." Clara turned away. "That's the only reason I agreed to this ridiculous quest of your king. I thought maybe I'd gain enough fame or prestige that I'd be granted some position of privilege in the Emestrian court. It was a long shot at best."

Clara turned back to Bronwyn suddenly, her fist tightly balled with her fingernails digging into her palm. "But you know what? When I asked Miro to help me, he didn't even ask who I wanted him to heal. And he didn't even want to know the name of the girl I asked him to treat, so you better goddess-damned believe my only, my truly only, desire is to see Miro check off enough boxes so he'll return to Corinthe with me and help Scarlette."

"I didn't know. How could I have known?"

"Save it, Bronwyn. All I care about is that you keep Miro safe so he can fulfill his promise. If Atien had any hand in what happened over the last couple of days, I'll put a load of lead in his forehead with no questions."

"Clara …."

"Go check on sleeping beauty. I'll talk to the god of poutiness."

Bronwyn put down her tin of potatoes and hesitated. She was ignored as Clara picked up strewn papers. After a minute, Bronwyn left to see if Miro had woken.

Clara was never an immature, carefree addition to their group. She wasn't along for the ride because of magic, money, or adventure. She was a grieving mother doing anything to save her child, and Bronwyn never saw it. Did any of them? Did Miro know? Is that why he was able to extend compassion, and not force Clara to tell him why it was so important that this one girl be treated?

Everything felt like a lie. The one thing she had always been able to rely on was her strength and skill with her weapon. The greatsword was impossible to wield with her right hand alone. Even with two hands, she struggled to maintain the balance she once commanded. If she wished to continue fighting, she would need to switch weapons. In basic, she learned to use a sword and shield. She could return to those weapons, or a simple spear if they were too unwieldy.

Bronwyn thought about attaching a targe to her forearm; she could wield that with three fingers. *Possibly a spiked targe*, she thought as she re-entered the tent and put her hand over Miro's chest to watch the little zigzags of static electricity jump between his body and hers. This was real.

Time to see what the gods have to say about this. Bronwyn placed her hand on his forehead, closed her eyes, and concentrated.

Bronwyn opened her eyes to find herself in the sea of ash, Naani standing by her side. The sky wasn't quite so red this time, but her knees sank further into the ground. Hundreds of feet in the distance, a solitary tree was surrounded by grass. Beneath it, one figure sat. Bronwyn could only make out the color of her hair from this distance—as gold as the sun.

"Has she always been here?" Bronwyn asked Naani.

"She showed up last night," Naani replied.

"Is it me, or is it Serra?" Bronwyn began walking toward the figure. With each step, her legs sank further into the ground.

"I don't know. The ash is too deep to reach her. Even when I try to go above, something pushes me away. Even Miro can't reach her when he tries. He just sinks." Naani let out a low grumble. "He doesn't want anything to touch her. He protected her from all the bad of this place."

"Or she decided to come here, to remind him that something good remains." The figure stood and turned toward them. She wore a plain white dress and stared back. Neither party made any motion to the other.

"Did you know what the gods and goddesses did, Naani? That Lynnfield is gone because of their plan? That the people you protected were killed by them?" Bronwyn breathed in heavily, listening to the wind as it whipped ash into swirling dervishes. Even they seemed to be repelled by whatever force protected this lone island.

"I found out after the last time you came. The nice man never relived that memory till then."

"I'm sorry, Naani. You know it wasn't him." Bronwyn looked to the sky. She couldn't see the island, but she knew it was hidden behind clouds. "They did this."

"I know. I don't want to see them anymore." Naani turned to walk away.

"I have to talk to them. One last time."

"I'll take you to the island in the sky, but I won't step foot on it ever again." Naani knelt in the ash and Bronwyn climbed on top of her.

"I understand." As Naani galloped through the sky, Bronwyn stared down at the woman standing beneath the tree. She knew that it was her, and she also knew that she was fine with solitude. Part of her wanted to remain here so that even in the worst of Miro's nightmares, he could look out and see there was one good thing he couldn't destroy.

Naani stopped short of the island, and Bronwyn had to balance on Naani's back and hoist herself up onto the island. Naani left the second Bronwyn's feet were off the great cat's back. As Bronwyn rose to her feet, Fria was already there.

Fria stepped forward with her arms extended. "My child, I'm sorry."

Bronwyn pushed Fria back. Fria was shorter than her now. "I'm not your child."

"But you are," Fria said. "You are a part of me."

"Yes, we're all your children and a bit of each god lives inside of us." Bronwyn rolled her eyes. "Keep your spiritual nonsense to yourself."

"It's not nonsense. You are the child of me and the void."

"I know my parents. They were good people. You are not." Bronwyn stared into Fria's one good eye, setting her jaw to prevent herself from losing her temper. She wouldn't give Fria the satisfaction.

"Your body may be of flesh, but your soul is of me and the void. You are a void walker." Fria cast her arm backward, gesturing to the swirling abyss already starting to eat at the island's edge.

Bronwyn shook her head dismissively. "What does that even mean?"

"I gave a part of myself to the origin of the gods, the void, to make you, so we could destroy the gem once and for all. You are my vigilance. I gave my Vigilant Eye to the void as a sacrifice to create your soul. I needed someone strong enough to walk the path."

"That doesn't mean anything. It's more of your smoke and smudged lies."

Fria shook her head. "The Ywaigwai were never obedient little pets. They are obstinate children who would have overthrown us if they figured out how to truly thrive without our power. One figured out how to make magi and survive without divine favor. My mother, Kyrie, sacrificed her eyesight to create the first void walker, Cassandra. She learned to hone her powers, to walk in the dreams of others, to redirect and absorb magic, and to even permanently silence a Ywagwai and rob them of their ability to make deals and cast."

"I'm tired of your games. That's all nonsense. Everything you say is nonsense. 'Don't use the Eye, it will only bring you pain.' How about, just telling me, 'Miro blames himself for Lynnfield because his Ywaigwai destroyed it. And if you use the Eye of Sleepless Dreams to find out, you'll be kidnapped by five psychopaths and have two fingers amputated.'"

Fria lowered her arms and her face grew stern. "Fate is a delicate web, and everything I say runs the risk of causing you to stray from your path. You have already made your path more complicated than you could ever imagine. You could never understand it."

"My path? I already strayed from my path. You want Miro to kill himself to correct your mistakes. Chivas is ultimately responsible for the creation of Defurge. Why didn't you just tell him not to play his little trick on Seraph?"

Fria sighed and hung her head. "Chivas and I never believed mortals were meant to be ruled by gods and goddesses. We could never convince enough of the others without something truly horrible being wrought by one of our hands. But we couldn't just destroy a city to make our point. We needed a mad god to do it for us."

Bronwyn's lips trembled. Somehow, in the back of her mind, she always knew this truth, but now with it laid plainly, she couldn't ignore it any longer. "You purposefully created Defurge to start the cataclysm. All those deaths, every city he attacked, the destruction of Dalmarask, Lynnfield, Seketh, and even the very war Emestria is now fighting is all your fault. And even with you not here, you're still trying to rule through manipulation. You're a monster."

"I am not the goddess of compassion. I'm the goddess of fate and death."

"I don't care if you gave your arm to make my soul. I only came here to say one thing. You try and act like the gods and goddesses are doing everything for the greater good. How was destroying an entire town, eliminating an entire nation of people, for the greater good?"

"One nation sacrificed to save a world. That's a fair trade."

"No. One nation destroyed because none of you dared to kill one of your own. That's not a trade. And you let Miro blame himself for your failures."

"We did not compel him to make the deal with Raithe. That was his own choice."

"You know that's a lie. You talk about paths open to us and how they're being closed off, but then you say you have no choice in the matter, that we're all just making our own decisions. When he wakes, I'll tell him exactly who is responsible for Lynnfield and for him killing people again." Bronwyn turned to leave.

"Three paths remain. The one you want is still open. If you tell him about us, then only one path will remain. He will take the gem to destroy us. You'll be forced to kill him. Then you will take the gem and live your life trying to keep it from others."

"And you telling me what happens, doesn't that close that path, so now only two remain?"

"No. Because you're still thinking of doing it."

"You're right. He should get to have his revenge against you. I'll bet that at the end of that path, when I'm forced to kill him, he'll smile because he knows he destroyed all of you."

"But you won't be smiling. You won't be happy. The only blessing will be you lose yourself to the gem and forget about everything in your life. At least you won't lose your sanity to it." There was nothing matronly about Fria's stare. She seemed to be daring Bronwyn to do it.

"Why won't I lose my mind?"

"The second time we made a void walker, Seraph gave up her ability to love to merge the soul of a Ywaigwai and a god. We thought the phoenix, Serina, would be able to keep the gem from others."

Bronwyn slowly blinked. *I've been such a fool. Everything I thought special about myself was a poorly concealed divine plan. I will not be a puppet.* "The next time you see me, I'll have figured out a way to force all of you gods into the void. As long as I'm alive, I will not let Miro die. Chivas was right. I'm too selfish to sacrifice Miro or myself to clean up your mistakes."

"If you will not listen to me, then you need to seek out the organization founded by the first void walker, The Mothers of Mercy. We created two artifacts to help void walkers hone their ability, Rune Blade and Armor. They still guard the blade. You mustn't stray from your path."

"I already have." Bronwyn stepped off the island, confident that Naani would catch her and carry her away from dreams, nightmares, and goddesses.

Defurge descended late in the night; Clara remained vigilant at the fire. She was burning papers from one of the hunter's packs. Defurge noticed she didn't toss one of the papers into the fire and instead folded it and tucked it into her blouse.

"What are those?" Defurge asked.

"Reports, journal entries, lists of crossed out names, bounty notices, and other accounts of their crimes."

"And you're getting rid of them? Isn't that evidence?"

"I'm not burning everything. Just the reports of what they did to their victims. No one should ever have to read about their loved ones dying like that."

"And what about that one?" Defurge pointed to the tip of the folded note, still not fully secured.

"Personal, but let's just say I'll be having some words with a certain pirate captain once I'm back in Newtonne."

Defurge took a leg off the cooking fowl and hastily ate the meat kept warm by a smattering of coals. They sat in silence as he consumed the meal. Bronwyn's presence wasn't missed. Her mind was frustratingly empty to him once again.

"How is the night sky?" Clara asked after Defurge discarded the meatless bone.

"Quiet, breezy, serene," he said.

"Make any progress?" Defurge raised an eyebrow at Clara's question, unsure of what she meant. "Thinking through whatever has been bugging you."

"I want to be alone for a while," he said before standing to leave camp.

"I'll tell you what I think," Clara said before he could. "I think you flew all the way to us with an idea in your head that you were going to come and be a hero. Then you got here and took out one enemy, but Miro decimated the others. When you thought it was your turn to step up and save the day, Miro royally kicked your butt, taking you out with a one-two punch. Bronwyn stepped in and stopped him with emotions and stuff." Clara held out her tongue and mocked gagging with her finger.

"Thanks, Clara, just what I needed," Defurge replied.

"But you killed the most important one," Clara added. "He may not have been the most vile, but he was top three. He had me and Bronwyn. Once Miro started his rampage, our captor would have killed us both before trying to run. With Bronwyn and I dead, Miro couldn't be stopped; he would have continued until he burned himself out and destroyed everything. Without you there, it would have all gone to shit," Clara confessed before Defurge sat back down.

"Bronwyn hasn't talked about it, but do you know what happened while you two were coming to find us?" Clara asked.

"No. Miro said I shouldn't peek in your heads too much," Defurge said, trying to mitigate how much he influenced them now that his secret was common knowledge.

"Bronwyn pissed off a sadist so that he would spend so much time beating her and drinking that he'd pass out before he could lay a finger on me. That's all she did—try and buy time for you and Miro to arrive. We knew that when you two arrived it was going to be scorched earth, fire, and brimstone—how right we were," Clara mused at the accuracy of their predictions.

"We tried to escape, but they had Gaebolg, and their daggers, and bolas. Enchanted weapons. Regardless of what the note said, you would come, and they would have no ability to fight you off. The magi hunters thought they had a weapon to neutralize Miro, so Bronwyn needed to buy you enough time to make your move."

Clara sighed. "Things are going to change around here, Defurge."

"How so?"

"For one, Miro will not be going anywhere near Emestria, or Newtonne for that matter. This group knew Miro was leaving Emestria, and even though Bronwyn denies it, I'm damned sure that her king had some hand in that. Bronwyn isn't going to give up on returning the Horn of Garanhir to Emestria, but she shouldn't return either. They'll need to go into hiding."

"And you?" Defurge asked.

"There is a certain pirate captain and his crew that I need to have words with. And I think I'd like to meet Amber's sister and determine how much she knew about this whole debacle. Bronwyn says you told her you can feel what Miro is thinking. Can you do that with anyone?"

"My link with Miro is strongest because of him trying to activate the curse inside the gem while the monks were probing his mind. It varies between others. Bronwyn is the most difficult to read, but with others, I can hear surface thoughts if I try, like you." Defurge grinned, knowing that Clara would now realize her secrets were known by him, but he never forced her to confront them.

"You'll be coming back to Newtonne with me. And, if safe, from there we'll return to the den of wolves Bronwyn calls her homeland and find out who betrayed her. That means possibly having to confront a bunch of pissed-off Emestrians. You see how hard Bronwyn hits; imagine a full complement of soldiers as strong as she. Me, what can I really do? I've got some magic but I'm not a heavy hitter like Miro or Bronwyn. If the last couple of days taught me anything, we need heavy hitters."

"But a god?" Defurge asked.

"A god would be a heavy hitter, but a god of fire. Not the god of self-pity and alone time in the sky." Clara let Defurge sit with the insult for a while. "Now, how would you like to return to Emestria and out some rats?"

Defurge smiled wildly.

CHAPTER 35

HEALING MAGIC HAD a certain feel. A firm but gentle tugging as your body stitched itself back together. It was that sensation that woke Bronwyn. She opened her eyes in time to see the green lines fade away from her hand. She unraveled the bandage. The wounds had closed over, new skin obscuring the bone and viscera that poked out from where her fingers used to be. Her face felt less puffy, and she turned her head as she ran her hand over her previously swollen eye.

"I healed all that I can. I'm sorry." Miro smiled as she turned up to look at him. She removed her hand from his chest, and he turned to her. They stayed, looking at each other, not speaking.

"I'd like to talk," Bronwyn said before adding, "but not here. Can we take a walk?"

Miro nodded, and he waited for Bronwyn to sit up before he did as well.

The empty camp didn't worry Bronwyn. Defurge and Ferdinand circled the skies, looking out for them. She and Miro walked along silently underneath the shaded trees for twenty minutes. Bronwyn had scouted this location out before. The trees parted, revealing a clearing. A flat rock buttressed a tree in the middle. Dappled sunlight pierced the canopy, offering both shade and subdued daylight. Bronwyn sat down on the smooth boulder and motioned for Miro to join her.

"Clara once told me that you and I always pushed and pulled against each other. Every time it was closer and further than the last. Those people were a level of deranged I have never experienced before; they called themselves magi hunters. They aren't the only ones. Clara thinks they operate semi-independently, but when they don't check in, others will come looking for them, and eventually you.

"They preyed on us when we were apart. Next time, they may come better prepared. They knew about the artifacts; if we're going to continue looking for relics, we might run into more people like them again." Instead of training yesterday, Bronwyn had rehearsed this speech all day.

"Bronwyn, I love you, but I don't deserve you and I can't put you in danger."

Bronwyn hadn't prepared for that response, and she took a moment to recalibrate. "I love you too. I deserve you." Bronwyn let that sink in. "Arguing you don't want to put me in danger is useless. We're both in danger. If we're together, we can keep each other safe long enough to figure things out."

"How, how can you deserve me? I'm a monster."

"I know you feel that way sometimes, but you also know you're not. The people we fought, they're the monsters."

A tear came to Miro's eye. "They're right Bronwyn. I'm a monster." He scoffed. "I committed genocide, an entire nation of people almost wiped off the map because of me."

"No!" Bronwyn shouted, surprising herself with her intensity. She lowered her voice back down to a normal tone. "You are not responsible for Lynnfield. That Ywaigwai, Raithe, is responsible."

"I knew I'd have to sacrifice myself to Raithe to save Serra and Bryant. I knew the deal I was making was going to hurt people. Issaroh may not have told me exactly what happened with his family, but he warned me that I would need to sacrifice everything I loved when I made that deal. I thought it meant I would lose Serra and Bryant, and in the end, I did."

"And did you think that meant the destruction of a town as well?" Miro didn't reply. "I know you, and I know you wouldn't have made the deal with Raithe if you had any idea that he was going to destroy Lynnfield."

"And Serra? I told her what I did."

"None of this is your fault, Miro. And I won't let you beat yourself up over it any longer. I'm sorry that I went poking around in your past. But my goal was that when you found out I knew about what happened and that I didn't blame you, you'd see that you're not a monster. My father died during the Battle of Lynnfield; maybe he died before you made your deal, or maybe Raithe killed him after he betrayed you, but I don't blame you for my father's death. Do you think if I did, I'd be able to love you?"

More tears fell from Miro's eyes, and Bronwyn wasn't sure if they were tears of sorrow or if he was moved by her acceptance of him. She wanted to tell him exactly who was responsible for Lynnfield—the gods and goddesses—but if that led to Miro taking the gem and Bronwyn having to kill him, she couldn't do it. But he needed to know something.

"Miro, I don't know why things happened the way they did or how we all got here, but there are way too many coincidences. You, a mage that epitomizes the goddess Seraph to such a degree that you willingly punish yourself for anything you believe yourself partially responsible for. A magus that loved so deeply he did what no magus had ever done before; he exited the curse rather than kill those that he loved. Clara, a smuggler who just happened to be the child of the priest who hid the mantle of Alcides and knew of its location, just tips over in her boat and is caught by the Emestrian army. Then I, someone that has an ability you've never encountered before, to resist magic, am the one that the king sends on this mission to join you."

Miro gave a biting, sarcastic laugh. "Bryant sent you because he knew you'd remind me of Serra. He sent Clara because he knew she'd feed into my guilt about Lynnfield."

Bronwyn shook her head. "No, he didn't Miro. Maybe King Bryant sent me because I looked somewhat similar to someone you knew long ago, or maybe he sent me because he knows how much I would sacrifice for Emestria.

"Your quest for the artifacts led us to Defurge, the last remaining god. And even when Defurge unleashed his full potential, you were still able to defeat him."

"Defurge and I fought?" Miro asked.

Bronwyn had momentarily forgotten the complete lack of awareness Miro had while in the curse. "Yes, and you defeated him pretty soundly. I'd suggest you steer clear for a little bit."

Miro smiled and she laid her hand on his thigh. The tingle of their energy reminded her. "And there's something else. Give me your hand."

Bronwyn raised her hand into the air, the palm flat and facing him. Miro copied the odd gesture, and as his hand grew closer, he withdrew it in alarm before moving the hand toward hers again. Between their bodies was a visible flow of electricity. Bronwyn couldn't tell the direction the energy traveled, whether it moved from her to him, vice versa, or both.

"What is it?" Miro said, moving his head around, examining the phenomenon.

"I don't know. I always felt something when I touched you or you touched me. Now it's much stronger. Do you have any idea what it might be?"

"I don't know," Miro said, still unable to take his eyes off the flashes of blue dancing between their fingers. "Is it just our hands?"

"No, I think the energy has something to do with your curse. When we kissed, your lightning passed through my body." Bronwyn removed her hand.

"We kissed?" Miro asked.

"I needed to shut you up somehow and my sword wasn't nearby." Bronwyn blushed. Miro stared at her right hand, the one she hadn't raised to touch his.

"I'm sorry." Miro broke his gaze. "Why did they do it?"

"To make you come. They knew if they threatened me, you'd charge in all self-sacrificing. We'll talk about how dumb of a move that was later," Bronwyn tried to joke.

"Just you, or Clara as well?"

"No, I kept them busy so they wouldn't touch her."

"How many were there?" Miro asked.

"Five, but they killed off two of their members before you even arrived, and Defurge killed one, so two."

"Two more lives. Two more that I never wanted to be responsible for." Miro sighed and hung his head.

"Two of the most disgusting, vile monsters imaginable. They lost their humanity long ago. They didn't restrict their activities to magi—whom they perceived to be evil—but enacted it on children and their loved ones if the end result met their goals or arbitrary code of rules. I found bodies before fighting the Cassolisk. Mutilated remains of a father and child with a note similar to the one written to you. Clara found lists, with locations, and crossed out names. Killing those two saved dozens, maybe hundreds, more."

Bronwyn went to lift Miro's face. She almost yanked her hand away when the energy shocked her, but she was trying to accept this as their new reality. He moved his head away from her hand defensively; he still hadn't adjusted to the experience. She tried again and he lifted his head like he always did.

"Were they from Loughlin? People who were mad because I didn't heal everyone?"

"They must have been in Loughlin at the same time as us, but they had been following us for much longer. They knew we were leaving Emestria before we even arrived in Newtonne. I still can't figure out how they were able to follow so closely without being noticed. Defurge should have sensed their campfire if they were camping close to us."

Miro seemed almost in a daze when he quietly muttered, "Crows …."

"What?" Bronwyn asked.

"Did any of them know magic?"

"One, yes, she could cast lightning magic, but I had bruised her larynx in our initial fight, so she wasn't able to cast after that. Why?"

"It's a scrying spell. Where the mage can look through the eyes of crows or ravens."

"The crows Ferdinand was killing," Bronwyn said, the same look of realization crossing her face. "He has been doing that since the library."

"I can't believe I didn't think about it. I didn't even think …." Miro placed his head in his hand and hung it in defeat.

"Miro, don't. There is no way that you could have known people were tracking us." Bronwyn reached over and tightly, reassuringly, gripped Miro's shoulder. "We should go talk to the others."

Bronwyn stood. She extended her hand to help him up as well. He took it, only flinching this time at the jolt. They returned to camp and waited for Clara to come back. When she did, Bronwyn called Defurge down so they could tell them both at the same time. Miro and she were still holding hands when she began speaking.

Bronwyn said, "Miro and I decided we're done—"

"Done fighting with each other?" Clara asked. "No more of this, 'we want to be together, but we can't'?"

Bronwyn shot Clara a look. "Yes, we're being hunted, and we can't afford to separate until we hunt down every last person who came after us."

"Good, because I'll be taking Defurge with me to Newtonne and Emestria," Clara said. "Miro, our deal still stands? Emestria, the gem, and your Ywaigwai—after that, you'll return with me to Corinthe?"

Before Miro could answer, Bronwyn squeezed his hand. "Yes, it still stands."

"Considering having a god of fire who can read people's minds, perhaps we hold off on the gem part until we've dealt with the hunter problem," Defurge said.

"Good point, but we'll figure that out later. Bronwyn, who can I trust in Emestria? No politicians, no kings—real people."

"My second, Lieutenant Narja Jakul, is my oldest friend and I trust her with my life. Zesh Shammei is a fellow guard whom we both trust implicitly. But Kaleb Dorn was the jailer when Miro was in the dungeons. The three of them are all friends, but Kaleb knows too much. He could be the one who sent the hunters after us."

Miro stammered, "Not Kaleb, he's a great guy. Wouldn't hurt a fly."

Clara held up her hand to stop Miro. "We'll start with Narja and Zesh. Defurge will find out who is trustworthy and who needs to be dealt with."

"What are you proposing?" Bronwyn asked.

"I'm proposing that we keep Miro alive and make sure no one else comes after us. We won't tell King Bryant we're returning with the artifacts. We need to find someplace for you two to hide out until Defurge and I get back."

"What about Corinthe?" Defurge suggested. "We were headed there, and they have a library to continue researching the artifacts."

Clara said, "No big cities. No capitals. You'll use fake names, get regular jobs, and stay incognito. Stone Ridge is a week out of Newtonne. It's a small town with a library and a booming gem trade. You'll keep him safe Bronwyn?"

Bronwyn gave a tight, reaffirming nod.

EPILOGUE

A SINISTER GRIN escaped Defurge's lips as he lay alone in his tent and searched for the font of his power, the gem around his neck. As his eyes closed, he found himself in the confines of the realm that existed inside the gem.

"What did you do?" the phoenix yelled. "You were not supposed to draw upon the gem's power. Was my power not enough to satisfy you?"

"I have no time for liars," Defurge said, turning to the multi-faceted prison of all the other previous incarnations. "My power never came from you. You cannot take it, and you cannot control me."

"You will not disobey me! I will command the monks to march you up to Bronwyn and have her take the gem."

"I don't think they actually can." Defurge raised his hand to the clear pane with a flame-wreathed, horned beast behind it. The pane shimmered and shattered. The inhabitant of the prison walked forward, nostrils flaring, and eyes filled with hate.

"I am Defurge," the bestial creature said as it approached.

"We are all Defurge. Bind these three and I will offer you the same deal I had with them." Defurge indicated toward the phoenix and two monks. "All my memories and experiences of the outside world, in exchange for your cooperation."

The beast stopped in its tracks, seeming to consider Defurge's offer. "Where is my sister?"

"Our sister is gone. She has left the mortal realm. We are the only god that remains—"

"Former incarnation, do not test us," One of the monks warned. The monk's interruption seemed to take the attention of the horned beast as it lowered its head and began to charge the plane where the monks meditated, and the phoenix lingered.

Defurge ignored the grunts of exertion from the monk who spoke as Defurge stepped to pane after pane, releasing each of the imprisoned incarnations and offering them the same bargain. By the time he turned around, the monks were both restrained, their arms held behind their backs and their heads pressed to the ground.

"You will rue this decision!" The phoenix shouted, flying high above where the monks were incapacitated.

"I think not," Defurge said, placing his hand on the surface of his next intended incarnation to release. Unlike the previously released prisoners, the dragon had to tuck its wings close to its body as it traversed through the gap in the wall.

"Bring the phoenix down," Defurge said.

"You do not command me," the dragon replied in a reptilian hiss.

"You may return to your cage and rage against captivity, or you can bring the phoenix down and live as a free resident of this realm. You shall feel the sun, the food, and the experiences I do."

The dragon responded with a frustrated snort as it squeezed through the exit of the gem. Several powerful flaps of its wings found it airborne and close on the phoenix's tail. Defurge watched with glee as each evasive action of the phoenix was closer and closer to the dragon's outstretched forelimbs. Finally, the phoenix tried to turn but found herself batted to the ground by powerful claws.

The dragon dove after her, pinning the bird-like form in a cage of scale and keratin. Defurge sauntered toward the prone phoenix. He wondered if the dragon was the incarnation that had previously stolen the gem from her.

"Now, this will be a lot easier if you tell me what you know. How was Bronwyn able to dodge the lightning?"

The phoenix shifted her form back into that of the long-limbed woman. "I'll tell you nothing. I'll rejoice when she finds out what you have done and slays you."

"Still being difficult? We'll see if living in chains improves your disposition." Defurge held his hand to the pane beneath his feet and drew it up, forming it into links of red metal. He handed them to another of the incarnations, a female form composed entirely of flame, and stepped toward the back center of the plane. A crimson throne rose from the surface. Defurge turned and sat, then looked out upon the other incarnations. They were quickly getting to work binding both the monks and phoenix.

Defurge announced, "Let the era of the God Defurge begin."

Afterward

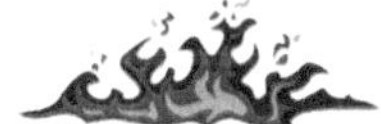

Thank you to all the beta readers, editors, and designers that helped make this book possible. And a special thank you so much to you for reading my novel, Of Hunters and Magi. As an indie-published author, reviews posted to Amazon or Goodreads are the primary way for me to get new readers. If you enjoyed my book or other books from indie-published authors, leaving a review is the biggest way you can help. If you somehow came upon this book without purchasing it or through an illegitimate source, i.e. piracy, you can offset the sale I didn't get by leaving a review.

If you'd like to know what's next in the Legendary Artifact series, check out my website: www.bookswithchris.com or my Instagram @ bookswithchristopher. I'm always looking for beta readers and ARC reviewers if you'd like get early access to the next installment in the series. Information about signing up to be part of my very infrequent newsletter can be found there.

www.ingramcontent.com/pod-product-compliance
Lightning Source LLC
Chambersburg PA
CBHW032340310726
48973CB00007B/1789